Fossil River

Fossil River

A Thriller

By Jock Miller

AEI/Story Merchant Books
Beverly Hills, CA

Story Merchant Books
9601 Wilshire Boulevard #1202
Beverly Hills CA 90210
http://www.storymerchant.com/books.html

To my wife, Kay, for being the compass in my life and encouraging me to do the things I love and cherish…Thank you for your patience and for being my best friend and life partner!

PART I

CHAPTER 1

Butch Gilselson's alarm sounded at 4:30 a.m. AKST, a two-hour time difference from his Mountain Time in Wyoming. But he was already awake, his chartered floatplane at ready.

Giselson had fantasized about this day for months. He'd studied the Orvis catalogue, selected the perfect gear, and read whatever he could get his hands on about fishing gold-medal rivers with the fervor of a kid obsessed with electronic games.

Two summers ago, he'd traveled to the Rio Grande River in Tierra del Fuego to fish for large sea-run brown trout at the southern tip of Argentina. Last summer he traveled to the Kenai River for big Russian rainbow trout, steelhead, Dolly Varden, and Chinook salmon. Now he was in quest of trophy native rainbows and oversized steelhead in the rarely-fished waters of Alaska's legendary Fossil River. It promised to be the most challenging of them all. In fact, Giselson wasn't even sure he could find the Fossil after poring over maps, satellite GPS pictures, and topographical charts. The thin blue river line in the Noatak National Preserve had no river name listed—but through the process of elimination, he assumed it had to be the Fossil.

Giselson had ventured into the wilderness many times before, but this time would be different, he told himself. When fishing the other famous rivers of the world, Giselson had fishing guides. But after countless calls to outfitters and guide services in the Noatak Preserve region, he found nobody willing to take him. Two of the five guides he'd contacted had never even heard of the Fossil River. Bottom line: there would be no guide.

Giselson's charter pilot would fly east up the Noatak River in a de Havilland Beaver DHC-2. He knew the plane well—no pontoons this time. He'd be dropped off between the Maiyu Merak Mountains and the Brooks Mountain Range, 136 miles upriver. Hopefully, there would be an ATV waiting for him when he arrived. He'd paid the rental fee the day before his arrival, and a riverboat was to make the ATV deposit on the south bank of the Noatak River.

The Fossil cut through wilderness that was so remote and inaccessible that tales of fishing the river were passed along as legend by the oldtimers who haunted the solitary fisherman's bar, The Master Baiter, on the outskirts of the small town of Noatak, population 510. The tales mesmerized Giselson. Not one of the fishermen Giselson had met the night before had actually ever fished the Fossil himself; their stories were all rumor and hearsay. But to Giselson, they were utterly irresistible.

He'd stayed up past midnight the night before reviewing old maps and double-checking his equipment: a five-weight impregnated bamboo fly rod, which had been a gift from his father on his sixteenth birthday; four-and five-weight tippets; a wicker creel with that wonderful smell that brought back memories of a great day fishing; a fly vest including dry and wet flies of all sizes; silicon dry fly dressing; a snap-free net attached to the back of his vest; a hunting knife; neoprene waders; a new Apple iPhone that he guessed might not have a signal deep into the wilderness; a satellite GPS.

And a Smith & Wesson SW1911DK his father gave him on his twenty-first birthday. It held one ten-round clip, which he zipped into the inside pocket of his vest with another box of shells. "Just in case," he said, shrugging, knowing that Noatak Park's six-and-a-half million acres contained the largest grizzly population in North America.

It was first light when Giselson's small plane touched down on the Noatak. A flock of mergansers took off from the river at the sound of the engine roar. The pilot negotiated a two-wheeled landing on a thin strip of shoreline not more than fifteen feet wide-confirming the agility of the de Havilland and its Pratt and Whitney engine. Giselson smiled with pleasure when he saw the ATV not thirty yards from the planned drop.

"Great job," Giselson chortled appreciatively.

"Great plane," the pilot grunted, his raspy voice confirming he could've used another two hours of sleep and two more cups of Joe.

"Great pilot."

"Up here, you have to be," the pilot responded with a nod. "But thanks."

The fisherman looked at his watch. "I'll be here at nine o'clock sharp tonight. Sun doesn't set until close to midnight so I've got extra time to fish. Not a bad deal for a fly fisherman," Giselson said.

The pilot exhaled. "You be careful in there. You got a gun?"

"Yes."

"Good luck," the pilot intoned.

The comment bothered Giselson. Something about it sounded a little more ominous than simply saying good luck in fishing. He decided to let it go and hopped out of the plane. Then he gathered his equipment and watched the pilot throttle up the engine into a roar of power. The small plane lifted off the thin strip of shoreline, circled once, than vanished into the western horizon.

The air was cool and the thought of large trout and steelhead gripped Giselson's mind. He loaded up the ATV. The engine came alive, and the GPS he held in his hand marked his exact spot. He took in a long breath of crisp mountain air and gunned the ATV up and over the south bank ledge in a high arc. Life was great, he told himself.

He cut a diagonal path toward the Maiyu Merak Mountain Range. On the map, there was no indication of any road or path beyond the river, but the rumors he'd heard mentioned a stretch of the southeast fork of the Fossil that was hidden somewhere between four mountains south of the Noatak River.

From the maps and history of the vast mountain range, he knew there were nine active glaciers, three active volcanoes of the thirty in Alaska, and more than 200 lakes within Noatak Park, sprawling 400 majestic miles across Alaska east to west. He knew that the Noatak River's origin began far to the east, high up in the mountains winding through the range until it spilled into the Chukchi Sea.

He pressed on in his ATV. It was smooth riding at first, then tougher,

3

and as he threaded his way between mountain ridges, it became almost impassable. By 8:20 a.m., Giselson had run up into a rock ravine so steep that he was forced to stop. He took a deep, frustrating breath of morning air and surveyed the sprawling mountain peaks up ahead.

One peak spewed a cloud of billowing smoke, and the fisherman realized he'd never before been this close to a live volcano. In the distance, he saw two Dall sheep butting heads.

He had no choice; he would have to hike toward the river with the hope of intersecting it. He marked the ATV on his GPS, shouldered his equipment, and began a slow, arduous climb.

Giselson walked for more than an hour. At first, he moved through the mountain vegetation with little resistance. But soon the mix of thick alders, Douglas fir, Ponderosa Pine, and Native Mountain Ash trees thickened and slowed his progress. The chokecherry that grew along the new path he was now blazing became almost impassible.

A machete would have been helpful, he thought, but carrying one would have been cumbersome. Then, in the distance, Giselson saw a wall of Fish & Wildlife Agency posters, each with a different message:

NO TRESPASSING!
DANGER AHEAD!
NO ACCESS!

Giselson had trespassed many times on private property to reach gold medal fishing streams, so he wasn't intimated. But how in the hell did the park rangers even find this place—and why such a strong warning?

Only one sign bothered him: a skull and crossbones with the message that, if he trespassed he was taking his life in his own hands and Noatak National Park would not be held responsible.

He walked around the sign and pressed forward.

Giselson maintained his relentless pace for another two hours, stopping only to read his compass, check his GPS, and scan his map. The promise of landing trophy native trout and steelhead pulled him through the dense terrain like a carrot leading a horse. He topped a high ridge and stopped to take in the view.

He heard something in the distance. It was faint at first, but it soon built to a thunderous roar.

4

Giselson walked cautiously toward the sound. He climbed atop the next ridge and peered down into the valley. What he saw coming around the valley bend below was a herd of caribou running in a stampede, dust swirling above them. Something had spooked them.

"Fucking reindeer," Giselson said in shocked surprise. The only thing missing was Santa Claus and his sleigh.

Giselson crossed three more ridges and stopped abruptly. In front of him stood a steep outcrop of rock, a thick ridge maybe 100 feet high that rose awkwardly from the dense forest.

The wall of rock and dirt rose up to form a jagged rim at the top of the incline and, for the first time, Giselson considered turning back. This outcrop must have been deposited by a glacier thousands of years before, he thought. He looked down mountain. The view was vast and desolate, as if an unseen hand had sculpted every gleaming snow-capped mountain in wondrous perfection. It took his breath away.

He walked sixty paces to the right but found no access. Too steep. He took a long swig of water from his canteen, then trudged back to the left. It was impossible. He'd never be able to scale this ridge.

But he kept following the wall of rock. He'd come too far to give up easily. Then he saw it: a crevice between two large boulders. He would have missed the opening were it not for the small streak of mid-morning sun that lit up the tiny slice in the rock wall. He went closer for a look.

Rusted steel bars had been bolted in place to prevent access.

Why would someone do that this far from civilization? He pulled on each one. They were firmly drilled into the rock.

Finally he found one bar, higher than the others, that was loose.

He climbed the ladder of bars and pushed and prodded on the loose bar until it snapped free.

He crawled into the narrow rock slit and wormed his way through it. Then he began to shimmy snake-like up through the tight crevice that wended back and forth across the wall.

An hour later, sweaty and out of breath, he reached the top of the jagged ridge, which seemed to stretch out for miles around him. A thick fog hovered over the forest canopy like white icing on a chocolate cake.

The trees atop the ridge seemed oddly out of place. They were taller even than the trees in the forest below, and he couldn't identify some of them. They were growing from the arid ridge in an irregular pattern, as if sewn by a drunken wind. This was truly virgin wilderness.

Something else struck him as odd. As he moved up and onto the ground of what he realized was a hanging mountain valley, he noticed the temperature was growing warmer, not cooler. Instead of sixty degrees Fahrenheit in June, it had to top seventy. Even stranger, the tree density seemed to thicken the higher he climbed.

Alaska has some strange country, he thought. He forged on, listening for any distant sound of a river. Nothing yet.

At one point, it had grown so warm and humid he considered taking off his fishing vest and stuffing it into his backpack. But the thought of suiting up and putting together his five-weight Orvis rod sent a surge of adrenaline into his step and he pressed on without removing his gear.

Pockets of deep snow, mostly on the north slope of the valley, still remained, but didn't seem to cool the temperate air. Up ahead, maybe 300 yards, a misty fog bank hung on the massive pine-tree canopy. Puffs of steamy vapor escaped from jagged crevasses in the earth's crust with an eerie hiss, thickening the fog.

Another hundred yards across the plateau, Giselson stopped and cocked his head. He could hear the whisper of moving water. He picked up his pace. Sweat was beading on his forehead.

As he pressed on, he began to think about what fly he would use. *Dry or wet? Deer-hair Royal Wolf, Rat-faced McDougal, or Bead-head Prince Nymph? Maybe both, with the wet serving as a trailer?* His pulse quickened as his mind raced through his options.

The thick underbrush was finally beginning to thin. Giselson stepped out into a clearing and caught his breath. Before him was a steep rushing gorge. He raised his eyes and took in the spray of white water plunging down between the huge mountain boulders.

In the distance, far to the east, rose Mount St. Lincoln. He realized that the small thin, jagged line that broke the face of the peak was another massive waterfall. Fossil River Falls, the highest natural waterfall in Alaska. At 814 feet it was triple the height of Colorado's Telluride Bridal Falls that fed into its San Juan River, which he had also fished.

Giselson made his way carefully down the slick rocks. His neoprene boots gripped the mossy surface without fault. He knelt down and took two cans of Coors Lite from his fishing vest and placed them carefully into the river for cooling, but the temperature of the Fossil surprised him. The water was warm, almost hot from volcanic activity, he thought, just like the Fire Hole River in Yellowstone Park, Wyoming. The rainbows he'd caught there were warm to the touch. He took his beers out of the river and set them on a rock slab.

He stepped within twelve feet of the first pool and stripped out line while false casting across the bottom part of the pool, knowing that feeding trout and steelhead would always face upstream. His #18 Royal Wolf dry fly hit the water with hardly a dimple and floated downstream.

The man stared at the fly, waiting. Out of the corner of his eye, he tracked a large shadow moving beneath the surface, a silhouette of wild perfection. The shadow rose and hesitated for a split second before the enormous trout sipped the fly into its mouth.

Instinctively, he lifted his rod tip until he hit resistance. The muscular rainbow leapt from the water and Giselson watched, eyes wide, as if he were in a trance. Eight minutes passed, then another ten, before the fish turned ashore, jumping three more times.

When Giselson was certain the fish was tired, he kneaded the line through his fingers, and slowly, carefully brought the fish in, where it flopped extravagantly on the river rocks. He dropped his reel to the ground, leaned over, and held the fish with both hands—the girth was that thick—while he worked his measuring tape from his vest pocket. The trout measured twenty-nine-and-a-half inches and the flesh was warm. He guessed its weight at over twelve pounds. Breathless, he stood mesmerized by the kaleidoscope that radiated across its shimmering flesh, the rainbow streak on its side the richest he had ever seen.

Giselson was usually a catch-and-release man. But he longed to taste the native pink meat, so he quickly gutted the fish and slipped it into the creel he wore slung across his back, ten inches of fish and tail poking out of the creel hole.

I'll go to The Master Baiter tonight when I return and play show-and-tell with the old-timers. A broad grin spread across his face. He rewarded himself with a cool beer, leaving the other can on the slab of red rock for when he returned.

He moved upstream, hugging the bank, carefully placing his fly along the far wall of the next pool. The moment the fly hit the water, a steelhead sipped the fly into its gaping mouth. The sound of the splash broke the tranquility of the scene like a slap across the face. He grinned with appreciation.

Now he was completely lost in the beauty of the sport. He landed the fish, which he guessed to weigh fifteen pounds, then released it back into the river.

He fished the next two pools upriver, catching two more fish of equal size, both rainbows. The trip into the valley between mountains had been well worth the risk. He walked around the gorge, having to go inland somewhat to negotiate the expanded width of the river.

He felt like the only man to have ever fished here, and he knew this feeling was what gave the Fossil River its reputation. He felt like he'd just scaled Everest or landed on the moon.

As Giselson forged the left side of the river, he heard a strange, unfamiliar sound that stopped him short.

It was coming from upriver.

At first, he thought it sounded like an elk's bugle, but it was too high-pitched and sharp. Whatever it was, its call sent a shudder down his spine.

He stopped and waited for another call. Nothing came. Slowly now as he advanced upriver, his eyes combed the thick woods that hugged the banks on both sides.

The next pool he came upon was large and enclosed by a high ridge of boulders that seemed to form an almost perfect circle. He peered down into the crystal clear water, which was about ten feet deep.

Rocks littered the bottom. Some were round sandstone, others gray with sharp edges, still others pink. He could see the shadow of large fish hovering behind a cluster of stones.

He stepped down to the very edge of the pool and raised his rod, stripping out line in a perfect arc, front-to-back, double hauling for distance.

Just before his fly hit the water, a high-pitched screech startled him. What was meant to be a smooth silent cast collapsed into a tangle of green line, and Giselson knew he had spooked the pool.

But he also knew that something was terribly wrong.

His heart was pounding in his chest now. Beads of sweat rolled down his brow, stinging his eyes. He stepped out of the water and stood rigid, eyes scanning the deep woods on both sides of the river. He took two steps back and heard a rustle in the brush on the opposite bank. His mind filled with the image of a grizzly bear on the hunt. Bushes moved, branches snapped. His eyes widened.

He pulled his Smith & Wesson from his vest, unlocked the safety, and fired three quick rounds into the dense trees on the opposite river-bank. The report echoed across the valley. Then there was silence, save for the soft lulling sound of the Fossil River.

Nothing moved. Giselson turned slowly, 360 degrees. Then he cursed his overactive imagination.

"Don't be an asshole." He tucked the gun back into his vest and looked into the pool before him. His imagination was playing tricks on him, he thought. He coached himself to relax. Again, he felt for the gun in his vest pocket and took in a deep breath of mountain air.

Without warning, a deafening sound swept across the river, but this time it was familiar, and it came from the sky.

He looked up. A thin vale of fog still hovered over the valley, but he could now see specks of cerulean blue Alaskan sky peeking through the clouds. In the distance, he heard the din of jet engines and then the belly of a silver plane appeared above him. It's too low, Giselson thought—but just the sight of it gave him a new sense of security.

That was short-lived.

Giselson shook his head, trying to make sense of the lost-world feeling that enveloped him. There was something else eerie about this place: the smell. He tilted his nose upwind and took in another deep breath of mountain air.

It's oil. Yes, he decided, the smell was definitely oil, but it was faint and seemed to waft into his sensory system, then vanish. *How strange.* His GPS read 7,800 feet.

An eerie screeching that seemed to be coming from all directions at once shattered his reverie and filled him with unmitigated fear.

Something was stalking him.

9

And whatever it was had to be more than one. Maybe two or more. A shape streaked to his left.

Then he saw movement across the river so fast that he couldn't register what it was—yet he knew in an instant it was not a grizzly bear. He pulled his gun out again, this time aware his hand was shaking. He tried to steady the motion and, as he did, turned slowly, pointing the weapon. He fired a shot. The sound reverberated through the mountain valley and gave him a modicum of confidence.

There was another ear-piercing screech and movement to his left; to his right, a rustling behind him. Something upriver seemed to be gliding right-to-left across the stream. Something large. He thought he saw wings, but the fog had thickened and left him with a fuzzy image.

"Jesus Christ!" he yelled.

Then he saw another streak of motion in the distance, and his eyes widened in disbelief. He saw color: blackish brown with patches of blue, maybe some red. He thought he saw feathers, but wasn't sure. Feathers made no sense.

He'd seen the size of it this time and it was large: ten to twelve feet long, six to eight feet tall. Most terrifying was the creatures' speed and agility. Somehow, Giselson knew, they were communicating to each other.

And closing in fast.

The bushes rustled again and shook with intensity. He was encircled. In one panicked and desperate motion, Giselson emptied his remaining seven rounds in all directions. The Rocky Mountain range seemed to explode with the salvo.

Then it happened.

Before he could even reach for more ammo in his vest pocket, something enormous lunged at him and tore at his face, blinding him and spinning him around. He flailed wildly, arms wind-milling for balance.

The impact sent him falling backward toward the river. His legs churned to regain ground. He blinked in disbelief. Everything around him seemed to be tinted red. Then he realized blood was spurting from his scalp, down his forehead, and into his eyes.

He looked down at his chest and saw a gaping vertical wound that ran from his sternum to his crotch. His hands instinctively moved to cover his guts. He threw his head back and let out a gurgling scream for help.

That's when he was attacked and surrounded again.

Before his lacerated body fell into the Fossil River, Giselson's eyes went blank, and his mind had already been paralyzed by a sight that forced his heart to beat its last pulse in one convulsive shiver of dread.

The strong current pulled his mangled corpse toward the center of the fast-moving river. His fishing gear fell away and floated downstream, and the once gin-clear water of the Fossil was now the color of a cheap rosé wine.

Giselson's tattered, bloodied vest caught on a tree branch. His creel, heavy with the trout he'd gutted earlier, sank to the bottom.

Moments later, the dead fish slipped from the creel basket and floated toward the surface. There, caught in the strong swirl of undercurrent, it was swept down river and around the bend toward the Noatak.

CHAPTER 2

ONE HUNDRED AND FIFTY MILLION YEARS AGO, THE MAJESTIC MOUNTAINS OF the American Northwest were nothing more than sand ridges that rolled along the bottom of a vast ocean teeming with prehistoric life.

When the plates of the continent heaved and collided, the earth buckled and bent, creating a dramatically contoured landmass where once there was ocean.

Then came the dinosaurs—vast lumbering herbivore packs and carnivore colonies that roamed the region to hunt amid dense, giant forests. The pathway for this colossal land migration of flora and fauna leading from Siberia to North America was across the Bering Land Bridge that connected Asia to Alaska, surrounded by the Chukchi Sea.

Gently rolling lands pocked with ponds and swamps teemed with creatures feeding on a plethora of small protozoa. Vegetation burst into full bloom and the dinosaurs thrived. The region was overrun with thousands of species, including Tyrannosaurus Rex, Stegosaurus, Deinonychus, Triceratops, and the duck-billed Hadrosaurus. Teleost fish began to appear in tidal pools along with ammonites, belemnites, echinoids, and the first sponges.

Then, in the Cenozoic Era, a massive meteorite approached earth at an unimaginable velocity, imploding with devastating impact in the northwest corner of Mexico—and sending massive flames, fumes, and dark clouds encircling the globe. On impact, the crater was 100 miles long and six miles wide.

The reverberation must have been excruciating to all living things. The heat from the explosion was beyond measure. Everything in the meteorite's wake was torched within a nanosecond.

Iridium, found in the shale near the site of implosion, confirmed that the massive object was from outer space. Iridium was also discovered at other points around the earth, including the Burgess Shale Quarry in Alberta, Canada where 60,000 fossils were found, and further north into Alaska in the mountain banks of the Colville River and on the north shore of the Beaufort Sea.

On all seven continents, living creatures lay in piles of slowly rotting flesh, bone, and waste, together with withering and smoldering vegetation and forestation. Over time, the decaying mass oozed beneath the earth's crust. During the Carboniferous era, it would be buried for one hundred million years, slowly to percolate into fossil fuel.

Approximately 170 million years ago, long before dinosaurs and tar sands existed, the plates of North America shifted and slid over one another with intense force. Layers of rock warped and folded like massive sheets of cauldron-hot steel. The slabs of ancient Protozoic rock lurched from the west and rolled over the younger, more supple, Mesozoic rock layers spilling from the east, creating the Lewis Overthrust. Ultimately, it would become the vast Rocky Mountain Range.

Thousands of years later, the human race's demand on the global energy supply of fossil fuel was slowly destroying the global landscape. The Industrial Revolution had left an indelible mark. Smokestacks belched carbon dioxide into the atmosphere and greenhouse gases began taking a toll on all living things.

To protect the ozone layer and avoid global warming, environmentalists had succeeded in blocking expanded production of coal gasification plants. Operating costs had become prohibitive. The environmentalists of E.L.F., The Sierra Club, and Greenpeace also worked to prevent oil exploration of all public and private lands. When the earthquake hit Japan in 2011, the tsunami that followed killed thousands.

Similarly, TEPCO's six Fukushima nuclear reactor plants sent a tidal wave of fear around the earth as the nuclear meltdown sent radioactivity into the water and atmosphere. Across the Pacific, it was found in cow's milk. As a result, the United States reevaluated its entire nuclear program.

Over 100 U.S. nuclear power plants provided the nation with more than twenty percent of the nation's electric energy. The disaster forced each of them to reevaluate their safety regulations. Some shut down. None were allowed to expand.

Solar and wind energy had proven too inefficient and costly to produce enough energy to make a short-term difference. But politicians were desperate to appease the public so they pushed for approval of any energy program that held any promise.

What no one knew was that the United States' strategic oil reserves were riding on empty—and supplies from all over the world were dwindling with surprising rapidity.

The nation was on the verge of losing power.

Military-fueled demands to carry out international missions on land, sea, and air cut deeply into domestic fuel supplies. Cars, trucks, buses, and commercial airlines were sacrificed in favor of military mobility fuels to protect the nation. Gas at the pumps doubled, then tripled in price. Worse, it was being rationed and lines at gas stations were slowly causing consumers to panic. As desperate consumers fought to fill up their tanks, riots broke out.

The commercial airline industry, unable to get enough jet fuel to keep up with flight demand, was beginning to unravel, cutting back flight schedules, raising prices dramatically, and laying off employees.

Without gas, industries all over the nation began to announce mass layoffs. It was a crisis of epic proportions. And it had come on fast.

The President of the United States, Peter Barton, summoned an *ad hoc* cabinet in hopes of diverting the perfect storm. Barton's Department of Defense was guzzling fifty-eight percent of every barrel of fossil fuel to power his military. Barton had named his last-ditch agenda *Operation Torch.*

As President Barton lifted the weekly energy report off his desk to study it, the phone rang.

"Morning, Mr. President." It was Secretary of Energy Tyler Conlon.

"It's getting worse, isn't it?" the President said. "A lot faster than we expected."

"Yes, sir. Time's running out. We'll be lucky if we can last another three months with current inventory. Operation Torch has to succeed. There are spot outages across the country already," said Conlon.

Barton took in a deep, labored breath. "I know," he said. "We only have one option."

CHAPTER 3

An ALPINE-GREEN SIKORSKY HELICOPTER BEARING THE U.S. FISH & WILDLIFE Agency logo on both sides flew low over the southern mountain range of Noatak National Park, northwestern Alaska. Prisms of sparkling light from the morning sun danced off dashboard instruments inside the cabin.

The chopper dipped into deep-ridged valley pockets, then climbed vertically to avoid the sprawling range of sharp peaks. Alaska contained 373 mountain peaks over 10,000 feet. Mt. McKinley towered over them all at 20,320 feet.

Forty-eight percent of all Alaskan mountains have yet to be climbed. Scott Chandler had researched that fact when he got the assignment. Noatak Preserve, the crown jewel of the U.S. Department of Interior's inventory of public parks, was the most scenic of them all. It contained twenty-three mountains above 10,000 feet.

Chandler peered from the glass-bubbled cabin, taking in the thick blanket of fog that hovered over the mountain canopy like puffs of cotton candy.

Two years ago, Chandler had been Manager of Wildlife and Senior Zoologist with the Department of Interior's Fish and Wildlife Agency in Glacier National Park, Montana. It was a job he remembered coveting with great excitement when he'd first received the offer on F&W letterhead while recovering in rehab. It was a dream come true, and his

Masters in zoology from the University of Montana, Missoula, clinched the position.

Chandler liked to think his academic credentials and piloting skills were the sole reason he landed the job—not the fact that he was also eligible under Section 508, which provided preferential employment for disabled veterans returning home from Iraq and Afghanistan.

But what bothered Chandler lately was that wounded warriors were being sent home in increased numbers from other Arab countries. "We're there to protect our interests," was the trite phrase used by presidents. Chandler had told his friends in the bars of St. Mary's. "It's all bullshit. We're there for the fucking oil," he'd held up his prosthesis for emphasis. "It's blood for oil, plain and simple. I'd like to see President Barton level with the people."

It had been a busy seven years at Glacier: taking surveys, monitoring elk and mule deer herds, checking for disease, and studying the living habits of the park's wildlife. Chandler applied the same obsessive quest for knowledge and detail, how everything survived and how it died, as he did to his work in Afghanistan where his obsessiveness saved his life many times. He committed to memory every mountain, ridge, glacier, river, lake, trail, and valley within the park's 3,000 square miles. After rigid tests affirming his ability to pilot a helicopter, he'd finally convinced the Interior that he could still fly with his prosthetic left arm. Two years ago, Interior Secretary Lauren Zollar gave him control of a Fish and Wildlife Sikorsky to manage the park's wildlife—then he got the call he dreaded.

"We need your talents in Alaska, Scott," Chandler remembered Zollar telling him.

"It must have been very important," Chandler told his park partner, Brave Wolf Whitman. "The call should have come from my boss, Trent Schneider."

Robert Brave Wolf Whitman was a Blackfoot Indian from the reservation near Browning, Montana, east of Glacier. As biologist with Interior's Fish and Wildlife, Brave Wolf assisted Chandler in managing the park's wildlife. Over the past seven years, they'd become professional friends. Brave Wolf was steeped in the lore of the area he'd learned from his ancestors reaching back to the Paleo Indians that had once inhabited the land in 13,000 B.C by crossing a land bridge that connected eastern Siberia with Alaska during the late Pleistocene.

"What's so urgent up there?" Wolf queried.

"Something about the caribou herd shrinking. This place is somewhere near the Arctic Circle, Noatak it's called. Zollar said there's a herd of 450,000 caribou in the Park. At least that's what they started out with, Zollar claims. The herd's down 75,000. Anyway, she wants us to take on a two-year assignment with the promise we'll come back to Glacier at the end of it."

"What do you mean, us?" Wolf stammered in disbelief. "No way am I going back there."

"That's precisely why I need you, Wolf. You might be a true-blood Blackfoot here in Montana, but they found out your great-grandfather was Inuit. Besides, you're the best tracker in the agency."

"Damn it to hell," Wolf spat, his voice thin. "Invasion of privacy."

"Hell no, my friend. When you work for the U.S. Government, nothing's private. You're stripped whistle-clean."

After they moved to Noatak, Alaska, Chandler and Wolf had taken over a small log cabin F&W field office 150 miles west of the small town of Noatak.

"You'll be closer to the caribou," Zollar told Chandler. As far as Chandler was concerned, it was all scrambled political bullshit. They rented two log cabins east of Noatak, 1.3 miles northeast of town, and within walking distance to the nearest grocery store.

They commuted to work using the Sikorsky. This made their existence somewhat tolerable compared to Glacier National Park, but they both bitched to each other about the lack of women in Noatak. Chandler told Wolf that nobody here was attractive enough to hit on. Then it happened: one night at The Master Baiter, he met an Eskimo woman. "She's reasonable," he told Wolf with mild interest.

"Don't hit on my people," Wolf complained.

"Don't flatter yourself, Wolf. I'd have to slam down three single malts to even consider it."

In March, Chandler won the *Employee of the Year Award* at

CAREERS & the disABLED Magazine's Twenty-first Annual Awards Ceremony recognizing the nation's top ten employees with disabilities.

To Chandler, it meant more than his Purple Hearts and Bronze Stars, because it validated his employment and reason for being. Chandler became the poster child of success for Interior's Fish & Wildlife Agency, and his picture and profile appeared on Interior's Internet job board, and in full-page ads in CAREERS & the disABLED Magazine. Far from Chandler's sock drawer where he kept his combat medals, this Award was mounted above the Sikorsky's instrument panel.

Chandler banked the chopper sharply to the left and dropped into a thick fog bank. Wolf sat next to him. As Wolf accepted the move from Glacier to Noatak, he grew more comfortable with his surroundings. It gave him a chance to research the Inuit Indians that surrounded Noatak. The thought that he was related to Alaska's Eskimo tribe through his great grandfather now took on new meaning, and he found himself poring over books and Googling his ancestors. Tomorrow, he promised himself, he would meet an elder of the local tribe and connect with his roots.

"This park is changing, my friend," Brave Wolf said. "Something's not right."

Chandler's helicopter flew down the center of the Noatak River. Then he headed south at the point the outfitter had dropped off the fisherman's ATV. He lowered the chopper so they could make out objects on the ground. Wolf pointed to a grizzly and two cubs and Chandler hovered briefly, then flew southeast toward a thick fog bank.

They vanished into the dark grey cloud. He was flying by instrument now, visibility zero, but his Simulated Vision Data System displayed the contour of the land below with uncanny accuracy.

"Another MIA fisherman. That makes four in less than a year. The police should be doing this gig, not us."

"Yeah, you're right," Brave Wolf said, his eyes leveling on Chandler. "But nobody can get in there like you. It's not exactly easy flying."

"Not the easiest hike, either," Chandler said, looking at the instrument panel. "And posted all to hell for over a hundred years. These damned fly fishing purists are going to a hell of a lot of trouble to get themselves lost and killed."

Brave Wolf frowned. "Yeah. To tell you the truth—not that I don't like people and all-but frankly, I'm more concerned with the caribou than the poachers. The herd count is down by at least another sixty, maybe more. Some of them must be separating from the herd and wandering into this area. They're not coming out. I don't know if they're getting lost, eating something that's poisoning them—or if some very hungry predator's doing the job. Hell, they could be falling off a cliff into a big hole for all we know. If we could at least find a carcass…right now it's like they're just disappearing. Spooky."

"We'll find something," Chandler said. "Whatever it is."

Moments later, both men spotted the south fork of the Fossil River, a white fuzzy meandering line through thick fog. Chandler dropped to thirty feet and wove his way along the river, looking for some trace of the missing fisherman. He was peering out of the port side of the chopper when two distinct magenta blips appeared on his sonar rig. By the time he turned back to face the instrument panel, they'd vanished.

"Nothing here," he said. "Still pissing me off."

"Leave it, Scott. Let's try upriver. We'll just do a mile of it." Brave Wolf looked down on the fast-moving water that rippled white at the next bend. As Chandler veered sharply right, a large Blue Spruce that had angled halfway across the river in a windstorm appeared directly in front of him. He pulled up quickly and banked to the left. Brave Wolf threw up his hands to cover his face.

Chandler gave him a quick glance. "You trust me?"

"Shit, man. That was close," Wolf complained.

"You haven't seen close, my friend. Not to worry."

Did I look worried?" Wolf said, falling back into his seat. "But maybe you could pick up just a little altitude?"

"I'm doing the flying here. You do what you do best-use those eagle eyes and find us something."

Brave Wolf watched his friend deftly handle the controls with his prosthesis. Around the next bend, he pointed and said, "Wait. Hold here."

Chandler brought the chopper to a stationery hover. "What?" he said, studying the altimeter.

Brave Wolf pointed out the copter bubble glass. "Put it down. There's something over on the far bank."

"I see it," Chandler said after studying the area hard. He had better than 20-20 eyesight, but nobody saw things like the Wolf. Chandler flew the chopper over to the opposite side of the Fossil and set it down on the rocky north bank of the river, engine still roaring above the sound of the water, which was in a white froth from the whirl of the blades.

"Check it out!"

Wolf bounded out of the helicopter and hopped over the rock-laden riverbank. He bent over and picked up what was left of a fishing creel. It was crushed. The leather sling used as a shoulder strap to carry it was torn in half, its rough edges like strings of spaghetti.

Wolf stood up, creel in hand, and looked downriver, inspecting each rock, looking for tracks. He walked forty yards, then peered into the thick underbrush. He looked toward the woods, but fog had settled low to the ground and discouraged him from moving out of sight of the helicopter. He turned around, walked back to the Fossil, and shrugging his shoulders, held up the creel to show Chandler.

Wolf turned upriver and paced out about fifty yards, maybe sixty. He studied the riverbank, walked up to a small pool of calm water. He saw two trout feeding at the base of the pool.

And then he saw something else. It was white, about a foot-and-a-half long. He knew it was a bone. It seemed to be suspended in the current, twirling in a circle.

At first, he thought it might be a bone from a caribou or mule deer, but it was shorter. About the size of a human femur. Brave Wolf looked behind him in an effort to find a stick long enough to prod the object closer to shore. When he turned back to the river pool, the white object had vanished downriver in the current.

"Damn," he said.

Wolf walked back to the helicopter, its powerful engines drowning out the eerie screech he thought he heard from 200 yards upriver. He wasn't sure. This was the first time that he and Chandler had reason to try and penetrate this remote area of the southeastern fork of the Fossil.

Brave Wolf lifted his nose high into the air. He drank in a long breath of air and his brow furrowed. *Oil.* The faint smell of oil wafted in and

21

out of the soft breeze out of the west, baffling him. It was quickly diffused and replaced by the strong scent of pine from the evergreen trees that hovered along the river shore.

He entered the whirling wind of the chopper blades. Wolf looked around the site one last time, inspecting everything he could. Then he hoisted himself through the hatch back into the cabin.

"This is new territory to me," Wolf said, shaking his head. He held up what was left of the creel.

"Me, too," Chandler grunted. He took the mangled creel and studied it. "If we assume this was the guy's creel from yesterday—he's toast. What the hell destroyed it? Looks like something tried to eat it."

"Don't know," Wolf said. "There was something else."

"What?"

"Thought I saw a bone. Almost a foot long. In the Fossil. The current got it. There was no flesh. Whatever got it must have eaten the meat off it."

"Christ."

Wolf closed his eyes tightly and Chandler watched his face twitch.

"There are ancient spirits in these mountains. I feel them."

As the helicopter lifted off the ground to head back to the Fish & Wildlife headquarters, Chandler looked at Wolf and said, "So your people are talking—the spirits again?"

"You mock me?"

"Easy, Wolf. I don't understand your culture, that's all. My point was, what the hell do we put in the report? Ancient evil spirits ate another trespasser? That'll go over well," Chandler said.

CHAPTER 4

I<small>T WAS STILL PITCH DARK OUTSIDE WHEN</small> P<small>RESIDENT</small> B<small>ARTON MADE HIS WAY</small> down the long, quiet corridor of the West Wing to the Oval Office. Although he was now several months into his second term, Barton still felt like he was just visiting, that somehow he had come in on a White House tour and had never left.

It was how he'd felt the entire time he was at Taft boarding school as a teenager. He'd been sent away to be shielded from the fallout of his parents' bitter divorce. It was then that he'd adopted the habit of waking up before first light to sit and collect his thoughts before the rest of the world was up and active.

Being awake while his family, his staff, and the rest of the country slept gave him the feeling that he was actually in control of his own destiny and the country he served. During these moments before dawn, Peter Barton felt most at ease.

It was also the hour when he made the toughest decisions of his career.

Barton had tried to break the U.S. dependency on foreign oil supplies and end the "wars for oil" that had been ravaging the Middle East for decades.

During his first term, he renewed a number of alternative energy resource programs that had been launched by previous administrations: wind, solar, water, gasification of coal, and biofuels. But they'd yet to deliver any substantial energy source that could divert the crisis that was now threatening the nation's electric power grid and causing havoc at the gas pumps. Energy Secretary Conlin was desperately trying to keep the nation's overextended and antiquated power grid balanced to prevent the lights from dimming. So far, he had succeeded with only minor outages.

But things were changing fast.

As President Barton approached the Oval Office, his long-time friend and senior member of his security detail, Johnny Styk, a Marine Purple Heart veteran from the Iraq war, saluted him with dramatic raising of his eyebrows. Officer Styk was used to seeing his boss early. But not this early. It was just after five a.m.

Barton smiled, returned the salute, and entered his office. Before turning to his desk, he looked out the window and gazed onto the empty, well-lit streets of the city that stretched out before him. He couldn't help but wonder how long it would be before this kind of urban tableau of brightly illuminated roadways and buildings would be a thing of the past.

Barton wasn't at his desk at this hour simply to get a jump on routine business. Today was no ordinary day at the office—even for the President of the United States. *Operation Torch*, if successful, would erase any remaining memories of how poorly past Presidents had responded to the spate of hurricanes that had thrashed the Gulf Coast and battered the domestic oil industry over the past two decades. If *Torch* was successful, it would not only solve the current oil crisis, it could also salvage his reputation. It might also secure his place as the greatest President of all time.

If it failed, on the other hand, he and his administration would be ruined.

For the past three years, Barton had been fleshing out the specifics of *Operation Torch*, under the aegis of the National Geospatial & Intelligence Agency under the Department of Defense. He'd had even gone so far as to clandestinely commission the development of new technologies that would be used exclusively for *Operation Torch*. It was time to put that technology into high gear.

The contract had been awarded to Lockheed Martin, Northrop

Grumman, and Raytheon to perfect penetrating technology and systems that could see twenty miles below the earth's crust. When the project was complete, the new technology was retrofitted onto Boeing OC135B jets. Under Barton's watchful eye, the departments of Energy, Defense, and Interior had worked tirelessly in concert to make it happen.

The most recent reports were on his desk. They'd been delivered by messenger just before midnight. Barton had stayed up most of the night reading them, and sat down now to review them again. On top of the three officially-sealed documents was one other report: a summary, from the department of Homeland Security, which outlined the billions of dollars—in lives lost, property damaged, toll on the domestic oil supply, and overall rebuilding and recovery expenses—that the string of hurricanes that had battered the Gulf Coast states had cost the country over the past fifteen years.

Barton took a deep breath and opened the first folder.

The title of the Homeland Security report said it all: "The Devastating Costs of Domestic Hurricanes."

Over the past fifteen years, it had become clear that the steady annual increase in the number of serious tropical storms that hit the U.S. appeared to be no accident or statistical blip. Barton knew it was due to global warming.

The warming climate had permanently changed the nature of hurricane activity in the Atlantic. Tropical storms that arose from the Atlantic Basin off the Cape Verde Islands of Africa were now routinely battering the U.S. Gulf Coast with a vengeance. Two years ago, it happened: a category five hurricane, Juan, slammed into the Gulf of Mexico with ravaging 180-mile-an-hour winds.

Seventy percent of the deep-water oil rigs had vanished, wiping out most of the domestic oil that the United States relied on for thirty percent of its energy supply. It left twenty-six oil refineries in Houston, Texas limping along at forty percent capacity. Now, each time a storm gained enough momentum to earn a name, the nation cringed. The explosion on BP's oil rig that left the Gulf of Mexico covered in a black sheet of oil back in 2010 only exacerbated a growing crisis that was on the brink of collapsing the United States economy.

Barton thought in the short term he could simply print more money to buy more oil from OPEC to make up for the thirty percent loss from the Gulf supply.

But three weeks ago, the worst energy crisis in history had exploded, shocking the world.

China, the world's second largest consumer of fossil fuel at 6.6 million barrels a day, had struck a deal with OPEC: guarantee China a supply of fifteen million barrels of oil a day in exchange for China's aggressive purchase of exports from all participating OPEC countries. The deal precluded any increase in OPEC's sale of oil to the United States.

People in China were suffering from inhaling deadly coal-laden oxygen and pollutants. They were caused by the intensive burning of coal gasification plants blackening the skies—the same harbinger of death that almost forced closure of the world's summer Olympics in Beijing, 2008. Tuberculosis, once the number one cause of death in the United States among coal miners, had killed over 2,000 people last year in China.

Gao Ziying, President of China, had promised his people that he would cut production from coal gasification plants in half, making up the shortfall with fossil fuel from the Arab Oil Cartel.

When President Barton called Ziying demanding he nullify the contract with OPEC or the United States would cut off imports from China, Ziying's angered response was decisive: "You cut off our exports to your country, and we'll call 376 billion dollars in U.S. Government issued security loans."

Barton hounded Saudi Arabia's Minister of Oil, Akhmed Naimi, with repeated calls for more oil, but each time Naimi refused to change the United States allotment. The perfect energy storm was in play, and Barton had only one option: find fossil fuel within the United States to save his country from unmitigated disaster, or enter into an energy-induced depression that would make 1929 look like child's play.

The cost of filling a tank of gas now hovered at $150, with the average cost per gallon not dipping below $7.25 in more than six months. Lines at the gas pumps were burgeoning out of control. Many gas stations were doling out gas in allotments: half tanks, quarter tanks, and some were forced to close down altogether.

The report prepared by Tyler Conlon, Secretary of the Department of Energy, was the grimmest of all. Most of the country's international oil partners did business with the U.S. only grudgingly. For many of these corporations and the governments that oversaw them, it was only worth doing business with the U.S. in order to see the richest country on earth squirm while handing over fistfuls of dollars. But the deal China struck with OPEC changed the international energy landscape. The only partner who still supplied a significant amount of oil without inflicting additional torment on the U.S. was Canada.

At nine a.m. sharp, there was a knock on the Oval Office door. The President stood and straightened his tie. For a brief moment, he felt the fatigue of having already been up and at work for four hours. But he was just hitting his stride: he was only a third of the way through a typical workday. He shook his head, sucked in a deep breath, and buttoned his suit jacket. Then he gathered up the briefing papers on his desk, walked across his office and stood at the head of a large conference table. He waited for his secretary, Lucretia Sanders, to open the door and enter.

"Mr. President, members of your Cabinet are here, sir." She walked toward him and placed three sets of the reports Barton had just studied on the table beside him. "Shall I bring you some coffee, sir?"

"Just water, Lucretia. Send them in, please."

Sanders nodded and left the office. Moments later, the door opened and three Senior Cabinet members entered: Zollar, Robinson, and Conlon.

Barton wasted no time. He gave concise yet sweeping summaries of the departmental reports that were now being scanned by his cabinet members. After going over these briefs, he paused momentarily, then told his staff that, from this point forward, the meeting would be confidential. There would be no documentation of the agenda and there would be no discussion of it outside the Oval Office. He then posed a series of questions, beginning with one for the secretary of Energy.

"Tyler. Given what we know of OPEC's reluctance to lower oil prices, Arab political turmoil, and their contract with China, what can we expect in terms of oil prices for the upcoming winter months?"

Conlon took a deep breath and shook his head before speaking. "Mr. President, this year it could top $200 a barrel."

Conlon's voice rose in pitch as he displayed maps and reviewed all major oil deposits now identified throughout the world. With a black magic marker, the Secretary methodically circled them: Alaska's Prudhoe Sound deposits under Gull Island, and the Gulf of Mexico's oil production providing the United States with thirty percent of their daily crude oil supply until Hurricane Juan cut production by sixty percent.

Conlon paused, took a long sip of water, then pointed again to Alaska's Prudhoe Sound deposit. With a pointer, he tapped Gull Island twice for emphasis.

"Prudhoe Bay oil field is a massive deposit on Alaska's North Slope. It's the largest oil field in both the United States and in North America. covering 213,543 acres and containing approximately 25 billion barrels of oil. The amount of recoverable oil in the field is more than double that of the next largest field in the United States, the East Texas oil field. The field is operated by BP and its partners are ExxonMobil and ConocoPhillips Alaska. Alaska, obviously, deserves our utmost attention along with the central western states, with a focus on Montana and the Rockies."

He pointed to the Kazakhstan twelve-billion-barrel oil field discovered in 2000. Then, back in 2008, the discovery by Brazil's Petrobras National Oil Company of the Tupi deposit near the Santos Basin.

Barton, Zollar and Robinson sat rigid, faces drawn. Conlon reported that Brazil promised to produce, within ten years, 17.2 billion barrels of oil, putting it ahead of Canada's 17.1 billion barrels, and Mexico's 12.9 billion barrels.

Conlon continued the statistics, his voice tense. "Venezuela has eighty billion barrels of proven reserves, and Saudi Arabia, controlling 26.3% of global oil reserves, has 216 billion barrels and a lock on OPEC and the Arab Oil Cartel that's driving the crude oil price per barrel up at will. But the Arab countries are in utter chaos now—so who knows what kind of production we'll get."

The strain on Conlon's face was evident as he circled a large oval area over the northwestern United States including Utah, Colorado, Wyoming, North Dakota, Montana, Idaho, and Alaska. "We've been over this before. It's critical—absolutely vital—that we focus on this particular region again. All our research from the Energy Department," said

Conlon frowning, "points to this area. Nowhere else on earth had such vast populations of dinosaurs roaming the area during the Jurassic and Cretaceous period. Many of the beasts apparently migrated over the Bering Land Bridge connecting Asia with Alaska. The irony of this crisis is that we hold sixty-two percent of the world's oil shale reserves. And most of it is in this area. But we don't have the technology to tap into it. Most of it's in tar sands. Very hard to extract and very costly. The one good thing about tar sand is that it's organic. Over time, it gives off shale gas, but we've yet to master the process of its release. But the Energy department is convinced that there should be more here than just the shale. We think there has to be oil. A lot of it."

"But," Conlon said, with an edge of frustration in his voice, "why haven't we been able to locate the single source that feeds these tar sands and shale deposits? Because we just haven't had the imaging technology that could look deep enough or wide enough, with sufficient sensitivity to cover every square inch of promising ground. Until now. Thanks to NGA we've got better imaging than ever before, and we're ready to deploy immediately. This is very serious. We are running out of time, gentlemen. We've got one card left to throw down—and this is it," said Conlon. "We can't afford to blow it."

With confidence in his voice, he again circled the large area on the map of the Western Frontier, including Alaska. "Somewhere within this area has to be the mother lode of oil. We have to find it. And we have to find it quickly."

Defense Secretary Robinson slapped his hand on the table loud enough to startle the President. "We're barely able to keep a full complement of planes, ships, tanks, and vehicles in motion now, Mr. President. We can't compromise our troops. At all costs, our mobility fuel must not be sacrificed. Any fuel shortage must come from consumers and industry," Robinson said resolutely. "Not from the military."

The President stood up. "With our jets equipped with this new technology, intensively covering the western states, we'll know soon enough if it all works," he said. "We'll alert each of you as things develop. God willing, we'll keep the lights from going out, and the military's fuel tanks filled."

CHAPTER 5

JUST AFTER SUNRISE ON A CLOUDLESS, CRISP MORNING, FOUR STATE-OF-THE-art Boeing OC-135B US Air Force jets lifted off the tarmac at Peterson Air Force Base. The jets were each retrofitted with the new systems. Defense Secretary Robinson had told President Barton that Peterson AFB, home of the 21st Space Wing, Air Force Space Command, and the North American Aerospace Defense Command (NORAD), would provide the perfect location to coordinate the launch of *Operation Torch* into western air space.

The jets lifted off in tight formation toward the northwest corner of Colorado. Precisely when they reached the border, they broke formation: two flew north, one flew due west into Utah, and the other headed south, canvassing the western border of Colorado before slipping into New Mexico airspace.

The two northerly-flying jets edged into Wyoming until one veered off sharply heading north by northwest toward Alaska, descending low over the state border. The other held altitude and continued west, heading for Montana airspace. On board each jet was a team of technicians from the National Geospatial and Intelligence Agency, a geologist and a petroleum engineer from the Department of Energy, an officer from Homeland Security, and a representative from the Department of Defense.

The National Geospatial-Intelligence Agency (NGA), was responsible for overseeing Operation Torch under Robinson's Department of Defense. NGA's roots reached back to President Thomas Jefferson, who realized that it was no longer strategically wise for the U.S. and its Army, which was overseeing much of the westward expansion, including the Lewis and Clark expedition, to rely on maps created by the British or by commercial cartographers. Jefferson, and all Presidents who followed him, had the good sense to know that the U.S. Military had to have its own mapmaking agency in order to promote and protect national interests.

The task force included state-of-the art satellite imagery, cutting edge GPS systems, an advanced sonar sound rig, heat seeking technology, and high-tech geospatial tools that would, it was hoped, enable the agency for the first time to make visual imaging of the layers of sediment beneath the earth's crust possible.

Sonar and image resonating photography could now capture the substance of all rock strata detail with vivid color-coded charts: gypsum, sandstone, mudstone, shale, granite, quartz, and dozens of other geological formations could now be coded, classified, and recorded. Each substance had a different density display to label whether it was oil, H2O, tar sands, shale, clear gas, or salt water.

Of the four pilots on the mission, Vance Keegan was the most experienced, having been with the Air Force for almost twenty years. His jet crossed into Canadian airspace and headed toward Alaska.

Though Keegan had retired from full-time duty a few years back, he was still on call for strategic flight missions. He'd been tapped for several classified flights in the past, but had never before been asked to sign a confidentiality agreement with such tough language as this one. The thought of going to prison for treason, just as he was easing into retirement, was not on his "things I must-do before I die" list. He'd hesitated for a moment, but then he had gone ahead and signed the agreement. After all, he thought, the flight plan said he was to make a routine pass over Alaska. What risk was there in that?

He pushed thoughts of the legal paperwork out of his mind and nodded at the pilot flying in tandem with him. When they reached the southern edge of Alaskan airspace, Keegan gave a thumbs-up wave to the navigator as he saw the massive peaks of Mt. McKinley.

"That's one hell of a mountain," Keegan said looking at the altimeter.

Keegan dropped the plane down to a cruising altitude of 18,000 feet, two thousand feet below the mountain, but well to the east of it. The navigator instructed him to fly due north toward Prudhoe Bay, then cut west toward the Chukchi Sea.

"We'll crisscross Alaska to make sure we don't miss anything," the navigator said purposefully.

The cartographers on board watched the large LED screens with focused intensity. The equipment had been turned on the moment the wheels lifted off the tarmac. Now the plane was approaching the northwestern edge of the state.

Keegan dropped the plane down another 3,000 feet as the navigator instructed Keegan to bank south and maintain course. Even at that elevation, the panel of computers and infrared cameras that had been bolted into the midsection began to whir and buzz with activity. The large LED screen showed a series of brightly colored images, the smaller screens measured substrata layers in brilliantly distinguished colors, and the NGA crew studied the instruments with intense focus.

The lead technician, Chip Rusbasan conferred with Dale Sloan, the geophysicist from Energy. Rusbasan scribbled something on the clipboard in his hand, then looked up at the navigator, "We're over something, but I can't get definition yet."

"What does it show?" the navigator asked, running his hand through his red hair.

"Holy shit. It's a massive salt deposit," Sloan, who was also busy making notes, said. "This can't be right."

"What is it?" Rusbasan asked.

"Well…this has to be right. The equipment is functioning perfectly. But I wasn't expecting this. I just can't believe we've never seen it before. If these readings are accurate, we're over one of the largest salt deposits in the world. It appears to cover the entire Maiyu Merak mountain range."

"Mark it," Rusbasan commanded the navigator as they flew southeast toward Mount St. Lincoln.

"Done." The navigator picked up the flight plan and looked up in surprise. "Christ, the average elevation of that cluster of mountains is 10,000 feet. To cover the range, we've got to thread four of those babies and into the valley."

"You need to take her down to 4,000 if you can," Rusbasan said to the pilot, "We need to get a look at what's beneath the salt."

"Four thousand?" the navigator said. "There's not much space between those peaks."

Rusbasan tried not to sound anxious. "This technology's good, but it's not perfect. We won't get adequate penetration unless you can put us within 4,000 feet of the valley floor."

Keegan pushed the plane down through the thick wall of clouds. Four snow-covered peaks appeared faintly in the distance above a bed of fog that seemed to be stretched between them like a massive white tarp.

He whistled between his teeth, then turned toward Rusbasan. "I'm not interested in doing any stunt flying today. I'll give you what I can, Rusbasan, but I'm not willing to die so you can get a gold star for proving your fancy new computers work."

Rusbasan knew he had to be diplomatic. "We just need to be a little closer, Vance. Can you drop between those peaks? Then I can get the reading we need and you can take her home."

Keegan turned to his navigator. "How much room do we have once we're between the four mountains?"

The navigator studied the map. "Not much. The valley rests at 3,700 feet."

"If we don't get within 4,000 feet of the valley floor, we won't get the goods," Rusbasan said.

"Fuck the goods," said Keegan. "Fog's too thick. I need a visual to make it at that height. I'm not sure I trust this new Simulation Vision Data Screen. If its reading of the contours is off by a few hundred feet, we're screwed."

The navigator glanced over his shoulder at Rusbasan, then looked back at Keegan. He leaned over and adjusted the controls in front of him. The altimeter spun from 18,000 down to 12,000.

The pilot's hands tightened on the controls. He banked the plane northeast and circled back around Mt. St. Nicholas, banked northwest and dropped past Mt. Stimson, then flew toward Mt. St. Lincoln. The

OC-135B banked hard to the left and toward Mt. Jackson, but St. Lincoln's jagged peaks were too close for comfort. The pilot corrected sharply to the left, and the plane entered a rough chop, its wings yawing back and forth. The jet bounced up and down in stiff mountain air currents.

"Say your prayers," Keegan muttered. "This one's for Uncle Sam."

He dipped the plane's nose farther below the fog bank and the cockpit went dark, as if a switch had been flipped. The brilliant blue of the Alaskan sky had vanished in an instant.

The navigator began to track the plane's descent and talked Keegan through it. "Get ready, Vance." The jet fell sharply in uneven air currents, its altimeter spinning.

Long training kept the navigator's voice professional and steady, but he couldn't help shouting the first word. "Up! Take it up! We're not going to make it." Then under his breath he spat, "Fuck!"

Keegan felt a shiver of fear skitter down his back and his adrenalin spiked. Instinctively he pulled back on the yoke. The jet's four engines vibrated violently as the nose of the plane tipped up. A sharp peak appeared out of the mist and seemed to almost touch the left wing. Stunned, the crew watched in horror as snow blanketed the window and the fuselage trembled violently. Keegan made another sharp correction before the plane leveled out. He looked out the cockpit window, peering at the left wing, and saw a jagged two-foot section of the wing missing.

"Jesus Christ," Keegan spat through clenched teeth. "Unfucking-believable. I thought we were gone. We lost a section of the starboard wing." There was organized panic in the cabin as Keegan frantically checked the instruments. He said in astonishment, "We're okay. We'll make it."

His eyes still glued to his GPS and LED screens, Rusbasan barked, "Keep it steady and make the same pass. We're tracking it."

Keegan finally lost his temper. He ripped his speakerphone away from his face and shouted over his shoulder, "I don't give a fuck what we're looking for. We're not going to die trying to find it."

Rusbasan didn't raise his voice in return. "This is vital, Captain. It could be a total game changer. If this means what I think it does, somebody's coming back here to find out exactly what this is. Do you want to make someone else do the job? Because it's going to get done, for Chrissake."

Keegan took in a deep, labored breath, gritted his teeth and said, "One more pass, and that's all you get. Then I'm taking us out of this hellhole."

The navigator, trained to stay calm even when flying combat missions, had quickly regained his own composure. "It's okay, Vance. The equipment's working."

Now the fog thinned. Through broken cloud cover, a verdant valley emerged below the plane cut through by the dazzling white line of a river.

"It's the Noatak," the navigator said, relieved to have a site fix on location.

Keegan flew the aircraft in a straight line between the four mountains. The navigator pointed through the windshield, then turned to Rusbasan and Sloan and nodded.

Rusbasan worked one of the computers on his lap, typing in commands as if his life depended on it. "Okay. Let's see what's holding up these mountains." The lifeless screen gave way to a multicolored, detailed topography of the land below.

"There's a lot of something down there," one of the NGA techs said, as he pushed a button on another computer panel and the screen lit up money-green indicating the first strata of matter beneath the salt cover.

"Damn. Look at this!" Rusbasan said, barely able to contain his excitement.

"What are you seeing?" Keegan couldn't help reacting to Rusbasan's enthusiasm.

"Whatever it is, there's a lot of it. A minute more, and we'll know," Sloan was peering over the shoulders of the NGA techs as they worked switches and knobs on the new high tech equipment. Another NGA tech pushed a button on the large LCD computer that was built into the console. They all listened and watched when the computer beneath his hands began to vibrate and hum.

The screen became a blur of data and images scrolling down through layers of salt, rock, and sediment. In unison, three printers began spewing massive reams of data and images in different colors.

"Holy shit," Sloan grunted.

"What is it?" pressed the navigator.

"I don't fucking believe it." Rusbasan stared at the geologist bug-eyed, his mind swimming in a sea of hopeful thoughts.

Even Keegan couldn't bear the suspense. "We're flying through death valley here, pal. Whatever it is better be worth it."

Sloan turned toward the computer console and high-fived Rusbasan before delivering the stunning news. "Gentlemen—it looks like we've just discovered a massive oil deposit."

"Well, it better be the mother lode," the pilot said, thinking about the near collision with the mountain.

"It just may be," Sloan said. He could barely contain his excitement. During the past three years, he had given up hope of ever finding a significant new deposit anywhere on the continental United States. "Jesus H. Christ. It looks like a bonanza. Buried under a pile of mountains in Noatak National Park."

"That's one hell of a big Park," the navigator said, staring at the chart, "and it's in the middle of nowhere."

But as they watched the data and images, something else was coming onto the screen. Oil was color-coded black, but beneath the oil was another color: amber. And there was something else beneath the amber, but it was colorless.

Sloan said to Rusbasan, "What the hell's that?"

Rusbasan flipped through his technical manuals, trying to find definition for the amber. He found nothing coded for both images showing on the chart.

Keegan banked the plane to the right, then pulled the OC-135B up to 9,000 feet and leveled off. In the distance he saw sharp peaks. An active volcano spewed smoke and the morning sun peeked over the north side of jagged cliffs. He pulled the nose up fast to clear the summit, but this time he was ready.

The navigator squinted out the window, shaking his head in disbelief. "A massive oil deposit protected by four huge mountain peaks. I don't envy whoever has to try and tap it."

Once the plane reached 15,000 feet, it left the mountains of Noatak behind. Now the late morning sun bathed the slick OC-135B in dazzling white light. Keegan flipped down his shades and maintained a southeasterly course back toward Peterson Air Force Base. This would be his last freelance mission, he swore.

CHAPTER 6

THE OIL DISCOVERY IN NOATAK NATIONAL PRESERVE WAS QUICKLY TRANSMITTED back to NGA headquarters, the Department of Energy, and the Department of Interior. The Cabinet members of the Operation Torch team now sat in the Oval Office reviewing details with President Barton.

Barton turned to Conlon, his voice brimming with excitement. He said, "This is accurate, Tyler?"

"Mr. President, the images and data confirm a massive fossil fuel deposit in Noatak National Park," Conlon said. "There's no question about it. I'm just as stunned as you that, of all places we've been looking for oil, and all the time we've been looking, we should find an oil field of this magnitude 7,800 feet above sea level. We just never had the technology—and the motivation—before. I'm sure there's an explanation, but it defies all scientific logic. Maybe the oil field has some kind of link to the Prudhoe Bay and Kuparuk River oil deposits, northeast of the field on the North Slope along the Arctic Coastal Plain. Those two oil fields were the largest in the United States until now. We don't know. I'm not sure we can ever prove any connection to those two oil fields, but it's in northern Alaska on the same longitude."

Conlon held up two charts graphing the results and pointed to the estimated size and depth of the oil field and its geographic relationship to the Alaskan pipeline and the Prudhoe Bay and Kuparuk River deposits.

"If this data's accurate, we're talking about the largest fossil fuel discovery in history. Substantially larger than Saudi Arabia's inventory. Maybe double. The good news, Mr. President, is that the 800-mile Alaskan pipeline starts in Prudhoe Bay and runs south to the Port of Valdez where we have shipping access through Prince William Sound. We can surely tap into the pipeline from the Fossil River deposit and send the oil south."

"Astounding, Tyler. But I see two challenges," said Barton. "First is how to gain access to the oil field—then once in, how to extract it."

"There's a third challenge, Mr. President," interrupted Zollar, "Keeping the environmentalists out of it. We have to be prepared for them to go ballistic over this."

"We've got the Alaskan pipeline that was pushing 2.2 million barrels of oil a day from Alaska's North Slope to Valdez," Conlon said, trying to be positive. "The volume today is one third of that volume when the pipeline opened in 1977—so that would be our strategy to bring it back to life," Conlon said.

"Environmentalists know that if the pipeline is shut down, by law it must be dismantled," Zollar said. "We bring the pipeline back to life with this new Fossil River oil field, keep the pipeline filled to capacity-and save the nation from economic ruin."

"Can the pipeline handle this much volume?" Barton queried.

"Probably not, but if it's running to capacity, they can't shut it down legally," Conlon said. "We control the flow."

"The fact is our nation's on the verge of an energy collapse that'll take everybody down—including the environmentalists," Conlon said. "Let's remember that we've just found the largest fossil fuel deposit in the world—and it promises to change everything in our favor."

Barton nodded. "Including bringing our troops home for good. Absolutely incredible. Before we announce it to the press, we've got to send in a research team to confirm the findings on the ground. There's too much at risk if word gets out and we find the technology has erred."

"Precisely, Mr. President," Conlon said. "I'll work with Lauren. We'll put together the team to confirm all this immediately. But there's something else."

"What's that?"

"There's another massive layer of something below the fossil fuel. We haven't identified it yet. It's liquid, we know that much. Hopefully, the team can identify what it is when they land in the oil field tomorrow. There's something else, too."

Barton lowered his head toward the Defense Secretary.

"We can't yet get a fix on it. It's below the liquid," Conlon continued.

Zollar leaned into the table forcing a challenging stare into Robinson's impenetrable eyes. "Maybe it's easier for you, Shawn, to overlook the impending impact that the environmentalists will have on this project, but this is all about the protected land that Interior manages. All of it is pristine and off limits for what we're about to do," Zollar said without a flinch. "And I'm responsible for all of it—not you. I'll arrange transportation into the area, but there's a major challenge getting in there. It's in the middle of nowhere in the western Brooks Range. Wild and very remote."

Robinson sat back digesting what Zollar said. Changing the subject, he said, "We've got some gutsy combat chopper pilots."

"So do we," Zollar said. "The best." She rolled out a large map of Noatak National Preserve and circled an area with a green magic marker that was nestled between four large mountains, hanging valleys, and three active glaciers. She circled one of the four mountains in red. "This one's an active volcano, billowing smoke and occasionally lava. Potentially very dangerous."

"It's huge," Robinson said surveying the chart.

"It's tough getting in there on foot," Zollar said, her eyes leveling on Robinson. "Maybe impossible."

"Anybody ever tried?" Conlon queried, leaning forward.

"A few hardcore fly fishermen have hiked in," Zollar said. "The weird thing is—none of them apparently ever came back out."

"Proving the place is remote with a capital R," Robinson blurted out.

Barton held up his hand for silence.

"The only way to get a lot of stuff in there is by chopper. Landing is problematic. Might have to drop in our team from the chopper. Either way, it's very high risk. I'll try to line up transportation when I get back to the office, and I'll get back to you. If the person I have in mind isn't available, I'll call you, Shawn, and you can round someone else up. But if I can't get him, whoever you get has to be the best. This isn't amateur flying. We're talking steep sharp mountains, fog, and high-level winds. It's the Arctic at its harshest."

"I'll assemble the research team," Conlon said, but the moment the words spilled out of his mouth, he felt a twinge of unease.

Barton stood up and said, "I'll hold off on the champagne—but it certainly seems we've got something to celebrate today."

"Finally," Conlon added. "A bird in the hand is worth a hell of a big flock in the bush. If it's there…we still have to figure out how to get it out."

Suddenly, the lights in the Oval Office flickered and dimmed.

It was a brief moment, but the room fell silent when it happened.

CHAPTER 7

Scott Chandler took a long swig of his latté. He finished filling out the last page of his F&W Form 309 Search Report. It bothered him that they had come back from the mission with no tangible results except a crushed fishing creel. The one crucial piece of evidence they might have had was the bleached bone that Wolf thought he'd seen in the Fossil.

Chandler had already decided not to give up the search. Leaving the scene of any man or woman missing in action was unthinkable to the former captain. In all the sorties he'd run in Iraq and Afghanistan, it was the Marine credo not to return back to base without a body, dead or alive. Chandler looked up from the report after affixing his signature and said to Brave Wolf, "As much as I hate to set those damn bear traps, maybe we should get a few out there."

Brave Wolf's head bowed slightly. He sat rigid at his desk, his mind drifting off into another world. His eyelids fluttered, then his liquid brown eyes seemed to glaze over.

Chandler studied his friend's face and thought about startling the man out of his trance. Instead, he just sat still and stared, aware that Wolf's body was twitching as if something was gnawing at the core of his subconscious mind.

Brave Wolf was drifting off into his past. Slowly and deliberately he was willing himself into a vision quest, remembering the ceremonies of his Blackfoot tribal chief, Red Horn, who would stand in the middle of the ceremonial teepee next to his medicine man shaking a rattle filled with stones. He remembered streaks of light emanating from the rattle, and the words of healing coming from the medicine man in a chant that pierced the darkness with eerie promise.

The vision quest was so vivid in Brave Wolf's mind now that he was convinced he heard Chief Red Horn's voice talking about the Lowampi, the healing ceremony in the Valley of the Chiefs where the Crow, Comanche, and his own Blackfoot tribe were praying to their father, the sky; their mother, the earth; their grandfather, the sun; and their grandmother, the moon.

Red Horn was puffing on the chief's bark-filled pipe and sipping from the communal water jug. They were talking about the curse on their forefathers' land amidst the Inuit tribal range in northern Alaska. It was a faraway place that was referred to in an effort to communicate to the spirits of their ancestors. Wolf's body felt like it was suspended above the ground in ethereal flight. He was now looking over some unidentifiable range of mountains as an omniscient observer, peering into every nook and cranny with GPS accuracy. Something was terribly wrong, and his vision urgently bore into an area of the mountain range appearing to be all black, as if someone had willed a plague over the area.

Wolf's body began to shake, his arms flailing at his sides. Chandler stared at the man. The image of his friend in such a state was very unsettling.

When the phone on Chandler's desk rang, Brave Wolf jolted in his chair. His eyes opened wide, filled with terror. Seeing the mask of dread on his face startled Chandler.

He picked up the phone. "Chandler here."

It was a woman's voice, the tone low and steady, filled with authority. "Scott Chandler?"

"Yes, ma'am."

"Lauren Zollar, Secretary of the Interior."

Chandler sat bolt upright in his chair, knocking his logbook onto the floor. He leaned toward his desk. "Yes, ma'am."

"I need your help in running a mission tomorrow for the Interior. I know you're the best person we've got to fly in and out of a remote quadrant of Noatak. It's tough flying."

"I know the Park very well, ma'am: every Mountain, river, valley, and lake. You can count on me."

"Your military record's outstanding, Scott. It's good to have you on our team. I remember reviewing your CV, and recommending we hire you. I'm glad we did. Fish & Wildlife says you're doing a superb job for us since you and Brave Wolf made the move from Glacier to Noatak. We very much appreciate your service."

Chandler forced out a thank you.

By this time Wolf had snapped out of his reverie and was watching the sweat form on Chandler's brow.

"Normally, we would've used the Air Force for this mission but, after we studied the area, I concluded you're the only pilot who can get us in and out of there safely on such short notice—but it's highly classified, Scott," Zollar said. "Even so, if you help us out, I'll make sure it becomes part of your record at review time."

There was a long silence. Finally, Chandler said, "Thanks, ma'am. Could you tell me where we're going?"

"We need to fly a research team into the area southeast of the Noatak River. About 150 miles or so east of the town of Noatak. We have the coordinates. It's near a hanging valley between four mountains and three glaciers, inaccessible by foot and air. We're hoping you can find a place to land in there. It's flanking the southeastern fork of the Fossil River."

Chandler thought about yesterday's flight into the dense fog, trying to follow the Fossil River, the near miss with a pine tree and the haunting feeling that something wasn't right about the area. This wasn't so far from there.

"I know the quadrant. It's remote, all right. But we've got a problem."

"Yes?"

"Fuel. We're severely limited here."

"Not to worry. This is top priority. We're sending a tanker of Jet-A along with the team."

"Don't think we'll need that much," Chandler said. Actually, he was surprised she could get any fuel at all. Chandler had watched all the news channels report car lines at the nation's gas pumps across the country were now clogged with half-empty tanks and enraged consumers.

Commercial jets were killing flights with increased intensity.

"It's less than an hour flight," Chandler added.

"You never know," Zollar said. It didn't sound like a joke.

"What's in there that's so important?" Chandler pressed.

"Like I said—it's classified, Scott. But trust me on this. It's a critical mission and we need your help." Chandler studied her voice and knew she was hiding something of importance. He decided not to press.

Brave Wolf watched the expression on his colleague's face. It was tense and full of concern.

"I'll get your people in and out safely, ma'am."

"Good," Zollar said. "The insertion team will be waiting for you at 0800 hours tomorrow. Where should they rendezvous?"

"Tell them to meet me at the helipad at the Noatak airport strip. They'll see the green chopper."

"Thanks, Scott. They'll be there. Thanks for your help."

"No problem, ma'am."

Chandler put the phone back on the cradle. Wolf leaned toward him. "You're sweating, my friend. Why?"

"That was the Secretary of the Interior."

"That sounds serious."

"It is," Chandler said. "It's classified.

"I take it it's a flying assignment."

"Like I said, Wolf. Classified. If I told you I'd have to kill you."

"So I take it I'm not invited."

"I wish you could come, pal. Not enough room."

Wolf stared at him in silence.

Chandler returned the glance and said, "What were you spacing out about before? I haven't seen you do that in a long time. Spooked me out."

Wolf hesitated. "You don't want to know."

"It wasn't one of your visions, was it?"

"If I told you I'd have to kill you," Brave Wolf said. He wasn't smiling.

"Right," Chandler said. "Well maybe we could swap classified info?"

"Okay. You first."

"Fine. I'm taking some kind of team down to the south fork of the Fossil," Chandler said. "Very urgent."

"Well, that's interesting. Because my little space-out was all about that…area. About what's making the caribou and humans…disappear."

"Great. You know what it is?"

"You really want to know?"

"Sure. Why not."

"Okay. Fine. A demon from another world."

"Right. Jesus Christ, Wolf. Is that the best you can do?"

Brave Wolf winced. "Look. You asked. All I can say is it feels very real to me, my friend. And I think there's danger. Very real, very big danger. So you'd better watch your white ass."

Chandler wanted to dig deeper, but thought better of it. Wolf's visions all too often came true soon enough. "Spooky," he told his friend.

Brave Wolf looked purposefully into Chandler's eyes.

"You have no idea."

CHAPTER 8

CHANDLER STOOD BESIDE THE OPEN DOOR OF HIS SIKORSKY, GREETING EACH of the six research personnel, helping them board the chopper. As the men entered the craft, Chandler took note of the equipment each carried: computers, ICOM five-watt transceivers, manual Raytheon GPS gear, Samsung satellite phones, and other strange-looking handheld gear, all snapped onto their field jackets for easy access.

Chandler sensed the excitement of his passengers. He also felt their tension. He learned that two of them were from the Department of Energy and one from Interior, a young man with tortoise-shell glasses, probably in his twenties. Chandler heard someone say his name, Cooper Windham. Another man, red freckles sprinkled across his face, was from the Department of Defense. There was also an older man from the NGA with gray, curly hair wearing a floppy hat with the agency logo on it.

The last man entering the craft, Tom Riley, appeared to Chandler to be the leader of the mission. Also from Energy, this man wore puffy field pants laden with bulging pockets, and an Alpine field jacket that was packed with small electronic instruments.

Chandler told himself that had he seen this eclectic group of people on a street corner in mainstream U.S.A, he would have concluded they were all...nerds. He hopped aboard his craft and slammed the cabin door shut.

Once strapped into the pilot's seat, Chandler said, "Good morning gentlemen. Welcome to the most scenic park in America. Another lovely day in Arctic paradise."

"Thank you, sir," the lead man said.

"How far from here to the drop-off point?" asked the young man from Interior. He adjusted his horn rims.

Chandler studied the dashboard instruments, flipping switches and tapping meters. He turned the ignition switch on, and the large rotor blades began to whirl.

"ETA forty-seven minutes," Chandler said. "And I'm not dropping you off. We're landing together. I'll be there with you through the mission. Not to worry. Everybody buckled up? Enjoy the views, gentlemen. It doesn't get any better than this."

The men in the back of the helicopter checked their shoulder harnesses and belt buckles, and the Sikorsky lifted off the helipad, rose 500 feet, then headed due east following the Noatak River.

At first, the air was crystal clear and calm, and the research team peered out the window, marveling at the views of the Noatak Range. But twenty-seven minutes later, Chandler cut south of the River and entered a rough area with mountains jutting high above the helicopter in every direction. Everybody stared at the blanket of dense fog snuggling the peaks.

Someone sitting behind Chandler said, "Hope to God we're not flying into the soup."

"Amen to that." The man sitting next to him swallowed to clear his ears from the pressure.

The wind picked up and the chopper jostled through rough air. It got worse quickly, and the chopper started pitching and yawing, dropping and rising violently.

Chandler passed a small plastic bucket to the back. "Here, use this," he offered. His timing was perfect. One more violent yaw, and Chandler heard two men puking in the back, the smell filling the cabin.

Fortunately, the turbulence didn't last long. The helicopter leveled out and entered a calm stretch of air. Another two miles and the copter dropped down into the fog. The cabin went dark. Chandler's radar screen was complex, and he had insisted that his Sikorsky be equipped with the same technology he had used in Afghanistan, enabling him to read and interpret the contours of the terrain below, highlighting any unusual spike or abutment. They called it the SVDS, Simulated Vision Data System. Even at night, it was like flying in daylight.

Someone in the back said, "Shit."

"Hold on, gentlemen. It's probably going to get choppy again."

"They didn't tell us about this," said the young man from Interior.

The helicopter dropped fast through the soupy fog. Finally, it fell beneath it until the low white ceiling was just above the whirling blades of the craft.

He was flying along the Fossil River now, following its bends and stretches. Parts of it were flat and calm. Other segments were riddled with massive glacier rocks and boulders, whitewater flushing around them. Chandler pushed the helicopter forward and entered a clearing. He hovered, checking the coordinates, then moved to another clearing, passing the spot where he'd landed yesterday, deeper into the mountain crevasse cut by the Fossil over millions of years.

As he negotiated the sharp turns, Chandler's chopper rattled in protest.

The scientist from Energy was tracking the coordinates and shouted above the engine din, "Another mile."

Chandler nodded. Through the fog, he couldn't see the next bend. He relied on the three-dimensional GPS to run the coordinates for him and the SVDS to pilot the terrain. Both systems were doing their job.

He looked back at the men and said, "No place to land here. The ground's too rough."

Somebody from Interior said, "How the hell can you land *anywhere* in here? I can't see a thing. I hope to Christ you can."

The research mission leader from Energy, Tom Riley, held up his right hand to calm the crew. "I have the fix, gentlemen. Another half mile to go. Our pilot's on course. Not to worry."

"Looks like a lost world," the petroleum engineer said, his body jumping with tension.

Chandler lifted the copter up and over the trees, searching for a place to land. Nothing here, he determined. He sucked in a deep breath and then saw it: beneath the hovering fog bank, a distant plateau.

At the same time, three distinct magenta blips appeared on his sonar screen, like the ones he had seen with Wolf. Chandler hovered and leaned forward to study the screen. Something was out there, but it baffled him. Two images flanked his copter, then a third twenty feet above the chopper's whirling blades. A shrill alarm sounded.

The petroleum engineer said, "What the hell's that?"

Chandler turned off the alarm with the quick flip of a switch. "Radar," he said as the images vanished off the screen. "Sensitive to motion."

"What motion?" the engineer followed, his voice tinged with concern.

"Don't sweat it. Nothing to worry about. Happens a lot when we move through tight passages."

In Afghan combat, Chandler had seen incoming missile blips on his sonar screen many times, but this was the Noatak National Preserve. Something wasn't right but Chandler held his comments in check.

Riley interrupted the incident with, "We're here guys, on target." As he spoke, the GPS equipment on his lap gave a loud confirming beep. At the same time, Chandler's GPS sounded the spot-on coordinates with a long, high-pitched whistle.

"Everybody ready?" Riley asked.

Nobody answered.

CHAPTER 9

Dense fog spiderwebbed the tall white-bark pines that outlined the rock-strewn plateau just north of the Fossil River. Chandler had to navigate a tight circle before setting the Sikorsky down.

When the helicopter doors were thrust open, an unmistakable smell drifted into the cabin.

"Ah! The sweet perfume of oil, gentlemen," Riley said, his eyes going wide. "Can you smell it? Man, that's simply unbelievable! It must be sitting very near the surface. Clearly, we're on the mark."

The remark clued Chandler in on what the mission was about. It also awakened his anxiety about the future of this mysterious Park that was now his charge.

Secretary Zollar must have known he would find out once the mission was underway. He'd seen firsthand the ecological damage the U.S. had inflicted in the Arab oil countries, the lives lost and land ruined, all in pursuit of fossil fuels. Now the same government was about to violate the crown jewel of the Interior. The impact of discovering oil here sent a cold chill down his spine. What would happen to the wildlife, the flora, the pristine lakes and rivers that were his responsibility to protect? Would all be sacrificed to maintain a lifestyle of excess, when alternate energy sources could be developed instead?

One-by-one, the D.C. scientists exited the craft and stood close around Riley as he reviewed their mission.

Chandler, from the flight deck, half-listened as he checked his instruments and equipment. The mission was inevitable, he knew, and logical enough from the government's point of view. But as he scanned the faces of the assembled team, he wondered if he was the only one who sensed that something very wrong was about to happen. From behind the chopper's bubbled glass, he thought the distorted expressions on the faces of the men mirrored his own building anxiety. For a moment, he wished the wind would pick up and dissipate the scent of oil.

"Each of you is equipped with a digital recorder," Riley was saying. "Switch it on now. It will record our communications as we probe for the oil field. We don't want to miss a word of the mission. The sounding technology you're wearing will monitor the depth and width of any fossil fuel beneath us. Spread out. Think of where we're standing as the hub of a wheel, with each of us the spokes. I want 360 degrees of this turf covered. You all know the drill. We'll consolidate all the images we capture of the sediment layers to determine the field's exact depth and diameter. Any questions?"

Cooper Windham, the young geologist from Interior, peered at Riley over the rims of his glasses. "The forest up here's dense. The fog's thick. What if we lose our way?"

"You can't get lost," Riley responded. "Use your ICOM transceiver. Anybody troubled by anything, just pipe up and transmit. We'll all hear you and restore your bearings. If for some strange reason we don't, every GPS has been individually preprogrammed with a built-in pedometer. Just push the find button and listen. She'll tell you the exact direction to head.

"This entire operation has been meticulously planned and calibrated, gentlemen. Once you flip on your tracking rig, the directional imaging process begins. Under no circumstances should you take it upon yourselves to veer off-track. Understand?"

"How far out from here do we go?" asked the geophysicist from Energy, his voice unsteady.

"About a mile and a half, three miles round-trip. Your distance traveled appears on the screen in meters. Okay, gentlemen." Riley held up his chronometer. "It's exactly 0846. I want to see all of your asses back here at the chopper at 1030 hours for a delicious government-issue box lunch."

"Shit," someone said. The sentiment was repeated all around.

Riley turned toward the copter door and peered inside at Chandler.

"You can monitor us on channel nine and observe our deployment on your GPS screen. Use your ICOM if you need to reach us for any reason."

Chandler studied Riley's face. He saw no sign of fear. He nodded and watched Riley and his six men spread out, then vanish into the dense pine forest. From his cockpit seat he continued following the seven red dots marking human heat fan out across his screen. They moved in an expanding field that formed a perfect wheel—with his own red dot as the center hub.

For some reason, Chandler's mind drifted back to his childhood. Thirty-six miles southeast of St. Mary's, Montana was his grandfather's cattle farm, Serendipity Ranch: 780 acres that spilled out over flat land seven miles below the southern tip of the Blackfoot reservation, with Glacier National Park's snowcapped peaks looming majestically in the distance. At Serendipity, his assigned responsibilities included feeding the cattle and chickens, collecting the eggs, and helping his father take the steers to slaughter when their weight peaked at 800 pounds. Working with animals had fascinated him as a teenager, bringing with it a sense of peace and rightness that stayed with him.

It was this experience that encouraged him to study science: biology, animal husbandry, zoology, ornithology, entomology, paleontology, and geology.

A noise outside the chopper broke Chandler's reverie, and he looked down at the GPS to see that the red dots were still spaced apart, equidistant. He heard the static of someone's transceiver click on.

A muffled voice broke the silence. "This is one helluva spooky place."

He recognized the voice as the young geologist from Interior, Cooper Windham. Other voices came on the air, acknowledging.

Of the seven red dots, the one closest to the helicopter was Windham. He was the hesitant one, moving slower than the others.

As Chandler was working his way toward the back of the chopper to get his own backpack, he heard a loud, echoing screech.

It was unnatural. Unlike anything in Noatak or Glacier Park he'd ever heard before.

Quickly, he was out of the copter, standing beneath the massive blades, tilting his head into the soft mountain breeze, listening intently.

He looked down at his GPS and took note of the red dots. None of them were moving now.

It came again: an ear-splitting screech that reverberated through the hanging valley.

The screech was answered by another unearthly call in the distance. The ICOM transceivers came alive.

"What the fuck was that?" someone shouted into his hand mike. Another voice crackled on the air. "Jesus Christ."

Riley barked an order. "Keep moving. We're making progress. We've got to finish the mission. Whatever it was, it's not going to bother us. Stay focused."

Chandler felt the knot in his stomach he got before entering battle. He picked up the ICOM transceiver and pushed the words out of his mouth, trying hard to lace them with calm: "Listen up. Chandler here. Tom Riley out there?"

"Roger that," Riley's voice came.

"Tom, I recommend you marshal your men back to the helicopter."

"I'll give the orders, thank you," Riley snapped. "We've got to finish the mission."

Chandler's voice was clear, without hesitation, "Sir, your men are in…"

A blood-curdling shriek sounded to the west, breaking up Chandler's transmission with a startling punch of silence.

It was answered by an even louder screech from the east, and yet another, closer in, from the north.

Chandler's eyes were wide and fixed on the GPS screen where the almost perfect work of art in the form of a wheel and hub of red dots had now turned into a chaotic disarray swirling swiftly in all different directions. Chandler heard Riley shout, "Stay the course. Finish the god-damned mission. That's an order."

He watched the screen, where another five dots now surrounded the seven humans.

Two more screeches sounded before he heard the first guttural scream for help.

Chandler's heart raced. He climbed back into the helicopter and reached under the seat for his M4A1 carbine. He'd requested and been granted permission to keep the weapon after his discharge from the Corps and assignment to Glacier, then Noatak, in case he needed to take down wounded or attacking animals.

He'd used the rifle in Iraq to defend his position when his attack helicopter had gone down, but had never had to use it in either park. Now he was thankful he'd kept the carbine with him.

Snapping a thirty round clip into the rifle, he ran toward the sound. From the haunting cacophony of human cries and the piercing screeches, he knew a full-scale hunt was underway. He glanced down at the GPS. Some of the dots were utterly still. Some seemed to have vanished—and others were moving erratically through the dense fog which had descended from treetop level and was now hovering just above the ground.

In seconds he was bounding over rock and bush, weaving his way through the thick evergreens and mountain alders. Suddenly, he saw it, streaking through the fog, barely visible.

Whatever it had been, there was more than one—maybe three, maybe a half-dozen. He squinted for a better fix.

They were moving too fast. His carbine at ready, he thought about shooting into the thick undergrowth, but feared hitting one of the men.

Their screams filled the air, echoing hopelessly through the small valley. A blur of faint images dodged in and out from behind thick tree trunks.

But now the human screams of terror were muffled by bone-chilling screeches so loud and close that the hair on the back of his neck rose as if an electric shock had just surged through his body.

That was when he almost stumbled on the remains of the floppy-hat-wearing NGA engineer.

The man's body had been eviscerated, ripped apart limb-by-limb. His remains lay in scattered sections, littering the bloodied ground.

The engineer's head rested against a massive white pine.

Chandler flashed back to all the Marines he'd seen blown apart—

guts streaming down walls, hanging from ceilings and doors, splattered on the pavement.

But to see such slaughter here in his park, on his turf, made him clutch his throat to choke off the first taste of bile.

Reacting to a sound, he spun around. Nothing in sight.

But wait—more movement off to the left. He looked down at his GPS, leaped over a dead stump, and ran toward the direction of the closest red dot.

He rounded a giant pine, and there in front of him was something that defied description.

Half the body of the research mission leader, Tom Riley, had been tossed over a large rock outcrop. The lower half, hip-to-toe, lay in a bloodied heap at his feet.

Chandler gave quick thought about firing his weapon blindly into the thick woods without target, but the risk seemed too high in hitting one of the men. Yet he had just seen Riley's guts splayed on the ground in grotesque clumps. Instinct told him to fire, and he raised his M4A1 carbine and pulled the trigger sending a stream of bullets in all directions.

Then there was silence.

One by one he tracked the scientists down, moving through the fog-laden mountain forest with the skill of an experienced Marine sweeping through a minefield.

Heads, arms, torsos, and legs were lying in all different directions, twisted and torn. No sign of life.

He'd located the bodies of five of the team. But the younger man, Cooper Windham, was unaccounted for. Chandler remembered that Windham's dot, the one he guessed was closest to the helicopter, had been off to the left, so he made his way back in that direction. He feared Windham would be dead like the others, mangled beyond description.

Chandler could now sense that he, too, was being stalked, just as the others had been. He swung his carbine left to right, right to left and, just to keep his enemy off guard, fired a few more rounds.

In the distance he could see shapes slipping in and out of the fog. He saw color—brown, some black, and, he imagined, red and blue—but couldn't be certain. Maybe ten feet long, whatever the creature was stood taller than a mule deer, even taller than an elk or caribou. That realization pumped adrenaline through his body. Larger by far than anything he'd ever before encountered in Noatak. The great balance of nature was unraveling before him, and he was losing control of his protective mission.

The predator he was facing was one of savage speed, cunning, and ferocity.

The last still red dot was closer now, and Chandler quickened his pace. On the final bushy stretch before the clearing where the Sikorsky awaited he found Cooper Windham lying prone.

Chandler could hear a gurgling sound that must be Windham's labored breathing. Blood everywhere and a missing right hand-but the man was alive.

Setting his carbine aside, he tore off his own Pendleton shirt and used his field knife to slice it into ribbons to make a tourniquet.

Then Chandler gathered Windham off the ground and jogged with him in his arms back toward the chopper, grateful that the strength of his prosthetic left arm made the carry easier.

"I have you, man. You're going to make it." Chandler willed him to breathe. "Breathe. That's it. We're going home."

They broke into the clearing.

The screeching of the predators behind him rent the damp air.

In a desperate final burst of effort, Chandler reached the craft, opened the cockpit hatch, and slung Windham onto the flight deck. The man's face was white with shock. He draped an olive green blanket over him, then slammed the hatch shut and climbed behind the controls, started the engine, and checked the instruments to make sure the coordinates for getting out of the area were accurate.

All Chandler could see through the cabin bubble was a blur of movement in the distance.

Something moving fast. Still too fast to identify what it was, but coming straight at him. Nothing in his inventory of mammals in the Park even came close to matching what was out there.

Then he thought he saw movement overhead. A creature with a large wingspan had just flown over his craft, larger than any bird of prey in Noatak-or in the entire known world of winged creatures.

Chandler's mind was spinning. There was no standard operating procedure for what was happening. He knew only that he had split seconds to lift his craft off.

Just as the Sikorsky lumbered from the ground, the creature, in a shrieking attack, lunged at the cabin door below Chandler's line of sight with such force that he felt the copter chassis tremble. The beast was slashing at the hatch, denting the strong metal. Chandler had to hold it shut.

The beast was trying to pry the handle open to get at him.

Chandler peered out the window and caught a brief glimpse of fierce yellow eyes glaring up at him. The handle was flipping rapidly. Now the copter was hesitating, a few feet off the ground.

Then the hatch was ripped open, Chandler's prosthetic arm in the jaws of the predator. The beast's teeth punctured the titanium prosthetic and tore off the hand, but somehow left the lacerated arm attached to Chandler's shoulder.

Releasing the joystick, Chandler thrust what was left of his prosthetic arm back into the cabin, and with his good right hand yanked the hatch shut, then hooked his mechanical forearm into the door brace and pulled hard. His right hand grasped the collective and coaxed the huge machine to lift.

Again the door was ripped open.

This time Chandler, in one motion, used his right hand to slam the hatch shut on the creature's foreleg and to urge the throttle all the way forward. What was left of his left arm was still entwined in the handle.

But at last he could feel the craft rise.

The beast was trying to cling to the rising helicopter, but finally lost its grip and tumbled ten feet to the ground with a blood-curdling screech that would surely haunt Chandler's dreams—if he lived.

Suddenly he noticed, on the floor of the flight deck, a sickle-shaped eight-inch talon attached to a thin, ragged, bloody piece of flesh-ribbed knuckles. The limb attached to the menacing talon was still moving, twitching.

It was covered with feathers.

Chandler focused on the instrument panel, lifting the Sikorsky through the dense fog, dodging the tall trees and sharp peaks, until it climbed above the forest canopy into the dazzling mid-morning Alaskan sun.

Secretary Zollar had given him her direct dial number in case there were any questions before or during the mission. Enroute to the small barracks hospital in Noatak, Chandler reached her on the voice-activated satellite phone. "We've been attacked," he said, his voice shaking.

"Who's this?" Zollar demanded.

"It's Scott Chandler. Your Noatak mission."

"You're breaking up. Where are you?"

"We've been attacked. Five dead. One still alive, but barely. I'm flying him to the hospital in Noatak. Do you copy?"

"I copy," Zollar finally said. "Attacked by who?"

"Not who—what. And I don't know what the hell it was. Nothing I've seen before."

Windham, behind him, uttered a horrendous wail, as though he were still being menaced.

"You're going to make it, Cooper," Chandler shouted back at him.

"What's happening, Scott?" Zollar's voice could have been a million miles away. "Talk to me."

The line went dead.

Chandler was on final approach to the Noatak helipad, and braced himself for the landing. With both feet operating the pedals, his right hand handled the controls. As the tarmac rose to meet the Sikorsky, he was somehow able to lean down and work the collective next to his left leg.

As the chopper's wheels met the ground, it didn't even occur to him that he was probably the first pilot in history to negotiate a safe helicopter landing with one arm.

CHAPTER 10

Chandler had radioed Noatak Hospital that he was returning with a near-death patient. When the Sikorsky set down, two medics pushed a gurney beneath the still-whirling blades. The hatch swung open and Chandler hopped out, motioning them to enter. "He's lost a lot of blood!" he said, though it was all too obvious.

They lifted Windham's body out of the helicopter. He was practically unrecognizable. One of the medics hissed through his teeth, "Holy Christ. What the hell happened?" The other medic, an Inuit, stood fast, mouth agape in astonishment.

The medics rushed Windham through the emergency room doors and whisked him down a narrow, dimly lit hallway into an operating room. Chandler stood outside. Moments later, two surgeons, one a woman in her early forties, the other an older, gray-haired man of Inuit descent with spectacles, came running down the hall. The surgical team entered the operating room. Chandler could hear their voices through the door, but couldn't understand what they were saying.

What seemed like moments later, Chandler looked down at his watch to see that forty-seven minutes had passed since Windham had been wheeled into the operating room. The female doctor opened the operating room door, faced Chandler, and said, "I'm sorry." Her face was pale and she was out of breath.

Chandler stalked away without a word. He walked out of the hospital and across the parking lot toward the helipad where his chopper rested. He looked east toward the towering mountain range, a spiral of dark smoke touching the cloudbank from an active volcano spiking in the distance.

Chandler took in a long, deep breath of cool air and looked down at the ground. His eyes filled with tears. Cooper Windham, like so many Marines he had seen killed in Iraq and Afghanistan, was a young man. As Chandler pulled a handkerchief from his back pocket, he felt a hand on his shoulder. A familiar voice said, "It's okay to cry, my friend." Chandler turned and Wolf put a strong hand firmly on his shoulders.

"I heard your transmission back at headquarters. It was hell to have to listen," his friend said. "Man, I'm so sorry I didn't force you to take me along. Hope you had insurance on that arm," he added.

Chandler swept what was left of his prosthetic arm across his eyes.

"I have no earthly idea what it was. Nothing I've ever seen before. Whatever it was slaughtered the entire research team. I mean…literally dismembered…" Scott had to stop and recompose himself. "I really thought you were bullshitting me with that evil spirit stuff. Now I'm not so sure."

Chandler motioned Wolf over to his helicopter and pointed to the hatch. Wolf walked up to the hatch and studied the long, jagged, diagonal gash that streaked across the door. He slowly ran his hand along the two-foot dent as if searching for a body print that could identify whatever had attacked them. Brave Wolf leaned in closer to the hatch, taking in a long, studied breath of air. His nose wrinkled. "Whatever did this is wounded. It's losing blood as we speak. So it's…mortal."

Wolf peered at the torn section of door hatch, then plucked two small feathers still clinging to dried blood from inside the gash. He cupped them in his hand and shook his head. "Holy shit," the Indian said. "It has feathers."

"Yeah," Chandler said as he moved around Brave Wolf to open the door to the cockpit. "And it uses them to fly, for Chrissakes."

They both heard the screaming roar of two F-18 Hornet jets sweeping low over the hospital. They watched the twin jet trails soar over them at mach II toward the Chukchi Sea, then circle heading back toward them. Within moments they were on the ground at the Noatak airport.

"What the hell was that?" Brave Wolf said cupping his ears.

"I have a hunch," Chandler said hopefully.

"Who?"

"Only the military would fly that low and that fast. I spoke to Zollar. I'll bet it's her. She had to panic after my phone call."

Chandler hoisted himself up into the Sikorsky cockpit, motioning Wolf to follow. "I want to show you something," he said.

Wolf climbed in and Chandler poked what was left of his prosthetic arm toward his friend for inspection. Wolf held the arm in both hands, inspecting the damage to the titanium. "Where's the hand?" he asked.

"In the stomach of the beast," Chandler said.

"He bit it off?" Wolf said in disbelief. "Jesus—does he know where that thing's been? I'd hate to have his indigestion."

Chandler reached into his pocket and extracted three sharp, two-inch teeth. "I found them in my forearm."

"My God," Wolf held them in his hand, studying them closely. He poked the sharp end of one of the teeth with his left index finger and a small drop of blood appeared. He winced in pain. "But if it has feathers, how can it have teeth?" Brave Wolf asked, a faint hint of terror appearing on his face.

Chandler reached behind the seat to pull out a bloodied cloth. He handed it to his friend. "This ripped off the creature when it attacked the helicopter. It got caught in the hatch. Damn thing was trying to get at me."

Wolf held the bloodied cloth in the palms of his hands, hesitant to unfold it.

"Go ahead," Chandler urged.

Wolf slowly unwrapped the cloth—and dropped it on the floor of the copter when he felt a small unmistakable twinge of movement. "It's still alive."

"No, it's not," Chandler reassured him. "Reflexes."

"Jesus. That's a hell of a long time for a piece of it to still be twitching. Okay. Now I am really freaked out."

"Hey, Chief. You were the one with the vision."

The Wolf picked up the claw with the cloth and studied it, careful not to touch the tough keratin of the knife-sharp talon. "Oh my God," he said, his eyes blinking in disbelief. "I have seen this before."

"Where?" Chandler asked incredulously.

"On ancient pottery. Passed down over generations. Nobody knows how long. It's true. Whatever's alive in those mountains is something that…" he hesitated. "I'll show you a piece I have in my cabin. This was my vision. I guess…the legend's true."

Chandler said, "There's more." He pulled out Windham's recorder and pressed play.

The two men listened as the sounds of terror played out in the cockpit: the screaming calls for help, the eerie, high-pitched shrieks from the predator pack as they stalked and attacked each of the six scientists. And the excruciating sounds of a human being dismembered. Chandler pressed stop and said, "Enough. It's God-awful."

Brave Wolf just stared at his colleague and friend in silence. "It has feathers. It has jaws. It has sharp talons, scaly skin—and it flies."

Chandler nodded affirmatively. "Not it. They. Half bird, half—" he hesitated. "Half reptile or—or alien."

"Whatever it is, it's not friendly."

"It has amazing speed. And stealth," Chandler said. "The attack was a blur. Maybe ten feet long, six- to eight-feet tall. That's all I can remember." He paused, then added, "And the eyes."

"What about them?"

"They were large, oval—piercing yellow."

"Dear God."

Chandler secreted the claw, teeth, and recorder in a leather pouch and drew the strings tightly around the mouth of the bag in a knot. They both stepped out of the helicopter.

In the distance they watched an olive drab military van pull up to the hospital. Three people exited. A woman looked around as two men stood, apparently waiting for something. Then the woman saw Wolf and Chandler and walked toward them.

Wolf and Chandler stood motionless as the Secretary of the Interior, Lauren Zollar, greeted them.

"Scott? Scott Chandler?" He recognized her immediately.

"Yes, ma'am. This is my friend and colleague, Brave Wolf Whitman."

She shook their hands. She looked askance after noticing that Chandler's left hand was missing. She composed herself.

"Are you alright, Mr. Chandler? Do you need medical assistance?"

"I'm fine for now, Ma'am. Perfect, actually. Lucky to be alive. Those F-18 Hornets got you here fast," Chandler said.

"First time I've ever flown in one. I'm only glad I was already in Seattle. The G-force probably did a job on my makeup," she smiled touching her face. Chandler grinned. "I want you to meet Secretary of Defense Robinson and Secretary of Energy Conlon."

"We need details about what happened today before we take military action," Robinson said in a deep, confident voice. "Let's find a room inside and talk. Time's limited."

Chandler nodded and looked at Brave Wolf. His eyes confirmed what Chandler knew: Whoever entered the park near the south fork of the Fossil River would engage a predator so powerful that survival would be a long shot—without some very heavy artillery.

CHAPTER 11

The dimly lit hospital hallway contained two small conference rooms used by doctors to consult with patients. Conlon had the same thought as Zollar: it reminded them of a typical U.S. government-issue building, dull and banal with sparse furniture, illuminated by forty-watt bulbs.

Robinson looked at Chandler. "Tell us what happened to the team," he said in a low contentious voice.

Chandler studied Robinson's face. He had the same chiseled jaw as the generals he served overseas: General David Petraeus in his second tour in Afghanistan, and his third tour under General Stanley McChrystal. Chandler pulled out the brown satchel and emptied the contents on the table. He identified each object.

Zollar said, "What is it?"

Chandler said, "I don't know."

Robinson asked, "You're the park's zoologist, right?"

"Yes, sir," Chandler answered.

"How could you not know what it is? You saw it, I assume."

"Part of it, yes."

"Which part?" Conlon asked.

"The part that ate my hand, sir." Conlon looked startled, and Chandler continued. "The head. Yellow eyes. It had feathers, wings, and jaws. The creatures moved too fast to see many details. There was thick ground fog. I was trying to save...it all happened so..."

Zollar interrupted him. "Take your time, Scott, please. Relax."

"It was terrible," Chandler said, as the memory hit him. "Worse than Iraq and Afghanistan. You know my record. I hope none of you ever see what I saw."

"What else did you see?" Robinson pressed, ignoring Chandler's discomfort. "We need the details, son. Try to remember every detail."

Chandler slowly spilled it out: the attacks, the screeches, the methodical way the pack of predators stalked and killed each one of the research team. As he played the digital recording as final proof that his story was true, Robinson, Zollar, and Conlon sat rigid in their chairs, eyes wide, mouths drawn tight.

The recorder played out, ending with a human cry that forced Conlon to push away from the table. Robinson flinched as if someone had just cuffed the back of his head. Zollar's mouth hung open.

A young, white-smocked orderly opened the conference door. "Excuse me," she said. "I'm supposed to tell you all that Cooper Windham's body's in the morgue now. Dr. Smythe is waiting for your permission to perform the autopsy. I believe one of you requested it."

Zollar turned around and faced the young woman. "Yes. I did. Thank you. We'll be right there." She got up and motioned everybody to the door.

"I think it important we see the autopsy," Chandler said. "It might shed more light on the creature if we can learn anything more about what the coroner thinks might have killed our men."

The recording had already convinced Zollar that she had to make a crucial, urgent decision. Noatak National Park had to be shut down. She'd already called the Fish & Wildlife Director, Tony Roberts, telling him to work with Interior's public relations director to prepare a press release announcing that the park would be closed at midnight on the day before the Park was to open for summer tourist traffic that would bring three thousand people into the park. In less than an hour, she had received a faxed copy of the release. It read:

Contact: Bruce Finley
Director, Public Relations,
U.S. Department of Interior

Fish & Wildlife Bureau
Washington, D.C. 20023-1436
202-346-3200, ext. 22

For Immediate Release

Due to the potential of a lethal virus affecting all mammals within Noatak National Preserve, the park will close until further notice effective midnight. This action has been taken to protect human life and to insure that the disease does not spread beyond the borders of Noatak National Park. The Department of the Interior is working closely with the Centers for Disease Control to identify the strain of virus causing the disease.

Noatak National Park will reopen as soon as it is determined that the Park is safe.

The gray cinderblock morgue building, with green and bronze colored lichens affixed to its sides, shone in the arctic sun like a jewel box. It was eighteen minutes north of Noatak Hospital. As Chandler opened the double doors leading to the pathology lab, Robinson coughed hard and Zollar covered her nose with a hankie. At the end of the hallway, at the basement level of the building, another large aluminum door appeared in the distance.

Brave Wolf pushed the door inward. The pathologist Burt Smythe was waiting standing over a gurney, which held a body wrapped in a green plastic sheath.

Robinson positioned himself at the head of the gurney. Conlon moved to the left side, and Zollar stepped off to the right. Wolf and Chandler stood together outside the tight circle. The coroner uncovered the body.

Atop the table lay the remains of Cooper Windham.

"He was still hanging on when I found him," said Chandler to the pathologist.

Zollar held her head high, breathing through her mouth so the smell of formaldehyde had the least impact. In a muffled nasal tone, she said to the pathologist, "What do you think killed him? We have a partial description from Mr. Chandler, but he couldn't identify what did this. His description—well, it makes no sense."

The coroner, a short, stocky man in his mid-fifties with half glasses perched on the tip of a pug nose, looked across the table with piercing grey eyes. "I've seen a lot of dead bodies in the past eighteen years," he said. "Car accidents, bodies falling from planes, off mountain peaks, frozen bodies, corpses gored by antlers from an angry bull moose. But nothing comes close to this. Whatever killed him, he was as good as dead when you brought him in. Still can't believe he breathed as long as he did."

He motioned them to step back from the gurney. "Let me show you something."

They all moved back from the table, staring at Smythe's latex-covered hands. Smythe grabbed Wyndham's stub of a left arm and what was left of his torso, and rolled the body onto its front. He pointed a scalpel to the nape of the neck down to the buttocks. His voice was steady, without emotion, but Chandler saw his grey eyes darting nervously over the body. "The ribs have been sliced clean through and splayed open like a hot knife through butter." The pathologist placed his left hand within the opened wound and ran it nape to butt in an unwavering, straight line.

He looked up at Robinson who stood rigid, eyes wide in disbelief, as he stared at the extent of the wound. "Whatever killed this young man did it swiftly. A butcher could not have done a better job."

Chandler stepped forward into the circle of Conlon, Zollar, and Robinson. "I saw enough to know it wasn't in the books. I'm the Park's zoologist. I know every living creature in the Noatak Preserve. A mutation, maybe. And there's not just one of them. There're many. More than a pack—I suspect a colony. It's got feathers, jaws, talons. And it's vicious."

"Scott," Zollar said, her voice barely above a whisper. "Do you think it's just confined to the southeast fork of the Fossil?"

"I hope to God," Chandler said. "If they're territorial, they might not be anywhere else, unless they run out of food. I saw one in flight. If it does fly, there could be others out of the territory, searching for food elsewhere in the Park. God help humanity if they can fly out of the Park. If that happens, they could be anywhere in Alaska."

Smythe looked at Chandler. "Did they eat the others?"

"Look. I was just trying to find anybody who was alive and get the hell out. Cooper Windham was the only one. The other bodies were torn apart and scattered in a wide area. It was like a bomb had exploded."

Chandler leaned over the gurney to give Smythe the talon. The pathologist studied it, peering over his glasses with a puzzled look in his weathered face. Chandler saw the man's darting gray eyes focus on the talon.

The room fell silent as the pathologist held the sharp edge of the talon against the gaping vertical wound in Cooper Windham's back. "Here's the lethal weapon. A perfect match." He shook his head in disbelief and looked at Chandler. "How the hell did you get out of there alive?"

They spilled out of the morgue into the small parking lot and stood in a tight circle.

Zollar spoke first, her voice unsteady. "Before we go back into Noatak again, I've got to close down the park. That'll play havoc with the press and summer vacationers. Thank God we're this far north. Fortunately, there aren't half as many as usual. Can't get the gas. I've already approved the press release and it's out. The park will be closed to the public midnight tonight."

Chandler looked at her. "What did you tell them?" he asked.

Zollar hesitated. "That we've got to do tests on some of the animals. Disease. Working it out with the CDC," she said. "There might be an epidemic that could spread to humans. They won't question it."

"Good idea," Robinson said. "When the park's shut down, we can launch the strike and clean those bastards out of there."

Wolf didn't like what he was hearing. "You'd be sacrificing hundreds of wild animals, birds, fish, and healthy trees, shrubs, and lichens."

Chandler added, "A military operation will turn the balance of nature upside down and take years to restore life as it exists today."

"We'll go as easy as we can until we know what's in there," Zollar agreed. "We've got a lot of healthy wildlife in that area and they've got to be protected." Zollar reached out and touched Chandler's good right arm. "Scott, you're the only person who confronted this thing and got out alive. It's critical that we find out what's in there."

Robinson looked at Zollar and nodded. "With the evidence you have already, is there anybody you know who could help us identify what we're dealing with? If we have to violate the park with a military invasion, we've got to understand our target."

"Yes. I happen to know the perfect person," Chandler answered. "I'll make a call today and try to locate her as quickly as possible."

"We don't have any more time left," Conlon said. "We've got to tap into that oil ASAP. We're falling apart at the seams."

Chandler escorted them to his helicopter so they could inspect the damaged door. Shawn Robinson peered at the thick slice in the shielding. "Fuck. Whatever it is, it's a powerful angry bastard."

"Out of curiosity," Zollar asked, "Who's this person you're contacting?"

"A paleontologist," Chandler said.

The group fell silent. His next comment left a perplexed look on everybody's face.

"She studies dinosaurs."

PART II

CHAPTER 1

Two girls, one four, the other two, blonde curly hair tipping their shoulders, stared at the head of a dinosaur fifty-six feet above them. Losing her balance, the younger one teetered. If she hadn't been holding her mother's hand she would have fallen over backwards and hit her head on the granite floor of the entrance rotunda of New York City's American Museum of Natural History, containing the world's most coveted fossil collection of dinosaurs.

From behind them, a woman's voice broke the silence. "Pretty amazing isn't it?"

The mother looked at the woman. "It's very big."

"The largest dinosaur on earth. It's a Sauropod. One hundred seventy million years ago. Family's Aptosaurus, but everybody knows it as Brontosaurus Excelsus."

The woman looked down at the two children. "Think of it as a Big Barney without teeth. Ninety feet long, thirty-eight tons. First one was found in a Dakota hogback quarry in 1879. Loved to eat plants. This one was brought here to the museum in 1938 from the Montana plains, east of the Rockies. At this size, we figure it probably lived 180 years."

The two girls stared at the dinosaur in awe, their eyes riveted on the massive skeleton. The four-year-old turned toward the woman. "Did they eat people?"

71

"People didn't exist back then," she smiled. "This one ate only vegetation. No meat."

The mother of the two girls said, "You know a lot about dinosaurs."

"It's my job," the woman said. "I'm one of the Curators of Paleontology, overseeing the Museum's dinosaur collection. Dr. Kimberly Fulton." She extended her hand and the mother pumped it firmly. "I'm always fascinated by the interest children have for dinosaurs."

"Adults, too," added the mother. "I can't believe the size of this thing."

Fulton grinned. "Enjoy the display. The real excitement starts on the fourth floor. Don't miss it!"

"Dinosaurs," the four-year-old said as she tugged on her mother's hand. "I want to see more dinosaurs, mommy."

Dr. Fulton grinned. "Yes. We have a T-Rex up there. Worth seeing." She pointed at the massive Allosaurus in front of them that was being attacked by a pack of three Veloceraptors. "Feisty little creatures, aren't they?"

The mother watched the curator vanish into a crowd of school children surrounding the central dinosaur display. A tour guide was lecturing them about how packs of small predators could take down large prey with vicious speed and precision.

The four-year-old stared at the Allosaurus and stepped back. She looked up at her mother and burst into tears. "Mommy, they're not alive, are they?" Her sister started to cry, and the mother sniffed the air. "Sophia. Did you go poopy?"

The two-year-old cried, nodding her head affirmatively.

The mother pulled both daughters protectively toward her. "No, Ella. They're not alive. They died millions of years ago."

Ella grimaced in doubt. "Promise?"

"Promise."

"What if they're still alive, Mommy? Would they eat us?"

Sophia, the two-year-old, was now whimpering in fear.

"Stop provoking your sister, Ella."

"How do you know they're not alive?" Ella persisted.

"Ella, enough already. Let it go."

"Why?"

The mother steered the girls away from the display, Sophia now sobbing uncontrollably. As she herded them into the ladies room, she worried that both her girls would have nightmares tonight.

Kimberley Fulton got off the elevator on the fourth floor and headed for the large dinosaur display hall. She walked briskly through the hall where the T-Rex hovered over her like an elephant over an ant. Now she was walking down another hallway and, at the far end of it, entered a large office and closed the door behind her.

Her office was filled with an assortment of fossils, all categorized in various stages of development, many of them still encased in plaster casts with orange tags.

As Fulton reached her desk, she saw three pink message slips stuck to the receiver. And the message light was flashing.

She picked up the first message and read: *Urgent. Please call Scott Chandler ASAP. 907-276-3888.* The second and third message slips had the same message.

At first she refused to recognize the name, couldn't really connect it with her past. Finally, she lifted the phone and dialed for the messages.

A man's voice said, "Dr. Fulton, I presume."

The voice was instantly familiar. It brought back a quick flood of memories from long ago. The sense of humor hasn't improved, she thought.

"I hope you remember me, Kimberly. It's Scott Chandler. I know it's been something like eighteen years. I hope you're well. I'm working in Noatak National Preserve, Alaska. Park Zoologist, head of wildlife.

"Listen, Kimberly. We urgently need your help. Something terrible happened. Six people were killed here yesterday. By something strange. I have kind of a—well it's a kind of crazy idea—that you might be able to identify the predator. I saw it...saw something, anyway. There was heavy fog. Whatever it is, it's bloodthirsty, and it's nothing like anything I've ever seen. It was like—like some kind of *living fossil*. That's why I'm calling you. I've FedExed a package. Contains some kind of talon, feathers, teeth, and a digital recording of the attack. Please call me ASAP, home or office. This is extremely urgent." There was a brief pause in the message.

"I have fond memories of you, my friend. I read about your success in *Paleontology World*. Call me."

Fulton sucked in a deep breath, her mind racing. She copied down the home and office numbers then placed the phone back on the cradle. On the corner of her desk rested a pile of FedEx packages. She stared at them, hesitating, then looked around her office. Two words in the voice-mail caught her full attention and her heart skipped a beat: *living fossil.*

Just the thought of it spiked her adrenalin.

But receiving surprise packages? Since she'd become curator of the Paleontology Department at the most famous museum in the world, she'd received more than her share of quack phone calls, letters, packages, and emails. But as she located Chandler's packet in the pile, she dismissed the thought of caution. Why would Scott contact her after eighteen years unless he was serious?

Uneasy memories rushed back. She remembered Chandler as a dear friend and reliable resource of information while both of them were studying science at the University of Montana. They'd lunched occasionally, picnic style, on the south campus lawn behind the library comparing scientific notes. On occasion dinner, but nothing formal: pizza or burgers at the Greasy Spoon, the local haunt off campus.

She remembered a scar on his chin like Harrison Ford's. She once told him, "Why don't you buy one of those brown fedoras?" She furrowed her brow in thought: is he married with a family by now? Silly thoughts from a middle-aged single mom, she scolded herself.

She picked up the FedEx package, and reached for the pull-tab strip at the end of the box. She pulled it hard to the right, the lid flipped open, and the contents, fogged in carbon dioxide mist, slid out onto her lab table.

"Oh my God," she gasped.

CHAPTER 13

A WILLY'S JEEP PULLED UP TO A SMALL LOG CABIN ON SOCKEYE COURT, fourteen minutes east of Noatak Hospital. Scott Chandler jumped out and followed his friend to the front door. Chandler had visited Wolf's home many times, but each time he discovered another intriguing bit of Indian lore. Wolf had successfully replicated the home he'd lived in back in Glacier National Park—it was as if he had never moved. The furniture and wall hangings were even in the same places. It was as if they'd airlifted Wolf's Glacier home and just plunked it down on Sockeye Court.

As they entered the small living room, Chandler remembered the first time he'd visited the place. The man was still living in the mid-eighteenth century, Chandler had thought, surrounding himself with old handmade Native American furniture, pottery, paintings, and beaded and turquoise talismans hanging from the walls in no pattern or order Chandler could make out. Three large red clay pots made by Wolf's Blackfoot ancestors perched on a hand-hewn spruce mantle over an oval hearth. A black kettle hung from an iron arm suspended over a stack of aged cedar firewood. Chandler wondered if Wolf still cooked his meals over the fire.

Today, Chandler spied two new additions on the mantle: a walrus tusk carved into a totem pole with Inuit inscriptions and a bright red Sockeye salmon with the hooked jaw of a male. Wolf claimed he caught it during the spawning run up the Noatak River on an eight-weight fly rod, but later confided to Chandler over drinks that he'd foul-hooked it in the dorsal fin.

The floor was thick red clay squares, each of them with some kind of imprint. Some were imprinted with the footprints of Inuit children who had once walked across them as they flipped more tiles to bake in the hot Alaskan sun. Others bore etched insect and animal prints. Chandler spied several dog prints along with some kind of insect impression.

"Your floor tells an interesting story," Chandler mused. He pointed to a light tan tile and said, "What's this?"

Wolf looked down at the tile and grinned. "Scorpion." He pointed to another tile. "Tarantula. The bite of a scorpion paralyzes the tarantula, then he eats it alive."

Chandler looked up at Wolf. "You know I hate spiders," he said.

"Wuss," the Indian laughed and walked out of the small living room into the kitchen. "Drink?"

"Water," Chandler studied a framed parchment hanging on the wall. Two quotes caught his eye. He read the second one:

"Peace comes within the souls of men, when they realize their oneness with the Universe, when they realize it is really everywhere…
it is within each of us.
—Black Elk, Medicine Man, Lakota Tribe, 1823"

Wolf came back into the room. "I read that every day," he said.

"Sad we White Men can't seem to grasp the meaning of peace. Your people knew the importance of these words," Chandler offered. "Somehow we've fucked it all up."

Wolf nodded and sank into a low brown hassock to face Chandler. He held up the small magenta bowl in his left hand and pointed to the images scrawled across it in red, blue, and black dies.

"My father said the story it tells comes from many generations ago, and was thought to be legend. But now I believe it tells the truth just as much as the wind blows from the west and the sun rises in the east." Wolf leaned over and passed the ancient bowl to Chandler. "My ancestors are from here. They crossed over on the Bering Land Bridge over the

Chukchi Sea into the arctic. It is good to be back with my people. Alaska's an amazing state. Most people know little about it."

He held the bowl carefully in his right hand, his left sleeve hanging limply by his side. He hoped his new prosthesis would arrive within the week. He slowly turned the bowl and examined the images. Half way around, his eyes widened and his face became rigid. The primitive stick figures were running for their lives. The predator pursuing them brandished a razor sharp talon that resembled the one that ripped off the beast when it tried to attack him in Noatak National Park. "Holy Christ. What the hell is this?"

Wolf lifted himself out of the hassock and walked over to the hearth mantle. He picked up an enormous seashell, put the small end of it to his lips, inhaled deeply, and blew into it.

Chandler cupped his ears in an effort to deafen the pulsating sound. "What are you doing?"

Wolf took the ancient conch shell away from his lips. "My people believe the sound scares away evil spirits. Keep turning the bowl around, and you'll see them running away. Watch for the conch."

Chandler twisted the bowl slowly to see the story continue. "Yes," he said. "There it is." His face was ashen.

"It's been a symbol of power to my people for as long as our history has been passed on."

Chandler remembered what he'd learned in Missoula. "Amazing to think that Alaska was once covered by the Pacific Ocean."

Wolf nodded. "When the water receded it left behind thousands of fossils from the sea high up in the mountains, including these conch shells." Wolf reached out toward Chandler and handed him the conch shell. "This one's yours," he said. "If you go back to the Fossil River, don't let it out of your sight. If you see them again, use it."

Chandler sat in silence turning the conch shell in his good hand. He lifted the shell to his pursed lips and blew hard.

A low muffled squeak filled the room and Wolf laughed. "Sounds like a grizzly fart. Blow harder and squiggle your lips like this." Wolf demonstrated by blowing into the air.

This time, when Chandler blew, the sound started in a low squeak then rose into a high pulsating rumble that rattled the windows of the small living room. He put the conch down as though it were alive. "Jesus. What a helluva sound. It's haunting," Chandler said.

Wolf grunted with pleasure, "Congratulations."

Chandler nodded at his colleague, then his face dissolved into a mask of concern. "If the Defense Secretary sends a Marine strike force in there," he hesitated, "to clear the area for oil…"

"They'll never get out alive," Wolf said, his eyes fixed on Chandler.

"It's imperative we identify this predator before it's too late. Maybe we can," he said.

"It's already too late," Wolf interrupted. He pointed to one of the images etched in the bowl. "It's them, all right. They're alive. They'll defend their territory to the death. Nothing can stop them. Not even military power."

"How do you know that?"

"My people know."

Chandler rose from the bench and walked toward the phone. The lights in the cabin flickered twice, dimmed, then glowed to life as if Wolf had willed them back with some ancient tribal chant. Chandler heard an electric click and the lights faded unevenly as if the power was slowly being sucked out of the home. He shook his head.

"Our country will do everything possible to get at that oil, you know that, Wolf. It took me two fucking hours to get gas yesterday, and the allotment only gave me a half tank, for Chrissake. There must have been twenty-five cars on line. Crazy shit."

Wolf shook his head. "So there's no hope of stopping Secretary Robinson from launching an attack?"

Chandler turned on his heel and responded angrily. "We've been in Arab oil countries for decades now. Lost 10,000 soldiers, 38,000 wounded. He held up what was left of his arm. "I know the price we're paying, and that we'll stop at nothing to get at the oil in Noatak. If Robinson thinks it's a walk in the park, he'll change his mind when he sends an attack force in there. What I saw at the Fossil River yesterday defies description. It'll be a fucking bloodbath."

CHAPTER 14

Fᴜʟᴛᴏɴ's ᴏꜰꜰɪᴄᴇ ɪɴᴛᴇʀɪᴏʀ ꜱᴇᴇᴍᴇᴅ ɪɴᴛᴇɴᴛɪᴏɴᴀʟʟʏ ᴅᴇꜱɪɢɴᴇᴅ ᴛᴏ ʀᴇꜱᴇᴍʙʟᴇ ᴀ rustic museum-within-a-museum. The floors were made of rough-hewn native woods and had been simply coated with a clear protective polyurethane finish. The custom print Scalimondri wallpaper showed fossil skeleton Therapods roaming in lifelike herds around her cave-like office walls. The only floor coverings were tarps spread beneath the legs of the two wooden lab tables in the center of the room facing her half-oval desk. On these tables, in artful, organized clusters, were fossilized bones of all shapes and sizes that she had personally collected from all over the world on her digs.

The walls were lined with bookshelves filled with dinosaur and paleontology books. Other shelves contained teeth, tiny bones, and skull fragments. A saber-toothed tiger fang, and the upper jaw of a dinosaur from the Order *Saurischia*, the Family of *Dromaeosauridae*, were carefully placed on long benches on either side of the bookcases. The orange tag on the jaw read, "Genus unknown. Coleville River bed, Alaska."

Another collection resting in the upper end of a long rectangular box contained a string of hollow tailbones. Directly beneath this arrangement was a large fossilized claw that sat beside a nearly complete skeleton of a three-toed foot. In the middle of the box rested a full set of sharp teeth jutting abruptly from a perfectly formed mandible. Fulton had laid out these bones as though they were part of a larger jigsaw puz-

79

zle that was missing the majority of its pieces. Off to the side of the box was a clutch of six fossilized eggs. Carbon fourteen testing confirmed that the fossil was from the lower Cretaceous period, 120 million years ago. The orange tag read that the species' Order was still in question.

The only piece of furniture that hinted this might be someone's office, and not the hideaway of a crazed fossil digger, was the rich, worn mohair sofa that faced the oversized fireplace.

When Fulton had been promoted to Curator five years ago, it seemed to the professional world to be the acme of her paleontology career. To her, it was only a step along the way. The Division of Paleontology encompassed the entire dinosaur collection, including Ancient Fossils and New Discoveries. She aimed to be the Division Chair. Today she was just one of three other curators. When she was passed over for the coveted Chair position in favor of Dr. George Crowl, she rationalized to herself that she was a victim of the glass ceiling. But she knew the truth. The man who got the job as Chair of the Dinosaur Division was fifteen years her senior, and understood the importance of politics as well as new discoveries.

In order to leapfrog out of her current position she knew she would have to either play politics, which she abhorred, or make a major discovery of her own. This goal had provided the motivation for her unrelenting fossil searches in all corners of the world: China, Mongolia, Patagonia, the Chilean Andes, the Sahara, and West Africa. She was a fellow of the Explorer's Club, and the Willi Hennig Society.

Maybe the package from Chandler would lead to the breakthrough she'd been waiting for.

After acquiring her Ph.D. in *living fossils* from the University of Idaho, Fulton had returned to her alma mater, the University of Montana, to become a full professor of Paleontology.

A rising star in her field, she didn't like staying indoors. Classrooms and labs had become increasingly frustrating to a woman who knew that it was out in the field, on the rich fossil plains of the western frontier, where the action was and where fossils were being discovered. After two and a half years of living in university-owned housing, she had used the money her mother left her to build a cabin in a wide-open prairie within an hour's drive of the campus.

She'd chosen Bitter Root Valley to build in because it had once hosted an ancient orchard and been the home of the Salish Indians, one of the great Western tribes that had been forced from the area during the Native American displacement at the end of the nineteenth century. The Bitterroot Valley was seen for the first time by white men when Lewis and Clark, along with Sacajawea and her baby, camped there. They'd been well looked after by the Salish during that year, 1805-06, but by 1877 the kinship the white settlers might have felt toward their welcoming hosts had vanished. First, the U.S. Army forced the Nez Perce, local brethren of the Salish, from the Valley. Just a few years later, at the turn of the new century, the Salish themselves were driven from the Valley and moved to a reservation in the northern part of the State.

Today, the rolling grasslands, once home to many native tribes that lived side by side in harmony, were being bulldozed for tract houses and strip malls. Fulton tried not to be disheartened by the rash of development. On her walks of the surrounding land in search of fossils and other artifacts, she felt a haunting kinship with the Salish, Nez Perce, and the other tribes that used to call the Bitterroot Valley home.

Fulton's reputation as an outsider began when she was just a young girl. She didn't behave the way people thought a young girl should. She was the quintessential tomboy who, often alone for hours, spent her time outdoors from dawn until dusk, exploring the woods and mountains around her home in the Catskills. She was far more athletic and outdoorsy than her two older brothers, whose influence on her, nonetheless, was profound.

For her sixth birthday, her eldest brother Quint, who had just turned twelve, gave her his collection of plastic dinosaurs. She immediately threw aside her dolls and tea parties to immerse herself in the world of the prehistoric giants. Her other brother, John, ten at the time, gave her a tattered, illustrated encyclopedia of dinosaurs, which had been their father's when he was a young boy. Her mother, initially dismayed by her only daughter's predilection for digging in dirt, burying the dinosaurs, then finding them again, soon realized that Kimberly's passion for this play was serious.

She actively began to encourage her. While her mother did chores, Kimberly would follow along behind her and recite the names of all the dinosaurs, and regale her mother with theories about how they ate, reared their young, and how they became extinct.

When she was eight, her father gave her a book entitled *The Unexplainable in Nature*, which detailed accounts of finding entombed animals. She would stay up late into the night, huddled under her blanket with a flashlight, and read tales of live animals who had lived millions of years ago but were found alive today. Young Kimberly was enthralled by the stories.

She loved the story of a live horned lizard being freed from a block of stone. But her favorite story of all recounted the discovery of a live pterodactyl found in France during the winter of 1856.

As the story went, workmen were digging a railway tunnel. They broke into a layer of Jurassic-age limestone and were terrified by an enormous creature that stumbled out of a giant split boulder.

The creature flapped massive wings, croaked a few times—then fell over dead. A local paleontologist identified the dead creature as a pterodactyl. The dating of the limestone confirmed that the animal would have been entombed during the Jurassic period.

The story left such an impression on eight-year-old Fulton that she decided at that moment that she would become a paleontologist—and that one day she'd find a living fossil.

Even then, Fulton knew her dream seemed wistful. But as she grew older and her studies became more sophisticated, she learned that the study of living fossils, plants, and animals that have remained unchanged for millions of years was a legitimate sub-discipline of Paleontology.

"We're surrounded by living fossils," she wrote in her journal. "crocodiles, cockroaches, ginkgo trees, lizards, and horseshoe crabs are among the most common."

Fulton's journal also recorded that the biological world was stunned when a fish long-thought extinct, and whose fossilized remains had become a benchmark for identifying other species, was found alive in 1938.

A live Coelacanth, predating the dinosaurs by 200 million years, and which was thought to have become extinct along with them sixty-five million years ago, was caught by a fisherman off the waters of South Africa and brought to a local museum.

The realization that this was a live specimen of a prehistoric fish that was known to be 400 million years old was hailed as "the most important paleontological discovery of the century." It was as significant as finding a live pterodactyl. Even more so, because unlike that isolated find in nineteenth century France, Coelacanths are alive today. In fact, she wrote in an article, "Over 500 living fossils thrive in modern times."

Fulton's interest in paleontology was enhanced by the study of two of the most prominent dinosaur luminaries of their time: Othniel Charles Marsh and Edward Drinker Cope. Bitter enemies, both were responsible in the 1880s for establishing and promoting the worldwide fascination with dinosaurs that still endures today. Fulton read their memoirs with avid interest, promising herself that some day she too would rise to their level of achievement and fame.

Marsh and Cope both raised money to explore the Western badlands for fossil remains. They hired their most prized bone collectors away from each other. They spied on each other's digs and paid people to smash each other's fossil discoveries.

Her interest in living fossils prompted Fulton to write her Ph.D. thesis on North American Theropods (three-toed, bipedal carnivores, such as T. Rex, that roamed the earth from the Early Jurassic until the late Cretaceous period, more than sixty-five million years ago) with an emphasis on the family *Dromaeosauridae,* the birdlike branch of the suborder, which includes Veloceraptors, and the granddaddy of them all, Archaeopteryx.

But the creature that most interested Fulton, and the one she focused on in her thesis, was one of the rarest and most confounding: *Deinonychus Antirrhopus,* the most vicious of the predatory Therapods.

Deinonychus, whose name meant "terrible claw" in Greek, was first discovered in south central Montana by the renowned paleontologist John H. Ostrom in 1964. Dr. Ostrom stunned the world of paleontology when he unearthed a complete skeleton of Deinonychus. When she was ten, her parents took her to the Museum of Natural History in New York City to see this marvel.

Fulton's career in paleontology at the University of Idaho would change dramatically when she got a call from the Chairman of the Geology Department at the University of Montana. He called with the offer of a lifetime: Just a year earlier, in 2006, the Montana State Board of Regents had approved a new Paleontology Center, which would be associated with the Fort Peck Station, the site of fossil-rich Cretaceous formations located in eastern Montana where Ostrom had found *Deinonychus*. Given her expertise in paleontology, he wanted to know if Fulton would be interested in a professorship that would entail teaching in Missoula during the academic year, then being out in the field in and around Fort Peck and other locations throughout the State during the summers.

Without hesitation, Fulton said yes.

After six years at UM, Fulton grew restless and sent out her resume to all the major museums in the country that were known for their dinosaur collections.

While she was passionate for digging in the field, the thought of being a curator for a museum's dinosaur collection heightened her curiosity. *I'll be able to get back out in the field for digs maybe more than I do now*, she had convinced herself. New York's Museum of Natural History was at the top of her list and when she got a call from the Human Resource department after her third interview, they offered her one of three Curator positions within the Dinosaur Division.

To Fulton, it was a stunning career achievement. The move to New York City was undertaken with the same feeling of excitement she'd experienced on receiving her first dinosaur book from her brother Quint.

Fulton sat rigid at her desk, her eyes still focused on the contents of the FedEx package. Her heart fluttered as if she'd inhaled a dozen cups of coffee. She looked up across her desk at the door to her office, then walked to the door, bolted it shut and turned the second lock hard to the right. Her mind was racing with only one thought: call Scott Chandler.

As she lifted the phone to dial, someone knocked on her office door. Fulton sat motionless, putting the phone back on the cradle. The knocking continued.

A muffled voice sounded. "Kimberly?"

Fulton didn't respond, but she knew who it was.

The knocking continued. "Kimberly? It's George."

Silence.

"Kimberly. Open up." Now the handle was turning back and forth.

Fulton sat rigid in her chair. Then she heard a key being placed in the lock. She swept the contents of the FedEx package back into the container, then hid the package in her lower left desk drawer. She walked briskly to the door and slid the lock bolt open.

Dr. George Crowl stepped inside her office. "It took you long enough to open the door," he said. There was not a wisp of humor in his voice.

The words were pushed out of her mouth with extreme effort, "I didn't hear you George. Sorry."

Crowl stood in place, staring at her through thick wire-rimmed glasses perched atop his bulbous nose. The sternness of his expression confirmed that he doubted her response. His white bristly beard and overweight five-foot-seven-inch frame made him look more like a troll than a stand-in for a German St. Nick, although he often arrived with a burled cherrywood pipe, empty of tobacco, stuck between his stained teeth.

Fulton spun on her heel, walked back to her desk and sat down, Crowl following. She shifted in her chair scanning the top of her desk.

"You know my open-door policy on this floor," he said.

"Yes, George. It was personal. I had to talk to my son," she lied.

"You don't have to lock your door to do that."

"I hear you, George."

"Then please. Keep your door open."

Fulton nodded, staring back at him with intensity, not wanting him to know she was hiding something—or that he intimidated her.

It was no secret to the employees in his department that Crowl suffered from an incessant fear that the people reporting to him were all trying to undermine his job and authority. Fulton counseled herself not to comment on his open-door policy. She knew what was behind the order.

Crowl stepped closer to her desk. He peered at its contents, then spun on his heel and slowly scanned her office, inspecting the fossils and plaster blocks as he walked toward the door. When he got to the door, he opened it, then looked back at her. He removed the pipe from his mouth. He smiled, but it was forced.

"You're not hiding anything, are you?"

"I'm offended you would imply that."

"Just a question, Dr. Fulton. No need to take offense."

Crowl pushed the office door wide open and vanished.

She waited for three minutes then dialed the number that Scott Chandler had given her. The phone rang but there was no answer.

She decided against leaving a message and hung up.

CHAPTER 15

SECRETARY CONLON AGREED WITH ZOLLAR AND ROBINSON TO NOT TELL Barton the gory details of the massacre in Noatak National Park until they were all together, and the two were now enroute to the Oval Office to join him. Conlon wanted to wrap up the research data quickly, and spoke with dispatch as he reviewed his notes.

"We got the data, Mr. President, from two portable computers that the pilot, Scott Chandler, was able to bring back from the research mission."

"And?"

"Based on preliminary calculations done at Energy's lab, sir, Noatak's oil field is unbelievably vast. It is almost double the size of the largest oil field in the world—Ghawar in Saudi Arabia. At 7,800-feet elevation, we estimate that the fossil fuel could run vertically for miles into the earth's core."

Conlon paused and looked directly at the President. "It could hold two trillion barrels of crude oil, Mr. President. Maybe more. We knew there had to be a massive oil deposit somewhere out there feeding the Baaken field that runs east of the Continental Divide into the Dakotas. But everything about this find is surprising. From Noatak to the western states, the oil would have to spread underground through Canada's northwest and spill into Montana and the Dakotas. Maybe that's why there's so much shale oil in the area. We just don't know." Conlon shook his head.

"This is amazing news, Tyler. Better than I could have imagined. Can we tap into it quickly?"

"I'd like to hold off answering that question until Lauren and Shawn arrive, sir. They'll have a better handle on it than I do," Conlon said.

Barton said, "If this is true, Tyler, it changes everything. We could bring our troops home. The economy, international relations—everything."

"Yes sir. It will. It'll change everything. I do believe this is a genuine find, sir. The data is pretty solid. Our worries over energy may soon be just a bad memory."

"I need to know how long—if we bring every conceivable resource to bear—it will take to get that oil out of the ground."

"Of course, Mr. President. We're working on some initial estimates now. But we really need to get onsite and do some more observation. If it's close enough to the surface, and if we really make an extraordinary effort, it is possible we could start pumping almost immediately. There's just one little problem, sir," Conlon said in an unguarded moment.

Barton adjusted his tie. "What's that, Tyler?"

There was a light tap on the door and Barton's appointment secretary poked her head in and said, "Excuse me, Mr. President. Secretaries Robinson and Zollar have arrived."

President Barton led the other two leaders of Operation Torch to the large conference table at the center of the room where Conlon was sitting.

"It's good to see you two back in one piece," Barton said to Zollar and Robinson. His smile confirmed his ebullience. "Tyler and I've been reviewing the data collected from Operation Torch. I'm assuming he hasn't yet shared it with you. But first, I want an update on our research team." He turned toward Secretary Zollar. "Lauren? I didn't get all the details. I heard there was some kind of problem. I trust everyone involved is recovering?" Barton caught a dark look wash over Robinson's face.

Zollar sat rigid in her chair, staring at Barton.

She inhaled deeply and said, "Actually sir, we have terrible news. Our team was ambushed shortly after the mission began. Only two of seven men who were on the ground got out of the park alive, and one of them died enroute to the Noatak Hospital. Only one survivor, Mr. President. Scott Chandler, our helicopter pilot—one of my employees."

She stopped talking when she saw the President's face.

"What are you saying, Lauren? That our research team was murdered? In Noatak National Park?"

"Murdered...may not be the right word, sir."

Zollar looked over at Robinson, who nodded. "Whatever attacked the men, sir. Well—it wasn't human. And it wasn't any animal we're familiar with..."

"What?" the President's brows were deeply furrowed. "What do you mean?"

"We think it was some kind of animal, sir. Some type of very powerful predator. But the forensic team and pathologist have not yet been able to identify what kind of predator's in there, or...."

Secretary of Defense Robinson interrupted Zollar mid-sentence. "*What* did this is pretty irrelevant at this point—isn't it? Clearly, what we need to do is get in there and secure the area as soon as possible."

The President looked over at his colleague, dumbfounded.

"Shawn. Please. Relax." He was still trying to absorb the fact that six people involved in Operation Torch were dead.

Robinson, who was now standing, could barely contain his anger. "I recommend we send a platoon of Marine Special Forces in there immediately. Annihilate the bastards that did this."

Robinson hadn't shared a word of his reaction at the morgue with her or on the flight back east, catching Zollar off guard. Her outrage barely containable, she leaned over the table toward Robinson.

"You can't send the military into Noatak National Park. Are you out of your mind, Shawn?"

"Shawn, sit down, please." The President turned back to Zollar. "Lauren. Tell us. It's your park. What's the strategy?"

Zollar had thought about nothing else on the interminably long trip back from Alaska. Her voice was now firm, unyielding. "We don't have a choice, Mr. President. We've got to close the Park. I've already issued a press release and given the orders to shut it down at midnight tonight. I'm afraid it'll be a public relations nightmare because one of our biggest weekends of the year, the long Memorial Day weekend, starts tomorrow."

She studied her hands, which were clutched in her lap.

"We'll be slamming the door on however many vacationers could afford $10 a gallon to get there. Not to mention the hundreds of employees we'll have to evacuate. At least it's not the 100,000 it would have been a year or two ago. The Press will be all over it—and us. Or, I should say, they'll be all over me."

"Is this really our only option?" The President thought about the headlines and the environmentalists.

"I'm afraid it is," Zollar said. "We'll have to work hard to minimize the damage."

"So what official reason did you give for closing it?"

Zollar shook her head.

"I've wracked my brain trying to come up with something plausible that wouldn't also cause a media frenzy. I thought about positioning it as routine census taking, but that wouldn't fly, and we'd have Park employees, who actually spend the winter months counting wild Doll sheep and herds of caribou and deer, crying foul."

She looked around the room. Her eyes searched her colleagues for some kind of help in justifying the sensitive decision she'd made. She poked copies of the press release across the table at the President and her two colleagues.

As they read, Zollar couldn't resist adding that there wasn't any way to handle this that wouldn't cause an outcry. She was quickly becoming resigned to the fact that she, personally, was about to become the latest punching bag for an Administration that was already skating on thin ice due to the energy crisis.

"Good, Lauren," said Barton. "I'm glad you took swift action." Barton looked at Conlon and said, "So. Do we have any idea—any idea at all—what kind of predator this is? You're sure it's some type of animal, correct? Something not seen before?"

Conlon looked at Zollar and Robinson, a look of deep concern spreading across his face. "Unfortunately, Mr. President, none of us know what the hell it was. Not even the surviving helicopter pilot could identify it, and he's the Park zoologist, head of wildlife. We all saw the

body of one of the scientists at the morgue. It was damned gruesome."
The color drained from Conlon's face as he recalled Cooper Windham's
lacerated corpse.

Robinson leaned across the table. "Whatever killed them has to be
taken out—and fast. I'd like your permission, Mr. President, to engage a
contained strike into Fossil to clear the Park before we go in for the oil,
sir. At the very least, we should position a military force in the Park so
we're ready to mobilize when you give the command."

Zollar gave Robinson a look. "Noatak National Preserve's the crown
jewel of our entire national park system. It's imperative we proceed cautiously. Before we do anything, we need to know what kind of predator
we're dealing with. Chandler's working on that as we speak. He was the
only person who got out alive and had a glimpse of the predator. He's a
trained zoologist and biologist. He has samples of whatever it was, and
we should have an answer within days."

Conlon took a quick look at the Strategic Oil Reserve inventories
and said, "We can't wait that long." His voice was thin and lacked confidence.

Zollar bristled. "There's a stringent law preventing the military from
violating any of our public parks, Shawn: The Posse Comitatus Act of
1878. Gives us no leeway to invade Noatak or any other park."

"Not when our nation's in a national oil crisis, cars and planes can't
get gas, and our military's threatened for lack of mobility fuel," Robinson
shot back with equal conviction.

Barton stood up and walked over to the window overlooking the
Rose Garden. Finally, he turned and faced the Operation Torch team.
"This helicopter pilot who got out alive, what's his name again?"

"Chandler, sir. Scott Chandler. Served in Iraq and Afghanistan. Two
Purple Hearts and two Bronze Stars," Zollar said.

"You have his number?"

"Yes, sir."

"Call him. Get him on speaker. I want to talk to him."

Zollar stared at him dumbfounded. All she could muster was,
"Now?"

"Now. We've no time to waste. We're running on fumes. Call him.
Use the red phone on my desk."

"Yes, sir." Zollar looked at her watch. It was eighteen minutes past midnight E.S.T. It would be 9:18 p.m. in Alaska. Her mind was racing: What if he's in bed asleep? This was an unrehearsed call, thought Zollar, and Chandler might say something that could throw the entire mission in jeopardy. It unnerved her, but she picked up the phone and dialed Chandler's home.

"It's ringing," she said.

"Put it on speaker," Barton said.

It rang for over a minute. As she was about to end the call, Barton said, "Let it ring. Don't hang up."

"Hello?" The voice was raspy.

Barton held up his hand to prevent anybody from talking. He said, "Scott?"

"Yes?"

"President Barton here."

Chandler sat up in bed and rubbed his eyes. "Is this a joke?" he asked.

Barton spoke firmly. "No joke, Scott. President Peter Barton here. I'm honored to talk to a soldier with such distinguished service. On behalf of our nation, I want to thank you for your tour of duty in Iraq and Afghanistan and for defending our country with such valor."

Chandler bolted out of bed, now standing at the window. A half moon lit up mountain peaks in the distance. He managed a subdued "Thank you, sir."

"Secretary Zollar tells me you're the best helicopter pilot we have."

"Thank you, sir."

"I'm here with Secretary Robinson and Secretary Conlon. They've informed me about your confrontation in Noatak National Park."

"Yes, sir."

"Since you got a glimpse of this predator, I want to hear from you as to what kind of danger we're facing before we consider sending in the military to clear the area."

"Yes, sir. I'm trying to connect with someone I think can identify what it is. I should have the person lined up by tomorrow."

"What do you think it is?"

"Whatever it is, it presents grave danger to anybody who goes back in there. It's a species I've never seen before—and I believe there's a colony of them in Noatak. How they could survive all these years without being detected provides some clue that they've obviously learned how to adapt unusually well. It's in a very remote area of the Park."

"If we were to send in a strike force, any suggestions for safety or strategy?"

"Only one suggestion, Mr. President." Chandler's voice was resolute.

"Yes."

"Don't do it."

Barton's eyes seemed to glaze over in disbelief. "Rest assured, we'll take your advice to heart. I want to thank you, Scott, for taking the time to share with us your thoughts. I'm sorry to call you this late."

"No problem, Mr. President," and the line went dead.

Barton walked back to the conference table and said, "It's clear what we have to do."

Robinson said, "Yes?"

"We wait until we know what kind of predator we're dealing with. We take the Marine war hero's advice. However, Shawn, I do think we should be prepared to do what you suggest. Send a company of your best Marines. Have them ready to strike on a moment's notice."

"Yes, sir," Robinson said. "Consider it done." He glanced at Zollar.

"Meeting adjourned," Barton said. As he walked toward the door, the lights dimmed.

"Jesus," he said.

Robinson bumped into a chair. Conlon stood in place, his heart racing. Zollar held onto the corner of something. A table maybe, she thought.

"Not good," Conlon said gloomily. "We've got to do a better job balancing the electricity over the power grid and transmission lines. When we power up the west, the east suffers, and vice versa. Feeding the electric system with more or less power is playing havoc with the old power network. The system's failing to redistribute the load evenly."

"We have a generator. Should kick on soon," Barton said.

Someone knocked on the door. A voice from outside said, "Mr. President?"

"Yes?"

"Security, sir. Lights will be on in a moment. System's booting up now. You okay?"

"Yes. Thank you."

The lights came on and the Oval Office now shone brightly. Robinson walked to the window and stared outside into the night. Squinting into the dark, he said, "It's fucking pitch black out there."

First light came at 5:48 a.m., Alaskan Time. Noatak National Park had officially shut down at midnight. Gates across each entrance had been chain-locked shut. Those already in the Park were methodically informed and ushered out—not without vehement objection. Following the vacationers, Park employees had been escorted from the Park before midnight by Alaska's National Guard, who were not informed that a Marine strike force would be encamped in the southeastern quadrant of the Park at combat readiness.

The press release announcing Noatak's closure hadn't hit local newspapers, radio, and TV news stations until after nine a.m. Memorial Day car and camper lines leading up to Noatak's entrances now stretched for miles from the east and south. More cars dotted the highways, having already run out of gas. Smaller lines were now building at the southeastern tip of the Park.

Horns honked and people got out of their cars, vans, and motorhomes asking questions, their engines turned off to save gas. Rumors spread back and forth. The most logical one was that a four-car collision had happened up ahead. But after two hours, the tourists' patience had vanished, and they began yelling at one another demanding answers.

As radio news stations announced Noatak's closure the cars that had enough gas to pull away turned around in disgust and drove away from the park. A single news helicopter arrived. It was exactly what Lauren Zollar had projected—and the frustration was just beginning to build.

By the time Zollar entered Interior's office building, reporters from Associated Press, The Washington Post, and The New York Times were staked outside her office waiting for interviews. Zollar's appointment secretary held up her hands in a helpless gesture. When Zollar opened her office door, pink message slips were piled high on her desk, her phone barely visible under a barrage of paper.

CHAPTER 16

Fᴜʟᴛᴏɴ ʀᴏsᴇ ꜰʀᴏᴍ ʜᴇʀ ᴅᴇsᴋ ᴀɴᴅ ʟᴏᴏᴋᴇᴅ ᴏᴜᴛsɪᴅᴇ ʜᴇʀ ᴏꜰꜰɪᴄᴇ. Cʀᴏᴡʟ ᴡᴀs nowhere in sight.

The lights dimmed briefly then came back on with full intensity. She walked down the hallway and glanced into Crowl's office to confirm. He was gone. She hurried back and dialed Chandler's phone number.

"Scott Chandler, please."

"Speaking."

Fulton's hand was shaking.

"Hello?"

"Scott. It's Kimberly."

"My God. It's you. How are you?"

"Glad to hear you're alive."

"Me, too. You got the Fed Ex?"

"Yes."

"What do you think?"

There was a long silence on the phone.

"Kimberly?"

"I'm here. My mind's blown, Scott. The stuff you sent...is it real? I mean, this isn't some kind of joke, is it?"

"I appreciate your doubt, Kimberly. No, it's not a joke. I wish it was. It's very real."

"And you saw one alive?"

"I saw many alive. A colony's in there, maybe more."

"Describe one to me."

"Walks upright on two powerful legs: feathers, teeth, yellow eyes, wings, and huge talons on its feet. Has two smaller appendages like arms jutting out of its shoulders, smaller talons. Alien-like."

"Shit, Scott. I can't believe this. Are you sure?"

"There's more. Thick fog—but I saw one gliding. I don't know if it was gliding or flying."

"How big was it?"

"The ones I saw were maybe six to eight feet tall. About nine to eleven feet long. But again, I just got a very brief visual. Couldn't be certain of the detail. Too fast."

"What about color?"

"Some blue, maybe pinkish-red. Some brown. Kind of a mix of those three colors. But there was one that was much bigger than the others."

"The alpha male," Fulton said in disbelief. "Aggressive?"

"It attacked my helicopter. Almost got me."

"Did you hear them communicating?" There were so many questions she wanted to ask, but she grabbed a quick deep breath and forced herself to slow down, her eyes wide with the possibility that this fantasy might actually be true.

"That was the most terrifying thing about them. The screech. Ear shattering. Different tones. Hard to describe—but they were communicating to one another. Moving through dense fog very fast, hunting. Any idea what it was?" Chandler asked.

"Yes."

"What?"

"Before I answer that, I want to complete lab tests on what you sent me—but it sounds like some kind of living fossil."

"That's what I thought, but I've no idea what species. There's no animal or bird in the park that even comes close to this thing."

"So when can you get out here? We're working on a tight schedule."

"What do you mean?"

"Kimberly, President Barton called me last night. I've already met with the Secretary of Interior, my boss, the Secretary of Energy, and the Secretary of Defense. They flew out here yesterday."

"To Noatak National Park?

"Yes."

"Jesus Christ. Why?"

"You won't believe this, either. Because there's oil in the preserve. A lot of it. And the oil field is dead center in the midst of the predators' territory."

"Dear God."

"They're talking about a strike."

"A military strike?"

"Yes."

"Into Noatak?"

"Yes."

"To do what?"

"To wipe out these things that killed six people."

Fulton was practically yelling into the phone. "They can't do that, Scott! We can't let them do that. If it's a living fossil, it might be the missing link between dinosaurs and birds!"

"When can you get out here?" Chandler pressed.

"Tomorrow. I'll get out there tomorrow. Hell," Fulton was shouting into the phone with uncontrolled excitement. Then it occurred to her and she blurted out, "I had a field trip at the Colville River working the fossil beds in Alaska. We found a lot of specimens, raptor bones—and talons too. Where's Noatak? Alaska's a huge state."

"In the northwest sector of Alaska. Over 400 square miles of arctic wilderness in a mountain range that will blow your mind," Chandler said with gathering expectation that Fulton would make the trip.

"Email me the details. Airport, your address, etc., but..."

"What?"

"There might be a complication."

"What's that?"

"I have a sixteen-year-old son. Ken. He's out of school—so I need to find a place for him to stay while I'm gone."

"When did you get married?"

"I never did. It's a long story."

"Oh."

"You?"

"Still single. Got engaged once. Didn't work out."

"If you can't find a place for Ken, bring him along. He can stay with a friend of mine. Brave Wolf."

"American native?"

"Yes."

"Ken will love that."

"Good."

Chandler gave his email to Fulton and said, "Let me know what flight you'll be on, and the ETA. You'll want to fly into Anchorage, then on to Kotzebue. Once in Kotzebue, you have to fly to the preserve with one of the air taxi operators."

"You still flying helicopters?" Fulton queried.

"Yes."

"Can you get me in there tomorrow?"

There was a long pause before Chandler said, "No."

Fulton said, "Why?"

"I barely got out alive, Kimberly."

"I know. I did my Ph.D. on the buggers. I'll have some answers by then, and I'll have all of my field equipment with me to prove what it is—but you've got to get me in there where they are."

"We'll talk about that when you arrive."

"Not good enough, Scott. How else can I identify the predator if I can't see what it is? I want your commitment now that we're going in there. I'm not going to fly my son and me to some remote Alaskan preserve on a puddle jumper and not see the critters."

"You haven't changed. And they're not critters, Kimberly. The damn things are alien," Chandler said uncomfortably as vivid memories flooded his mind.

"People don't change," Fulton said with professorial confidence.

"Okay, okay, but we stay in the chopper, engine on. Can you tell me now what you think it is?"

"Not yet."

"Still the same tease."

"I look forward to seeing you, Scott. Been seventeen years—or eighteen. Anyway, a hell of a long time. We have a lot to catch up on."

"Me, too. Good-night, Kimberly."

Chandler was lost in thought. Memories of their relationship vividly came back to him. It was as if he was living their last moments together now. Both were hesitant to express any feelings other than a genuine fondness. Both were afraid to cross the line into anything that might ruin their friendship.

Chandler remembered Fulton being surprised and disappointed that he had signed up for the Marine Corps overseas. Her response, strong and sensitive, gave him the feeling that there might be more than a casual, platonic link. When he told her he was flying out to Quantico, she flustered him with a comment: "You're not serious, are you?"

He'd poured more wine into both glasses, now into their second bottle. They were in his car, front seats, a Jeep Wrangler XL.

"Yeah, I'm serious. Those bastards killed over 3,000 innocent people when the towers came down, and they slammed into the Pentagon. Happened a long time ago, but I consider joining the Marines as payback." At least our Navy Seals killed the bastard Osama Bin Laden. The angry thought interrupted his reverie.

"You could be killed," he remembered Fulton telling him with a compassionate stare.

"Yes."

"So this is it?"

"What do you mean?"

She hesitated, her lips parted and she stared into his eyes. "I mean—" she did not finish the sentence, just kept staring at him in silence.

Chandler could hear her breath. He sat still, wanting to kiss her, embrace her, and tell her how much he cherished their friendship. Tomorrow he'd be leaving to join the Marines, but now they were together alone—and there was no guarantee they'd ever see each other again.

Fulton slid across the front seat. She'd put her hand behind his head. Gently, slowly, she'd pulled him toward her.

The kiss was soft.

Chandler remembered the sweet scent when their lips touched. In a matter of seconds, it seemed, their clothes were off and they were enjoined in what he now remembered was the most beautiful sexual moment of his entire life.

CHAPTER 17

Fᴜʟᴛᴏɴ ᴜɴʟᴏᴄᴋᴇᴅ ʜᴇʀ ᴅʀᴀᴡᴇʀ ᴀɴᴅ ᴘᴜʟʟᴇᴅ ᴏᴜᴛ ᴛʜᴇ FᴇᴅEx ᴘᴀᴄᴋᴀɢᴇ. Sʜᴇ carefully scraped small samples of chitin from the eight-inch talon. She did the same with dried blood from part of the webbed knuckle attached to the talon, then centrifuged the blood in a small test tube. Then she clipped a small specimen of the pinkish feather that was attached to the flesh of the knuckle.

She took the specimens to the Museum laboratory on the fourth floor that contained the world's most advanced computers, microscopes and lab equipment for testing every conceivable sample of flora, fauna, bird, fish, reptile, and fossil.

Fulton did her best to control her mind from exploring wild possibilities. "Stay focused," she said aloud. "Stay focused." She carefully mounted specimens of flesh from the torn appendage to paraffin blocks, and placed them into the microtone. She took paper-thin slices of the waxed specimens, and died them red with eosin so the computers and electron microscopes could read the cellular structure of each and classify the specimens. If it was indeed a living fossil, the vast inventory of fossil bone collections that had been globally collected and identified for over two hundred years should provide a species match in the data bank.

She placed all her specimens into three electron microscopes that were connected to the computer databank and flipped three switches. There was a quiet hum of activity. Green, white, and red lights flickered on the laboratory ceiling and walls in a kaleidoscope of colors.

She sat back and waited. It was, she thought, surrealistic.

Fulton had already made three calls to try and line up a home for her son Ken to stay during her absence. All three mothers of Ken's friends were unavailable. There was no other choice now: he would have to fly out to Alaska with her. To leave her son home alone in New York City in this climate was unthinkable, she told herself. High unemployment was ravaging the City and lights that normally bathed the skyline in gossamer splendor barely provided enough dull light to identify buildings. The power that lit up Times Square, normally flashing brilliant rainbow colors day and night, was now running at two-thirds power.

Most disturbing to Fulton was that people were being held up in broad daylight. The crime rate seemed to triple. Two armed robberies taking food, jewelry, clothes, and cash had happened last week only a block from her apartment. Just four blocks from Fulton's apartment, three weeks ago, seven cars on the block had all four tires and headlights stolen.

Fulton stood up to stretch. She thought she saw a shadow move outside the lab door. She moved closer to the door, squinting to see detail, but the glare from the neon lights overhead blocked part of the image of someone who was standing there, peering inside. Whoever it was tapped on the glass with a hard object.

Fulton spun to look back at the computer bank and it was still processing. Then the computers went silent, and a low-pitched sound came from the main terminal.

She watched three printers come alive simultaneously. The job was done and she quickly moved to collect the reports, stuffing them into her briefcase.

Now she turned around to confront whoever was waiting outside. It was a man, she could see that much. She thought she saw a pipe but wasn't sure.

As her hand touched the doorknob to unlock it, a voice said, "You're working late tonight, Dr. Fulton."

CHAPTER 18

When his mother first called to tell him that he was flying with her to Noatak National Park, Alaska, Ken Fulton replied, "No way, Mom. I'm not going." But when she described what the trip was about, there was a long silence on the phone. "Can Meghan come?" he pleaded.

"No," Fulton had said with maternal authority. "Not this time."

"Why not?"

"Because."

"Because why?

"Ken. Please. No."

Ken hung up the phone and said, "Crap." He went online and sent an email. He wrote:

"Hi beautiful. Got an awesome idea. Email me. Urgent. I love you! Ken."

Before he signed off, an answer popped up on his screen.

"Hi. What's the awesome idea? Love you back, Meghan."

"Have to go to Alaska tomorrow with Mom. Asked her if you could come with us. She said no. Going to Noatak National Park. Mom says she's researching a living fossil. Sounds awesome. Can you fly out there and join us? Maybe surprise her?"

Meghan wrote: "Your Mom said no. Alaska's a long way off!"

"So?" he wrote back.

"What's a living fossil?"

"A live dinosaur."

"Shut up. No way!"

"That's what I said."

"Where would I stay?"

"I'm staying with an Indian."

"A Native American Indian?" she wrote.

"Yes."

"That's sick. So cool."

He wrote, "So?"

Meghan wrote, "I'll get back to you."

"Good. Think how much fun we could have," Ken wrote.

"Sounds cool. I'll check it out. My parents are going to the Hamptons tomorrow for a week. I'm supposed to stay with Julianna McGuire so it might work. Maybe she'll cover for me :o)."

Ken wrote, "Awesome. I love you. XXOO, Ken."

"Love you back. XO."

The door opened and the man said, "Hi Dr. Fulton. Sorry to bother you. Mind if I clean the lab?"

Fulton took in a deep sigh of relief and said, "Good to see you Jeremy. The lab's all yours. Just finished."

"Thanks, Doctor. Have a good evening."

When she got back to her office, she sat down at her desk and pulled out the reports. Her eyes were wide, face taut. She unfolded the print out and flipped to the first report. It read:

SCIENTIFIC CLASSIFICATION

Kingdom: Animalia

Phylum: Chordata

Class: Sauropsida

Superorder: Dinosauria

Order: Saurischia

Suborder: Therapoda

Family: Dromaeosauridae

Trembling with excitement and utter awe, Fulton looked up from the report. She knew the genus and species before continuing:

Genus: Deinonychus

Species: D. Antirrhopus

Fulton picked up the second report. It read:

Deinonychus Antirrhopus: 3.4 meters long dinosaur. Lived during the early Cretaceous Period, 121 to 98.9 million years ago. Fossil parts of the species have been discovered in Montana, Wyoming, and Oklahoma, but teeth have been discovered as far north as Alaska, and east to Maryland.

"Deinonychus," Greek for "terrible claw," refers to the large sickle-shaped talon on the second toe of each hind foot. The species name "antirrhopus" means "counter balance" which refers to Dr. John Ostrom's conclusions about the function of the tail. It could swish to each side with acute flexibility, enabling the predator to change direction 180 degrees on command. Paleontologist John Ostrom's hypothesis of Deinonychus in the late 1960s revolutionized the way scientists thought about dinosaurs, igniting the debate on whether or not they were warm-blooded. Before Ostrom's theory, dinosaurs were thought to be plodding, reptilian giants. Ostrom taught that lightweight bones and raptorial claws on the feet, coupled with an agile tail, piston like legs, and sharp jaws with inverted teeth created the most vicious agile predator in the Therapoda suborder.

The report ended with what Fulton hoped would be the stunning siren of discovery: Ostrom's hypothesis declared that Deinonychus was the link between birds and dinosaurs.

"Jesus Christ. It's alive."

CHAPTER 19

CHANDLER PRINTED OUT FULTON'S ITINERARY AND READ IT TO BRAVE WOLF. The sun was a large day-glow red in the western sky. It was 4:21 p.m. and they were in the Fish & Wildlife log cabin office set back about 200 yards from the Noatak River.

"I have to ask you a big favor, my friend," Chandler said. "She has a teenage son who's coming with her."

"I get the picture. You want him to stay with me. Babysit."

"I'm not sure yet, but in case it works out that way, I'd be grateful."

"How old is he?"

"Sixteen, I think. Maybe seventeen."

"Better than thirteen."

"I wouldn't know the difference," Chandler said.

"At thirteen, they tell you to go to hell to your face. At sixteen, they don't tell you anything, but you know they're thinking 'go fuck yourself.' At twenty, my son finally admitted that I was right about a lot of things."

Chandler chuckled. "Thanks. Appreciate it."

Wolf looked up from his field report. "You hear that?"

"Hear what?"

"Rumbling."

"No."

Wolf stood up and walked outside. Chandler followed him.

"Hear it now?" Wolf said.

"No," said Chandler curiously.

Wolf got down on his hands and knees and put his left ear to the ground.

"At first I thought it might be an earthquake. But it's trucks. Lots of them, coming out of the west, our way." Wolf looked west at the horizon. "They're in the air, too." Wolf pointed.

"How the hell could they get this far upriver?" Chandler said. "We're 150 miles east of Noatak—wait. Yes. I hear it now. You're right. How'd you learn that?"

"My grandfather, Soaring Eagle. He lived on the Montana plains east of our reservation. He would tell me he could hear a buffalo herd ten miles away, and follow an antelope tracking it in circles for twenty miles until the animal fell to its knees in exhaustion. Then he'd skin it and eat it."

"Raw, like sushi?"

Wolf laughed. "No. He'd roast it on a spit."

"Amazing. When I think of the billions of dollars we spend on defense on high technology. Nothing in our arsenal of high tech could identify an enemy that far away. From the air, maybe the Predator drone could make a visual, but if the enemy's moving on foot and camouflaged, no way."

"Why do you think U.S. troops used our people to track for them back then? White people knew squat about how to find the enemy, let alone a trail." Wolf laughed at himself for saying it.

The sound grew louder into a reverberating rumble of clanking cacophony. "Christ, it's the military," Chandler said. "They've invaded Noatak. I'd hoped they'd wait."

Chandler and Wolf watched the convoy—jeeps, armored trucks, and communications vehicles—snake round the bend along the south bank of the Noatak and spill out into the clearing, lights on. He knew the make, model and structural detail of each armored vehicle. He'd seen them all blown apart in his combat missions in Iraq and Afghanistan.

"They came upriver in Marine LCVs. Smart move."

"What the hell's an LCV?" Wolf said.

"Marine Landing Craft Vehicles. Amphibious. They must have dropped all the equipment at Noatak airport and launched on the north bank."

A low grumble of engine power sounded overhead, west of their position.

"Here come their supplies," Chandler said. "Semper Fi."

"You and your credos," said Wolf, shaking his head.

"We win wars because of it, my friend."

Three Boeing CH-47 Chinook helicopters loomed toward them, double blades whirling the Noatak River surface into a white froth. They set down behind the F&W office cabin and the engines powered off.

On the ground, the lead jeep, with a vertical whip antenna swaying from the rear, pulled up in front of the log cabin. A man hopped out and swaggered over to greet them.

Chandler had the eerie feeling he was the Officer of the Day (OD), and the convoy was about to "pass in review," a daily military exercise he remembered from his days as a young Marine at Quantico. Reflexively, Chandler snapped a salute to the Marine officer.

The officer extended his hand to Chandler and said, "Major Michael Wong, sir. Here under orders."

"Scott Chandler." He nodded over at Wolf. "My colleague Brave Wolf Whitman."

"Glad to meet you. I've been briefed about your military service, Mr. Chandler. A pleasure to meet you, sir."

"Likewise, Major Wong, but please call me Scott."

"Yes, sir. We have orders to set up camp near your headquarters and hold till further notice."

"Have you been given any detail about what's in the Park?"

"All we know is six people were killed in there last week, and that the park's closed. Something about a disturbance with the wildlife, sir, but no detail yet. Whatever's in there, we'll wipe it out when the orders come down."

Chandler looked away from Wong and took notice of the Marines who were sitting in their vehicles. More Marines were streaming out of the three Chinooks. Most of them were young. Maybe late teens, early twenties.

"Any ideas of where to set up camp in the area?" Wong asked. "The chart I have indicates somewhere over there." The Major pointed to the left quadrant of the clearing, mountain peaks soaring beyond.

Chandler nodded. "There's a small dirt road used by ATVs at the end of the clearing. You can maneuver your convoy through there. About a quarter of a mile up-mountain you'll see another clearing where you'll be able to set up camp. Your troops will be on a thirty-degree incline, but that's probably as good as it gets up there."

"Thanks. Any hazards I should know about?"

"Not here," Chandler said.

"Good." Wong walked back to his Jeep and slid into the front seat.

The convoy slowly moved out toward the end of the clearing. Chandler counted fifty-seven vehicles when the last deuce-and-a-half vanished out of sight, their headlights casting an eerie glow as they moved off. He assumed that their gas tanks were filled to the brim.

"God help them," Wolf said.

CHAPTER 20

D<small>R. K</small>IMBERLY F<small>ULTON'S</small> A<small>MERICAN</small> F<small>LIGHT</small> 628 <small>OUT OF</small> JFK <small>WAS SUPPOSED</small> to land in Anchorage, Alaska at 3:46 p.m. Alaskan time, which it did. The connecting flight to Fairbanks, Alaska, America West flight 1428, took off on time. Upon landing, they were supposed to take off forty-nine minutes later to Kotzebue, where hopefully a chartered air taxi would be waiting to take them to Noatak.

But the Kotzebue flight never took off. When Fulton and her son Ken deplaned in Fairbanks, they stood in line at the ticket counter and waited twenty minutes before an agent was available. Fulton said, "Flight 1428 to Kotzebue was cancelled. We'd like to rebook on the next flight, please."

"I'm sorry, ma'am. Both flights into Kotzebue have been cancelled due to jet fuel inventories."

Ken stared at the ticket agent. "Excuse me, ma'am," he said, "but my mom has a very important meeting she has to be at today, not tomorrow."

The ticket agent didn't acknowledge Ken. Instead she mentioned a Holiday Inn where they could spend the night. "I could book you on the 8:42 a.m. flight to Kotzebue tomorrow morning. We've combined three cancelled flights into the one tomorrow, and we'll have enough jet fuel to take off."

"I don't think you understand my mom's predicament," Ken repeated. "She has a crucial presentation to make in Noatak National Park and it's very important she be there today, not tomorrow morning."

The agent finally looked at Ken. "There are no more flights into Kalispell today." she said. "We don't have enough fuel. Unfortunately, you have no choice."

Fulton nodded to the agent.

"Shall I write up the tickets?"

Fulton nodded.

Ken persisted. "There's got to be another way to get there," Ken said. "How about we drive to Noatak? We can make it there in time for your presentation."

Fulton looked at her son and nodded toward the rent-a-car counters. "You see what those signs say?"

The teenager walked toward the empty rental car counters and studied the signs at Hertz, Avis, National, Dollar, and Budget. He shrugged his shoulders in disappointment. All the signs had the same message: NO GAS.

"Book the flight for tomorrow," Fulton told the agent. "We'll take it."

CHAPTER 21

Major Michael Wong finished reading the orders he had just received from the commandant at 1330 hours and flipped them to his field sergeant Jack Roeder. "Study them carefully," Wong said. "I want the company inside this tent at 1400 hours. We've got orders to strike inside Noatak tonight and wipe out whatever's in there."

Roeder regarded Wong with a questioning look. "I thought we were waiting for some woman to I.D. the thing that killed the research team?"

"The orders reference that plan, but her plane was grounded in Fairbanks. No fuel. Robinson refuses to put the strike off and it's got President Barton's blessing. Our job's to wipe out whatever's in there fucking with human life so the country can tap into the oil before the lights go out for good. Understand? Memorize every detail, Roeder. On the ground at Fossil River, it's your mission, your men, your life."

Roeder said, "Yes, sir. Fourteen hundred hours."

As Roeder left the command tent in the Marine Noatak encampment, Wong called after him, "Roeder?"

Roeder spun on his heel and peered back into the tent. "Yes, sir?"

"You'll be in charge of sixty-eight Marine lives. When your men land in there, every second counts. You suggested we hold off the strike until this Fulton woman arrives. Never question an order from me again. No room for hesitation, Marine. Understood?"

The Marine field sergeant snapped a salute. "Yes, sir," he said crisply.

Major Wong stood at the head of a large field table in the command center tent. An overhead light shone on the table, illuminating the object resting on top. On his right was Sergeant Major Roeder. On his left, Scott Chandler leaned over studying the Miniature Unmanned Aerial Vehicle (MUAV) that perched on the table like a menacing praying mantis. Wolf stood quietly next to Chandler, looking thoughtful.

Chandler had relied on the data drones provided him during his helicopter missions in the mountains of Afghanistan. He knew this one well. It had saved his life many times: the Raven RQ 11B. It was launched by hand. Three-and-a-half feet long, it had a range of 11.2 miles per flight.

Someone would have to get dangerously close to the attack zone for a launch.

He also knew the drone's every detail: they'd used 1,200 of them in Iraq Pakistan, and Afghanistan. Each fuselage cost $75,000 to build, packing $250,000 of vital reconnaissance technology inside. To Chandler, it was a life-saving flying photo lab. Now he was about to witness the drone's reconnaissance ability yet again in his own Park.

The thought was unsettling.

The look on Wolf's face confirmed concern about what the Marine company commander was about to discuss: an strike deep into the Noatak National Park's most inaccessible area, the south fork of the Fossil River. Filling the rest of the seats around the twenty-by-ten-foot table were lieutenants, gunnery sergeants, lance corporals, and six squad leaders who would lead their men into battle with Roeder at the charge. Marine soldiers, eleven of them women, filled the rest of the seats surrounding the assembly.

Wong, a man in need of detail and fact to support his strategy, had asked Chandler and Wolf to join the meeting after he read the detailed report on the gruesome fate of the research party. Wong had reviewed every detail of Chandler's military history, and it was essential to have both F&W Agency men present at the meeting to lend support to what was about to happen. They both had valuable hands-on experience of the park. Maybe they could help save lives. More soldiers spilled into the tent to join the meeting.

The U.S. 3rd Marine Corps Special Operations Battalion had trained in the Black Rapids mountain region of Alaska to prepare themselves for the mountains of Afghanistan. This would be helpful as they prepared to engage their unknown enemy in Noatak.

The Marines sat down in the amphitheatre, staring at the screen showing a detailed full-color chart of the south fork of the Fossil River and surrounding mountains. A thick black line delineated the massive fossil fuel oil field. Wong pointed his infrared light at the landing point as he set the parameters for the recon coordinates that each of the six squads were to establish upon landing.

"The moment you land, it'll be pitch dark. Sun sets at 2214 hours. Lift off from here at 2245 hours. Spread out to these GPS coordinates and set the laser borders. Cover each others' backs. Nobody, I repeat, nobody walk. Run your asses off to get those borders in place, laser coordinates equidistant," Wong commanded. "When those bastards break the laser line, and you hear those loud beeps, open fire. You'll each be wearing night vision goggles so you'll see whatever violates your borders.

"Once your sector is secure, move into the next sector and establish the borders the same way as the first until all six squads, sixty-eight Marines, have wiped out every single living creature within this border. Sergeant Roeder will control the operation from this command point at the landing site—which is where you'll all return when you're done with the mission. Any questions?"

"No, sir!" a female Marine shouted and the entire company burst into "Hoo-ahh!"

He looked at his watch. "Listen up, Corps," Wong said. "We're about to engage an enemy that's not human. It's already demonstrated lethal force against six civilians, possibly more. The expert who's supposed to identify our enemy got delayed in Fairbanks. The importance of the mission is critical and our assignment is to wipe out whatever's in there so the United States government can gain access to the largest fossil fuel deposit in the world. Without access to the oil, our nation will soon be without power—so it's imperative that this mission succeeds. What does that mean to us? It means no mobility fuel for our military operations if we fail. So it's critical with a capital C. I've asked Scott Chandler and his colleague Brave Wolf Whitman of the Fish & Wildlife Agency, because they know every square inch of Noatak Park. Chandler's a decorated ex-

Marine with two Purple Hearts and two Bronze Stars and knows the…"

"Hoo-Ahh!" the Marines shouted.

Wong held up his hand for silence. "Chandler's the helicopter pilot who first confronted this thing. He's been trying to convince the military to cancel the mission. He says the predator in the Park's dangerous, beyond anything we've ever fought."

"We'll kill the fuckers," a Marine shouted and the crowd chanted with him.

Chandler stood up and said to Wong, "Mind if I talk?" Wong nodded.

"I've fought in tough battles like most of you. I've tried my best to persuade the military to stand down on this one until we confirm what this predator is. It's like nothing you or I've ever confronted in war. It's fast, smart, and equipped with sharp talons and jaws that can rip through human flesh and bone in one slash. If I sound like I'm trying to scare you, I am. To go into battle without fear of this thing would be a grave mistake. You'll be armed with the military's latest weaponry—but don't let that fool you into thinking you have the edge in battle. You won't."

Wong stood up, motioned Chandler to have a seat and nodded to the Raven on the table. "That's why we're sending in a drone to capture as much of the landscape as possible," he said. "When you land in there, you'll have a fix on the terrain."

Wong picked up the drone from the center of the table with little effort. He looked at his watch. "Approximately thirty minutes ago, two of our Marines took a Raven RQ 11B and drove an ATV to get close enough to the Fossil River for a launch. We'll be controlling the drone's speed, course, and altitude from here, so I want all of you to focus on the visual you're about see on the screen. Memorize it. Your lives may well depend on the images you're about to see."

The silence in the tent confirmed the tension. An ICOM transceiver suddenly barked to life. "Major Wong, Richardson here. You copy?"

"Affirmative, Richardson."

"We got as close as we could before launching, very rough terrain. There're a number of impasses. Some kind of glacial wall, couldn't get beyond it, but we just launched the drone. You should have a visual by now. Confirm, over."

The large screen burst into a colorful pan of Noatak's landscape.

"Roger that, Richardson," Wong said. "Come back to base. Ten-four."

"Roger that. Ten-four, Major."

Wong looked at Chandler and Wolf. "What are we looking at, gentlemen?"

Chandler pointed at the screen. "Passing over Red Eagle Lake now."

Brave Wolf stood up and pointed at the left side of the screen. "Coming up to Inuit Glacier. There's Mount Logan in the distance. You're now looking at the De Long Mountain Range. Great clarity."

The Marines moved closer to the screen and there was not a whisper in the room.

Chandler pointed. "That's Jackson Glacier over there."

"Pumpelly Glacier coming into view," Wolf said.

Wong appeared fidgety, tapping a swagger stick against the table. "How far to the Fossil?"

"Another two or three miles," Chandler said, "There's Walton Mountain within the Brook's Range," and he pointed to a small creek, "and Harrison Creek."

Wolf said, "Affirmative. And there's Thompson Creek. They both run into the Fossil River, so we're getting…"

Wolf stopped in mid-sentence. The image on the screen jumped as if the Raven had hit an air current.

Chandler said, "Air current. Major Wong, have the technicians zoom in on Triple Divide Creek."

A Lance Corporal pressed the zoom control and the detail was crystal clear. They could see the color of stones in the Creek, make out small bushes flanking it.

A Marine said, "Holy shit. The technology's amazing."

"Zoom back," Chandler said. "Mount Stimson's over there. Less than a mile from the Fossil."

A thin mist veiled the images below. Brave Wolf pointed. "Flying over Nyack Creek now. There's Caribou Lake." A thick fog bank covered the screen.

Chandler knew the drone technology could pierce any fog or weather disturbance. He looked at the Lance Corporal and said, "Press the 'WX' squelch knob."

The Corporal searched the compact control panel and found the knob. He pressed it and the fog vanished, illuminating the landscape below with clarity. As the image came into view, the picture screen became fuzzy then shook violently as if the drone had impacted something. Wavy black lines spread across the screen. It cleared briefly then the image, in one trembling instant, vanished.

"What happened?" Wong asked.

"I've never seen that happen," Chandler said. He walked over to Wong, who hovered over the technicians staring at the control panel. Chandler leaned over Wong's shoulder and pressed several buttons, but the screen was still blank, not even an altitude reading. "Something's badly wrong."

"Any ideas?"

"The drone is a sturdy plane, built to withstand all types of weather conditions. The only thing that could take it down would be a missile or a stream of bullets," Chandler said. "It flies like a glider. In these mountain currents at that altitude it should fly without fault."

Wolf read the nametag on one of the technicians and said, "What's your take, Kraus?"

The technician looked back at Wolf with a blank stare. "The manual's troubleshooting section reports nothing like this," he said. "We rebooted the flight program, tried to make signal contact, nothing. The damn drone just vanished out of thin air."

Brave Wolf knew what Chandler was thinking. He said, "The Raven was attacked."

"By what?" Wong asked, his eyes wide. The Marines in the tent sat rigid, leaning forward trying to grasp what was happening.

"By the predator in Noatak," Wolf said.

A Marine in the middle of the Corps said, "Bullshit. These things fly?"

"I told you it has feathers."

CHAPTER 22

Elmendorf Air Force Base is adjacent to Anchorage, the largest city in Alaska. It was named in honor of test pilot Captain Hugh M. Elmendorf and is the home of the Headquarters, Alaskan Command (ALCOM), Alaskan NORAD Region.

Elmendorf's mission is to support and defend U.S. interests in the Asia Pacific region and around the world by providing units ready for worldwide air power projection.

Seven Bell AH-1Z Viper combat helicopters sat on the tarmac, their pilots running toward them in full gear, gripping mission orders in their hands.

The engines came to life, gas tanks brimming with military fuel, and they lifted off the ground simultaneously, heading north by northwest. Destination: Noatak National Park. Orders: land at Marine encampment, deploy with full complement of Marines, and transport them into the attack zone: South Fork of the Fossil River. Mission: Drop soldiers into the area, then hover until Marines wipe out whatever life exists in attack zone; pick them up and fly them back to the encampment. ETA to Noatak: 1800 hours, night strike.

Captain Fenton, the lead chopper pilot, was a Gulf War vet, with two stints in Afghanistan. He'd served two years after Chandler finished his rehab at Montana's Fort Harrison Veterans Hospital. As Fenton led the squadron past the west face of Mt. McKinley, he said, "One hell of a mountain. They say it's taller than Everest because McKinley's base starts

117

at 2,000 feet above sea level. Everest starts at 17,000 feet above sea level. So do the math and McKinley tops Everest by 6,320 feet."

Fenton heard someone behind him say, "No shit?"

The Captain nodded and banked the squadron toward the Chukchi Sea.

Wong had just finished a strategic meeting with his tech sergeants, Chandler and Wolf listening with the corps behind them. Hopefully, the new strategy would confirm what happened to the first Raven drone: send out another ATV team of Marines to launch two more drones at the same time, one flying above the other to capture the drone below it in flight: a financial risk of $825,000 if all three drones disappeared, Wong thought.

But Wolf didn't need to be convinced with visual proof. He already knew what had happened. Eyes closed, face screwed up into a mask of anguish, he'd seen it unfold in a riveting vision he'd experienced moments before the strategic meeting even began.

Marine Lance Corporals Richardson and Clark had already taken off in their ATVs, each with a Raven drone, maintaining radio contact with headquarters. Thirty-nine minutes later Richardson's voice crackled over the command radio, "We just launched both drones, sir. You copy?"

"Copy that, Richardson. You and Clark hold your position and I'll tell you when to come back to base. We might still need you out there."

"Roger that," Clark said.

Two large LCD screens came to life, showing new images. The left screen displayed a vivid landscape below from the first drone as technicians manipulated the second drone 110 feet above it. The right screen displayed the landscape below, with the Raven drone below it flying effortlessly through the mountain air in the center of the screen, not a blip of disturbance apparent.

The large tented area again fell silent as everybody stared at both screens. When both drones glided closer to the Fossil River area, it happened so fast on the right screen that nobody caught it except Brave Wolf. "There," he pointed at the screen. "That's it."

"What's it?" said Wong, his voice agitated.

Chandler said, "Christ, I didn't see a thing."

Herbert Spencer coined the phrase, "survival of the fittest" in 1864 in his book, Principles of Biology, but Charles Darwin referenced it in his Theory of Evolution in 1869 when he talked about the "survival of dominance" among all living creatures. Darwin argued that certain species were capable of living hundreds of millions of years without perishing: they were the master predators who developed survival techniques over their class, order, and collateral species by territorial protection, hunting, and breeding.

What was happening in the sky, 600 feet above the Fossil River, had happened repeatedly in the Cretaceous era of dinosaurs 150 million years ago. Today's events gave proof to Darwin's theory that a living fossil could survive millions of years because it was the master of its territory and its progeny.

The predator's intelligence, cheetah-like speed, prehensile claws to climb trees, soar in the air with the ability to change direction or plunge into a spiral death dive like a raptor, combined with versatile defense mechanisms, had enabled the creature to be so highly developed and refined that nothing in Noatak's food chain could ever hope to compete with it. In the last 400,000 years, the creatures had even developed echolocation, like bats, and could now locate motion and objects in the dark of night or in extreme weather conditions including dense fog. It had become nature's ultimate predator.

A high-pitched sound, beyond human ability to hear, echoed across Noatak as a blur of winged creatures flew low above the mountain forest canopy toward the Fossil River, responding to a call for action. The two Raven drones had invaded their territory and soared evenly, one above the other, in slow concentric circles gliding above the Fossil.

Above the drones, seven predators broke off from their murderous flock and began an orchestrated attack in unison, their eerie calls confirming which one would take out the top encroacher, and which one would extinguish the drone below it. In what seemed like a blink of an eye, both Raven drones were attacked at exactly the same moment with such speed, force, and precision that both exploded into nothingness and drifted out of the sky like confetti over the river.

Both blank screens confirmed that something had gone terribly wrong. Major Wong stared at Chandler and his technicians as if expecting some simple answer that would explain how three of his drones could mysteriously vanish out of the sky without a trace of technical malfunction.

Nobody had answers, and the Marines were whispering questions and concerns to each other.

"It's them," Wolf said without hesitation. "They won't allow us to invade their territory."

Wong picked up the hand mike and pressed transmit. "Richardson. You copy? Major Wong here. Over."

There was no answer on his ICOM transceiver.

"Corporal Clark? Over."

Static filled the speaker.

"Richardson? Clark? You guys copy?"

No response.

"Clark? Richardson? Answer me, Goddamn it," Wong repeated impatiently.

Silence.

Wong looked up. "Sergeant Roeder."

"Yes, sir."

"Get a detail together and track down Clark and Richardson. Get on it fast. Send up a chopper to accompany the ATVs and report back ASAP."

Roeder snapped a salute and exited the tent with a complement of five Marines and a chopper pilot.

Wong shouted after them. "Keep in touch with me, Roeder."

Roeder nodded on the exit.

The five Marines jumped into two ATVs. The engines roared to life, and a Marine Bell Viper rose above them to shepherd their route.

Marine Squad Leader Peter Hall spun his wheels churning out of the clearing. The others followed in hot pursuit of Richardson and Clark, their GPS locked into a probable course for the two ATVs that had launched the drones less than an hour before.

Fifteen minutes passed, then twenty, twenty-five. The Bell Viper tracked their progress and reported back to Wong. Four extreme winding turns later, a deep crevice with a dangerous forty-five degree incline caused one of the ATVs to flip on its side. Quickly righted, the two Marines jumped back in and gave chase to catch up to Hall.

Corporal Hall spotted something ahead of the last sharp turn.

The Bell Viper above him saw it, too, and swept over him, taking the lead.

Something flew into the chopper blades with such force that the whirling fuselage jerked in midair and started spinning out of control. The pilot lurched forward, grabbing the cyclic in a clutching moment of terror. Blood covered the bubble glass. The blood was deep and dark and streaked the glass in clotting streams confirming that the throbbing heart of something monstrous had been pierced by the whirling blades on impact. The pilot strained to see detail.

As the pilot struggled to gain control of the craft, something slammed against his door, piercing the glass hatch with resounding impact.

The pilot turned with a sudden jerk of panic. Before his mind could lock into what had happened, vice-like jaws crashed through the hatch glass and enveloped his head. The pilot's lifeless body fell atop the controls just as the beast detached itself from the chopper and flew back to its flock.

The chopper fell out of the sky and burst into flames in a plume of black, billowing smoke.

Hall and his contingent of four drivers sat bug-eyed in their ATVs as they watched the Bell Viper hit a mountain ridge one hundred yards up-trail from their position.

"Stand fast, Marines. Wait," commanded Hall. "I want your weapons locked and loaded, finger on the trigger, grenades at the ready. This is tough shit, whatever it is."

"What the fuck is it?" Jim Cullen asked grimly.

"Christ if I know," Hall said. He looked at the billowing smoke ahead and shouted, "Follow me."

At full throttle, Hall lurched through the smoke and flame of the crash to the other side, his men following. When they got through the crash site, Hall saw something that defied description.

The two ATVs from the previous drone launch team were sprawled out ahead of them as if they had both been dropped from a forty-story skyscraper. The twisted steel chassis of the closest ATV lay overturned, its engine still steaming hot. Corporal Richardson's legs poked out from beneath the ATV. When a Marine poked his head under the twisted frame for a closer look to see if he was still alive, he found the other half of Richardson's body had vanished. Only blood and sinew marking the spot where it had been.

Corporal Clark's ATV was still upright, but the leather seats had been torn to small shreds, tethers of tan fabric blowing lightly in the mountain breeze.

Hall, his mouth dry and heart thumping in his chest, looked under the ATV for any sign of Clark's body. There was nothing except a blood trail that led away from the vehicle to a dense mountain bush. Hall motioned to Lance Corporal Latanzi and said, "Check it out."

Tony Latanazi gagged. "I don't think so," he said.

"Don't fuck with me, Marine. Get your ass over there and check it out. That's an order."

Latanzi pushed himself toward the thick bush, following the blood trail. When he reached the edge of the bush, he peered around it.

Something exploded at him with a deafening screech.

Latanzi's guts fell out of the deep slice that ran suddenly from his sternum to his crotch. His body fell backward to the ground next to Lance Corporal Clark, who lay in a bloodied heap behind the bush, half of him devoured. Latanzi's eyes rolled up into his skull.

Hall screamed: "Fire!"

A fusillade of Marine automatic weaponry echoed across the mountain valley. The bush vaporized in a biblical flame. In the distance, well beyond the bush, something had taken to flight and vanished out of sight.

Wong's voice sounded over the ICOM microphone. "Did you find them, Hall?"

Hall pressed the transmit button, clutching the hand mike as if his life depended on it. "We found them, sir. Nothing left."

"What do you mean?"

"I mean their bodies are mutilated, and one of our choppers fell out of the sky, pilot killed."

CHAPTER 23

THE SQUADRON OF BELL VIPERS FROM ELMENDORF AIR FORCE BASE WAS fourteen minutes to touchdown at the Fish and Wildlife Agency Park headquarters. Captain Fenton put a call into the Marine encampment to report his ETA: 1752 hours. "We'll be ready to deploy in twenty minutes, sir," he told Major Wong.

"Roger that, Captain Fenton. We'll be ready."

Wong conferred with his two lieutenants, Field Sergeant Roeder, and the six squad leaders, five men and a woman from Arkansas, Becky Lee Brown. They were all suited up for the mission into Noatak.

"Hall, do you have anything more to add before I review the mission orders?"

Hall's eyebrows furrowed into a twisted knot of concern. "Hell, Major, whatever it was took all of us by surprise. Richardson and Clark didn't have time to pull off a single shot. After a burst of fire from us, we still couldn't get a bead on whatever it was. It ripped Corporal Latanzi apart. Then it flew off and vanished as if nothing happened. But the sound it makes is fucking scary, some kind of alien shit. We still don't have a clue what happened to the chopper pilot. His gunship just fell out of the sky and burst into flames. When we land in there tonight, safeties better be off, night vision goggles on, bayonets fixed, and stay close with volumes maxed on the two-ways. We've got to be able to communicate. It's imperative all squads establish laser beam perimeters the moment we land. This is heavy-duty RECON shit, and if we let them pierce our space, we're all fucked probably within a matter of minutes."

Becky-Lee Brown tugged on a single blonde pigtail poking out of the back of her Marine cap. She leaned forward and said, "I'll take the alpha male."

Brown's comment caused a burst of levity until Hall spoke. "I don't know how these predators fuck, but if they fuck like they fight, you don't want to be on the bottom."

"I'm always on top, gentlemen," Brown said. "As I said, I'll take the alpha male." She held up her pinky and wagged it.

Wong, ignoring her comment, looked down at this watch. "Listen up, Marines. We've got one mission: wipe out whatever moves and secure the area so we can get to the oil. We don't want you shooting each other. We're using cutting edge weaponry in there—tracers, mortars, flamethrowers, grenades. You'll see each other on your vest pocket heat-seeking locators, all with a red X. Each of you is wearing a transponder. Any X you see in bright yellow is the body heat of the enemy. Shoot to kill."

As Wong finished reviewing the orders and mission details, the sound of approaching choppers filled the tent. Field Sergeant Roeder shouted, "Atten-hut! Listen up, Marines. Your squadron's here. You all know the mission. I'll be commanding the ground strike. The moment we land, stick with the drill. Stay with your squad at all times and obey orders. We're all going in there on tethers. Choppers can't land in the area so hang tight. The moment your feet touch the ground, safety off, all ammunition at the ready. Any questions?"

The Marine attack force burst out of the tent, shouting as they ran toward the squadron of choppers lined up in the clearing, engines on and ready for liftoff.

As the last Marine entered his Viper, the choppers lifted off the ground in unison and flew south by southeast away from the setting sun. In eight minutes it would be dusk. In another twenty, pitch black.

Chandler and Wolf stood on either side of Major Wong, who turned to Chandler. "I don't have a good feeling about this mission."

Chandler and Wolf stared at the setting sun, a gild-edged crimson, and did not respond.

CHAPTER 24

THE U.S. MARINE CORPS, FOUNDED NOVEMBER 10, 1775, HAS FOUGHT more battles on the ground than all U.S. armed forces combined.

Among the most famous: the battle of Chapultepec where the Marines stormed the Mexico City castle in 1847 and two days later captured it in a fierce battle that would inspire the first line, "From the halls of Montezuma," of the Marines famed hymn.

Almost 175 years later, it was not the excitement of winning wars on the ground that encouraged Sergeant Major Jack Roeder to enlist in the Marines. It was the slogans, "The Few, The Proud, The Marines," and "Semper Fidelis," always faithful.

Roeder liked that saying, and he also liked being a leader of the "Few." It gave him a feeling of superiority, of power, and of being endowed with a special Midas touch. He sat in the command gunship heading into the depths of Noatak National Park for a battle that already seemed like something from a lost world. Not knowing the enemy complicated the mission, thought Roeder, and he wondered if he would still have that Midas touch the moment his feet hit the ground.

In the few minutes remaining before the chopper squadron reached the mission area, Roeder took inventory of the soldiers who sat with him ready for battle. All of them were young, maybe eighteen to twenty-five, not one in their thirties. These were all hardcore Marines who'd trained in the rugged Black Mountain range of Alaska to prepare for battle in

Iraq and Afghanistan. Some of them had deep scars, Purple Hearts, one a Bronze Star.

Roeder had checked their equipment, all eighty-three pounds of it: M16; eleven of them also carrying the M249 SAW machine gun; Monocular Night Vision Device (MNVDs), a single-eyed night-vision scope; the M203 grenade launcher and grenades tied onto their field jackets like a string of jalapenos; the M9 Beretta; and the bayonet affixed to the M16 for hand-to-hand combat. Shoulder rocket launchers and flamethrowers completed the arsenal held by each of eleven special force Marines.

Roeder felt confident they would be victorious, just as they had been overseas. He took in a deep, labored breath, and as the bright yellow light flashed their arrival at the destination, he prepared himself for battle. The lead chopper hovered in place, signaling they were over the Fossil River coordinates.

But the pilot in the lead chopper had his eyes fixed on the radar screen. He didn't like what he saw: incoming blips of magenta light homing in on his location. He pressed the microphone transmit button and said, "Charlie-foxtrot-one-five-two, this is Bravo-niner-five-six. Over."

"Go ahead, Charlie-foxtrot."

"Something's out there. Sonar shows magenta blips all over our airspace."

"Roger that, Charlie. Show the same here. What is it?"

"Have no idea."

All the pilots came on the air and confirmed something strange had flown into their airspace and encircled their choppers.

Unaware of the transmission in the cockpit, Roeder shouted, "Heads up, Marines. You know the drill. I'll be first to land. Stay close, radios on." He vanished out of the port hatch and slid down the tether into the dense fog. Roeder heard the distant sound of the Fossil River, somewhat comforting before battle, but he was aware of a damp stillness that filled his senses with dread.

He looked through his night vision goggles and could see detail in the distance: trees, huge boulders, and thick mountain brush. Plenty of cover for a predator. A moment later, the next Marine slid down the tether and landed beside him, then another, and another. They kept coming, filling the ground around Roeder, restoring the power and excitement he always felt before going into a fight.

It took sixteen minutes for the eight choppers to empty their cargo of soldiers onto the ground, and another twenty for the Marines to spread out and set up their RECON laser beam perimeters.

Roeder said, "Squad One?"

"In place sergeant. Ready."

"Squad Two."

"Roger. Ready."

"Squad Three?"

No answer.

"Squad Three!" Roeder commanded.

"Affirmative, ready."

"Squad Four?"

"Ready."

"Squad Five?"

"Affirmative. No sign yet. Ready."

"Squad Six?"

"Roger. Ready."

"Okay. Don't fire until you see movement out there. We wait for the enemy to engage. Understand?"

Someone said, "Fucking spooky place."

"Roger that," one of the squad leaders said. "Fog sucks."

"Piece o' cake," squad leader Becky-Lee Brown said with confidence. "Ready to engage."

"Easy there, Brown. Hold off. They engage first. Remember that."

"Affirmative," she said, her voice thick with a southern drawl.

Each squad sat in a large circle facing outward, backs to the inner circle, weapons pointed, as planned, toward the infrared laser perimeter surrounding them. It was a beam, visible only through night vision goggles. Marines at the corners of their perimeter, had turned on the device and waited. Anything intersecting the beam would trigger a loud beeping sound to alert the forces their perimeter had been breached.

In the distance, a loud beep sounded. Roeder heard it and said, "Hold your fire till you have a visual."

"Something's out there."

"What do you see?" Roeder pressed.

"I don't know. Three magenta blips on my screen moving in fast. Something streaked across the perimeter. Wait."

"What?"

"Two of them."

"Where?"

A Marine in Squad Four heard a rush of movement above him and what sounded like wings flapping. "Christ!" he said over the air.

"What?"

"Something just flew over us. Something big. Fucking big."

Roeder said, "Next time, take it out."

"Too fast to get a bead on it."

A loud bleep sounded in Squad Six's quadrant, the infrared beam broken, ten o'clock high. "Holy shit!"

Roeder barked an order, "Take it out! Take it out!"

A burst of tracers ripped through the forest, followed by silence. A grenade exploded and the sound burst through the mountains.

"What the fuck was it?"

"I don't know."

Someone said, "Probably the fucking devil."

"Jesus," another voice croaked.

"Cut the shit," a squad leader commanded. "We're on a mission, not a Girl Scout overnight. Stay focused."

A bleep ripped the silence in Squad Two, then another in Squad Five, four in Squad Six. Shrill bleeps were heard in all sectors, cutting the damp fog like a knife with serrated edges.

Then, on the outer perimeter of the fossil fuel field, a loud piercing screech filled the air. It was followed by three others from different quadrants.

The entire oil field burst into a cacophonous sound of deafening screeches. Roeder bolted from his knees to his feet and shouted into his hand mike, "We're surrounded. Attack!"

Six squads of Marines began firing in unison, holding their tight circle, defending the perimeter. Tracers lit up the thick fog in an eerie mist-laden glow as if ghosts from the past were omniscient observers of something sinister about to happen. Someone from Squad Five fanned a flamethrower along the outer perimeter trying to scorch a flash of some-thing that ran in front of him, but it was so fast the flame was fifteen feet behind the target.

Two more grenades exploded in Squads Two and Four, and Hall in Squad Six unleashed his M249 SAW machine gun with a blast of one hundred bullets in less than thirty seconds.

Roeder had calculated with Major Wong that he could cover every square inch of land in the fossil fuel field using RECON maneuvers. He estimated it would take no more than thirty minutes to extinguish every living organism within the oil field. But the moment Roeder sprang to his feet he knew something was terribly wrong.

Major Wong sat motionless in his command center at the commu-nications table. It was as if he were in a pew about to take communion—hoping prayers could solve the problems that seemed to be on the threshold of spinning out of control.

He was nursing his fourth cold cup of coffee, tweaking the knobs on his ICOM, and holding the hand mike. The sound of an explosive battle filled the two speakers that flanked his transceiver. Chandler sat at his side, barking comments to Wong about his Park and how the Marines could still get out alive, but his comments fell on deaf ears. Wong's face was screwed up into a mask of hopeless despair.

"Report, Roeder," Wong said.

Roeder was on the run when he heard Wong's voice. "Roger."

"What's happening?" Wong barked into the mike. "Status?" Wong could hear Roeder's breathing.

"We've engaged the enemy, sir. Will report later. Over and out."

"Roger that, Roeder. Ten-four."

As Wong clicked off the transmission, the speakers on his command table filled with a rage of battle sounds so haunting and loud that Wong tasted bile in his throat. The lieutenant sitting beside him said, "I think we're going to need reinforcements, sir."

"I think we're going to need more than that," Chandler said. "Get them the hell out of there! Now, Major."

Chandler looked into Wong's eyes and realized the Marine Company Commander did not hear what he said. Chandler reached out

129

and grabbed the Major's arm. "Major," Chandler shouted. "Get them out of there! Now!"

"It's too late," Wong said.

Captain Fenton looked down from the lead Bell Viper and couldn't believe what he thought he saw. His screen showed warm bodies on the ground, red moving blips he knew were Marines in motion, their transponders sending up the signals. But his eyes focused on something else, and he almost dropped the microphone from his right hand. He toggled the mike. "Foxtrot-Romeo-seven-niner, Bravo-niner-five-six. Can you see what I'm seeing? They're surrounded by something."

"All I see is magenta dots surrounding them."

"Yeah—and whatever it is looks like our Marines are outnumbered six to one," another pilot said.

"Hold your positions, Marines," Fenton said. "We stay put until we get the order from Field Sergeant Roeder to pick them up."

Roeder's voice filled Fenton's cockpit. "We need support, Captain. We're surrounded. You see us?"

"Roger that, Sergeant."

"We need firepower on our perimeter so we can move out and kill these bastards. They have us pinned down. Copy?"

"Affirmative, Sergeant. Hold your position. We're on target. X minus sixty seconds. Copy that?"

"Affirmative Captain. We're locked down. Fire at will."

Five Bell Viper gun ships broke away from the hovering formation and unleashed a scorching burst of rocket fire into the area surrounding the Marine platoon. Fires broke out, shrapnel rained down, and rock fragments hurled through the air like missiles unguided.

Corporal Becky-Lee Brown had done three stints in the Afghan war and had taken two mountaintops filled with insurgent forces. The Purple Heart she received for the shrapnel wound she suffered to her left clavicle, steel fragments still embedded in her shoulder, was pinned over the wound on her uniform. The Bronze medal she got for bravery was affixed to the other shoulder as a badge of honor.

It was, as she had told her mom, "A pain in the ass to take the medals on and off my uniform, but it's my constant reminder to never let down my guard."

After the burst of firepower from the Vipers, Roeder shouted into his hand mike, "Spread out and secure the area."

Brown sprang into a run. The Marine platoon swarmed over the riddled ground in urgent attack mode. Through her night goggles, Brown felt she was in some strange land engaged in a battle on a distant planet in an environment like no other she had ever seen.

She could see all seven men in her squad sprinting through the dense underbrush on either side of her, all firing at will. Brown saw images of things streaming in and out of view so fast that nobody could get an accurate shot off.

Then she saw something swoop down from above and land atop one of her men, Corporal O'Neal. It grabbed O'Neal in flight—and with a flurry of flapping wings swept him off into the night, screaming a guttural cry of terror.

Brown took aim and ripped off fifteen shots in rapid succession, hoping not to hit O'Neal, but she had no choice. She knew she hit the predator because it faltered in flight and dropped him, but she saw the enemy still trying to gain altitude.

She ran toward O'Neal and found him lying face down on a rock slab, still quivering. She turned him over. He sucked in a terrorized breath of air and spat blood. His voice rattled a labored effort and Brown screamed, "Medic!"

The rest of Brown's Squad Four was engaged in a raging battle for survival.

"Medic!" Brown screamed again and, as she turned to scan the area looking for a medic, something bolted at her. In one motion she pulled out her Berretta and fired at the predator. Brown knew she was in trouble after the fourth shot because the predator held its ground and was still coming at her, twenty-five yards out.

She fired again. Only this time the predator threw its head back and gave an anguished screech for help.

Three other creatures surrounded her, two from the air, another from the woods. Brown pointed her Beretta at the larger predator and as she pulled the trigger, felt excruciating pain spread across her back. She folded to the ground like a deck of cards, bayonet now clutched in her right hand. The beast was atop her, making a deafening, high-pitched screeching sound. She thrust the bayonet upward trying to find a lethal spot. She felt flesh, but was shocked to feel feathers all around her, smothering her. With a final surge of adrenaline, she twisted herself atop the attacking predator and began stabbing it in the chest. But the other beasts jumped atop her, too and she felt the life draining out of her from cuts so deep and so painful that she knew she only had one option.

Brown thrust her left hand to the tether of grenades on her chest and clutched for as many pins as she could find. In a single moment of triumph, she let loose a scream that filled the air around her.

"Fuck you, you bastards! Eat this!"

She closed her eyes, pulling down on the pins of four grenades. Seconds later, the grenades went off, mercifully ending her life and killing six of the creatures mauling her.

The detonation was so loud and the reddish-yellow burst of flame so bright that when Roeder heard and felt shrapnel raining down on his position, he knew something horrific had happened. He shouted into his hand mike, "Squads One, Two and Three, finish your sweep and converge to your right. Report."

Roeder heard back from all but two of his squad leaders. "Hall and Brown, report back," he said.

Hall's voice sounded hollow. "They have us trapped, sergeant. Need help. Two men down. They're closing in."

A moment later, Hall screamed as if somebody had driven a hot spike into his eye.

Roeder clicked off, knowing the chance of finding Hall alive was remote. But sadly, it confirmed something else: Roeder knew it was Squad leader Brown who was responsible for the massive explosion. He guessed she had sacrificed herself to save the others in her squad. She was, thought Roeder, one of the few, the proud—and one of the best fighting Marines he had ever seen in the Corps.

Gunfire surrounded Roeder. It was a firefight worse than anything he had experienced in Iraq or the mountains of Afghanistan.

"I see your position, Hall. We're coming," he said, trying to convince himself and his Marines that Hall was still alive.

Roeder's squad stayed in tight formation, a half circle closing in on Hall's position. They were two hundred yards away, and it was comforting to Roeder to be able to see his soldiers charging through the dense tree-pack, the night vision goggles lighting up their way as if the sun was about to rise at first light.

"All squads converge on Hall's position," Roeder said. "You have his coordinates. On the double."

Roeder didn't know how many men he'd lost. But he knew from the brief squad reports that there were men down, many still alive, others perished in bloody encounters beyond description. "Hall, Roeder here. Over."

No answer.

"You there, Hall?"

Still no answer.

"Any Marine from Squad Six, answer."

Roeder heard a whispered response. He said, "Say again. Over."

"Milliken here. They have us pinned down, Sergeant."

"We're coming in. Explain your position."

"Up against a rock escarpment, a 300-foot drop behind us. They got Hall and two others. There are only five of us left."

A burst of tracer fire ripped through the woods, ricocheting off boulders in streaks of brilliant white light. Roeder said, "Milliken, give us the enemy's position."

"They're fucking everywhere, Sergeant," Milliken whispered. "They're flying over us right now. There must be a dozen or two out in front of us on the ground. No place to go."

"Milliken, listen to me," Roeder said. "Keep your men down. We're coming toward you now. We're going to trap them in a crossfire." To his men: "Heads up Marines. I want every damn weapon strapped to your body in action when I give the word."

Roeder looked up into the sky. There were no breaks in the thick fog, but he could hear the choppers hovering somewhere above him. On the designated frequency of 440 megahertz, every Marine could hear his voice, including all of the Viper pilots. He said, "Captain Fenton, Sergeant Major Roeder here, over."

"Roger, Sergeant Roeder, Captain Fenton on frequency. Your men okay?"

"Negative, sir. Here's the plan. Five of our men are trapped. You have our position on the ground?"

"We see five men on what looks like a cliff. A drop behind them," Fenton said.

"That's them. See us about 200 yards out from their position?"

Fenton said, "Roger that. It's 176 yards to be exact. Need a count?"

"Roger that."

Fenton pushed a button on the heat-seeking GPS monitor and a number blinked on the Bell Viper screen: "I count thirty-seven alive, all in. You want another round of firepower? Over."

"Negative, Captain. Too tight."

It was the first time Roeder had a grasp of his headcount loss. He said, "Christ. We're down thirty-one."

"You want up?" Fenton said. "Just give us the word."

"Not yet," Roeder said. "Give us ten and then get us the hell out of here. Here's the drill. We're going to trap these pricks in a crossfire and wipe them off the face of the earth. When done, go to coordinate seven-niner-six-eleven."

"Got it."

"What about the ones in the air? They're all over the place," Milliken whispered.

Roeder said, "Captain Fenton?"

"Go ahead."

"Keep your choppers away from these coordinates for about ten minutes. We're going to fill the ground and sky with every weapon we have. Copy that? We don't want to hit you guys."

"Roger that, Sergeant. Semper Fi. Ten minutes, over and out."

Fenton's sign-off filled Roeder with renewed strength, power, pride, and the will to win.

"Kill every last one of these fuckers." Roeder finished the pronouncement with, "Attack!"

As Fenton lead the eight Vipers away from the attack zone, the fog bank below him lit up in pinks, reds, and brilliant sparkling patterns as if it were the Fourth of July.

Roeder led the attack with an M249 SAW machine gun that lit a small fire in the thick mountain brush in front of them. Three flamethrowers scorched the earth, two flanking the attack and one in the center. With night vision, the attacking Marines could see flashes of movement in front of them, now tripping over wounded and dead predators. They seemed to be winning the war as Roeder pressed his men toward the escarpment.

Two Marines launched shoulder rockets that tore through the thick tree-pack and exploded into something with an ear splitting shockwave that echoed through the mountain valley below and shimmered the surface water in shallow pools of the Fossil River—as if a crack of thunder had bellowed out of the sky in protest.

They were almost at the median of the crossfire. Roeder knew it moments before he crossed the imaginary line of battle where their crossfire was to trap the enemy in the middle, and their foe would all be extinguished. Now, Roeder and his men had reached the center divide, fifty yards out from the escarpment. He shouted into his hand mike, "Hold your fire. Hold your fire."

A silence spread over the area as if an armistice had been declared. Roeder and his men could hear the Fossil River in the distance. He heard some of his men groaning in pain. "Milliken?" he called out.

Silence.

"Milliken. You there?"

"Over here," a voice said. "Here," Roeder and his men watched through their night goggles as Milliken stood up from the rocky escarpment.

The whooshing from a massive wingspan came to their ears a moment before Milliken was lifted off the ground and carried back over the cliff in a stunning display of speed and dexterity. The Marine's heartbeat had stopped only ten feet off the ground, his back splayed open from the base of his neck to the eleventh vertebrae of his spine.

Roeder shouted into his hand mike, "Captain Fenton. Roeder here. Request pickup ASAP. Under attack."

"On our way to your coordinates, sergeant."

"Move out to the coordinates. Fire at will," Roeder said as he heard the sound of the Vipers above him. Thirty Marines still alive, he thought. Got to get them all out of here before it's too late.

As they moved toward the escarpment, now thirty yards away, a screeching sound came from above and all around them. Whatever enemy this was, Roeder knew they'd been intelligent enough to set up a trap. There was no escape except the Vipers hovering above them.

The Marines hurled grenades in every direction as they tried desperately to set up a circle of protection. They emptied their ammunition into the night in a resounding paean for survival. Flamethrowers spewed liquid fire in all directions and M16s filled the air with tracers. The predators were communicating with each other from the air and ground, with a range of high- and low-pitched screeches. A Marine turned to shoot to his left, but was picked off by a diversionary ground attack from a predator that seemed to appear out of thin air. Another Marine thought he was shooting at a flash of movement in front of him, but was suddenly attacked from behind, plucked off the ground and swept away, screaming a cry of terror that haunted the Marines below.

Tethers and lift harnesses fell from the choppers above like strings of spaghetti, and Marines desperately lunged for their lives, grabbing hold and slowly being lifted to the Bell Vipers.

But as each of them vanished out of sight into the thick fog, they were being plucked off the tethers like grapes from a vine.

The Marine tech support in the chopper, manning the tethers, felt powerful tugs on each and then nothing, no weight, no movement—just an empty line by the time it reached the chopper.

Roeder waited until he judged that all thirty of his men had lifted off the ground. He held his M249 SAW machine gun at the ready, stepping into the harness and tugging on the tether for the lift. As his feet left the ground, he felt a strong sense of accomplishment. The feeling left him the moment he entered the thick damp fog surrounding him. He heard something like wings approaching him. Roeder pointed his machine gun in the direction of the sound and pulled off a hundred rounds. He was fifty-five feet off the ground, moving closer to the chopper, but the world around him was moving in slow motion.

Fifty feet from the Viper, forty, thirty, still surrounded by fog. Then he heard another set of wings, but this time it was closer. Too close. Roeder shouted into the fog, "Come on, you fucker! Come and get me, you bastard!"

It emerged from the dense fog like an apparition, and for the first time Roeder got a sharp glimpse of his attacker through his night vision goggles. His mind simply went blank. Nothing he had ever seen before came close to it. Roeder guessed the wingspan was over twelve feet, maybe fifteen. It veered sharply toward Roeder and he tried to pull off another round of fire, but it struck him on the right lower side, below his waist. The M249 SAW machine gun fell out of his arm from the impact, and he realized with horror he had no right leg, cut off just below the knee, and he was losing blood fast,.

As Roeder's head bobbed above the fog bank and the Marine Gunnery Sergeant from the chopper saw him below, he shouted, "Come on, Marine. We've got you."

The tether line slowly reeled onto the large spool. Then there was a loud snapping sound just as the Sergeant said, "Almost there."

Roeder was fighting unconsciousness as the blood drained out of the nub of his right leg.

When he reached the top of the fog bank, the Marine above got the eerie feeling Roeder was walking atop clouds as if he were in heaven. Now ten yards below the landing rungs of the craft, he could see Roeder had no right leg. "You're a Marine, Goddamn it. You're going to make it," he shouted at him.

The words drifted in and out of Roeder's mind as he fought to stay conscious. As the Sergeant reached out to grab Roeder's hand and hoist him through the chopper hatch, something streaked below the Bell Viper with such speed and power that the tether snapped back at the chopper door like a rubber band, the impact cracking the side window of the chopper. The sergeant leaned out of the chopper hatch trying to comprehend where Roeder had gone. He knew the tether would hold up to 700 pounds without breaking, so nothing made sense to the Marine except one thing: what had just happened didn't happen.

Major Wong received the call from the lead pilot of the eight-chopper squadron. "We lost all of them, Major," Captain Fenton said.

Chandler looked at Wong and said, "Fuck."

Wong could not find words to respond. Instead, he sat at his command desk beneath the large tent with two lieutenants, his E7 gunnery sergeant, and two E6 staff sergeants, his face ashen and his mind utterly empty of thought.

"If you strike inside the Park again, Major, the Marines will kill every living creature in the Fossil River plateau—if they haven't already. And," Chandler said, "the oil field will go up in flames. Imperative we convince Secretary Robinson we can still have access to the oil, and save the environment."

"How the Christ can we do that after what just happened?" Wong said in desperation.

"I'm hoping Dr. Fulton will have that answer, sir," Chandler said.

Somehow, Wong managed to pick up his field phone and place a call to Lt. General David Ottaway. He said, "Sir, Major Wong here, Operation Torch. We've suffered a catastrophe, sir. Lost all of our men in Noatak Park, sir."

Ottaway said, "Jesus. How?"

"I don't know, sir."

"What do you mean you don't know?"

"Sir, I lost all contact with my gunnery sergeant."

Ottaway said, "I'm conferencing in Secretary of Defense Robinson. Hold on."

"Yes, sir," Wong said, his heart pounding in his chest, sweat forming on his brow. He coughed twice.

Chandler looked at Wong with a hopeful nod, and gave a supportive thumbs up. "Hang tough, Marine," Chandler said.

Wolf nodded reluctantly, his face awash in angst.

Ottaway patched in Robinson. "I've informed the Secretary. He's on the line," he said.

Robinson said, "What the hell happened?"

"We lost all sixty-eight men, sir. Whatever's in Noatak wiped out all our Marines. I lost all communications with them."

"Goddamn it," Robinson said. "Get that Fulton woman in there to I.D. the bastards. What the hell is this enemy? We've got to get to the oil by the end of next week or this country's on its knees. It's war. I'll get President Barton to approve sending in a battalion force before the week's out."

Major Wong summoned all of his courage and said, "Sir—you'll destroy Noatak National Park if you do."

Ottaway said, "The Major's right, sir."

Robinson said, "To hell with Noatak, gentlemen. This country runs on oil, and we can't afford to lose sight of the mission here. Operation Torch must succeed."

Major Wong held the phone in his hand. He suddenly realized his entire body was trembling.

PART III

CHAPTER 25

AIR ALASKA FLIGHT 1410 FROM FAIRBANKS TO KOTZEBUE DEPARTED ON time, its fuel tank only three-quarters full of Grade A jet fuel. It was more than enough for a roundtrip to Kotzebue, unless something happened to divert it on the way back to Fairbanks. For the first hour, there was little disturbance, and Ken sat silent in a window seat tapping the keys of his laptop and checking his email. He sat motionless reading the one from Meghan Lastinger.

"I miss you, Ken. Working on flights to Kotzebue and Noatak. This place is in the boondocks. Have to connect through Seattle to get to Fairbanks. Will let you know the moment I book tickets. Mom told me I can't stay home alone so I called Juliana and set it up with her. She'll do it! She's all concerned about my safety. Afraid I'm going to get mugged or stranded somewhere. Anyway, Mom thinks I'm staying with the McGuires and she'll cover for me. Can't wait! See you tomorrow. Loving you, Meghan.'

Ken's mind was in overdrive. How the hell am I going to break the news to mom? She'll go ballistic. But he missed his girlfriend and the thought of being with her in this mountainous wilderness piqued his excitement. He glanced over at his mother. She seemed to be deep in thought. Maybe now's not the right time to tell her.

Fulton was studying the file she had brought with her. While she intimately knew the profile of what she was flying out to Noatak

141

to hopefully identify, she couldn't help but review it yet again.

A living fossil surviving over 100 million years and living inside Alaska's remote wilderness in the most coveted national park is utterly unthinkable, she kept telling herself. Only 500 living fossils in the world had been found. This could be the rarest discovery of them all. She scanned the pages she had printed out in the research lab at the Museum of Natural History only forty-eight hours before.

Fulton looked up, a blank stare in her face. One troubling thought kept coming back to her: that the military hadn't already gone into the Park to extinguish the living fossil colony because she was locked down in Fairbanks with no flight. She looked down at the file and finished the report, unaware that her son was staring at her.

Ken leaned over and said, "Mom?"

Fulton was startled by her son's voice and the file on her lap fell onto the floor at her feet, papers scattering out into the aisle.

"Mom, what's wrong?"

"Nothing," she said. "You spooked me."

"You okay?"

"Yes. I guess I'm just excited about the trip. This could be a major discovery, and I was …"

Ken interrupted her, "I want to be with you when you go into the Park. I'm worried about you." He hesitated. "I love you, mom. I'm very proud of you. I don't want anything to happen to you."

Fulton smiled, reached across the empty seat between them and put her hand on his left cheek. "And I love you, too, son. I feel the same way. If anything happened to you, I'd never recover."

"Then I can come with you into Noatak Park?"

Her smile vanished. "Not this time, darling. Maybe in the future. But not now."

"Why?"

"We've covered this already, Ken, and the answer's No. N-O. Please."

This would definitely not be a good time to tell her about Meghan Lastinger.

As the plane flew over jagged land below, Mountains seemed to sprawl everywhere with increased elevation. Ken stared out the window mesmerized.

"Mom, look! Awesome. It's a live volcano." Smoke was billowing out of the cone rising up into the cloudless cerulean blue Alaskan sky.

"A land from the past," Fulton said. "There're over thirty active volcanoes in Alaska."

Ken's eyes were wide with excitement. It was the first volcano he had ever seen.

Fulton turned away from the window. She closed her eyes in thought. Seeing the volcano took her back in time to vast green landscapes, towering trees, and huge lumbering dinosaurs amidst active volcanoes. Was it all as it had been back in the Jurassic and Cretaceous era? If Deinonychus had survived well over 100 million years, had things really changed that much over time? The thought swirled around in her mind and was unsettling to her. How much more did we not know about this vast earth of ours, she pondered.

A noticeable chop brought her out of her reverie as the craft took a sudden dip in a downdraft. The fasten seat belt sign flashed on and the pilot announced they were preparing to land in Kotzebue.

They made the transfer to a private air-taxi charter, Green Wilderness. As Ken and his mother approached the small six-passenger plane, Ken said, "The whole plane's green, Mom."

"Sign of the times, son. It's in to be green today. All about the environment."

The pilot greeted them. She was a husky Aleutian woman in her early thirties.

"Welcome to Kotzebue," she said.

"Thank you," Fulton smiled generously. "What's the flower painted on the plane?"

"It's Alaska's state flower. The Alpine Forget-Me-Not," the pilot said hoisting the luggage into the small compartment.

She closed the doors, revved up the engine and taxied down the small runway. They lifted off the tarmac and climbed to 4,000 feet. "It's a short flight, but lots to see."

Ken peered out his window. "Wow! Mom," he said. "What a view of the mountains. They're huge."

Fulton leaned over to take it all in.

The pilot was talking in a loud voice over the engine rumble, pointing to various sites below. Ken heard only part of what she was saying, his mind on overload. Wait until Meghan sees this, he thought.

The pilot dropped down to 2,000 feet and pointed out the small windshield to the right. Below, two grizzlies were in the middle of a large stream fishing for salmon. "What are they?" Ken said.

"Grizzly bears," Fulton said.

The pilot grinned, "Largest carnivore in North America." Then she announced, "Noatak National Park coming up. There it is," she said.

"Awesome. Is that where the thing lives?"

"Supposedly."

"Think you'll see one?"

"Hope so."

"What would it do if it saw you?"

"I'm not sure, but I'd be ecstatic. Take pictures. It would blow my mind."

"How big is it?"

"From all the fossil remains we've found in the west, our guess is about six- to eight-feet tall and nine- to eleven-feet long. About three times the size of a lion—and much bigger jaws."

"That's pretty big." Ken shook his head.

"Yes."

"Is it dangerous? I mean if you were close to one, would it attack you?"

"Yes. To both questions."

"I want to be with you when you go into the Park," he said protectively.

"You can't do that, Ken. We've already covered that. This is a very dangerous predator."

"So?"

"So you can't go there. Please drop it."

"When I Googled it, they said it might be related to birds. Does it fly?"

"I don't know. But if it's in there, I'll find out. If it does fly, that'll clinch the hypothesis that dinosaurs are related to birds."

"What does she look like?" Brave Wolf asked, standing at the edge of the small airport tarmac at Noatak's airport. The brilliant Alaskan sun beat down on Chandler and Wolf and the warmth on their backs felt good.

"I haven't seen her in seventeen years. A lot can happen in that time."

"Give it a shot. I'm curious what you remember about her."

"Cute face."

"That it?"

"Nice figure. I don't know. Quit drilling me. It was a long time ago."

"And?"

"Auburn hair. Christ, Wolf. We lost sixty-eight Marines last night and you ask me about what she looks like. Come on. Give me a break."

"Sorry," Wolf said. "Guess we'll know soon enough."

"She knows more about paleontology and dinosaurs than anybody else. That's what's important."

"Hopefully that'll discourage the military from going back into the Fossil," Wolf said.

Chandler looked at the approaching plane and said, "It's them. Don't you just love a green airplane? Only in Alaska."

"Nervous?" Wolf said.

"What kind of question is that? Of course I'm not nervous," he lied.

The small plane pulled up in front of them and the single prop feathered to a stop. The door opened. The small steps unfolded and tapped the ground.

The first passenger stepped down onto the tarmac, a man in his fifties, followed by a young girl, maybe seven, thought Chandler. Another young woman came out of the small charter plane, and then a boy appeared in the open door. He hesitated, looked up toward the mountain peaks to the west of the airport and Wolf heard him say, "Awesome."

"That's got to be her son," Wolf said.

Chandler let out a small chuckle. "He looks confident."

The boy hopped down the steps, two at a time, and Chandler called out to him, "Ken?"

The boy looked over at the small group of people assembled behind a yellow chain and singled out Chandler.

He waved at him, then turned back toward the plane. A woman was coming down the stairs wearing baggie pants with several stuffed pockets. She also wore light brown boots, a thick field jacket with sleeve and chest pockets, several equipment cases thrown over both shoulders. A shock of auburn hair pony tailed out of the back decorated with a fossil insignia—some kind of talon.

She stepped onto the tarmac. "It would have been nice if you helped your mom with all my stuff," Fulton said to her son.

The boy turned around. "You didn't ask."

"What kind of answer is that?" the woman said. "You could have offered," and she slung one of the heavy shoulder bags toward him.

He grabbed it and hoisted it over his left shoulder. "Okay, mom. You made your point."

Wolf nudged Chandler. "There she is. Not bad."

"I see her," Chandler said.

"Nervous, now?" Wolf grinned.

"Drop it," Chandler said.

The boy reached them first. He didn't wait for an introduction. He poked his hand at Chandler and said, "My mom told me about you."

"Some good stuff, I hope," Chandler said cheerfully.

"Yeah. But it's family talk," he teased. "Ken. Ken Fulton."

"Hi. Scott Chandler. This is my friend Brave Wolf."

"I know. You're the guy my mom told me about. Cool. I'm Ken."

The woman in the field jacket walked briskly up behind her son. She threw her arms around Chandler. "Seventeen years, my friend. Great to see you."

Chandler held her in his arms. She really hadn't changed too much, he thought. He felt awkward at first, but then pulled back from the embrace and looked into her green eyes.

"God, Kimberly!" he said. "You really look fabulous. I'm so glad you're here."

"Thanks! You, too. You met Ken?"

"Yes. This is…"

Ken interrupted him. "Brave Wolf."

She extended her hand. "Hi. Nice meeting you."

Fulton looked at Chandler. "You know where the Rising Sun Motel is?" she asked.

"Yes," said Chandler, "But you're not staying there."

"What do you mean?" Fulton asked.

"Change in plans. I've cancelled your reservation. You and Ken are staying in my home. It's inside Noatak. Not far from here. I'll be bunking with Brave Wolf. He lives just north of here. Not far," said Chandler.

"That's really nice of you, Scott. Appreciate it, but you don't have to do that," she said.

"Already done." Chandler grinned.

On the way to the Jeep, Fulton turned to Chandler. "I hope the Marines haven't invaded Noatak," she said.

Chandler stopped and confronted her. "Couldn't stop them, Kimberly. They went in last night."

"Jesus. What happened?"

"It was a catastrophe. They lost every Marine."

"How many?"

"Sixty-eight."

"Good God. I can't believe they went in there without knowing what it was."

"I tried to tell them, but the Secretary of Defense said they couldn't wait. Told me to stand down. The oil crisis and all that crap. Wolf tried to persuade them to hold off until you arrived. They didn't want to hear it."

"I could have saved them all if I'd…"

"It's history, Kimberly."

"Hey, Mom, let's go," shouted Ken in the distance.

They loaded their suitcases and equipment into Brave Wolf's Bronco. Wolf stared at his gas gauge, a habit he now embraced out of fear of getting stranded. One-quarter of a tank remaining, Wolf confirmed with a grimace. Eleven minutes later, now inside the Park, Wolf pulled up in front of Chandler's log cabin. The gas gauge had moved only fractionally. They helped Fulton and her son unload the Jeep. Chandler carried her suitcases inside and put her equipment on the couch.

"Kimberly, your bedroom's over there, on the right. Ken, you take the room on the left. There's a bed near the window so you can see the view."

Ken walked over to his room. He was already thinking about the sleeping arrangements for when Meghan arrived: he and his mom would sleep in his room, he decided. Mom would be next to the window to see the view—a peace offering—and he would sleep in the other bed. Meghan could sleep in his mom's bedroom. Just the thought of it gave Ken a jolt. He coughed reflexively. The same thought kept pulsing through his mind: how and when would he summon the courage to tell his mother about Meghan's arrival? Maybe he could confide in Brave Wolf. He would approach him later when they were alone, he decided.

"I love your home, Scott. Rustic and charming." She added with a grin, "A bit masculine."

Ken stared at the two mounts hanging from the living room wall, a Dall Mountain sheep head and a massive grizzly head, teeth flared.

"Cool," he said.

Over the fireplace, a caribou head rose majestically above the mantle, the antlers tipping the ceiling.

"Did you shoot him?" Ken asked, his eyes wide in wonder.

Chandler put his right hand on Ken's shoulder. "Nope," he said. "He was attacked by a Grizzly. It was a gift from a friend, as were the others. I protect the animals in the Park. Wouldn't dream of shooting one."

"Awesome," Ken said, his mouth agape.

"Make yourself at home. I've got sandwiches and sodas in the fridge for lunch. There're a number of dirt trails leading out from the back of the cabin." Chandler pointed out the picture window to the mountains. "The trailhead goes to the base of Mount Stimson. Beautiful views and you're safe here. Brave Wolf and I have to get back to the agency headquarters, so we'll see you guys for dinner," said Chandler. "I'll pick you both up at six."

He looked at Wolf hesitantly and whispered sheepishly, "The Master Baiter?"

Wolf nodded in agreement.

Ken heard him and chortled. "The Master Baiter? You're joking right?"

"Refers to fishing—as in being the master of baits for salmon and trout," Chandler tried.

"Yeah, right," Ken laughed.

Wolf gave him a firm pat on the back. "My main man. Six o'clock it is," and he walked out the front door motioning Chandler to join him.

Chandler held up his hand to Wolf. "In a moment." He tried hard not to stare at Fulton, but memories from the past kept tugging at his consciousness. She was really very attractive, he thought—maybe more so now than back at UM in Missoula.

As she walked toward her bedroom, she turned around and faced him. She looked down at her watch. "What time can you get us in there?"

"I don't think we have enough time today, Kimberly. I was thinking tomorrow morning, early. Maybe we lift off at 7:30 a.m.?"

"It's only eleven o'clock, Scott. We don't have the luxury of idle time. You told me the military wants to identify what's in there ASAP before they go in again. I don't think we should wait. I'm not even sure we'll have time for dinner tonight. What matters is that we I.D. this thing before it slaughters another human. How long does it take to get us in there from here?"

"Depends. If the fog's thick, might take forty-five minutes to an hour, maybe longer. If it's all clear, maybe thirty."

"Let's go for it. That's what I came out here to do. I can sightsee any time."

Chandler thought of the military's threat to go back into the Fossil. He knew if they did, it would be a major assault with potentially much higher casualties—and would devastate the ecosystem of Noatak National Preserve.

He had not yet told her that an entire Marine battalion had flown deep into Noatak National Park before sunrise, and was now camped out a half mile behind Interior's Fish and Wildlife headquarters waiting for orders to strike at Fossil River yet again.

Earlier in the day, Major Wong had convinced Robinson not to attack until the predator was identified. Reluctantly, Robinson had agreed, but only for seventy-two hours.

Chandler and Brave Wolf were both relying on Fulton to present convincing evidence for restraint.

"If we go back in there, Kimberly, we both stay inside the cockpit, engines on, and ready for take off. These bastards are ruthless predators. They destroyed three of our drones that were doing reconnaissance."

Fulton's eyes riveted on Chandler. "Scott. That confirms it. We have proof they couldn't fly a hundred million years ago. Maybe they morphed into flying dinosaurs millions of years later. Either way, they fly. There were feathers in your samples. Do you know what this means?"

"It means we're not getting out of the chopper, Kimberly. Not even for a quick photo op. Promise me that."

CHAPTER 26

KEN UNPACKED IN HIS ROOM. WHEN HE FLIPPED ON HIS iPHONE, HE WAS relieved to see four bars. It must be coming from a tower nearby, he thought.

When his mother entered his room, he was pleased when she said, "Scott and I are flying into the Fossil River in Noatak this afternoon. You'll be with Brave Wolf for the rest of the day until dinner. You okay with that?"

More than okay, he thought. All he said was, "Great, mom."

Fulton hesitated for a brief moment, suspicious of how quickly he agreed with her plan. An hour ago on the flight into Noatak he had insisted on going into the Park with her—yet now he seemed as if he didn't care one way or the other. But she was relieved at his response.

She walked up to him and kissed him on the cheek. "See you for dinner."

"At the Master Baiter," Ken teased.

"The Master what?" Fulton said, startled.

"The name of the restaurant we're eating at tonight."

"Really?" Fulton's nose crinkled curiously.

"Big fishing spot here," Ken said, fighting to keep a straight face and look innocent. "It's all about the baits...and the fish."

"Sure," Fulton grinned in disbelief. "Great name for a restaurant."

She was glad he was out here with her. He's very special, she thought. Raising a son without a husband and father had been very difficult after college, but moments like this reaffirmed just how special the relationship had become. Ken had been a joy to raise. Although he always questioned her judgment and decisions regarding his struggle for independence, Fulton knew that was just her son's silent effort to break away from her. That was natural for a teenager. Pubescence into adolescence, she had read, was always fraught with challenge, and now she was seeing positive signs that he might be on the other side of it.

Fulton walked out of their bedroom, slung her gear over both shoulders and left the cabin.

Chandler had already convinced Wolf to spend the day with Ken. Wolf walked into the livingroom. "Ken? It's you and me for the day, sport," he said.

"Cool," Ken replied with a smile.

Chandler showed Fulton the pilot's side of the copter where she inspected the jagged slice in the door made by the alpha male's eight-inch talon that he'd sent her by FedEx. She took pictures, then placed her camera back into its carrying case.

Chandler loaded Fulton's field equipment into the Sikorsky. Helping her into the cabin, he shut the hatch. "You really need all this equipment, Kimberly?"

"Trust me Scott. I do."

"Sure you're up for this?"

Fulton put on her headphones. "I've waited a lifetime for this moment."

"When we land in there, remember, do not open the hatch door. Take pictures from inside the cabin through the glass. If one of those bastards attacks us, we're off the ground in a heartbeat. Understand?"

"I know this predator, Scott. I got my doctorate on it: how it hunts, eats, sleeps, and breeds."

"You didn't see what I saw."

She was silent.

Chandler turned the key and the engine roared to life, the massive blades whirling into a blur of power. The helicopter lifted slowly off the tarmac at Noatak airport and swept off to the east over a wall of large pine trees that encircled the far end of the clearing, then headed upriver along the Noatak. Thirty minutes later, they passed over The Fish and Wildlife Agency headquarters.

When the chopper reached four hundred feet above the jagged terrain, Chandler hovered in place, pointed down to the right, and spoke through the headphones. "Look down there—Marine encampment."

Fulton moved the small speaker toward her mouth, and nodded. "We've got to stop them, Scott. How many men down there now?"

"A complete battalion. Anywhere between three hundred and a thousand soldiers."

"I know we shouldn't be going in there, but I've got to confirm with a sighting: pictures, video, and I'm hoping to get audio, sound bites. My lab work confirms what it should be, but we need to have absolute proof of what it is."

"You'll have it today. I just hope to God we can get out of there alive," Chandler said. "The nation's on its knees. That's all they see. Our country's desperate. After you get proof of what's in there, then you have to convince them that it's suicide to go back."

He looked over at Fulton who appeared to be mesmerized by the sweeping views of Noatak's mountains, lakes, valleys, glaciers, volcanoes, and rivers. She looked at him, shaking her head.

"God's country, Scott," she said. "It's so beautiful. I've missed it. No wonder you love it out here."

He pointed at the cloudbank ahead of them. "Hold on. It's going to get rough."

"We're going through that?" Fulton said, squinting at the ominous blanket of fog beneath them.

"Affirmative."

Fulton stared ahead at the mountains rising above the fogbank, knowing that what she might see in Glacier today promised to change her life. The helicopter dropped down and skimmed atop the thick blanket of fog. Seven minutes later, he said, "We're going down. Hold on."

The chopper vanished into dense cloud cover and began bumping up and down, then fell sharply at a left angle through a dark patch of thick mist. An air pocket pushed the craft back up in a sudden rise, and

Fulton gagged, trying to hold down the turkey sandwich she'd grabbed for lunch. "How much longer?"

"Soon."

For a moment Chandler thought the cyclic was jammed and his heart skipped a beat, but he thrust it up and it popped in place. Shit, he thought. that was too close.

He pushed the helicopter to its limit and it dove into a deep descent through the thick vog created from sulfur dioxide and other gases and particles emitted by an erupting volcano reacting with oxygen and moisture.

Fulton clutched her stomach again, but the expectation of what she might see forced her to focus on readying her equipment. She pulled her Canon out of its case and checked the function. Next, the video camera and her recorder. She was ready. Her breath came in deep pulls of excitement.

The cockpit was brighter now and Fulton was aware they were flying below the fog bank just above the timberline. Chandler was reading the GPS and had charted the flight before takeoff. The colorful display showed them moments away from the river. As he dodged a large tree to his right, he saw the white line of the river below, and thrust the engine into high torque to hold his position.

He aimed the nose downward at the river and, as he did, four bright magenta images streamed onto his radar scope, moving directly toward his craft. Chandler pointed to the screen. "See these blips?"

"Yes. What are they?"

"It's them. They know we're here."

"Incredible," she took six quick shots with her camera through the window. "Will they attack us in the air like the drones?"

"No."

"Why not?"

"Because they've already learned the chopper's a dangerous predator to avoid when it's in the air."

"How do you know that?"

"When they took down the drones, they also took down a chopper pilot. When the Marines checked the crash sight, they found blood and guts all over the rotary blades. The predators have learned it's lethal if they get too close and the engine's on. Let's hope they remember that when we're on the ground. That's why it's important to keep the blades spinning. The alpha male that attacked my helicopter had no fear of anything."

"That's how they've lasted 100 million years," Fulton said. "The species has learned how to survive through communication, and has passed knowledge on to their progeny. It becomes etched in their genetic fiber." She looked down. "Is this the Fossil?"

"Yes."

"Are we at the landing site yet?"

"No." Chandler knew the toughest part of the trip was ahead of them. Following the river was fraught with challenges at each bend, even though the SVDS helped him read the contours with pinpoint accuracy.

"It's great being with you again, Scott." She touched his shoulder.

"Me too, Kimberly," he said through the headphones. "Ken seems like a nice kid. I'm glad you brought him with you."

Fulton nodded.

The helicopter skimmed the whitewater and flew upriver to the next turn. As it hovered at the bend, Chandler looked for the clearing he remembered from the last time he'd been here. He didn't see it. He maneuvered along a narrow stretch of the river where trees grew on both banks, so thick they barely cleared the diameter of his whirling blades.

"Another five minutes, Kimberly. Hang in there."

Fulton stared at the four magenta blips on the screen and was surprised to see three more appear. She reached for her camera and snapped off two more shots of the screen. "Three more, Scott. Coming into range." She peered out into the dense ground fog, her nose against the bubble glass, trying to see something.

Chandler took the chopper up in a sudden ascent to avoid a fallen tree, but he didn't see the broad reach of spruce branches poking out over the Fossil to his left, stretching out toward the center of the river. The cockpit shook violently and a shower of branches, cones, and needles spewed out over the river in an arc of green. The helicopter vibrated in response and Chandler hovered in place, testing the rotary engine and blades. "We're okay."

Fulton sat silently, filled with awe as she studied the blips. Fear hadn't even occurred to her. It was like a dream coming true. She let it spread over her like a warm blanket.

The helicopter sped forward to the next two bends, rose above the treetops, pressed forward another half mile, then dropped down on a swath of river that was clear on both banks. The chopper was flying only fifteen feet above the churning river when a loud GPS bleep sounded.

Fulton jerked her head up. Chandler hovered in place, inspecting the large clearing before him. He flew over to the far bank, held position above a slight incline, and slowly let the chopper down atop a slab of rock.

He took his headphones off, zipped open his jacket. "We're here," he said.

Fulton peeled her headphones off and swiped her right arm across her face. It was wet with perspiration. "What a rush." She looked at the radar screen. "They've vanished," she said. "Where are they?"

"They're out there Kimberly, trust me. They know we've landed. Get your camera ready and turn on your recorder."

CHAPTER 27

KEN FULTON STARED AT THE TURQUOISE TALISMAN HANGING FROM THE WALL of Wolf's home. "Where'd you find this?"

"It was my great grandfather's."

"What's it mean?"

Wolf pointed to the accented colors of the talisman as he spoke. "The colors tell a story of the wind, sun, moon, mountains, and stars— the powers that make up our faith."

Wolf watched the teenager's curiosity unfold as he looked down at the tiled floor. "Is this a real footprint?" he asked.

"Yes. The tiles were made by boys and girls your age from my tribe. As the tiles baked in the sun, our children walked across them, leaving their foot- and handprints in the clay as they flip each tile to bake in the sun."

Ken studied the tiles and saw spiders, lizard-tail tracks, and one that looked like a snake track. His stomach responded with a churn of angst as he thought of eating snake. He turned to Brave Wolf. "What does snake taste like?" he asked.

"Chicken."

Ken shrugged his shoulders. "Everything tastes like chicken. Seriously, what does it taste like?"

Wolf pointed down at the tiled floor. "See that one?"

"Yes."

"Know what it is?"

"Scorpion?"

"Good. You know your stuff, Ken. That's what it tastes like."

"Snake tastes like scorpion?"

"Yes. It's sweet, but not crunchy like scorpion. Lizard meat is sweet, too. Kind of squishy until the juice hits your tongue." Wolf pointed to a lizard impression in one of the tiles. "If you can get past the mental image of eating it, and the crunchy sound of chewing it, it's really quite tasty. In fact, it's better than chicken." Wolf grinned broadly, showing irregular teeth. The incisor on the left side of his mouth was gold.

He walked over to the hearth mantle and picked up a small clay pot. "I'll tell you a story about my people."

As Wolf turned the pot slowly in his hands, he pointed to the ancient images scrolled on the pot in blue, black, and red dies, describing each image to the teenager as he had done with Chandler. The stick figures were running from a pursuing beast, razor sharp talons clawing at the air.

"What's this?" Ken voiced.

"Sharp as a sickle. It's a hook like talon the beast uses to kill its prey."

"Did this really happen?"

"You know what a legend is?"

"A story from the past?"

"Yes, a story that might be true, or might not. This is a legend from my people, thousands of years ago."

"You think it's true?" Ken said, staring at the Indian in questioning wonder.

"Good question. When I was your age, and I first heard about the legend from my great grandfather, I didn't believe him. But I believe it now."

He studied Brave Wolf's mocha tan face, made leathery by years of exposure to the wind and sun.

"Keep turning the pot," Wolf said, "and tell me what you see."

"A beast with sharp teeth."

"Yes. Keep turning."

"What's this?"

"A conch shell."

Ken turned the pot yet again and furrowed his brow. "What are they doing?"

Wolf took a conch shell from the mantle. "This is what scares off the beast in the legend shown on the clay pot. See it?"

The teenager nodded. "How does it scare them off?"

"Ever heard a conch shell before?"

"No," Ken said curiously. But he hesitated in thought because he saw something in Wolf's face that was unsettling. It forced him to say, "Why are you telling me all this, Brave Wolf? I get the feeling you're worried about something that might happen in the future. Talk to me."

"You're very insightful, Ken. Yes, I am worried. Not necessarily about you. But if you go into the Park, I want to make sure you're prepared."

"Prepared for what? The dino?"

"Yes."

Wolf turned away from Ken, held the shell up to his lips, and blew into the massive conch. The sound started off low and haunting.

Ken stared at Brave Wolf in disbelief. As the sound grew in intensity he had to cup his ears. The windows started to rattle.

"Awesome," he shouted. "Truly awesome."

Wolf sat down next to Ken and handed him the conch.

"Can you teach me?"

"Sure. Purse your lips and blow out slowly at first, then intensify the wind through the shell to cause the loud, pulsating sound. In the legend, this sound scares away the beast."

Ken stared at Wolf, concentrating on every word as if his life depended on it..

"Watch me," Wolf said. "You can push your hand into the conch opening like this to change the tone, which gives it an eerie effect. Scott and I recorded the conch so that it can be amplified and played back when they see the predator."

"Blow it again, Brave Wolf. I want to get it on my iPhone."

Wolf picked up the shell and blew into it again as Ken recorded.

"I didn't know you could record with the iPhone," Wolf said.

"New model, just got it for my birthday. Does everything. High volume, too." Ken reversed the recording and played back the haunting sound, turning up the volume. The conch filled the room yet again with perfect pitch. "This is sick, Brave Wolf."

Wolf smiled.

Ken picked up the shell again and put it to his lips. He blew into it and a balloon squeak escaped into the shell chamber.

Wolf laughed. "Now that's sick," he said.

Ken put the shell to his lips yet again, this time tightening his lips, blowing harder until the sound emanating from the chamber built into a low rumble that intensified into a shrill resonating siren like pitch. The windows rattled in response.

Triumphantly, the boy put down the shell. "Thanks, Wolf. Where can I get one of these? I'd love to blow it in Central Park and watch people freak out. "

"Take this one," Wolf said.

"No way. You serious?"

"It's yours. I have more of them down on my reservation. If you go into Noatak, make sure you take it with you."

"Mom is convinced there are dinosaurs in there. You think she's right?"

"If she is, the legend's true."

"You didn't answer my question."

"I guess I'm afraid to answer, Ken. Whatever's in there is bad, real bad. Let's have lunch."

"No scorpion," Ken said without a smile.

"Promise. No scorpion. After lunch, how'd you like to take a drive down to the Inupiat Tribal Reservation outside Noatak? I can introduce you to some of my friends and relatives."

"Awesome, how cool is that? I've never been to a reservation. Are Inupiats Eskimos?"

"Yes. My people are probably all related to the Eskimos. We're Inuit. It means, 'the people,' but the terms Inuit and Inupiat are technically the same people. We're all Eskimos. Although my mom and dad were true Blackfoot from Montana, we all probably came over to Alaska across the Bering Land Bridge from Asia."

Ken carefully placed the conch shell into his backpack and set it down on the coffee table. He looked out Wolf's window at the snow-capped mountain peaks in the distance. Somehow he would find his way into Noatak and find out for himself if the legend was true. Meghan would love it, he thought. While Wolf went into the kitchen to make sandwiches and get sodas, Ken opened his laptop to check his messages. There was one from Meghan:

Good news, Ken! Cleared everything with Juliana McGuire. Already spoken to my mom. She's okay with it, but doesn't know anything about Alaska. Juliana will cover. Confirmed the flight to Kotzebue via Fairbanks. Got a Green something charter into Noatak. Covered the cost with babysitting money, thank God! Landing at Noatak airport at 4:20 p.m. Alaskan time tomorrow afternoon. Hoping you can pick me up at airport.

Have you been to Noatak National Park yet and seen the thing? Can't wait to see you both! I Googled living fossil and it says it's a living prehistoric creature, fish, plant, or bird that lived back in the dinosaur age and is still alive today! How cool is that? I wonder what it looks like?

Love you, Meghan.

Ken texted back:

Can't wait either. I'll be at airport. You'll love the Eskimo pilot and green plane. Love you back.

Ken looked out the window again. He wondered how he was going to pick up Meghan.

CHAPTER 28

CHANDLER OPENED A SMALL TRIANGULAR APERTURE IN THE DOOR TO VENTI-LATE the cabin. A puff of pine-scented mountain air filled the cockpit. "The engine stays on."

Fulton nodded.

Chandler poked his left arm toward her. "You see this?"

"See what?"

"My arm."

"What about it?"

"It's a prosthesis. You didn't notice?"

"No. Why would I? It looks like your other arm." She reached out and touched it. "How do you fly a helicopter?"

"Nerves of steel."

"And determination. You haven't changed." Fulton laughed at his joke and searched his eyes.

"Neither have you."

She ran her fingers over his hand, felt each of the fingers, then lightly squeezed the arm. "A stupid question, but can you feel this?"

"No, but seeing you touch my arm, I can feel it in my mind." He hesitated.

"I'm sorry. Was it Iraq?"

"No, Afghanistan. And don't feel sorry for me. I'm lucky to be alive."

His comment flustered her and snapped her back to the moment.

"I don't feel sorry for you at all—just pisses me off you lost your arm in that damned war. It must have been crazy over there."

"It was."

She looked into his eyes, again searching for old memories. She remembered the attention he gave his research in Missoula, his compulsive need to master every detail of his work, and the passionate way he listened and learned. All of it came back to her. They were all good feelings, including their last night together.

Chandler scanned the bank of the Fossil.

She pulled out her field bag filled with still and video cameras, recorders, and a collection of paleontology field gear: picks, brushes, orange tags, small hammers, a field microscope, a bag of white plaster for impressions, sharp knives, scalpels, and binoculars.

Fulton studied the open field, the trees and bushes that lined the banks of the river. "They not only know we're here," she said, "they've already surrounded us and communicated a plan of attack: which ones will charge, which ones will decoy the attack. It's a precision death trap."

Chandler pulled his carbine from underneath the pilot's seat and slammed in a full clip.

"You're not planning to use that, I hope," Fulton said.

"If we're under attack, I sure as hell will. We won't get into a save-the-species mode when our lives are at stake. You haven't seen the carnage these bastards levied on the research team. I have. God only knows how sixty-eight Marines died last night."

"Okay, but restrain yourself as long as you can."

"Don't worry. I don't like killing."

Fulton took her cameras out of their cases and slung them over her shoulder. She placed a recorder around her neck and turned it on.

"Testing, testing," she said. The red light blinked to confirm her voice was being recorded. "Tuesday, June ninth, 12:48 p.m. We've landed next to the Fossil River in the southeast quadrant of Noatak National Park, Alaska. We've not seen signs yet of the predator, but we know it's out there. We're not getting out of the helicopter because it's not safe, so we're going to try and capture pictures of the living fossil from inside. Stand by." She turned off the recorder.

"Nothing's on the radar yet," she said.

"They're all around us—just not moving."

"Maybe the engine's too loud. We're scaring them off," Fulton said.

"The engine stays alive."

Chandler pointed at the rocky hill that ran up to an outcrop approximately forty-five yards away from the craft. Behind the slab of rock was a 200-foot drop. "This clearing gives us perfect position to capture them on film."

"But the sound of the engine will ruin my audio, Scott. It's too loud to record them. Please turn it off."

"No. When they start communicating, trust me, you'll hear them loud and clear. If we turn the engine off, we risk them charging us. If that happens, there's not enough time to get the engine restarted and up to speed for lift off. They'll be all over us in a second."

"They won't charge us, Scott. They're going to watch us first. Feel us out. They'll surround us, alright, but they'll stay at the edge of the clearing, waiting, studying us. I know their habits, especially hunting and tracking."

"Being in the field and seeing them hunt and kill firsthand is a lot different than being in the museum and hypothecating. No offense, but I've seen these demons up close and personal. Felt their breath on my face, seen their snapping jaws, and stared into their piercing yellow eyes. It's no fucking picnic with ants. It's heart-pounding terror with aliens."

"No argument, but I know my raptors. The big difference with this one is intelligence."

"Stay ready," Chandler said as he rested his carbine across his lap.

"We're making history, Scott, and…" She stopped midsentence and touched his leg. "Thanks for taking me in here. I just wanted to say that before…"

"If we lose focus, we're dead. It's okay to open the window hatches a little, but both doors stay locked and bolted from inside."

They both sat motionless, scanning the open field for movement. Fulton took her field glasses out and scanned the trees, the river, then the terrain on both sides. Forty yards from the Fossil she fixed onto something on the ground. She adjusted the focus and gasped.

"Oh my God, Scott. There's a half-eaten body out there. A head and shoulders, I think an arm." She handed the binoculars to Chandler.

"It's one of the Marines from last night. I see part of a flack jacket and two stripes on the shirt, a Lance Corporal. Jesus, it's a woman. Goddamn it!"

He fought the temptation to investigate, but spied something else. "Look to the left of her body. Five yards out. What's all that stuff around her?"

Fulton squinted through her binoculars. "I see a wing, feathers all over the place. Scattered Deino remains. Looks like a graveyard," Fulton said in disbelief.

Chandler kept staring at all of the body parts surrounding her body then nodded knowing what happened. "Son of a bitch. She took them all out."

"What do you mean?" asked Fulton.

"She blew herself up with grenades knowing she'd take her attackers with her. One helluva Marine."

"God. How awful," Fulton said shaking her head.

"She's a hero," Chandler said.

Fulton moved her attention from the corpse to the thick slab of rock atop which the chopper had landed. Crustaceans were etched in the Cretaceous rock, one Trilobite in perfect fossilized condition. Breathless, she whispered into the recorder. "Beautiful specimens. Decapod crustaceans. The extant Genera are of the Callianassidae found from the Northern Rockies to British Columbia north to Alaska."

She took out her camera and shot four quick pictures of the fossils in the rock. As she snapped a series of pictures she talked quietly into the recorder.

"Anomalous environment, like a lost world. Temperature at this altitude should be cool at this time of year. Some patches of snow on the north face, but not here. Instead it's temperate, seventy-four degrees Fahrenheit. I can see three active glaciers in the distance and a live volcano close by, probably too close. Smoke rising from the cone. Feels like I'm in the Jurassic era. Nothing seems changed."

She looked down at her altimeter gauge and read aloud.

"Seventy-eight hundred feet. The trees are huge. Taxodium, and Metasequioia. Also see Ginkgo, a dioecious gymnosperm, and

Taeniopteris. Tall conifers, palmlike cycads, too. Some deciduous trees totally out of place. Amazing collection of ferns. Bryophytes, and—oh my God—I see *Equisetites* showing partially fused leaves of an extinct horsetail—but here it's alive and thriving. Another undiscovered living fossil!"

Chandler pulled out the giant conch shell that Wolf had given him and set it on the cockpit floor. Fulton looked at him.

"Do you think the sound from that actually works?" she whispered. "Scares them away?"

"Brave Wolf claims his ancestors swore by it. We'll see soon enough if it works." Chandler pulled out the recording device he and Wolf had constructed, lowered a speaker outside the hatch, and dangled it half way down to the ground.

Fulton began filming a span of the clearing from left to right, down to the river's edge, scanning the bushes, pointing the camera up at the treetops. "There's still no movement," she said into the recorder. "Eighteen minutes and no sign of life. If they're here, we know they're watching us. But the helicopter engine's still on. Maybe keeping them away."

Another ten minutes passed. "Scott, please turn the engine off," Fulton pleaded with a soft, persistent voice. "You have a loaded gun and the sound system to scare them away. They're not coming any closer because of the helicopter. When you turn it off, how long does it take to get the engines back up to speed for lift off?"

"About three minutes to liftoff. It stays on. That was the deal. You have no idea how powerful and fast these bastards are. They'd be on us in less than thirty seconds."

Another fourteen minutes passed and Fulton pleaded yet again. Chandler sat bolt upright. He stared long and hard at Fulton, then studied the GPS. No blips. He clutched his carbine and snapped the safety off.

"I'll give you fifteen minutes without the engine on—then we're out of here. Deal?"

Fulton checked her equipment. "Deal."

Chandler turned the ignition off and the engine wound down to a purr before going silent. An eerie stillness filled the cockpit and Fulton thought she heard the slow tick-tick of her chronometer.

Chandler studied the radar with renewed focus. The screen was blank.

Then one magenta blip moved onto the screen, a loud chirp sounding from the trees to announce it. Chandler snapped his head to the left.

"Don't move," he whispered.

Fulton's heart skipped a beat, her right finger poised on the shutter button.

"Shhh."

"Where?"

"To your left, across the clearing."

Fulton didn't see anything, but pointed her camera to the left and clicked off a dozen or so pictures hoping to capture whatever Chandler saw.

"I don't see it."

"Just came out into the clearing. Watching us. God, it's big. Not moving, to the left of the white pine, holding its position."

"Oh my God. I see it."

She pointed her camera and clicked off eight shots, then held her camcorder up and started recording. Into the recorder: "It's bigger than I thought. Colorful plumage, reds, blues, and a shock of black before the tail. The tail's long and thick, maybe six- to eight-feet long, at least six inches in diameter. No feathers on the tail. Very muscular. Just like the fossil fragments we've found on the Montana plains, only bigger and more developed. Can't believe what I'm seeing. Deinonychus is alive. It's alive and thriving in Noatak National Park."

Chandler slowly raised his carbine to his shoulder, his finger on the trigger.

"Please don't shoot."

"I'm not," he whispered. "Just aiming. Getting ready, just in case."

Something moved. Chandler turned to the right. "Christ."

"What?"

"Two o'clock. Two more."

Fulton's heart thumped so hard in her chest she had trouble operating the camera. But she did, and she was capturing every moment on video.

"Two more now in view," she said, eyes riveted on what looked like an alien with aggressive purpose, "about the same size and shape as the other one. Same color on the plumage. Probably females. The eyes are big, size of a chicken egg, and yellow, proving what we always thought: They've got binocular night vision to hunt prey."

Fulton zoomed in on the two predators to her right.

"Notice size of head and jaws. Much bigger than we hypothesized. They stand about six- and-a-half-feet tall, some of them maybe up to eight, hard to tell in the fog."

Fulton put the video camera down, adjusted her backpack, and picked up her still camera to reload. As she opened up the film compartment of her field pack, an ear shattering screech sounded from somewhere high in the trees. Fulton lurched backward, almost dropping her camera, and smacked her head on the seat brace bar.

Another screech sounded and the three Deinos in the clearing dashed closer to the helicopter and spread out in one coordinated motion. The one in the center issued a bellowing screech that was different in tone from the first sounds. Fulton chattered quickly with excitement into the recorder while trying to film the predators. "

They're communicating to each other, planning an attack, maybe sixty yards out."

Chandler's right hand was on the ignition switch. Again he checked the safety of his carbine.

In a blur of rapid motion, another seven predators dashed into the clearing, fog swirling behind them, forming a half moon around them. The helicopter was encircled by three Deinos only forty-five yards away, seven behind them.

"Don't touch the ignition. Let me capture it all," Fulton insisted, her eyes confirming she was living a life of dreams coming true.

Beyond the clearing, somewhere off to the right, a sound pierced the silence with such decibel force that Fulton and Chandler flinched at the same moment.

The sound reverberated across the mountain range into the valley below. The other predators responded with a clicking noise that sounded to Chandler like a thousand crickets. Fulton knew it was an alarm to signal the hunt. She described it into the recorder.

"We're seeing proof surrounding us that Deinos hunt in packs, communicating with precision about each individual's role in the hunt. There are two males in the clearing, flanking the females, but none of them seem to be leading the charge. They're behind the females that have formed a circle around us."

Chandler shouldered his carbine. Something bounded out into the center of the clearing with such speed and force that Chandler and Fulton had to blink their eyes to gain focus. The other creatures flanked it in a phalanx of support.

"Holy shit," Fulton said. "It's the alpha male. It's huge! Look at it, Scott."

"I'm looking, for Chrissakes."

Fulton's cameras were a blur of motion as she tried to capture the scene. The alpha male's powerful legs churned in place, high kicking its razor sharp talons into the air and bellowing a low pitched screech that rose in a crescendo of dread. But Chandler spied the left muscular foot that was missing a talon. "It's the same one that attacked my chopper. See, it's missing a talon."

The alpha male displayed expansive wings and colorful plumage, jumping up and down and swaying sideways.

"It's going to feign an attack," Fulton said. "Don't shoot. Let it charge. I've got to get this on film."

The Alpha looked at the others flanking it, issued a bloodthirsty cry that deafened Chandler and Fulton, then broke loose into charge straight at the Sikorsky.

"Don't shoot."

Thirty yards out.

"Don't shoot."

Twenty.

"Don't shoot."

Fifteen yards out and Chandler felt the steel trigger on his right index finger. He had a bead on its head.

The Alpha stopped in a flurry of motion and stood rigid, its streamlined body pulsating in brilliant colors. It looked back at the others, then began snapping its jaws in defiance, fury glaring from its bulbous yellow eyes. When it let out another shrill screech, the ten Deinos behind it emitted a cacophony that flooded the humans' senses with fear.

Fulton spoke rapidly into the recorder, her voice at high pitch.

"It's feigning another attack, trying to paralyze us. Wingspan at least twelve feet wide, maybe fifteen. Its massive jaws display rows of sharp jagged teeth, maybe three inches long, much bigger than the fossil collections back at the Museum, incredible. Absolutely mind blow…"

Chandler heard the rushing sound of wind above the chopper before Fulton did. Fulton felt a sudden jolt of the fuselage and Chandler knew that a predator had just landed atop the still chopper blades.

He turned on the sound recorder, volume at full force. The eerie sound of the conch shell filled the air and the Deino atop the chopper flew down to the ground and ran toward the alpha male.

The pack of Deino predators, now numbering seventeen, vanished from the clearing. The magenta blips on the radar screen rapidly moved off the scope in one deliberate unified motion.

Chandler flipped the ignition switch on and the engine came to life, the chopper blades whirling into a high pitched torque.

Fulton was in a state of utter excitement and awe.

Chandler turned off the wailing sound device and pulled it back into the cabin. Just to aggravate the enemy, he picked up the conch shell on the cockpit floor, swung open the hatch door to its full extension, and leaned outside the craft. He blew into it with all the lung power he could muster. The sound, pulsating and deafening, filled the clearing and echoed through the mountain valley below.

Her eyes wide and filled with wonder, Fulton stared at him.

Chandler closed the hatch, put the conch shell back onto the cabin floor, and the Sikorsky lifted off the ground and swept across the Fossil River, then rose vertically through the thick fog, leaving the scene behind, the surface water white-capping from the craft's windy ascent.

Fulton could not speak into the recorder around her neck, but it was still rolling, capturing the surrealistic details of the trip into Noatak's Fossil River she knew had changed her life forever.

"Thank God the sound device works. Brave Wolf was right about the legend," Chandler said.

Fulton nodded appreciatively.

The helicopter rose above the cloud cover, prisms of the late afternoon sun dazzling the cabin with flashes of bright light.

He touched Fulton's hand. She squeezed his and said, "To quote my son Ken, you're truly awesome."

"Thanks," Chandler said. "So are you." He looked at his watch. It was 4:48 p.m. "I've got good news, Kimberly." He grinned broadly. "We'll be home just in time for a caribou dinner."

Fulton looked at him and smiled. "Funny man. I don't think I'll eat one of Santa's reindeer tonight."

"I think you've captured enough vivid evidence to make a very convincing argument for the military not to invade Noatak again."

"I hope you're right."

CHAPTER 29

FULTON AND CHANDLER EXITED THE SIKORSKY. CHANDLER WALKED AROUND the craft inspecting the fuselage and blades for damage. Fortunately, thought Chandler, there was only a small nick in one of the blades that had clipped the pine tree hanging over the Fossil River.

When he climbed atop the chopper blades, he discovered a section on one of them where the tough resin paint had been scraped down to the metal base. Chandler knew the moment he saw the damage that it was made by the razor-sharp talons of the Deino that had landed atop his craft. The helicopter was, Chandler concluded, still safe and in good working order.

They hopped into an ATV parked at the side of the F&W headquarters, and sped out of the clearing toward the military encampment.

"Glad you're back here alive," Major Wong said as they walked into the command center tent.

Chandler nodded. "Thanks. Meet Dr. Kimberly Fulton, from New York City's Museum of Natural History. She's the best in her field. She's got the proof we needed to enlighten your superiors, sir."

Fulton pumped Wong's hand with a confident shake, then cut to the chase. "When can I make the presentation to your soldiers, Major Wong?"

"Day after tomorrow, Dr. Fulton. We've got forty-eight hours to prepare our Marines for the strike."

"Why not tomorrow?" Fulton pressed.

"Because all the troops are not here yet and I need to review the strategy with my men: training, drills, coordination, armor and offensive tactics, based on our first failure. We don't want a second loss of life on the magnitude of the first."

"I understand, Major," Fulton offered, "but after my presentation you won't need to a second time. I'll promise you that."

"It's under review. I'll make the decision after your presentation, Dr. Fulton."

Fulton took a step back from Wong. "Yes, sir. What time shall we be here for the presentation?"

"Make it fourteen hundred hours," Wong said. "I'll have the battalion superiors assembled here under the tent."

"Can I view the area for the presentation?" Fulton asked.

"Of course."

Fulton ducked back inside the massive umbrella tent and studied the staging area at the front of what she guessed was close to eight hundred chairs. Chandler came to stand beside her. "We'll put the screen here and flank it with speakers," she said. "I'll move the podium to the center."

Chandler studied her face and saw the muscles in her cheeks flex, a sign of steadfast determination. But he saw something else: a sense of dread in her eyes confirming that if she failed to convince the military it was not necessary to invade Noatak's Fossil River, hundreds of Marines would perish and the Park's pristine ecology and wildlife would be devastated.

It even occurred to him that his career might be over.

When Fulton got back to Chandler's home, she carefully placed all of her equipment on the floor next to the plaid sofa, walked into the kitchen to grab a bottle of Diet Peach Snapple from the refrigerator. "Can I get you anything?" she called back.

Chandler was already viewing the camera shots that she had taken. "A Coke, thank you."

Fulton came back into the livingroom and looked at her watch. "Where are Ken and Brave Wolf?"

"Don't know, but Ken's safe with Wolf. They know we're going to dinner at 6:30. They'll be here shortly."

"Good," Fulton said hopefully, but Chandler picked up a note of concern in her voice.

"Your nerves are shot, Kimberly. We've experienced one hell of an afternoon. They'll be here on time. I trust Wolf. He's the most responsible guy I know."

"If anything ever happened to Ken, I'd be lost. He means everything to me."

"He seems like a great kid. You've done a good job raising him."

"Thanks, Scott. It wasn't easy, with my career."

"I'm sure it wasn't." Chandler hesitated. "You haven't told me about his father."

"It was a long time ago. I'd rather not talk about it right now."

"Okay."

"Thank you. I appreciate that," Fulton said.

"These pictures are incredible," Chandler said viewing the Canon. Especially the ones of the alpha male. When they're blown up full-size on the big screen on Thursday, your audience won't believe their eyes. They'll be riveted."

"They'd better be," Fulton said. "And I hope to God I can convince them. There's close to a thousand chairs in there, Scott. After losing all sixty-eight Marines, I find it hard to believe they'd go back in."

The Secretary of Defense is, pardon my French, a prick. He doesn't give a damn about Marine lives or the environment. He just wants the oil at all cost. "

"No pressure," Fulton said. "Jesus."

"You can do it, Kimberly. You're the authority in the field and now you've got the proof you need to make the case for not striking again."

"There'll be a lot of questions."

"I'm sure. But you have all of the answers."

Wolf's Bronco wove slowly through the back roads of the Inupiat reservation northeast of Noatak, his tank running on empty. Some of the roads were simply widened dirt paths, wending toward the northern slope of the vast Brooks Mountain range within Noatak National Preserve. The snowcapped peaks towered over the sprawl of HUD houses and makeshift shacks that dotted the reservation.

Old cars and trucks without wheels were perched on cinder blocks, giving Ken the feeling he was touring a place from a distant past. Young children kicking a ball behind a rickety shack. Strands of dried sockeye salmon hung on clotheslines by the hundreds. Two walrus tusks leaned lazily against a rickety old doorframe.

"How can your people live like this, Brave Wolf?"

"We have our own school, educate our own people, and they work on the reservation."

Ken's eyes were wide as he scanned the small village landscape.

"They work very hard at what they do. We might seem poor to you, but we're a very industrious people who have learned to survive in this tough arctic climate for a very long time."

"But I saw some people drunk, and in the middle of the day."

"That's been a problem, yes. Some see no hope, especially the younger ones, but there're many opportunities out there. Just depends on what you make of it. We have many role models that help prove to our younger people they can support themselves and make a go of it. Some leave the small villages and go to college like I did."

How could you afford college?"

"Full scholarship. Hearst Foundation. Even paid for my books. Many companies and government programs provide our people with scholarships. A wonderful man, Max Frehse, set it all up for me. I still write him, affirming how he's changed my life for the better."

"I admire you, Brave Wolf," Ken said affectionately.

Ken sat in silence taking in a civilization he only knew through reading history books and seeing pictures. Eskimos lived only in igloos, he had thought, but this was real-life stuff and the sights made him anxious. It all seemed so harsh, and yet the people were surviving rather well, he concluded.

Wolf drove through the Inupiat reservation entrance, leaving it all behind, and headed west toward the small village of Noatak. He counted six cars abandoned on the highway and knew they'd run out of gas. The sun was low on the Chukchi Sea and it lit up with scintillating brilliance.

Ken fidgeted in his seat. Finally, he almost whispered the words, "I need your help."

"With what?" Wolf asked.

"I have a girlfriend."

"This is good."

"She's flying out here tomorrow."

"Even better."

Ken's heart was thumping so hard in his chest he thought he couldn't finish the sentence. He took in a deep breath. "Could you help me pick her up at the airport when she arrives?" He slumped back in his car seat and exhaled, drops of sweat beading on his forehead.

"Does your mom know about this?"

"No."

"Not good."

"I know. I thought you might be able to help me work it out."

"Tell me more."

"There's not much more to it. Her name's Meghan Lastinger. She's smart. Real smart, very cute, red hair. Got early acceptance to Yale. Loves the environment. Not a green freak, but close to it. She'll flip out when she finds out the military's invaded Noatak. Anyway, we thought it would be cool to surprise mom and get a chance to be together in some place we've both never seen before."

"Some surprises are good, son. This one's real iffy," said Wolf evenly. They were approaching the sign reading, Noatak Two Miles. "Did you ask your mom, already?"

"Unfortunately, yes."

"And she said no, of course."

"Correct."

"Does Meghan's mom know about this?" Wolf said.

"No. She thinks Meghan's staying with a friend, Julianna McGuire."

Wolf took a deep breath as he registered the complexity of the plot.

"So, let's sum it up: your mom says no. But you and Meghan decide to surprise her, anyway. Right?"

"Yes."

"Then Meghan lies to her mom telling her she's staying with a friend while they're in the Hamptons, and the friend's supposed to lie to her if her mom calls. Right?"

"Kind of like that," Ken said nervously shifting in his seat.

"This is some pretty serious shit, son. I'd call that a breach of trust with your mom and Meghan's mom."

The comment angered Ken. "I don't need a lecture."

"I'm not lecturing you, son. I'm empathizing with you, and with your mom, too. She'll be pissed at you for disobeying her when she's already said no, right?"

Ken hesitated.

Wolf sensed his anguish. "It's okay, son," he said. "God knows we've all made mistakes with our parents at one time or another."

Wolf saw tears forming in the corner of Ken's eyes. He instinctively stopped the car and reached over, embracing the boy in a warm, loving hug.

Wolf felt Ken's chest heave in a burst of emotion. "Hey, no sweat," he said. "We'll work this out together. I'm there for yah."

Ken's composure returned as if someone had just given him a hundred dollar bill with no payback.

Wolf started the Bronco and pulled back onto the road. The yellow gas light flashed empty.

"Damn," Wolf said impatiently. "We've got to stop in Noatak and grub some gas,"

"So what do I tell my mom?"

"The truth."

"About Meghan's parents not knowing, either?"

"I'm guessing your mom will want to call Meghan's mother. The truth from both of you. I don't know your mom, Ken, but from what little I've seen of her, she's a woman of resolve and substance and substance is truth. Always truth."

"So when do I tell her?"

"What do you think?"

Ken shrugged his shoulders, stalling for what he knew was the answer.

"Soon, I guess," he said, not wanting to hear how soon.

"Tell her when we walk through the door of Scott Chandler's home with your girlfriend. Your mom will be shocked enough to see Meghan. Maybe she'll think it's just coincidence. But if you lie to her, she'll be disappointed and angry. Moms and dads don't like to be disappointed by their sons or daughters—especially by not being told the truth."

Ken did not answer the question until the Bronco turned left onto Main Street in Noatak. Wolf pulled into a small ExxonMobil station, one pump, lowered the window and said, "Can you spare me ten gallons, Charlie?"

"We're almost out, Wolf. I can spare five. That's it. You gotta wait in line."

"Thanks. I'll take it."

Wolf had four cars in front of him, but he knew Charlie would save him five. Wolf turned to Ken and said with a grin, "It pays to know people in high places."

Ken nodded nervously. As they waited in line, Wolf forced a smile to put the boy at ease.

"What time is the flight tomorrow?"

"Twenty after four at Noatak Airport."

Wolf's Bronco guzzled five gallons and he pulled back onto the road heading home. Wolf put his right arm around Ken. "We have a deal, son."

"Cool," Ken said triumphantly. Drying his eyes with his sleeve, it occurred to him that he had never shed a tear before over not having a dad. He wished Wolf could be his father.

CHAPTER 30

Whale meat really did taste like chicken, Ken decided as they supped at The Master Baiter restaurant with his mom, Chandler, and Wolf.

His mom refused the whale and seal combo, choosing caribou steak instead, since Beluga whales are protected and muktuk sounded to her like some kind of mush. Chandler ordered a grizzly steak.

Chandler and Fulton both refused Wolf's suggested appetizer, walrus tartar, served in a hallowed out walrus tusk, but Ken tried it. They watched the look on Ken's face, his eyes watering, as he munched on the blubber-like globule for what seemed like an inordinate amount of time. Fulton put her hands over her eyes in disbelief. Chandler just shook his head back and forth and grinned.

Finally, Ken gulped it down and gagged. "It's not bad," he announced. Brave Wolf was right. But it tastes more like tuna than chicken." A loud belch escaped from his throat and his face lit up with embarrassment.

The dinner conversation was consumed with Deino talk and military invasion. Ken's eyes widened as he viewed the pictures from his mom's camera. How awesome it would be if he and Meghan could possibly get close enough to see a live Deino, he thought as he clicked from picture to picture. The thought of danger was miles away as he finished the last section of whale meat.

179

Meghan Lastinger had printed out Noatak National Park's profile from Google and was scanning the map of Alaska she'd bought at a Barnes and Noble in preparation for the trip.

Her backpack, stuffed into the overhead compartment, contained a plethora of additional research papers she had gleaned from the New York Library to read on the plane. Her selection covered all the sciences relevant to Noatak National Park.

It was just like the teenager to gather in-depth research before she immersed herself into the realm of anything to do with science: ecology, biology, geology, botany, ornithology, herpetology, entomology, paleon-tology, and husbandry of every living and breathing animal, insect, bird, fish, and flora that lived in Noatak. The thought of seeing a real live herd of reindeer titillated her mind—but to see a live dinosaur in the flesh was an unheard of fantasy that she promised herself she had to see, regardless of the risk.

But Lastinger's interests focused on ecology. Saving the environment was the backdrop for her thesis that had secured an early decision from Yale.

She looked up from a printout on the ozone layer, and stared out the window at the thick, billowing cumulus clouds. In the distance, she thought she glimpsed a mountaintop, but it vanished when the jet flew into another thick cloud bank.

As the plane emerged into the cerulean sky on the other side of it, she saw it: the Alaskan horizon exploded with sharp-peaked mountains, some of them volcanoes with billowing smoke, gracing the landscape below with unending beauty. Then Mount McKinley came into view, towering over the others in majestic splendor, its snowcapped peaks daz-zling in the noon sunlight. She knew they were near Fairbanks and it would not be long before landing.

Thoughts of Ken filled her with excitement. They'd known each other for seven years, meeting in church school at Old Brick Presbyterian on Park and 92nd. It was fate, she'd told Ken, when they later both enrolled at Horace Mann, a private school on the west side of Manhattan.

Her mind drifted warmly over their relationship as she sat in her seat thinking back on what it was that attracted her to Ken: he was cute, yes, she thought, but it was his adventurous and independent spirit that really kept her on her cell phone sending a constant flow of romantic texts. He had a propensity to analyze and memorize details of obscure facts that always intrigued her. But, best of all, was comfort. He seemed to always be there for her, encouraging and challenging.

The flight attendant announced the preparation for landing and Meghan's reverie brought her back to the reality of what she was doing. Whatever happened on this trip, she knew, promised to bring excitement.

Danger was not even a remote consideration.

The flight out of Fairbanks to Kotzebue was on time and the small six-passenger green charter flight was there waiting for her when she landed, just as Ken had promised. And Ken was right, she loved the vivid green plane. Yes, she told herself, this trip was fate.

As the green charter pulled up to the yellow line at Noatak airport and stopped, Brave Wolf watched Ken push to the front of the small crowd and bolt across the tarmac before a security guard could stop him. Wolf stepped back into a shadow to observe the teenagers' warm embrace. It was as if the two were totally alone on the tarmac without a soul watching.

Ken slung Meghan's backpack over his shoulder. They locked arms as they walked toward the small airport. Wolf stepped out of the shadows, watching Meghan pointing toward the majestic Mt. St. Lincoln in the distance. Wolf could see the sweeping gestures of Ken's right hand as he told her about Noatak National Park.

"Meet Brave Wolf," Ken said.

"Ken texted me how excited he was to meet you." Meghan shook Wolf's hand and appraised him. "Now I know why. Thanks for picking me up."

When they walked through the small airport, Meghan excused herself to use the bathroom.

Ken turned to Wolf.

"What do you think?" he asked.

"Forthright and confident. I like her. And like you said—she's very cute."

"I knew you'd like her. Everybody likes her."

"Let's see what your mom thinks when Meghan walks through the door."

The peaceful look in Ken's eyes dissolved behind a mask of angst.

CHAPTER 31

Chandler sat in his living room nursing his second single-malt Glenmorangie. A warm fire of alpine wood blazed in the fireplace.

Fulton sat next to him, enjoying an extra dry martini, Ketel One, one olive. Chandler had hooked up Fulton's player to his forty-inch plasma screen and they were watching the footage Fulton had shot on their foray into the Fossil. The volume was on high.

When the room filled with the Deinos' first shriek, the windows rattled and the crystal vase atop the mantle seemed to move in place.

"Jesus Christ," Chandler said.

Fulton's eyes were riveted on the screen as she took a long sip of her martini. Just as the alpha male dashed into the clearing, confronting the helicopter, the front door of the cabin opened and Ken appeared, Wolf and Meghan behind him.

On the screen, the alpha male was displaying brilliant plumage and bellowing a deafening roar that filled the room with terror. Wolf and Ken took two steps back, inadvertently concealing Meghan.

Chandler clicked off the player and Fulton stood up.

"I'm glad you're back. I was worried."

"Gas at the pump. Had to wait on line to squeeze only five gallons from Charlie. Crazy times," Wolf complained.

"What the heck was that on the screen?" Ken asked in disbelief.

"What we saw in Noatak this afternoon," his mom said.

"Oh, my God."

Wolf now stood between Ken and Meghan, blocking Fulton's line of sight.

"Took Ken to the Inupiat reservation for the afternoon," Wolf said.

"It was dynamite, mom."

"I'm glad," Fulton responded.

Meghan stepped out from behind Wolf. "Hi, Mrs. Fulton," she said as if she'd just come from next door to ask for a cup of sugar.

"Meghan?" Fulton's voice registered her surprise. She embraced the teenager stiffly.

"I can explain," Ken said, his face flushing.

Wolf stepped toward him protectively.

Chandler, still holding the remote control, sat on the sofa, taking it all in. He took another pull on his Glenmorangie.

"Mr. Chandler, this is Meghan Lastinger," Ken said.

Meghan stepped toward the couch as Chandler rose to greet her. "Pleased to meet you," he said.

"Pleased to meet you, too." Meghan offered, then stepped back politely.

"Are your parents here?" Fulton asked.

"No."

"How did you get out here?"

"Several flights. This place is hard to get to, that's for sure," Meghan said in an effort to break the stiff silence.

"From New York?"

"She flew United from LaGuardia to Seattle," Ken explained, "then to Kotzebue, then to Noatak."

"Who picked her up at the airport?"

"Brave Wolf and I did."

"Nice of him." Chandler turned to Wolf. "Explains why you vanished at four o'clock."

"The boy needed a lift. I offered one."

Ken saw the muscles in her jaw tighten and knew his mom was putting it all together.

Fulton turned to her son. "You knew about Meghan coming here?"

"Yes."

"Even after you asked me if she could come out here with us and I said no, not this time?"

Ken's eyes shifted to Meghan and then sheepishly back to his mom. "Yes."

Fulton turned to Meghan. "Do your parents know you're here?"

"Not really. They're in South Hampton for the week."

"And so you took off out here to be with Ken?" Fulton said, the look in her eyes now showing her anger and disappointment.

"And to be with you, Mrs. Fulton. Ken and I thought that…"

"Your parents wouldn't leave you alone in New York City, Meghan. Even though you're eighteen, these are not safe times for anybody. Especially not with what's happening in the city now with the energy crisis."

"No," Meghan said. "You're right. They wouldn't."

"Who do they think you're staying with?" Fulton pressed.

"Julianna McGuire."

"Does Julianna know you're here?"

"Yes."

"So if your parents call Julianna and ask to speak with you, she lies? Is that the intent?" Fulton said crisply, her voice laced in building anger.

"Yes," Meghan said. "I thought that…"

Fulton held up her right hand, silencing Meghan, and turned back to her son. "I'd like a word with you privately, Ken."

Ken nodded, looking at Wolf for guidance. Wolf encouraged him with a single nod toward the bedroom door.

His mom motioned him to the bedroom on the right and walked in front of Chandler and Wolf, leaving them with Meghan, who stood rigid, her backpack still clutched in her left hand.

Ken followed his mom. The door was shut loud enough to confirm Fulton was pissed.

"I'm sorry, mom. It's my fault," Ken said. "She shouldn't have come here. It was my idea and I was wrong. I know that, but…"

Fulton walked in silence past her son over to the window staring at the snowcapped peak of Mt. Stimson, her back to him. When she spoke, she did not turn around to face him.

"For seventeen years, I've desperately tried to teach you the meaning of trust and integrity. The truth, for God's sake."

"I'm sorry, mom. I know what it is."

"Then why did you do this to me when you asked me if Meghan could join us out here? What did I tell you?"

"Not this time, you said."

"Correct. And yet you not only disobeyed me—you lied to me," Fulton said. "And so did Meghan. I have to call her parents, you know."

"Please don't. I disobeyed you, mom, but I didn't lie to you. I told you the truth. I could have lied," Ken said, remembering Wolf's advice.

"Don't be smart with me, Ken." Fulton turned around to face her son. "You think it's been easy raising a son without a husband all these years?"

"No, mom. And it hasn't been easy to go through my life without a father, either," said Ken, his eyes welling up in tears. "That was your choice, mom—not mine."

Fulton saw the tears in his eyes, and she saw something else for the first time: pain.

"I didn't have a choice, Ken." She fought back tears. "Your father left me. He just vanished out of our lives."

"But you could have…"

"Could have what?"

"Could have told me about him."

"I could have done nothing," she repeated. "I didn't even get a chance to tell him I was pregnant. He just disappeared."

Ken wiped the tears from his face and said, "Please don't call her parents. Let her stay, mom. I love her and she won't be any trouble. I promise."

"I've got to call her mom."

"Please don't."

"Jesus, Ken. I can't believe this. What the hell were you both thinking?"

Fulton stood still for a moment, thinking. She turned around to face the window again, staring at the mountains in the distance.

Ken stared at her. Then her shoulders began to shake. He heard her labored breathing and knew she was crying. He walked slowly up to her, putting both hands on her shoulders. He hesitated for a moment, then said, "I love you so much." He gently squeezed her shoulders and burst into tears.

Outside the closed door, Wolf had walked into the kitchen to fix himself a glass of ice water. Chandler had gone outside to inhale a long breath of cool mountain air. Meghan was listening at the bedroom door.

As Chandler reentered his home, the bedroom door opened. Fulton stood in silence at the doorway. Then a broad grin appeared on her face.

"I'm starving. Let's call for pizza," she said.

"It'll take a little longer. They don't deliver by car anymore. They bike it here," Chandler said shaking his head.

Ken walked to Meghan. "It's mom's idea you sleep in that room." He pointed to the other bedroom. "My mom and I'll be sleeping in the room with double beds." He gave her a quick hug and whispered in her ear. "Everything's cool."

"Is she calling my mom?"

"Everything's cool," Ken said yet again.

"Thank God!" Meghan said, with a relieved sigh.

Chandler picked up the phone. "Great idea on the pizza." He called Noatak's only Pizza store, the Sockeye Pizza shop.

Wolf came out from the kitchen. "Hold the anchovies," he said.

"I love anchovies," Ken said.

"So do I," Meghan added.

Fulton looked at Chandler.

"It's been a very long day. Could you make me another martini? One olive, only this time just a drop of vermouth, extra dry, not shaken."

Chandler passed in front of Fulton, heading toward the bar. He saw that her eyes were red.

"You did the right thing, Kimberly. I'm very proud of you," he said.

Fulton sighed. "You really think?"

He looked into her green eyes. "I know you did."

Fulton stood in front of the crackling fire, looking up at the massive caribou above the hearth, its antlers wide with sharp points, a Santa stocking hanging from one of the prongs. It brought her back to the flying Deinos, the sharp talons, the vicious jaws, screeches of horror, the dead Marines—and the fact that tomorrow she had to make the most convincing presentation of her life to the battalion. Could she save the rarest and most valuable living fossil of them all, *Deinonychus Antirrhopus*?

"Here's your martini. You okay?"

"Yes. Just uptight about tomorrow's presentation."

"You'll convince them. Especially after they see and hear the Deinos in action and the sound of the conch."

Wolf overheard the conversation and sidled up to them. "So the legend of the conch is true?"

"Indeed," Chandler said. "It works beautifully. They're terrified of the sound."

While Meghan was unpacking in her room, Ken Fulton had positioned himself off to the side of the adults. He managed to hear every word.

As the sun dropped below the mountain range off to the west, darkness enveloped Noatak.

The pizza was delivered. The five of them sat around the dining room table helping themselves, memories of beluga and walrus tartare fading with each bite.

The lights flickered three times, extinguished quickly, then came back on with a dull, shimmering glow.

"You have a generator?" Fulton asked.

"No," Chandler said. "I prefer candles." He stood up and lit seven, placing them strategically around the livingroom. With the fire ablaze in the hearth, the candles gave off enough light to cast an eerie glow upon their faces as if a séance was about to begin.

"Hard to believe that just east of here is enough fossil fuel to light up the world," Meghan said. "And yet here we sit without enough power to light up a single room."

"How did you know about the oil?" Fulton asked.

Meghan hesitated. "Ken told me. But I've been studying the dendrite networks of fossil fuel in the Bakkan shale range for years in my environmental studies. Alaska's loaded with oil. I knew it was a matter of time before they'd find the mother lode."

"An educated guess," Wolf said.

Her comment surprised Chandler and Fulton. "No wonder you got early acceptance to Yale," Fulton said raising her martini glass. "To education."

And the room burst into laughter.

"Thank you," Meghan said.

Ken beamed silently. Being cute helped, "but this one has it all," he'd told his mom. "She's a keeper."

CHAPTER 32

W̲O̲L̲F̲'S̲ S̲IKORSKY̲ L̲ANDED̲ I̲N̲ F̲RONT̲ O̲F̲ N̲OATAK̲'S̲ F̲ISH̲ & W̲ILDLIFE̲ A̲GENCY̲ headquarters. Chandler and Fulton spilled out of the helicopter with Ken and Meghan following.

As they entered the log cabin, Ken saw a row of ATVs parked on the left side of the cabin. There were five of them. They were all Polaris Sportsman XP 500s.

His eyes widened and he nudged Meghan on the way inside. "Look at that," he said. "ATVs."

His mom didn't hear him. "We should be back in a couple of hours, maybe less," Fulton said.

"We've got sodas in the refrigerator," Chandler said. "Television's over there in the cabinet, but reception sucks. Lots of maps and charts you might find interesting—especially the big one on the wall that shows the entire Park."

"So where's the Fossil River?" Ken asked.

Chandler pointed to it. "Here."

"Awesome. That's where you guys were, right?"

"Yes," Fulton said. "That's what the presentation's all about. Saving the Deinos."

"What about the oil?" Meghan persisted.

"That, too," Chandler added.

"Good luck," Meghan said.

"You'll be awesome, mom."

"Thanks. We'll be back soon."

Beneath a large olive-drab military tent, a battalion of 849 strike force Marines, twenty-seven of them women, sat silent in their chairs waiting for orders.

First, they would hear what Major Wong had promised to be a riveting presentation about the enemy.

In front of the Marines stood a ten- by twenty-foot screen flanked by two self-standing speaker systems. A slide and video projector system was connected to a PowerPoint presentation on Fulton's Toshiba laptop.

She'd tested the system earlier and everything worked. "I'm ready," she had told Chandler. "Bring them on."

Major Wong had arranged for a debriefing of all officers in the field, the high command of the Marine Corps in Noatak, to be held in his headquarters tent, prior to Fulton addressing the Battalion. "They don't want any surprises they can't answer for the troops," Wong had told Fulton and Chandler.

"It'll give me a practice run before the Battalion presentation," Fulton told Wong.

Fulton handled the request deftly with slides, video, and audio. There were many questions, but Fulton glibly answered each one with the confidence of a well-educated college professor.

It was enough proof to convince Brigadier General Robert Pine to recommend that Wong proceed with Fulton's presentation to the full Battalion. Colonels Jeff Fox and Laurie Cohen agreed. They also agreed that this alien-like creature gave valid reasons for more discussion about whether or not high command should order another invasion. They would reserve that judgment until after Fulton's presentation to the full Battalion.

"Our Marines' reaction to the enemy will play an important part in our decision," Pine had commented to his command team. "Losing one Marine is painful enough. Losing sixty-eight of our finest is over-the-top sacrifice."

As Fulton and Chandler walked into the tent, she said, "Scott, I don't feel comfortable leaving Ken and Meghan back there alone. Would you mind asking Major Wong if he could send someone back to Fish & Wildlife to look after them until we get back, please? Just until I'm done with the presentation."

"Sure," Chandler said. He walked over to Wong and made the request. The look on Wong's face was one of surprise. "She brought her kids with her?"

"Yes."

"Out here in Noatak?"

"Yes."

"But she's here on a mission for us and…"

Chandler interrupted Wong. "She's a single mom, Major. She had no choice, and it was the responsible thing to do. It is what it is. She's uncomfortable leaving them alone while she's here. Consider it a favor for her sacrifice being here."

Wong shrugged his shoulders, confirming the query presented a pain in the ass. "Let me check with the new Field Sergeant. I'll make sure he takes care of it."

"Thanks," Chandler said and he walked back to Fulton. "Done. You're a great mom, Kimberly. I like that about you."

"Appreciate it."

Marine Corporal Hank Rubin muttered silently to himself when the field sergeant asked him to double back to the F&W headquarters and look after two teenagers.

"You're off duty when Dr. Fulton finishes her presentation and returns to her kids. Keep them safe," the sergeant had told him. Rubin wanted to say, "Fuck that, Sarge. I'm a goddamn Marine, not a baby sitter," but he thought better of it.

The sergeant knew he was pissed and said, "Get on it, Marine. That's an order. Snap to."

Three people entered the tent from the rear, and Major Michael Wong stood at attention shouting, "Atten-hut!"

The entire Marine battalion rose to their feet and stood motionless as Defense Secretary Shawn Robinson walked to the front of the staging area and stood behind the podium facing the Marines.

Robinson gave a quick salute. "As you were," he commanded and they sat down in unison.

Secretary of the Interior Lauren Zollar entered, accompanied by Energy Secretary Tyler Conlon, discreetly positioning herself at the back of the room.

"Good morning, Marines," Robinson said.

"Good morning, sir," the Marines shouted back with a show of esprit de corps.

"Your Marine Commandant, General Gordon Hargraves, could not be here today because he's in Afghanistan overseeing our liason operators there. He's been fully apprised of your presence in Noatak National Park, and asked me to convey to you his thanks for your service to the Corps, our country, and to this mission. As all of you know, our nation's experiencing a crippling energy crisis. We've barely enough fuel to carry out our mission over there, and it has forced us to curtail our sorties and long-range ground assaults. Fortunately, within Noatak, our government has discovered the largest fossil fuel deposit in the world—twice the size of Saudi Arabia's Garwar deposit."

Someone from the back whistled and the Marines responded with applause.

Robinson nodded. "But as you've heard, we have a problem: how to get into the area where the fossil fuel field is without losing any more Marines. Only seventy-two hours ago, sixty-eight of our Marines were slaughtered by something in Noatak that's not yet been identified. We're hoping this afternoon to find out what kind of predator's living in there and take out the bastards.

To understand our enemy, we've got a curator from the Museum of Natural History in New York City, Dr. Kimberly Fulton. She flew into the area yesterday to confront and identify the predator. She'll show you the results of her trip into the Fossil River. But before I introduce her, I want to introduce one of our own, retired captain Scott Chandler. Would you please stand up and be recognized, captain?"

Chandler stood up, snapped a salute and said, "Thank you, sir."

"Captain Chandler's a helicopter pilot who served four tours in Iraq and Afghanistan, saving many of our troops. He's been awarded two Purple Hearts and a Bronze Star."

The Marines shouted, "Hoo-ahh," and stood up simultaneously and saluted Chandler.

"Captain Chandler works for Interior's Fish and Wildlife Agency," Robinson said. "He manages the Park's wildlife. He flew Dr. Fulton into the Fossil River area yesterday, and I understand they confronted the predator. Fortunately, they made it back here alive—unlike the Marines before them. It's of critical importance for each of you to listen carefully to her presentation. If President Barton issues the order to secure the Park, your lives will be in danger. So listen up." Robinson nodded to Dr. Fulton, who approached the podium.

Fulton picked up the laptop remote control and pressed the forward button.

The screen came alive with eight Deinos surrounding Scott's helicopter. With the volume on high, the sound of screeching filled the tent.

"Holy shit," someone said.

Fulton pushed the button again and the screen filled with a full-color still shot of the alpha male displaying its brilliant plumage.

"Good morning, ladies and gentlemen," said Fulton. "I have two objectives this morning: The first is to save your lives by convincing you we can get into the Fossil River area to tap the oil field without another strike. My second objective is to save and protect the colony of living fossils, the Deinonycus, while we harvest the oil. What you're looking at now is an alpha male in threat mode. It's a living wild dinosaur, and there's an entire colony of them thriving in a remote mountainous area of Noatak National Preserve on the south fork of the Fossil River.

"The dinosaur colony is protecting its territory that, unfortunately, happens to surround the fossil fuel field the government is targeting. This species is the link between dinosaurs and birds. Living proof, ladies and gentlemen, that the birds you see today flying around you are descended from dinosaurs.

It's name is Deinonychus Antirrhopus. Deinonychus is Greek for "terrible claw" and Antirrhopus for "counterbalance" because its tail can swish back and forth helping it turn on a dime as it pursues its prey by land or air. We saw one today negotiate a 180-degree turn in the blink of an eye. It's the most dangerous predator of the dinosaurs, and it hunts in packs, communicating with a series of high- and low-pitched screeches, chirps, and rasping sounds. The sound you heard before is as paralyzing as it is terrifying. Scott Chandler and I heard and saw it only forty-eight hours ago."

Fulton walked up to the screen and circled the talons, jaws, and wings with a large pointer.

"Its intelligence," she said, "is extremely high. It eviscerates its prey with these sharp talons. Then, when the life is drained out, it eats the remains with these razor sharp teeth. That's including the bones." She paused and looked at her audience. The Marines sat transfixed.

"It runs faster than a cheetah, over sixty miles an hour, climbs trees, has binocular night vision, and, over the past 100 million years, it has evolved enough feathers to give it lift. The wingspan is up to fifteen feet, which means it not only soars on the mountain air currents, but can go into a spiral death dive to seize prey or, hypothetically, avoid predators. Truthfully, there aren't any in nature. It is, ladies and gentlemen, the perfect zoological weapon of mass destruction and sits at the very top of the food chain."

Fulton paused and took a long drink of water. From the silence, Fulton knew she had her audience engaged.

"Major Wong informed me that Raven Drones were sent into the Fossil River area to survey. All three were taken out by this predator. The intelligence and stealth of these creatures also explains why they've probably killed four fly fishermen last year, killed six researchers when Scott Chandler flew them into Noatak to track the oil field, then butchered sixty-eight Marines only forty-eight hours ago. Nobody got out alive. I'm told the last Marine up the tether, Field Sergeant Major Roeder, got plucked off like a grape from a vine only thirty feet below the chopper. They can strike on the fly with incredible accuracy."

As Fulton spoke, the PowerPoint presentation continued to hum, reviewing on the big screen all the pictures and videos Fulton had taken on the trip into the Fossil, confirming with terrifying visuals that everything she was telling them was true.

"You're probably saying to each other that there's no way in hell that a battalion of Marines, equipped with the latest arsenal of cutting-edge weaponry, can't go in there and wipe out every last one of them." Fulton looked up and did not see any movement in the audience. She hesitated

195

for a purposeful minute, took another sip of water, then continued.

"You've seen the pictures, heard the soundtrack, seen the video, and you already know the loss of lives. Yet, you're still thinking that the United States is capable of wiping them off the face of the earth. Right? Wrong."

Fulton gripped the sides of the podium and studied her audience yet again. What she saw was utter disbelief. Marines were sitting on the edge of their chairs, mouths agape, eyes wide as if they had just seen an alien from another planet.

CHAPTER 33

Ken and Meghan had pored over Noatak's maps and charts for twenty minutes. Their excitement over the size and scope of the Park was building. Ken pinpointed the exact location, based on notes found on Chandler's desk, where his mom and Chandler had flown into Noatak's Fossil River area the day before last. When Ken found the longitude and latitude coordinates of the Fossil, his heart raced.

Meghan opened the front door of the F&W headquarters and peered outside at the line of parked ATVs. "Let's go for a ride," she said. "It's so beautiful out here." She hopped down three steps and stood next to an ATV.

Ken seemed hesitant. "I don't think it's a good idea."

"Why?"

"Because it's not safe, Meghan. That dinosaur's vicious—and it flies. What if it sees us?"

"I'm not suggesting we go close to the Fossil River, Ken. Just a joy ride. Look at the beauty of this place." Meghan swept her right hand across the mountain range in the distance. An active volcano rose above the mountain range with smoke spewing out of its cone. "I'm just suggesting we explore a little, not far." She pointed to the southeast at the four mountain peaks. "Over that way. Come on."

"My mom will lose it if we're not here when she gets back."

"You worry about her too much. We'll just take a short ride. We're almost adults, for Christ's sake. I've never been in one of these. They look neat. Come on."

Ken debated her plea.

"What, are you a wuss?"

"No. I just don't think…"

"You're a wuss, Ken! At least, let's check out what's beyond this clearing. It'll help me better understand what's at stake if the Marines go back in and ravage the Park. Let's go."

Ken walked down the steps, sidled up to the ATV and studied it. He'd always wanted to ride one, and now that he had the chance to do it the temptation was building. He stared at the controls.

"The key's in the ignition. Come on. Let's go for it. Blame it on me. Tell your mom I wanted to study the environment. It's true. I'll have a hcad start at Yale because of this. Start the engine."

"I'm thinking," he said. Ken was wait-listed at Williams, and had Wake Forrest for a backup. But he had no academic agenda, at least not yet.

"This is sick," he said. He'd studied the Polaris on Google, knew every detail, but his mother's lecture and disappointment in him still hung on his conscience like a shroud of bad news.

The thought passed, and he leaned on the Polaris studying the roll bars for safety, the digital fuel gauge filled to three quarters, odometer, tachometer, clock, all-wheel drive and the analogue speedometer with a top speed of fifty MPH.

"Awesome," he said. He looked at the engine. "Forty HP, 700 twin EFT. I have to admit this is cool, Meghan. The total package."

"Let's take it for a spin."

"It has IRS."

"Internal Revenue Service?" Meghan asked. "What the hell's that? What are you talking about?"

"Independent Rear Suspension," Ken chuckled.

Then Ken saw it: the GPS on the dashboard, its screen reading, OTSL, "On-The-Spot Location."

"Too cool," she said. "Come on, wuss. Let's go."

"Stop calling me wuss!"

He hopped into the seat and turned the key in the ignition. The engine roared to life. He flipped the toggle switch on the GPS on and plugged in the coordinates he had written down from the logbook on Chandler's desk. The system responded with a blur of motion as it calculated the detailed chart pinpointing the south fork of the Fossil River. But it was inaccessible, except by air. When the GPS had finished, a bleep sounded and Ken said, "Hang on. We're in. But we're not going near the River. Just part way, then we turn around."

"Let's go," Meghan persisted.

"My mom will kill us if we're not back in time."

"We'll make it back. Stop worrying." She leaned over and kissed his neck. "Maybe we can do it in the mountains."

Just the thought of it gave him a tingle. He kissed her. "Maybe," he teased. "But let's first get our backpacks and some food and water, just in case we get thirsty."

"Good idea," Meghan said.

They slid off the Polaris, engine still purring, and ran back into the F&W cabin searching the refrigerator for bottled water, food, and snacks.

"Bingo," said Meghan as she rifled seven energy bars off a shelf and stuffed them into her backpack.

Ken picked up his backpack and carefully checked the contents. The conch shell Wolf had given him was neatly packed at the bottom, wrapped in a green sweater. The thought occurred to him that he might have fun blowing it when they got farther into the mountain range. Meghan had not yet seen or heard it. He called out, "Did you bring a sweater, Meghan? It might get cold up there."

"Yes."

"Good."

As Ken passed Chandler's desk he saw a jar of matches and grabbed two packs, not really knowing what he might need them for. It seemed like a good idea. He unplugged his iPhone from the charger sitting atop the windowsill and slid it into his pocket. He went back to the refrigerator and grabbed four bottles of Poland Spring water and stuffed them into his backpack. He looked at his watch and said, "We have about an hour and a half left. Let's split."

Meghan was closing her backpack when an idle thought popped

into her mind. "Should I bring toilet paper?" she called out.

"We're not going to be gone that long. Go now if you have too."

"No. I'm good," she said. Then she changed her mind and went into the bathroom. When she finished, she peeled about three feet of toilet paper off the roll and stuffed it into her backpack. Easy for a guy, she thought, not so for a girl. They ran out the front door with such bounding energy that Meghan stumbled and almost fell down. Ken helped her up, then wriggled onto the seat and gripped the wheel. "What if it sees us?"

"What sees us?"

"The dinosaur."

"Will you let it go, Ken? Jesus. Come on, let's get outta here." She looked at her watch. "Less than an hour and a half now. We're not going that far. I never knew you to be such a worrier."

"I'm not a worrier. But that thing out there's dangerous and it flies. It eats people—killed all those Marines."

"So what do you want to do now? Not go for a ride?"

Ken looked at the Polaris dash, his eyes wide with possibilities. The sound of the engine teased his mind. In neutral, he stepped on the gas pedal and heard a grumble of power, took the brake off, and slammed the gear into low. The Polaris lurched forward and sped across the clearing, dust swirling behind them.

Corporal Rubin's quarter-ton jeep pulled up in front of the F&W cabin just in time to see a swath of swirling dust at the end of the clearing. He saw the line of ATVs parked in front of the building and thought the ATV in the distance might be the kids. He slid out of the jeep and ran quickly into the office. He called out, "Ken? Meghan?"

No answer. He ran into the two back rooms, checked the bathroom, looked out back through the large window and called out again.

No answer.

If he lost the kids on his watch, his ass would be in a sling. Rubin ran up to the first ATV and hopped onto the seat.

He thought quickly about taking his jeep, but he knew the ATV would be much better if the trailway narrowed and rocks and boulders blocked his way. The differential on the jeep was high, Rubin thought, but the Polaris could move around and through challenging areas much more easily. Rubin squealed away from the F&W cabin and gave chase.

Rubin tore through the end of the clearing. In the distance he could see a dust cloud from the other ATV. He looked down at the speedometer: 46 MPH. A mile behind, he guessed, maybe two, tops. He jumped up off the seat to avoid the impact of a mogul, his ATV airborne by three feet. He was glad he chose the Polaris.

He pressed the gas pedal to the floor. His senses filled with the sight of the afternoon sun lighting up the snowcapped peaks and the glistening tundra surrounding him.

Ahead, way off into the mountain range, he saw a fog bank hanging in a distant valley. It was, thought the Marine, a place from a different era.

Fulton took another long drink of water before continuing.

"When we landed near the south fork of the Fossil River yesterday, our mission was to identify the predator with pictures, audio, and video to prove this creature in Noatak exists. Scott Chandler had sent me blood samples, a talon, and some feathers. I ran tests back at the Museum of Natural History in New York, and they proved positive that the samples came from Deinonychus, a dinosaur raptor from the Cretaceous era. This, ladies and gentlemen, is an astounding discovery. But we had to get into Noatak and capture living proof. That mission was successful yesterday, and the answer is a definite yes. Deinonychus is the living link."

"We tested the sounding device to see if it worked. Had we not had the sound of this conch shell recorded and playing from outside the helicopter when we got to the Fossil, we would not be alive today."

Fulton held up the large conch. "The sound of the conch actually scares this predator away. I want to introduce Brave Wolf Whitman, Scott Chandler's colleague who works for the Fish and Wildlife Agency. Brave Wolf's relatives are native Inupiat born near Noatak. He will tell you about the Inupiat legend of the conch shell."

Wolf's now-familiar tale, including blowing the conch and sharing his pottery illustrating his people's beliefs, had the desired effect. The Marines were spellbound.

"Thank you, Brave Wolf," Fulton said. She pushed the remote control and the screen lit up with a live video of eighteen Deinonychus predators encircling the helicopter, threatening.

The alpha male burst onto the video field and took center stage, commanding the others with a screech so loud that the Marines were disoriented. Some of them sat back in their seats in utter shock; others turned away from the screen in disbelief.

Then the video shifted to an inside shot of the chopper cabin as the sounding device was hooked up and the speakers were strung outside the chopper's hatch window.

Fulton pointed to the speaker system. "Watch what happens when the system's turned on," she said

The Marines sat in silence as the sound of the conch shell echoed across the clearing and the Deinos vanished, nine of them taking to flight, the others bounding off into the mountain woods.

Fulton took another long drink of water, flipped to the next picture and said, "This is a shot of the terrain showing the creature and the surrounding rugged mountain forest. Note the size of the trees. They knew we were there the moment we landed. For some strange reason, maybe the oil, the climate at this altitude is temperate, not cool like it should be this time of year. The foggy mist, we call it vog, consists of volcanic gases that hover on the ground. Because of volcanic activity beneath the earth's crust, the water flowing out of the Fossil River is almost hot, like the Fire Hole River in Yellowstone Park, Wyoming. The large native fish caught in both of these rivers are actually warm to the touch, yet they thrive. There are, believe it or not, large coniferous specimens growing up there that thrived back in the Cretaceous era. The area surrounding the Fossil River truly is a lost world."

"This is fucking incredible," a Marine said.

"Watch them now. Look at the one in the center. See how they're trying to confuse us. The one in the center's going to feign an attack. Listen to the different sounds they make while orchestrating a unified assault."

The alpha male charged their position but halted twenty yards in front of them, leaping into the air and screeching.

"Why doesn't he shoot the fucker?" a Marine in the back asked.

Chandler wanted to say something but held his comment.

"Ladies and gentlemen, this is an unprecedented opportunity to experience a living dinosaur species in the wild. We have over 500 pre-historic species today throughout the world—but this is the only live dinosaur. Truly a miracle, and it must be protected."

It was the first time she'd mentioned saving the creature, and Robinson and Conlon shifted uncomfortably in their chairs. Zollar breathed a sigh of relief. Maybe the crown jewel of Interior's park system would be spared after all, she thought.

Fulton flipped through a sequence of photos and videos until she got to the end of her presentation. "This is the last shot before one of the Deinos landed on top of our helicopter. The entire chopper shook when it clung to our rotor blades. It glided in from behind us. Note the faint shadow in the picture. That's the Deino in flight before it struck the copter."

There was an audible sigh of disbelief from the Marines who sat motionless in a state of collective awe.

"Take them out," someone in the front yelled.

"Kill the fuckers," someone shouted from the back. "They killed our Marines. I say kill them all."

"As you were, soldiers," Major Wong stood up.

"Not so easy," Fulton said. "The colony is protecting their territory. It happens to be the exact location of the fossil fuel deposit. I know there's consideration to launch a second invasion to wipe out the pred-ator force, but I urge restraint. First, you're risking your lives against a hunting pack of the world's most aggressive predators, and you've already seen what happened to sixty-eight of your Marines. With all your firepower and military technology, not one of them got out alive."

"What happened when we turned the conch sound device on? The Deinos vanished."

"And you got out alive," a woman shouted from the left side of the audience, obviously in favor of not going back in there.

Fulton was relieved. That was the reaction she wanted to hear.

"Precisely," said Fulton. "Because we proved, just as they were about to attack, that the sound of the conch scares them away. It associates the sound from the conch as extreme danger. We've proven it works. What we're suggesting here is that simply by employing the sound of the conch, we can cause the predators to leave us alone.

"Ladies and gentlemen, we can go in there tomorrow and, as long as the sound of the conch is heard, we can tap into the fossil fuel and save this rare colony from extinction at the same time. Not one life will be lost and you'll not be destroying the ecology and the wildlife in America's most beautiful public park. We must protect this species, save your lives, and still be able to tap into the oil supply."

"But we'll have power again. Electricity and gasoline," a Marine lieutenant called out. "Fuck the public."

Major Wong thought about reprimanding his Marines from further outbursts, but concluded it was important to let them vent.

"We want lights in our homes and gas in our cars. How else can we survive?" a Marine shouted from the second row.

Major Wong shook his head and stood up again. "As you were, Marines!" he ordered. "As you were!"

The audience silenced.

Fulton entertained a few questions, then thanked the Marines for listening and left the podium.

Secretary of Defense Robinson took her place. "Thank you, Dr. Fulton. It may be very difficult to believe that there's a live dinosaur colony living inside Noatak National Park. But after Dr. Fulton's presentation this morning, I have to say pictures and videos don't lie. Admittedly, it will be a tough call to send our Marines back into the area to destroy the creatures, knowing how many we've already lost. I thank Dr. Fulton, Scott Chandler, and Brave Wolf Whitman for their time and their risk of life for enlightening us today. I will confer with President Barton and get back to your company commander within twenty-four hours. Until then, stand ready. Thank you."

The Marines broke into a round of applause and stood up as Dr. Fulton walked out of the tent with Chandler and Wolf.

Major Wong stood at attention. "Marine Corps, atten-hut!" he barked as Robinson, Conlon, and Zollar exited the tent behind them.

When the three of them got outside, Conlon looked at Robinson. "We've no time left, Shawn," he said. "We're tapping the bottom of the barrel now. Before the week's out, the entire nation will be out of oil. Our transportation and your military's mobility will be paralyzed."

CHAPTER 34

Ken pulled the ATV atop a plateau and slammed the gear into neutral, shimmering heat rising off the engine cowl.

"Why are you stopping?" asked Meghan. "Keep going."

"No way. This is as far as we go. Any closer and we're in danger," Ken said.

Meghan pointed to the next mountain ridge, less than a mile away. "Go to the next ridge so I can get a view of the valley on the other side. I've never seen a live glacier or been this close to an active volcano. Ultra cool. According to the map, there's one on the other side of that ridge. I want to take a picture. Then we can turn around."

"No. It's too close to the Fossil River, Meghan, and we've taken an ATV without permission. We're screwed if we don't get it back in time. We never should have done this. Damn," he said disappointed in himself for giving into the temptation of it all.

"I can't believe you Ken. Jesus. You are a wu…" Meghan stopped in mid-sentence. She tilted her head over her right shoulder. "You hear that?"

"No," Ken said. "Hear what?"

When Meghan turned around in the ATV trying to get a fix on the sound, and how far away they had traveled from the F&W log cabin, she saw a speck of something in the distance. It was moving toward them fast.

205

"Somebody's chasing us," she shouted. "Go."

Ken hesitated, fear flashing across his eyes. Meghan sensed he was paralyzed, but he wasn't. He was weighing options—and none of them seemed promising.

Ken slapped the palm of his hand on the gearshift and the ATV lurched off the plateau in a lunging charge toward the next mountain ridge. Driving the ATV had become more challenging to Ken with the passing of each bend in the rock-laden road, which had narrowed into a path just wide enough for its passage. He was struggling to keep up the speed as well as to avoid turning the vehicle over on the hairpin turns he was negotiating.

"Who is it?" Ken shouted back.

Meghan turned around again and squinted to see through the dust swirling behind them. She almost fell off the vehicle as Ken turned sharply to the right, then left, then into a bumpy washboard straight-away filled with sharp rocks and boulders. Meghan gripped the side bar. "I don't know, but they're gaining on us. Speed up."

Ken pushed the gas pedal to the floor and the ATV seemed to be air-borne, gliding from mogul to mogul, bouncing off small rocks, ridges, and stumps.

"I can't go any faster, Meghan. Too rocky," Ken said.

"He's gaining."

"Is it my mom?"

"No. It's a man."

"Who?"

"I can't see. Too much dust."

"Is it Scott Chandler?"

"I don't think so. I don't know."

"What's he wearing?"

"I can't see."

Ken's knees were bent as if he were skiing down a double diamond slope, foot on the gas pedal, bouncing back and forth, up and down, as the ATV wound its way through the dense mountain forest, climbing higher at one point, then dipping into a deep gulch, then rising sharply up a slant so steep Ken thought they might fall over backwards.

Corporal Rubin knew he was losing ground behind the ATV in front of him because he lost sight of the vehicle when it vanished over a distant ridge into a deep valley. He didn't see it emerge on the opposite bank. His foot pressed the gas pedal to the floor and his vehicle responded, wheels spraying chunks of dirt and rock behind him. Then he had an idea: shoot a couple of rounds of bullets into the air to scare them into stopping.

Rubin pulled his M1911A1 .45 Caliber pistol out of his holster and fired three shots into the air, hoping the report would cause them to stop.

"That'll scare the shit out of them," he muttered. They'll stop now for sure, he thought. The shots rang out across the mountain, breaking peaceful silence with a punch.

"Jesus Christ. He's shooting at us. What the hell for?" Ken shouted.

"He's gaining, Ken. Hurry."

"What's he want?"

"I have no clue, but I'm scared." Her voice was shrill. "He's going to kill us."

Ken's heart was racing in his chest. "Maybe we should stop and turn around," he said. "Find out what he wants."

"No. Faster, Ken. He shot at us, for God's sake," she pleaded. "Floor it."

The ATV was moving toward a sharp precipice dead ahead then, beyond it, a massive wall of glacial rock seemed to explode out of the earth like a giant tombstone. A slab of glacier spilled down the valley to their right.

"He's got us. We're trapped." As Ken slammed the automatic transmission gear into low, the ATV lurched up mountain and seemed to hang atop a large oval boulder, wheels spinning in place.

"Lean forward, Meghan," Ken commanded, and the quadrunner came off the rocky fulcrum. Its front and rear wheels tore into the earth, sending the vehicle into wild gyrations that propelled them forward.

Meghan, hanging onto the roll bar with clenched fists, spun around for another look at their pursuer. "He's a hundred yards behind us. Faster! Please!"

Then she looked back again and saw something soaring behind the other ATV, swooping down. It seemed huge, with a wingspan wider than the dirt path. It glided close, its talons extended, jaws snapping. Meghan threw her head back and gave a guttural scream of terror that filled the air with such dread that Ken lost grip of the wheel.

They careened down a thin steep pass, pine branches snapping and slapping at them with stinging sharpness.

Then they heard a hideous screech that made Meghan's scream seem like a baby's whimper.

Their ATV flipped over before coming to a sudden lurching stop against a large hemlock stump on the right side of the narrow passage. Ken and Meghan were pinned beneath its chassis, which poked out over a 100-foot-deep ravine.

"Shhhh," Ken whispered. "I'm okay. Are you?"

"I think so."

Ken felt liquid dripping on his forehead. It had a strong smell, and was warm.

Then he heard a noise above them, outside the protective ATV frame that arced over them like a turtle shell. The Polaris roll bar had saved them from disaster.

Ken could hear his heart beating in his chest. "Don't move," he said. Drip, drip, drip.

"I can't." Lying on her back, Meghan's eyes were wide as saucers as she peered out from beneath the ATV. She could see the sharp drop. Her right shoulder was resting on the cliff's edge, which was sharp and cutting. "It's out there," she whispered, "Did you hear that?"

Ken pulled her close to him and whispered, "Yes. Shhhh. Don't shift your weight."

CHAPTER 35

A FEELING OF SUCCESS WASHED OVER FULTON LIKE A WARM BLANKET AS Chandler lauded her presentation.

"Incredible, convincing, riveting, and terrifying" were the four words he used to describe the impact of her delivery on the Marines, who stood outside the large olive-drab umbrella tent after her presentation.

Chandler saw Secretaries Robinson, Zollar, and Conlon off to the side of the flow of Marines still spilling out of the tent into the clearing. They were engaged in what appeared to be a debate. Major Wong was in the group too, shaking his fist in a circular motion.

Fulton broke his focus. "I've got to get back to Ken and Meghan."

Chandler nodded. "Of course," he said. "And I'm sure the Marine babysitting them can't wait to get out of the gig."

Seven Marines in a tight circle were talking under a large cedar tree, its feathery branches spreading out over them like tendrils. They were rehashing Fulton's presentation and, as they walked past, Chandler and Fulton were sucked into the fold. Fulton tugged on Chandler's prosthetic arm. "We can't wait too much longer, Scott. The kids are expecting us back."

A Marine sergeant waved at Fulton. "Incredible presentation—but how can this shit be real?"

"You saw the pictures, heard the video? It's real," Fulton shot back resolutely. "All of it."

"If it was all a hoax," Fulton added, "Sixty-eight of your Marines would still be alive. This shit you reference is real."

She looked down at her watch. What else could convince them? Then she reached into her field pack and pulled out the evidence. She had decided not to use it in front of the large audience because it could not be seen or appreciated except up close.

It was the eight-inch talon with the dried blood and feathers attached to it. The stench that wafted into the air when she pulled it out of her backpack was convincing enough. It brought an instant reaction from the Marines.

"This is what you're dealing with, Marines, if you go back in there," Fulton said. "It can slice and dice viscera into jelly with one stroke. Then your mind goes blank. But your eyes stay open and take it all in, seeing the way this predator rips your body apart and eats you alive."

Fulton extracted one more piece of evidence and held it out to the Marines. It was a three-inch, dagger-like dinosaur tooth. She swiped it across the thigh of her jeans. It tore a neat three-inch slice through the fabric. Fulton winced as a streak of bright red blood shown through her torn jeans, a sacrifice she was willing to make to drive home the reality that all of it was true.

Chandler stepped back. "Jesus," he said. "You didn't have to do that."

"Yes I did, Scott. They had to see it to believe it. I don't think any of you want to meet this creature face to face even if you had a grenade in your hand with the pin pulled," Fulton said.

As she finished her last sentence, six Marines backed away from her and walked off, leaving only the Marine who'd challenged her.

Shaking his head, he said, "Unbelievable, lady! It's really true isn't it? Dinosaurs in Noatak-fucking-Park!"

Fulton took two steps into the Marine's space. "It's all fucking true, soldier. Every last word of it." The sergeant took a step back. "You don't want to be in the food line when this baby's hungry."

Chandler was shaking his head in disbelief. The Marine towered above her an easy foot, and yet she stood her ground. He'll spread the word fast, Chandler thought, and it won't be rumor. It'll be hard fact spread like falling dominos through the entire battalion before sunset.

He shrugged his shoulders. What an incredible woman. She wasn't like this back in college.

When they pulled up to the F&W headquarters, Wolf was standing on the front steps. From the look on his face Chandler knew something was wrong.

Fulton got it out first. "Where're the kids?"

"I don't know," Wolf said. "Two of our ATVs are missing."

Chandler looked over his shoulder at his Sikorsky.

Fulton said nothing as she walked past Wolf into the cabin. She searched the office, the back rooms, then the small kitchen off the large office quarters looking for any sign that would assuage her growing concern. Nothing. Her heartbeat quickened. What concerned her most were their backpacks. She remembered Ken and Meghan placing them on the red leather couch that sat squarely in front of two office desks, Chandler's and Wolf's, and they were missing. Not a good sign.

She tried to control herself, but the worst crept into her mind. When she approached the front door to exit, she burst outside.

"Call the major now, Scott. We have a big problem. They're gone. Tell him his Marine is missing, too. Hurry, please."

Wolf stood there watching her reaction, instinctive as a mother bear chasing after her cubs. This woman was claws out and ready to attack, and he knew she was about to lose it.

Wolf went inside to make the call. He was thankful he'd given Major Wong the matching transceiver he held in his hand: an ICOM IC92 five-watt submersible. It was capable of sending a signal up to fifteen miles, even through the mountains.

Wolf pressed PTT (Push-To-Talk). "Major Wong. Brave Wolf here. Over."

"Reading you loud and clear, Brave Wolf. Over."

"We have an urgent problem, sir. Your Marine, Sergeant Rubin, is missing—and so are the two teenagers. We need your help."

"Christ," Wong said, his voice full of concern. All he needed was another crisis, with the Secretary of Defense, Shawn Robinson, still in the encampment and due to leave in less than an hour.

"Any idea where they've headed?"

"Two of our ATVs are missing," Wolf said. "They're both two-seaters. My guess is the kids took off for a joyride in one of them and your sergeant took off after them in the other when he discovered they were missing."

Wolf heard F&W's Sikorsky power up. Chandler and Fulton were already on board. "We're heading out to search for them in our helicopter now. If you can send a couple of more choppers to aid in the search, we'll stand a better chance of finding them before dark."

"Affirmative," said Wong. "ASAP. Copy?"

"Roger that. Tell the pilots to use our F&W frequency so we've got contact. Over and out."

Every second counted. A Marine battalion was on the verge of a second invasion unless Defense Secretary Robinson and President Barton bought into Fulton's sound device strategy to gain access to the oil field.

Two teenagers missing could stall the entire project.

"Over and out." Wolf clipped the ICOM back on his belt and dashed out the door to the awaiting chopper. The moment he closed the hatch, the Sikorsky lifted off the ground and swept over the clearing, over the vast pine tree pack, and headed southeast, toward the four snow-capped mountain peaks in the distance.

CHAPTER 36

W<small>HEN THE ACCIDENT HAPPENED AND THEY WERE PINNED UNDER THE</small> ATV, Ken and Meghan were happy to be alive. Ken was also relieved when he swiped his index finger across his face to find out what was dripping onto his forehead and streaming down his cheeks—oil from the engine.

Ken was holding Meghan in a tight bear hug when he heard the wind from flapping leathery wings as a Deino landed, not 20 feet from their wreck.

There wasn't much time. As the viscous liquid, still warm from an overheated engine, continued to drip onto his forehead, Ken began rubbing it all over his face, ears, neck, bare arms, legs, and every exposed crevice of his body. Meghan didn't resist when he motioned for her to do the same. She quickly cupped a free hand under the syrupy spill, and spread Pennsylvania twenty wt. oil over all exposed body parts.

Oil. Created from the ancestors of what was now breathing and thriving in Noatak National Park. A creature that would gladly devour them now if it had a chance.

There was a snort, a cricket-like purring, then the puffing. It was sniffing the ground, moving closer.

What was it doing outside its territory? Ken knew it was confused, or maybe curious—or just maybe it knew its next prey was nearby, beneath the wreckage. But the human scent was diffused by the strong smell of oil, and the creature's brain was trying to sort it out. As it approached the ATV, a thin veil of human scent filled its senses. Enough to make it hesitate. It stood fast, processing the scent as if mesmerized by the oil containing the spirits of its ancestors.

Very close—less than two feet away now—and what human scent it had taken in moments ago had vanished in the strong engine oil scent.

Then Ken heard a slow scratch that sounded at first like the squeak of chalk against a slate.

Ken knew what it was. He'd held the eight-inch talon of the alpha male in his hands along with the feathery knuckles that his mom had given him to experience the smelly reality of it all.

The Deino was scratching the underbelly of the ATV, exploring every square inch of the steel chassis.

They had to be smelling oil constantly, every day, every hour, every second. It was their territory, part of their environment. If they were smeared with oil, Ken prayed, they would blend in.

The dinosaur kept sniffing. Then it nudged the chassis, enough to lift it up six inches off the ground. Ken's mouth was up against Meghan's ear when he whispered, "Close your eyes. Don't let it see your eyes. Do not look. Do not move."

Meghan could hear her pulse, hear Ken's breathing, hear the irritable scratching of icepick-like talon against steel, and the purring click of a thousand crickets. Suddenly, the Deino lifted the chassis higher and its yellow squinting eyes peered beneath the wreckage. It snorted air, cocking its head like a mad dog treeing a raccoon.

It was cogitating, Ken thought, because it hesitated. Long enough to somehow reason there was no threat, maybe no food. Its jaws were under the wreckage and Ken could feel its hot breath on his face. The smell was ugly and he choked off a cough, gritting his teeth and holding his breath.

Meghan felt his body tense and knew it was close. Too close. She held her breath too, but screaming was only a breath away, maybe the next. The scent of engine oil filled the air around them like a cocoon protecting a chrysalis.

With enormous relief, they heard the sound of a helicopter in the distance. As the helicopter passed over their position, Ken wanted to dash out from under the ATV, wave his arms and scream for help. But he couldn't—not when they were pinned down at the door of death by a dinosaur.

Nothing awesome about this now, no way, thought Ken.

The Deino looked up into the sky, saw the helicopter circling above it, and opened its massive jaws. A sound came out that caused Ken and Meghan's skin to prickle and the hair on the back of their necks to rise.

The Deino held its ground like a vulture in the middle of the road hovering protectively over carrion, watching the helicopter pass over, its massive wings cupped over the ATV, camouflaging the chassis.

Instinct controlled the predator's senses. The will to survive dominated its reason. It had come out of its mountain lair to tread outside its territory for the first time because the colony was now at risk. Sentinels had been dispatched to defend its borders surrounding the oil field.

It was the first time the Deinos had breached the perimeter.

"Those little devils," said Robinson when Major Wong told him about the missing teenagers and Sergeant Rubin. "What the hell are they doing in the Park?"

"I don't know, sir."

"Find them and get them the hell out of there before I send in the whole battalion. Shit," Robinson said. "Our entire nation is about to go down the tubes and a couple of fucking kids throw a wrench into our plans. Hell, it's a bomb, not a wrench. God damn it to hell. Use as many choppers as you need to find those undisciplined brats. And, when you find them, bring them to me. I'll set them straight. Now I've got to cancel my flight plans and stay here. Major, get me President Barton on the phone."

"Yes, sir."

"Get them the hell out of the Park. Now."

Chandler dropped the helicopter down low as they tried to follow a small dirt passage that had been wide enough for a jeep to pass through two miles back, but was now a narrow ATV path that vanished into the thick mountain underbrush.

"I don't see anything, yet," Chandler said. "Do the kids know where the dinosaurs are?"

"Yes, I think so," Fulton said. "I remember telling them about the Fossil River. They asked me a lot of questions. Ken might have seen my map. I had circled the area where the oil field and dinosaurs are, and you circled it on the big map. Remember?"

"Yes," said Chandler. "Unfortunately."

"Ken doesn't forget details like that."

"Not good, Kimberly. That's probably where they're headed," Chandler said.

"Don't say that, Scott. You don't know." Fulton leaned forward, her eyes stinging from staring through the bubble glass, searching for any sign of life. She thought she'd seen something ten minutes ago, but it turned out to be a cairn, a pile of rocks built up into a cone to mark a long forgotten mountain trail.

"Where else could they have gone?" Fulton asked. "We've got to find them before dark."

Her voice broke, and Chandler saw tears in the corner of her eyes. He reached over and touched her hand. She took it and squeezed as if it were a lifeline. "We'll find them, Kimberly." He wasn't sure they would, but he said it anyway hoping to give her a modicum of hope. "I don't think they can get there on foot. The cliffs are too high."

Wolf took in a 180-degree sweep of the land below, then looked north. "We've got help," he said. "A dozen Bell Vipers, two o'clock high. Coming in fast."

"They see us," Chandler said. He swung the microphone piece toward his mouth and pressed the talk button. "This is Glacier-Kilo-two-niner-five-Foxtrot. You copy? Over."

"Roger that, Glacier-Kilo-two-niner-five-Foxtrot. Lead chopper here. We've got a visual on you. I'll coordinate the search from our end. Over."

"Affirmative. Over."

"We've been following a trail branching out from the F&W cabin. Just lost sight of it. Narrows down into an obscure path. Dropped down low to follow it, then we lost it. Over."

"Roger. We'll search the southeast slope then swing over the Fossil River. Two hours to sunset. We've got to work fast. Have the heat-seeking equipment on. Anything alive down there, we'll find it. Over."

"Got mine on, too. Nothing yet. We'll do a sweep over the big glacier ridge at the end of the trail around the volcano. Map shows an escarpment, then a higher ridge down range. I don't think they can get back there on foot. If they get up there, it'll be tough to track them from the air. Over."

"Affirmative. We'll keep in touch. God speed."

"Let us know if you get onto a track. Over and out."

The Sikorsky helicopter split from the approaching formation of Marine Bell Vipers. Chandler pushed his chopper down into a culvert, then up and over a sharp ridge and down again into a hanging valley. A herd of caribou scattered. By the time he circled the area twice, the sun was low on the horizon.

The look on Fulton's face betrayed tension and desperation.

Wolf saw something else: fear. He touched her shoulder. "They're alive."

Fulton turned around and said, "How do you know that?"

Wolf was about to answer her question when he pointed out the port window. "Down there," he said. "See it?"

Chandler swooped down and hovered one hundred feet off the rough terrain. Now they could spot what was left of a thin, almost invisible trail. There was a speck of something dark amidst pine-green foliage. To the right of it was a sheer drop-off into a deep ravine.

"I see it," said Fulton, with hope in her voice. "What is it?"

"An ATV," Wolf said. "Look fifty yards behind it. There's another one."

What Wolf didn't say was that both of them looked like they had been dropped off a ten-story building.

"Can you land in there?" Fulton said, pointing at what looked like a small clearing cluttered with large boulders.

"Too tough." Chandler scoured the area for any stretch of flat land. There was no clear place to set down. "It's not safe."

"We have to," Fulton pleaded. "Please try."

CHAPTER 37

Ken and Meghan heard the helicopter.

It seemed to hover, then circle, hover again, then circle again. What's taking them so long? Ken thought. Land, for God's sake. Land and save us.

He wanted to get out from under the ATV and throw his arms up in desperation and shout, but the thought of the Deino still out there somewhere held him in check.

After the deafening screech, the creature had vanished—or maybe it hadn't. Just maybe it was still out there lurking. The oil on their bodies, he knew, had saved them. But what now? Meghan was clinging to him, terrified to let go.

"We're okay, Meghan," Ken kept whispering softly. "We're going to make it. Shhhh. Shhhh. They're right above us."

But that was five minutes ago, maybe ten. The helicopter had changed its position and the sound of the engine was off somewhere to the south of them.

"Over there," Wolf said. "To the right of the larch tree. Looks possible."

Chandler drifted the Sikorsky over the spot. "Might be enough room for the blades to clear. It's a close call."

Fulton looked down and studied the mangled wreckage. "They can't be alive," she cried.

"I think that's the Marine's ATV, not the kid's," Chandler said.

"How do you know?" cried Fulton.

Wolf pointed to a limb poking from beneath the wreckage, a Marine's mottled camouflage pant leg.

Fulton held her head in the palms of her hands. "They're both dead," she moaned. "I just know it."

Chandler followed the narrow ATV path that ran straight along the top of a narrow ridge, then plummeted down hill in a sharp slant to a rocky ledge. At the bottom of it, Chandler hovered his craft staring at a basin empty of water that he guessed was once a catch pool for a waterfall, now dry. "It'll work," Chandler declared as he pushed a GPS button to mark the spot for landing.

Fulton looked up. "Can we land there?"

"Yes," Chandler confirmed.

"Thank God," Fulton said.

"It's a tough climb back up to the ATVs—but it's our only chance to reach them on foot."

"Do it," Fulton said.

"Kimberly," Wolf's voice was low and confident. "Your son is alive, and the girl is, too. Their ATV was turned over, but it had a roll bar. The other one was crushed. The Marine's dead, but the kids are still alive."

"Could they still be trapped beneath the wreckage?" she asked.

"Maybe. Hard to tell. They're probably long gone."

"Where could they go?" she said.

"We don't know yet, but we'll find out soon enough," said Wolf.

As the helicopter slowly descended toward the empty basin, Chandler took stock of provisions. Thank God, he thought, he'd put the sound device back into the chopper when they loaded up. The stash of provisions he kept on board were stuffed in the back compartment but it had been a long time since he had taken inventory: food, water, flashlights, First-Aid kits. Knives and matches, too, he remembered.

The landing bars of the craft tapped the rocky basin and Chandler turned off the engine.

"We stay tight," Chandler said. "Gather up our supplies and let's go for it. I'm out first, Brave Wolf second. Kimberly, follow Wolf. Understood?"

They nodded and gathered their gear. Chandler opened the hatch. And heard the crickets.

On the last pass, the sound of the chopper engine was very loud. Ken knew it was low. He also guessed they had spotted their ATV, maybe the other one too. But then the helicopter swept away and the sound of the droning engine slowly ebbed until there was nothing. Nothing except the soft sound of the mountain breeze and the awful sick feeling creeping through Meghan's stomach.

Ken sensed there was something wrong and said, "Shhh. Shhh. You okay?"

"No."

"Neither am I—but we're going to make it."

Then they waited, their eyes straining to see outside from beneath the Polaris' overturned chassis. Nothing was moving save for the wind, which was steady out of the west. Not even a twig breaking. Silence.

It seemed like two hours, but it was only minutes since the drone of the chopper engine ceased. They emerged from beneath the Polaris. Ken slid out first, his arms, legs, and face pitch black from the oil.

Then came Meghan, Ken pulling her by the arm to help her slither over the rough mountain turf until she was free. The moment they stood, their plan was in motion.

Crouching down on their knees, they ran into the evergreen thicket covering the left side of the narrow path. They waited a few minutes, then were up again on the run, weaving back and forth tree to bush, bush to tree, listening for any sound that might alert them to danger.

The sun was a ball of crimson yellow as it touched the tip of Mount St. Lincoln and slid behind the mountain. Meghan shivered.

"Put your sweater on," Ken whispered, pulling his out of the backpack. Then he changed his mind. It was bright orange.

"Wait. Don't put it on yet. Not until dark. It might blow our cover. We got out of there because of oil on our skin. Let's not cover our skin until it's safe. Wait until dark."

"It'll never be safe, Ken. How're we going to survive? They're all over the place. In the air, up in the trees, on the ground—and they know we're here. They must know we're here by this time."

"I don't think they do, Meghan," Ken whispered. "Or if they do, the oil on our bodies makes us blend in. If they did know, we'd be dead. That's for sure." For the first time since the accident he looked at her and grinned.

"What's so funny?"

"I've never met a black redhead. You're really cute."

Meghan didn't laugh. "There's nothing funny about this. We could be dead by nightfall."

They burst out from behind a large boulder and ran in a jagged dash down mountain, then up a sharp embankment that lead toward a massive wall of rock seeming to rise up and touch the sky.

They worked their way around the massive glacial wall checking each crevasse for a passage.

Nothing. They kept inching their way around it, backs pressed to the wall so they could keep their eyes on the landscape out ahead of them. Stopping, listening, then moving forward, sidestepping, always conscious of crouching down low if they saw movement or standing bolt upright behind trees that had rooted up against the massive wall.

Then they heard something. Off in the distance, faint at first, now stronger: Helicopters. Many of them coming straight at them across the hanging valley below.

Ken counted fifteen. The sky was black with them, flying low over the mountain canopy of thick pines, spotlights now penetrating the thick forest as dusk settled in and the air chilled.

At one point, they hovered in unison for a brief moment, then swept up and over the sharp wall of rock, their spotlights fanning the massive wall. Ken wanted to scream. Wanted to run out from the rock wall and wave a sweater, but to be exposed out in the open, away from the protection of the wall and its dark green forest undergrowth that crept up the edifice he knew would be a death trap.

Instead, he and Meghan held firm against the rock wall until the sound of engines faded off into the distance somewhere above them.

As the sun set, dusk made it harder to see, and they groped their way,

221

hugging the vast wall hoping to find someplace to hide for the night. Then they heard something again, but it wasn't a helicopter. Off in the distance, they heard a familiar sound, and with it a burst of hopeful adrenalin surged through the teenagers as the faint sound of a conch shell bellowed its protective alarm across the valley below. It was faint, very faint, but Ken recognized the distinct sound.

"Answer it, Ken," pleaded Meghan. "Let them know we're alive."

"Shhh," Ken said. They crouched down against the rock wall. Ken opened his backpack and pulled out his conch. The sound of the distant conch seemed to ebb and flow on the wind currents that blew out of the west. One moment it filled their space as if it were a hundred yards away, and the next moment it was barely audible.

Meghan watched Ken hold the massive shell up to his mouth. He sucked in a deep drink of cool mountain air, pursed his lips and blew hard into the shell. The sound began as a rattling bellow, but its intensity grew into a long, low, cacophonous crescendo that echoed across the valley. The rock wall behind them helped push the sound outward and magnify its intensity.

What surprised Ken and Meghan was that when Ken finally ran out of breath, the sound of the conch ricocheted back to them in a pulsating, eerie response louder than the first call. Ken thought the conch sound might be coming from someone out there calling them, but Meghan knew it was an echo because there were so many rock peaks and walls across the valley. She knew echoes were common in wide open places when the distance between sound source and surface resistance was more than fifty-five feet away.

After the echo ceased, there was no response. Nothing. Only an eerie silence that crept over them confirming they were alone.

CHAPTER 38

When Chandler turned on the electronic conch device, the sound of the crickets outside his chopper abruptly ceased. They exited the Sikorsky and trekked up-mountain toward the two ATVs they had spied from the air a half hour ago.

When they arrived at the first vehicle, Wolf felt the undercarriage covering the engine and said, "Cold."

Chandler leaned down, peered beneath the roll bar, and pulled something out from under the ATV. It was a purse and it had Meghan's New York State driver's license in it. "They're gone." He hesitated, looking up at Kimberly. "They're alive."

Fulton leaned over the ATV and found a fallen ski cap. "It's Ken's hat," she cried, her voice cracking.

Wolf gave a thumbs-up and walked around the overturned ATV, studying it for clues. He saw the oil spill from the engine and looked under the chassis. Oil was still slowly but steadily dripping out of the crankcase, but there was very little on the ground. There should have been a pool of it by now, thought Wolf. He sniffed the ground, then noticed the earth away from the drip was covered with oil, as if someone had taken a paintbrush and bathed the dirt-covered area leading to the outside. He gave a knowing smile. "These kids are very bright—and very clever," he said.

Chandler dipped his index finger into a swath of the liquid outside the chassis. He held it up to his nose and said, "Not gasoline."

Fulton watched the two men, trying to understand what they were doing.

"Oil from the crankcase," Wolf declared. "They rubbed it all over their bodies."

"Why would they do that?" Fulton asked.

"Camouflage," said Chandler.

"And impossible to smell human flesh. That's the best reason," Wolf added.

"Brilliant," Fulton said proudly. "Leave it to my son to figure it out," she added, feeling a modicum of relief. "What if it rains and washes it off?"

"Oil doesn't wash off easily," Chandler said. "Trust me. It would take a torrential downpour."

Wolf walked away from the ATV and studied the landscape. He walked over to a clump of three pine trees directly on the other side of the narrow path and held one of the evergreen branches in his hand. "See this? It's broken. They went this way."

"How do you know it's them?" Fulton asked. "It could be from an animal, or one of the Deinos."

"Not when the branch has a taste of motor oil on it. It's the kids—and it's Pennzoil twenty weight."

Chandler grinned and Fulton shook her head in disbelief. She had walked many mountain and desert trails, but had never before been with a tracker. "How did you learn to track?" she asked.

"From my grandfather. He was the best there was."

They walked back seventy-five yards behind the teenagers' ATV and came upon the Marine's ATV. It had been destroyed almost beyond recognition. Chandler looked at the leg they had seen from the air and gave it a tug. Fulton was standing on the other side of the wreckage and didn't see the leg slide out from beneath the chassis, unattached to the body.

"Don't look, Kimberly," he said protectively. "It's bad, real bad."

Chandler leaned over and looked beneath the Polaris. The rest of the body had vanished.

Wolf knew what Chandler saw—or more precisely what he didn't see—and was relieved he chose not to tell Fulton. Panic was not something they needed right now.

Wolf studied the seats. They were soaked with blood. The leather was ripped to shreds. The steering wheel was bent and the small hood covering the Polaris engine had a massive dent in it where Fulton guessed the Deino had landed when it attacked from the air. Talons had scraped the brown lacquered paint off the hood. The roll bar had been ripped off and lay on the ground like a twisted pretzel.

Chandler walked a short distance away so Fulton wouldn't hear. He unclipped his ICOM transceiver from his belt and pressed PTT. "Major Wong, Scott Chandler here. You copy?"

"Affirmative, Scott. Go ahead. Over."

"Bad news here, sir. Found Sergeant Rubin's remains, sir. But we only found the leg. Over."

"Did you say, 'only a leg?' Over."

"Affirmative."

"Son of a bitch. We've lost one shy of seventy," Wong said.

"What are the coordinates, Scott? We'll send out a chopper and pick him up. Over."

Chandler gave Wong the coordinates, clicked off the air, and walked over to Fulton.

They turned away from the Marine's ATV and walked back to the other one.

"Where could they have gone?" Fulton asked.

"Anywhere," Chandler said. "Vast area out here—but the Fossil might be a good bet. They had the coordinates."

"Tough to get there from here," Wolf said. "But why would they want to head in that direction, knowing the Deinos live there? It would be a death sentence."

"Unless they were being chased," Chandler said.

"By the Deinos?" Fulton said.

"Maybe the Marine who was sent back to watch them," Wolf said.

The sun had set. Wolf had tracked the kids for the last ninety minutes, his flashlight swinging back and forth, trying to keep the trail. It was easy all the way through dusk, but as it grew pitch dark the trail was tough to follow.

Wolf would walk ten paces, sniff the air like a hungry dog, retreat five paces, then move forward with renewed proof that they were on track, touching and feeling every leaf, twig, or broken branch that seemed to lead in a certain direction. Then he would study the ground, fall to his knees and examine a footprint, measure the size of it, determining whether it was Meghan's or Ken's.

Then, atop a flat rock, he spotted an arrow made from broken sticks. He picked up one of the sticks and examined it in the light. It glistened, confirming Ken had purposely rubbed motor oil on it, leaving clues like Hansel and Gretel breadcrumbs.

The recorded sound of the conch shell maintained a constant low frequency bellow that was loud enough to insure their safety. They were traversing another ridge that led them higher into the mountains. Chandler had stopped to read his chart using his GPS to confirm the fix on their location. They were heading toward a massive wall less than a mile and a half ahead. As they started their ascent, Wolf found another arrow tipped with motor oil. It was pointing up-mountain toward the massive wall.

Fulton heard something in the distance, "It's them," she said. "It's another conch. Listen."

The eerie, unmistakable bellow filled them with hope.

"It's definitely a conch," Chandler said. "It's them. They're alive. Let's go."

Ken had blown the shell once more in response to the steady conch sound that was drifting up mountain. But, with nightfall, the acoustics changed, and they could no longer hear it in the distance. The wind had shifted and was coming out of the northwest blowing at their backs.

"There's no point in blowing it now," Ken said.

"Why not? How are they going to find us then?" Meghan said. "We should turn around and follow the sound down into the valley."

"The sound won't carry, Meghan." Ken said. "They're behind us and the wind's blowing the sound away from them. We turn around now and get off track, we're totally exposed."

Ken put the shell back into his backpack and they concentrated on finding a safe place to spend the night.

With the massive wall of rock at their backs, they wended their way side stepping and searching for some safe place to bed down. There wasn't any. As they rounded a sharp corner of mountainous rock, Meghan said, "Did you hear that?"

"No," said Ken. "Hear what?"

Meghan nodded off to the left, afraid to say another word.

Ken cocked his head and listened. Something was out there—and whatever it was seemed like it was heading straight at them.

"Shhh," Ken said. "Keep moving. Faster."

In the distance, a low guttural growl broke the silence. It was more than a growl, thought Ken. It was a panting, heaving bellow of dread, and it was moving toward them fast, on the run, branches snapping, snorting on the way as if highly agitated.

Ken and Meghan quickened their pace, hearts pounding, eyes searching out from the rock wall.

Meghan saw it first and gasped, "Oh my God. It's a bear, Ken."

"Jesus," said Ken. "It's huge. Crouch down and don't move."

The 1,100-pound grizzly tore up the mountainside moving at thirty-five miles an hour. Chandler and Wolf had tagged and logged what they believed to be every grizzly bear in Noatak—486 of them—but this one, *Ursus Arctos Horribilis,* had no tag. It had strayed into the area four months ago.

Named grizzly by George Ord in 1815, the species got its name because of the grizzled gray hairs in its fur. This one had killed and eaten a Dall Sheep eight days ago. It was starving for meat again, and it hadn't yet found the south fork of the Fossil River to fish. Coming out of hibernation forty days ago, its body needed nourishment now.

It was coincidence that the grizzly ran straight into the teenagers, for it hadn't sniffed human scent, the oil on their bodies diffusing it. But the bear stopped short close enough to see their eyes, hair and clothing, and its throbbing empty stomach sent an urgent message to its large brain: eat.

Announcing its presence with a deafening roar, the grizzly ran head-on at them, its thundering paws pounding at the ground in a sudden, purposeful charge. At thirty yards out, Ken and Meghan watched in horror as its massive head shook back and forth in an attacking rage. At twenty yards from the rock wall, it skidded another ten yards to an abrupt stop then rose on its muscular hind legs towering eleven feet over them, its long forearms outstretched and ready for the kill.

Meghan's hand cupped her mouth. Her life flashed before her in one agonizing moment. Ken's eyes were riveted on the size of the creature and realized in one shiver that he and his girlfriend were about to be consumed. It was over, he concluded. The thought of blowing the conch did occur to him, but the loud bellowing call would probably do more to agitate the bear than scare it away. Ken's mind exploded with options for survival. They couldn't run, couldn't scream for help, and they had no weapons of defense.

Ken stared at the massive jaws which hung open, revealing four-inch fangs for tearing flesh—their flesh. But he studied something else that reminded him of all the teddy bears adorning Meghan's bed back in New York City. Attached to this massive head were two blonde ears that seemed to soften the ferocity of this enormous carnivore that was about to consume them. The ears were fuzzy puffs of blonde fir. The sight was surreal to Ken.

The grizzly leaned over the teenagers and let out a deafening growl, shaking its head and snapping its massive jaws.

Its right forepaw swept behind its back, and as it started the death slap, capable of breaking a 1,500-pound bull elk's neck with one swing, it hesitated and arched back in pain. It shrieked a blood-curdling cry, and spun around shaking its massive body in a convulsive shutter.

An alpha male Deino in flight had attacked the grizzly from behind, tearing a deep vertical wound on the bear's back. The grizzly tried to shake the Deino off, but its talons had torn through the thick brown coat of fur through bone and flesh. The jaws of the Deino ripped and tore at the grizzly's head.

Ken and Meghan stared up at the raging battle, paralyzed in fear. The grizzly was swaying back and forth, the sound from its throat filling the air with dread.

The massive bear fell backwards atop the Deino, forcing the raptor to release its grip. It sprang to its feet and issued a shrieking call for help.

The bear righted itself and faced the Deino, its powerful forearms swinging in vicious arcs trying to connect with the Deino. The Deino dodged the massive paws, springing in and out of range, its talons striking the air, searching for flesh.

The Deino flapped its wings in an effort to distract the bear, but the grizzly moved in, growling and swinging its paws. As the Deino dodged a left hook from the bear's massive paw, it ducked beneath the swing and thrust its jaws up and into the bear's neck. The grizzly had already begun a slap from its right paw and caught the Deino on the side of its head with such powerful force that the Deino's body was hurled through the air twelve yards from the battle zone. It lay on the ground writhing in pain, its body twitching. Then, in one last gasp of breath, its head rose from the ground and gave a mucus-laden cry before it collapsed in a pool of blood.

The grizzly turned toward Ken and Meghan and let out a defiant growl of victory then, upright on its hind legs, walked toward the teenagers again, determined to finish the job.

As it bent down, it was ravaged again from the back, only this time, three Deinos, having heard the call for help, were atop the towering bear and gorging on flesh and fur.

Still upright, the bear stumbled. It turned a tight circle twice, three Deinos attached to the giant carnivore. The bear's front legs were flailing wildly. When it rolled over on its back yet again, the Deinos viciously charged.

When the grizzly uttered a death rattle from its throat, Ken elbowed Meghan, grabbed her hand. "Let's go, now. Follow me," he said.

They moved in unison, crouched down, resuming their side-stepping motion to freedom. Five yards away, ten yards, now twenty, than thirty yards.

They moved around another corner of mountain wall and their pace quickened into a full desperate run, searching for a safe place to take cover. In the distance, they heard the last, painful cry of life from the grizzly and knew it had taken its last breath.

Forty minutes later, they found a narrow vertical vein in the thick rock wall they were following. It seemed large enough for passage, maybe large enough to squirm inside and bed down. As Ken put his foot into the small opening to hoist himself up into the crevice, they heard the sound of helicopters in the distance yet again; more than one, more than three, enough to send a course of hope through their veins and for Ken to say, "See, I told you we'd be okay. They're searching for us."

Meghan did not answer.

She heard something behind them. It sounded like crickets, a lot of them, and it got closer and louder as they tried to hide inside the rock tunnel. She gave Ken a boost up, then dragged herself up and into the small crevice, Ken pulling on her oil-soaked arms, losing grip, then pulling hard only to slip again and have her slide backward toward the opening. Her nails clawed at the sharp rock floor of the tunnel to gain grip, blood dotting her fingertips. Her legs were still dangling outside of the opening.

Behind her, something nudged her sneakers. It was too dark to see what it was, but her heart thumped like a drum in her chest. She heard the breath behind her, and felt its warmth, a distinct vulgar stench filling the air. She reached out to grab Ken, her hands slipping away on his greased legs, but then she got his mountain boot with her left hand and it was void of oil. Ken heard the breathing too, and knew what it was. When he felt her hands on his boot, he clawed upward, pulling and grunting, trying to hold his breath as he struggled with all his might to crawl upward, deeper into the crevice, hoping the Deino was too big to gain entrance.

The Deino sniffed and nudged Meghan's sneaker, then her leg, its yellow piercing eyes squinting to see detail in the dark. A pink tongue protruded from between razor sharp jaws, the tip touching Meghan's oiled leg and sending a confused message back to its well-developed brain. Binocular night vision helped the process. Something was different about this prey, something that gave the creature a pondering pause. The strong, familiar smell of oil filtered into its flared nostrils.

No, the dinosaur processed. This was not food, the taste of oil on its slithery tongue confirmed. It was not edible.

The Deino gave a loud snort of approval as the object slowly, ever so slowly, was pulling away from the tip of its rough leathery nose. Then the legs were gone, disappearing inside the crevice.

It tried poking its massive open-jawed head deeper into the hole, but its muscular winged shoulders prevented ingress. It turned away from the crevice, let out a shriek of bewilderment, and vanished into the night.

There was no light to see anything inside the crevice that led deeper and higher up into the tunnel of stone and glacial rock. Ken and Meghan groped the inner walls, trying to find an area of flatness, some place to rest for the night. There wasn't any.

Ken thought about lighting a match or turning on a brief flick of light from his flashlight, but if there was anything alive in this tunnel of darkness, he did not want to draw its attention to them.

They closed their eyes and fell into a fitful sleep.

CHAPTER 39

A THICK, DAMP FOG HAD SETTLED UPON THE GROUND.

"Impossible to see anything now," Wolf said, squinting into the fog.

An arrow formed of tree branches had been found twenty minutes before the fog settled in. Chandler walked in a widening circle, searching for shelter.

They had adjusted to the constant dull bellow of the conch sound system. Chandler had a dozen extra batteries in his field pack just in case they lost charge. Since it was a new device, nobody knew how long the batteries would last, but they hoped they could install new ones in time.

"Over here," Wolf said, standing in front of a thick clump of cedar trees. Large boulders deposited by a glacier encircled the trees to provide a modicum of protection. Chandler and Fulton followed Wolf into the fold of dense evergreen.

Inside, Wolf turned his flashlight on. It was obvious that some other creature had the same idea.

"Whatever slept here was big," Wolf said sweeping his flashlight in an arc across the indentation of boughs that lay on the ground. Chandler bent down and looked at the nest, studying it for signs of something. He looked up into Wolf's light and said, "Grizzly."

Wolf walked to the edge of the teepee-like tent of evergreen bows and thick bark peeling tree trunks. He played his light on a clump of scatter. "You're right. A grizzly—but look at the blood trail."

"What?" Fulton said, her voice a frightened whisper of concern.

"Deino's the only predator in Noatak—or anywhere—that could take on a grizzly," Chandler said.

Wolf followed the trail leading away from the tent of evergreens. His flashlight lit up the ground at the base of a hemlock.

"Jesus. Look at this."

Chandler walked over and said, "My God." He scanned the area with his light. "Looks like the grizzly got two Deinos and feasted. Feathers all over the place."

Wolf nodded in agreement and they walked back to the tent of greens.

Chandler placed the sound device atop one of the large boulders outside of the protective cover and came back inside beneath the bows. "We'll be okay in here. We'll resume at first light."

Wolf nodded in the dull flickering light of the Coleman lantern and they curled up in a tight circle, Wolf's feet almost touching Fulton's head, and her feet three inches shy of Chandler's head. In a circle, they had a better chance to spring into action should there be an incoming threat, Chandler had told them.

Chandler's carbine was tucked against chest. His eyes closed and he fell into a deep sleep.

When Ken and Meghan burst into the open, it was first light. The fog was still thick, soup-like. They heard the sound of a river in the distance. The teenagers dashed across a small clearing toward a glacial outcrop, then hid in a rock laden culvert crouching down low, eyes wide, searching for motion.

Nothing. The scent of pine filled the air.

From across the clearing, it had watched them, alerting the others with a loud purring sound, followed by rapid clicks deep from its throat, like a drum stick tapping on a marble countertop.

The hunt was on. A large Deino was leading the charge with uncanny precision. Too heavy to fly, it had mastered speed and deception on the ground.

Ken heard the clicking sound first, then Meghan. They were still in the culvert, flat against the ground and peering over a small ridge. They did not think to turn around when they heard it because what swooped out of the dark fog laden sky was coming at them with unmeasured speed.

Its claws extended, it dug into Meghan's back and its massive wings flogged the air, clutching her in its talons like an eagle with a rainbow trout.

Meghan let out a scream and reached for Ken. But it was too late. The girl was lifted off into the fog and disappeared.

When Ken turned around, fifteen feet in front of him stood the alpha male, its jaws agape. It uttered an unrelenting screech.

Ken reached for his conch shell so fast that it fell out of his hands and cracked into three pieces. The alpha male leaped across the culvert and engulfed Ken's head in its jaws.

There was a sharp cracking sound and his body fell limp.

Kimberly Fulton's body twitched violently back and forth on the ground, her eyes opening and shutting, fists clenched across her chest as her arms flailed outward. She let out a low wail of horror that began deep in her throat and built into a terrifying, gut-wrenching scream that jolted Chandler and Wolf out of a deep sleep.

Chandler covered her mouth and held her close, rocking her.

"It's okay, Kimberly. You were dreaming. It's all a dream. Wake up."

Fulton moaned, clutching him, not yet awake. Her body was trembling and she held onto Chandler.

When her trembling stopped, she burst into tears and her grip on Chandler tightened.

"It's okay. You had a nightmare."

"It was real," she sobbed. "Ken and Meghan are dead. The dream was real, Scott. I know it happened."

"It was a bad dream. Just a bad dream. Let it go."

Wolf tried to reassure her. "You're okay, and so are the kids. Try to get some sleep."

Fulton began to cry. Not the hysterical cry of someone who has just lost a friend or family member, but the steady cry of someone whose heart had been in deep grief over a long period of time, the kind of grief suppressed deep within one's soul.

Chandler knew something was terribly wrong beyond even the two missing teenagers. He held her, swinging her around so that her head was cradled in his lap, her eyes staring up at him.

"What's wrong? Talk to me," Chandler said.

Fulton was staring into Chandler's brown eyes, the lantern's flickering light dancing between them.

"It's okay," Chandler said. "It's okay."

"It's not okay, Scott," she cried. "He's your son."

"What?"

"Ken's your son, Scott."

Chandler couldn't process what she was saying. It didn't make sense. "I...don't understand," he finally said.

She stared up at him, her head still cradled in his lap, the Coleman lantern splashing streaks of light across his face as if he were an apparition. Maybe this was a dream, too, he told himself, and somehow they had linked together in another life and were sharing it.

He tried to think back to the last time they were together at the University of Montana in Missoula, seventeen years ago.

Ken was seventeen.

"The last night we were together?"

"Yes."

"But we only did it that once," he said without thinking.

"Once is all it takes," Fulton said.

"Why didn't you tell me?"

Wolf was listening to every word, but he lay still, feigning sleep. This was their secret, he told himself, not his. He crawled outside of the protective evergreen encasement undetected, and sucked in a deep breath of cool mountain air.

The fog was thicker and the sound of the conch seemed muted, almost like a distant call from another shore, another mountain.

"By the time I found out I was pregnant," said Fulton, "you'd joined the Marines and were already on your way to Afghanistan. I assumed that's where you were. Or Iraq."

"Yes," Chandler said. "Afghanistan." He held up his left arm.

"I tried to find you. Called the Marines, but they kept telling me they had nobody enlisted by that name. Maybe it was security after 9/11, but they told me they couldn't find you. I called them three more times, each time futile."

Chandler hesitated. "He's…my son? Ken is my son?"

"I was a virgin when we were together, Scott," she said.

"This is a lot to take in after seventeen years, Kimberly."

"I know. I've been living with it all this time. I thought you were dead. Killed by Al-Qaeda, or killed by all the bombing after the towers collapsed."

Chandler lay still staring into the flickering light for a long time then he rolled over and stood up.

"What are you doing?"

"I'm going to find our son."

She stood up and faced him.

He held her face in his hands, not thinking about his prosthetic. It was a spontaneous moment, and he kissed her.

It sent a warm chill through her body. She kissed him back.

A loud, haunting screech sounded in the distance, bringing them both back to Noatak and the Fossil River, the Deinos—and the fact that their son and his girlfriend were on the run, lost somewhere in the Park, their lives in jeopardy.

Wolf ducked back into the circle of evergreens. "It's first light," he said. We've got to get on the trail fast. If we don't find them soon…"

CHAPTER 40

THEY'D SLEPT AT A FORTY-DEGREE ANGLE INSIDE THE ROCK CREVICE. WHEN Ken woke up it was as pitch black as it was when they'd entered the tunnel of rock at nightfall. It was damp, and condensation formed drops of water that dripped on his face when he looked up. A speck of motor oil seeped into the corner of his right eye, stinging, and he blinked to clear it.

Meghan was still asleep. The sound of her deep breathing filled the rock tunnel around them.

Something was crawling up his leg. He swatted it with his left hand and felt a crunch. It was big—creepy crawly big. Ken reached into his backpack and extracted another power bar from a plastic bag. Whatever had crawled up his leg, he reached around in the dark, found it, and shoved it into the bag. He only had three bars left. If they ran out of food they would have to eat off the land.

He peeled off the wrapping and took a large bite, munching slowly. They'd have to find a water source soon, he knew, and hoped the Fossil River might be reasonably close once they exited the tunnel to the top. When the water dripping from the rock ceiling touched his tongue, his first thought was to collect it in the empty bottle he kept, but the water tasted of sulfur and he spat it out.

He guessed it was close to first light and nudged Meghan. She groaned and turned in place. "We've got to get out of here."

237

She moaned a sleepy response and he nudged her again. "Meghan."

"What?" she said, her voice low and gravelly.

"Let's go."

"I want to stay here. It's safe."

"They won't find us unless we get out of this tunnel. Come on."

"No."

"If we stay here, we die. We're almost out of food and water."

"If we stay here, at least we're safe. You can blow the conch from here."

"They won't hear it. No way. We have a life together, Meghan. If we don't get out of here soon…"

"If we go out of here, they'll find us and kill us."

"We stand a better chance of living if we're above ground," Ken said. But he wasn't sure.

"Mom, Scott, and Wolf are looking for us now. They won't find us in here. And the Marines are looking for us, too," he said, hoping it was true. "You heard the helicopters. Nobody will find us in here. Come on."

"I have to pee."

"What does that have to do with anything? Pee, then let's get the hell out here. Please. Hurry."

"No. I'm staying here."

"Then I'm going."

"Without me?"

"Yes. Without you."

Silence.

"So? Are you coming or not?"

"You'd leave me alone?"

"Yes. We've got to be found, Meghan—and there's no way they'll find us in here."

"The Deinos will get us."

"Maybe, but maybe not. We have the conch."

"They'll find us."

"They found us yesterday, and they didn't eat us. We're covered with oil. Let's get out of here. Now!"

"No."

"That's your choice. I'm sorry, Meghan. I'm leaving." Ken reached

238

into his backpack and pulled out another power bar and one of two remaining bottles of water. "Here, take these." He reached out to find her in the dark.

"What is it?"

"Water and a power bar."

"You're sweet, Ken. That's why I love you. Don't leave me. Please don't leave me."

"One of us has to get to the top of this tunnel. I hope it leads to an opening above the rock wall. It's our only chance. We've got to get above ground. Backing out of the tunnel's not an option. The Deinos might be waiting for us."

"They'll be waiting for us at the top too," she said.

"We don't know that. Either way, we've got to find out."

Ken crawled upward, away from Meghan. She sat rigid, her mind filled with fear. "Ken?"

"Yes?"

"I love you."

"I love you, too, Meghan. I'll be back for you."

Then the tunnel became silent.

Ken had turned a sharp corner in the rocky wall and waited, hoping his leaving her would convince her to follow him up and out of the tunnel. He waited five minutes.

Meghan sat still listening to her heartbeat pounding in her chest, her mind trying to replay her life. She thought about her love for Ken, her studies, her incessant passion for the environment, and her early acceptance at Yale. I don't want to die, she thought.

Ten minutes passed. Another few minutes and Ken heard movement below him.

Meghan heard a sound below her. It was the sound of crickets. She heard heavy breathing and a snort.

"Ken?" she called above her.

Ken heard the sound of someone clawing her way upward through the pitch black tunnel toward him. It worked, he thought with great relief.

"I'm up here," he said.

"They're back at the entrance," she said.

It took twenty minutes for Wolf to find the next arrow, the tip of it showing a small smudge of Pennzoil. They were still on track. They trudged up-mountain for forty-five minutes. The faint glow of hazy sun penetrated the thick fog that hovered above the ground. It was easier to see, and there was enough light to aid Wolf's search for the next trail marker.

It came when they reached a massive wall of rock leading two hundred feet above them. There was an arrow to the right, and they quickly worked their way along the towering mountain wall. Fifteen minutes passed, and they found nothing until they rounded a clump of four cedar trees growing against the rock wall.

Fulton saw it first.

Chandler and Wolf walked out twenty yards to a large circle of feathers, bone, and fur. Blood covered everything on the ground in a fifteen-foot circle of torment. In the middle of it lay the tortured carcass of the grizzly bear, its jaws still fixed on a Deino's neck that died in battle. The lower half of the bear's body had been eaten, leaving the head, shoulders and chest in a grizzled soup of its own blood.

"I've never seen a battle this bloody before, not even in Afghanistan," said Chandler. "Let's get the hell out of here. The stench's bad enough."

"It confirms one thing we've always known in Noatak," Wolf said.

"What's that," Fulton asked.

"The grizzly's the most ferocious carnivore in North America."

"Not now," offered Fulton. "Deino is."

"You got that right," said Chandler.

Wolf tracked another thirty minutes until they came upon a vertical opening, a crevice that led deeper into the mountain wall. At the foot of the crevice was an arrow made of pine boughs, a smudge of oil on the tip of it.

"Bingo," said Wolf. "Here's where they escaped. Probably spent the night inside."

Chandler studied the entrance along with Fulton. "Not big enough for a Deino to enter, thank God," Fulton said with a sigh.

"They're safe inside," Chandler added.

Wolf poked his head inside the crevice and shouted. "Ken. Meghan." No answer.

Wolf pointed the speaker of the sound system inside the rock tunnel and turned it on high, then turned it off.

They leaned toward the opening and heard no response. Wolf turned the sound system on and adjusted the speakers over his back.

"They're not in there now," Wolf said. "They're gone."

"Let's go after them," Chandler said. He stuck his right foot up into the V of the crevice and hoisted himself into the rocky opening.

"I have a better idea," Wolf said.

"What?"

"We go back to the Sikorsky and fly up and over the cliff. We'll need the chopper to get out of there once we find the kids, anyway. Much faster, more efficient," Wolf said.

Fulton nodded. "I'm for it."

"Makes sense," Chandler added.

"If we go in there now on foot, we'll have to crawl our way up. It'll take hours to reach the top, maybe more. And, what if it doesn't lead to the summit? Then we're stuck and have to come all the way back down. My guess is that it does lead to the top because we'd have run into the kids by now if they couldn't get to the summit through here." Wolf pointed to the entrance.

It took them almost three hours to get back to the Sikorsky, but only four minutes to fly up and over the mountain wall. Chandler circled over the Fossil River, then flew back toward the precipice that contained the crevice leading to the top of the mountain plateau. As they flew atop the plateau, they scanned the area for any sign of the teenagers.

They saw nothing.

"We've got to land and search on foot," Wolf said. "That's the only way."

Chandler nodded and flew 200 yards inland to set the chopper down on the same slab of cretaceous rock that he and Fulton had landed on only seventy-two hours ago.

When the blades ceased whirling and they opened the hatches, the scent of oil filled the cockpit.

But there was another distinct smell, the scent of decay: Marine bodies slowly rotting on the ground all around them, Deino carcasses strewn among them as if a flamethrower had torched the area leaving nothing alive.

241

Fulton saw the remains of a corpse off to the left of the chopper maybe forty feet away: a torso, no head. Part of an arm lay five feet from what was left of the body. Something had eaten the meat off the skeleton. The head of a Deino's jaws with no body was still attached to the Marine's torso—as if it was trying to gorge and swallow its last morsel before its body was blown apart by mortar fire.

Chandler said, "Shit. This is tough to see. Don't look at it, Kimberly."

"I already did," she said.

"Let's move out," Chandler announced, and pushed the hatch door outward. He stepped out of the craft.

Wolf strapped the sound device onto his back and turned it on. He'd replaced the batteries. The low bellowing sound came to life and the conch's eerie noise filled the clearing.

Fulton jumped down onto the landing gear. As her feet touched the ground, a shrill shriek sounded down valley.

"A warning," Fulton said. "They're telling us they're here. It's their territory."

"It's ours together now—and they'd better get used to it," Chandler said as he punched a thirty round clip of shells into his carbine's chamber and checked the safety. "Today we're finding our son, and they'd better not get in our way."

Wolf spun on his heel and walked across the clearing, his backpack carrying the conch device blaring a warning to the colony of predators.

Fulton fell into step behind them, and they walked toward the mountain precipice looking for an opening in the rock that would announce the escape route that Ken and Meghan hopefully would have taken on their way to the top.

Chandler trailed Fulton. "I want you in the middle, Kimberly," he said. "I don't like you exposed at the back. That's my job." He held up his carbine as he finished the sentence.

Above them a formation of Marine Bell Viper helicopters swept over the mountain ridge and hovered above them.

Chandler's ICOM came alive.

"Glacier-Kilo-two-niner-five-Foxtrot. This is Alpha-Bravo-Niner-six-Charlie. Over."

"Roger that, John. We've picked up a trail down-mountain. Nothing here yet. How'd you get my ICOM frequency?"

"Major Wong gave me your frequency. We have four Marine squads behind you on the ground. We dropped them down-mountain."

"Thanks for the support. I hope they have the sound device with them."

"Roger that, Scott. It's a helluva noise. Scare the shit out of anybody after awhile. Let us know when you pick up their trail again."

"Affirmative, John. Over and out."

Wolf walked behind a large hemlock tree growing on the edge of the precipice, its roots splayed atop the cretaceous rock searching for soil and water. "I found their trail," Wolf said. "And the opening to the tunnel from below. They exited here."

Chandler and Fulton ran over to Wolf and stared at the small opening in the rock surface.

"How do you know they came up here, Brave Wolf?"

Wolf pointed to a small arrow made by a finger dipped in oil. "See it?"

Fulton leaned over and said, "God. I can't believe you found that. Great."

"Well done, partner. You'll find them."

Wolf stood up and stared at Chandler. "We'd better."

Fulton looked at Wolf, then at Chandler. "You heard?"

"Yes. You guys are lucky. Ken's one hell of a guy. I wish he were my son," Wolf said.

Chandler felt a rush of emotion and choked it off by walking away from the opening, heading in the direction of the arrow: toward the Fossil River.

As Fulton walked past Wolf, she put her hand on his shoulder and said,

"Thanks, Brave Wolf. You're a very special man."

Wolf nodded and walked swiftly past Chandler to take the lead. "They headed to the Fossil to get water."

CHAPTER 41

K~EN AND MEGHAN CROUCHED LOW AND CRAWLED INTO THE THICK BRUSH~ that flanked the north side of the river, each clutching two empty plastic bottles, caps off, ready to fill.

The only question now was how to run out from the heavy brush, fill the bottles, and get back into cover before the Deinos got to them. Their bodies glistened in the hazy midmorning sun, the smell of thick motor oil rising from their exposed arms, legs, necks, and faces. An unexpected blessing, Ken told Meghan, was that the oil kept the black flies away from them.

They sat in the same place for twenty minutes, listening, hoping, and planning. Ken whispered to Meghan that it was a good omen they had gotten this far and survived. How they had managed to find their way up and into the inaccessible area of the Fossil River plateau was a wild coincidence, Ken had told her. If they hadn't found the small opening slice in the rock wall enabling them to escape from the grizzly and Deinos, they probably would be dead by now.

"Thank God we're here," Ken whispered. "We're out of water and there's the river."

They'd seen the Marine helicopter formation fly to the west of their position, too far away to leap out into the open and flag them down.

"With what?" Ken told Meghan who insisted they take the risk. "Our black arms? Forget it. We'll be toast."

They froze, falling silent.

Across the Fossil, a Deino came out into the open and looked up and down the river, then to the south riverbank.

Meghan clutched Ken in horror. "Shhh. Don't move," Ken said. "The wind's blowing cross-river. It can't smell us. The smell of oil's all around us. Shhh."

They watched the Deino walk up to the river's edge and stare into the water.

"It's hunting," Ken whispered.

"For us?"

"No, for fish. It's fishing. Watch it. Shhh."

The Deino waded out into the Fossil and peered into the water. It probed the pristine pool with the talons of its three-toed feet. Then, in a split second, it thrust its leg outward into the water and spun around toward shore. Speared on the end of a talon was a thirty-inch steelhead trout, its sides glistening. The Deino's jaws ripped a slice of the fish in one motion. In another blink of the eye, it filleted both sides of the fish.

"Awesome," Ken whispered. "Did you see that?"

Meghan didn't look up. Her body trembled in his arms. "Hold me," she whispered.

Ken pulled her close and continued to watch, transfixed at the speed and agility of the predator. The Deino stepped back into the Fossil and fanned its fifteen-foot wings over the water. Ken tried to figure out what it was doing. Then he knew. It was herding fish. Spooking them, getting them to swim in circles. That gave the Deino the decisive edge. As they swam within the Deino's reach, its talons were poised to pierce them like spears.

Ken watched the Deino pluck seven trout out of the Fossil, one after the other, filleting each as it flopped onto the riverbank. He shook his head in disbelief. This was one intelligent beast, he told himself.

It heightened his will to survive. Could he outsmart it?

Maybe. He knew that one wrong move would signal his death, and that of the girl he loved.

Ken pulled out his iPhone. The GPS pinpointed their exact location in Noatak National Park, but there was no signal strength for a phone call.

He remembered the conch. The recording he made. He'd taped the sound of the conch when Brave Wolf blew into the massive shell. He flipped the recording on and turned the volume on high.

The wind shifted, coming out of the north at their backs, and it magnified the sound across the river. The moment he turned the sound on, the Deino across the Fossil vanished into the thick forest on the south bank.

For the moment, Ken thought, they were safe.

"Come on. Let's go. Now," Ken commanded. They bolted out from thick evergreen cover running toward the Fossil. Once there, Meghan quickly filled up their bottles with river water, clearer than Poland Springs but the water was not cold. It was hot. Ken pointed his iPhone toward the thick tree pack on the opposite bank.

CHAPTER 42

WOLF KNELT DOWN AND FELT A BED OF THICK MOUNTAIN BRUSH WITH THE palm of his hand. It had been flattened down by the weight of an animal, and he knew the animal was human. There were two impressions, not one, and the brush was cold to the touch.

"They lay here, but awhile ago, two to three hours, maybe more," Wolf finally said.

He indicated another arrow, made from Fossil River bedrock and pine cones, pointing north, away from the river. Wolf found it approximately three feet from where Ken and Meghan had lain. There was a smudge of motor oil on the tip of the stone that completed the arrow and an empty Snicker's bar wrapper beside it, rolled into a small tight ball of glistening aluminum.

Wolf stood up and pointed to southeast.

"They're going that way, up-mountain." He turned up the volume on the sound device. "We have to move."

"Why don't they hold their position?" Fulton said, "So we can catch up with them?"

"They're probably afraid that if they wait in any one place too long the Deinos will find them," Wolf said. "The oil they rubbed on their bodies is probably the only reason they're alive."

"The sound of the conch is loud. Can't they hear it?" Fulton pressed.

"Not when the wind's blowing from the north. These trade winds normally blow from the west, but there's a storm coming in," Wolf said. He held his head high and took in a long drink of mountain air. "By tonight there'll be heavy rain, strong winds."

Chandler stood off to the side taking it all in. "We've got to find them before the storm hits. If we get heavy rain, it'll wash the oil off their skin."

"It'll take a lot of rain to do that," Wolf said. "Ken's smart. He'll figure that out and take shelter before the storm rolls in."

The reality of Ken being his son was now settling into Chandler's every move, every thought. The idea of losing a son he never knew he had was chipping away his hope, and he knew the chances of Ken being killed by a Deino were growing with the passage of every moment they weren't on the search. "We've got to keep moving."

In the distance a crack of gunfire sounded in the valley below, breaking Chandler's reverie. He flipped his carbine's safety off and cradled it at the ready.

"What's happening?" Fulton whispered.

"There's been a breach," Wolf said. He looked back at Chandler.

"Call Major Wong and check the status. Confirm they've got the sound devices on at all times."

Chandler nodded and flipped on his ICOM transceiver. "Major Wong. Scott Chandler here. Over."

"Copy that, Scott. Go ahead."

"Just heard gunfire below us, down-mountain. Confirm use of sound devices. Confirm their location, too. Over."

"Roger that. Lost entire squad. Eight men. Sound device malfunction. Dropping more recorders into the area. About three miles behind your location, in a valley below you." Wong gave him the GPS coordinates. "We're going to drop another platoon one mile northwest of your position up-range. Rendezvous at new coordinates." Wong repeated the new position, Chandler locking it into his GPS.

But time was running out, and the storm clouds were thickening.

More gunfire sounded and Chandler heard helicopters approaching. From the sound of the engines, he knew they were Black Hawks, not Bell Vipers. They were parachuting sound devices to the platoon of Marines now searching the thick mountain woods north of the Fossil River below them.

An ear-shattering screech ripped through the thick woods in front of them and another burst of gunfire broke the silence.

Then a rip of bullets shattered the whisper of mountain breezes. Chandler heard a grenade explode.

Wolf ran up ahead crouching low, tree to tree, signaling them forward, his index finger touching his lips for silence. Fulton and Chandler rushed forward and vanished into a thick tunnel of overgrown cedar and larch trees.

They didn't see the flash of movement behind them, nor the span of feathery wings above them.

Ken felt the first drop of rain on his forehead, another splashing on Meghan's wrist.

"We've got a problem," Ken said. They were ascending a steep rugged crag of mountain rock leading up to a massive ridge of overhanging cliffs.

"It won't wash off, will it?" Meghan's voice pleaded for Ken to say no.

"I'm not sure. Maybe. We've got to find shelter fast," Ken said. "Before it opens up."

"Where can we hide?"

"Up there," Ken nodded up toward the top of the cliff. "Looks like an entrance. Maybe a cave."

"My legs are killing me, Ken."

"So are mine. We've got to keep moving."

Meghan had just eaten the last half of a power bar and they had only a half bottle of river water left in Ken's back pack. They had heard the sound of gunfire, but it seemed far off in the distance. An occasional faint conch sound drifted across the mountain, but then was silenced as the wind shifted.

They climbed up to a plateau, hid behind a large boulder, and waited. The rain did not come, at least not yet. The few drops they'd felt earlier were harbingers of a distant storm that was gathering strength over the Chukchi Sea and sweeping in over northern Alaska.

Off to his right, Ken heard a snort. Loud enough to send a jolt of fear through his tired body.

Meghan heard it, too, and moved closer to Ken, clutching his right arm in both hands. "What was that?" she said.

"I don't know."

Then a high-pitched whistling broke the silence, followed by another snort. Ken peered out from behind the massive boulder and jerked back. "Jesus," he said.

"What is it?" Meghan whispered, her heart pounding in her chest.

"An elk. Don't move. It's huge."

The 1,300-pound bull elk lifted its massive rack of antlers high into the air and gave a loud bugling that pierced their ears.

Then Meghan heard the sound of crickets, lots of them.

"It's them," she whispered. "What do we do now?" she pleaded.

Ken turned his head sharply toward Meghan. "Shhh. Don't move."

Her body froze, her eyes wide with terror.

Something shuffled in front of the boulder. A loud snort sounded, then a loud shriek knifed through the silence, filling their senses.

The elk shook its large head trying to spear its attackers with its massive rack of antlers, but a Deino had already affixed its talons deep into the elk's flank and it tore through flesh and bone like jelly, its shark-like jaws tearing raw meat from the huge beast.

It bugled a painful cry and in one final, powerful, neck-snapping lunge, managed to gore a female Deino that had lifted off the ground in an effort to grab hold of the elk's throat. It caught the Deino squarely in the chest plate, impaling it in flight. It gave a loud squawk and its body fell limp. The elk's head twirled the dinosaur in circles before throwing it down on the ground and stomping its lifeless body with thrashing hoofs.

Ken peered out from the corner of the boulder and his eyes widened. Twenty yards in front of the boulder, three Deinos had surrounded the massive bull elk and an alpha male had the elk's throat in its jaws, peeling the flesh off its neck, exposing its trachea. Ken saw a missing talon on its left foreleg. The other two Deinos ripped the flanks of the elk with razor sharp talons.

Ken was paralyzed with the sight and did not see a fourth Deino swoop down over them onto the wounded animal's back.

The elk gave a last doomed, garbled call before its throat was ripped from its body, and fell with such force that Meghan and Ken felt the earth tremble.

The alpha male Deino threw its head back and issued a call of victory that echoed across the mountains, summoning others to join the feast.

Ken pulled back from the sight and sat motionless.

They could hear bones crunching, and meat being ripped from the carcass. "Stay close to me," Ken said.

"I'm not leaving. They'll kill us."

"Shhh. Listen to me, Meghan. They're eating the elk. They can't smell us and to them we're not prey."

A band of heavy rain pushed its way across the clearing. Ken felt the first few drops dissolve into a heavy downpour. He looked down at his arms and watched the drops splash onto his skin.

At first the water washed over his oiled skin, but then something happened that sent a shock of fear through him. Oil was starting to drip off his body.

Meghan saw it, too.

Ken tapped her arm and pointed to the cliffs. "Stay down," he whispered. "Follow me. Don't look back."

As Ken and Meghan vanished out of sight, heading for the cliffs above, a Bell Viper helicopter swooped up and over the plateau they'd just abandoned.

"What the hell's that?" the pilot said.

"Looks like an elk carcass. Helluva rack of antlers. Something ate the shit out of it," the Marine co-pilot said.

"Christ," the pilot said as he swung back over the plateau for a better look, hovering over the sight. "I hope the fuck those kids didn't see that."

"They can't still be alive down there," the Marine lieutenant said. "If those creatures don't get them, fear will."

CHAPTER 43

Wolf said, "We must move faster. The storm's gathering strength."

The rain was pelting down at a slant from the north, and the wind picked up, blowing what was left of the ground fog out of the area. Visibility was better, and Wolf had just found another arrow pointing northeast, but the rain was unrelenting.

Wolf set off at a blistering pace. Chandler and Fulton fell in behind him. They pressed forward, the forty-five degree incline of the mountain taking a toll on their energy. The sound device gave off a continuing haunting bellow, and Wolf knew they were safe as long as the device delivered the dreaded call.

As Wolf approached a large boulder atop a plateau, he dropped to his knees and froze. Something was not right.

He caught the wet scent of a kill. He turned back to Fulton and Chandler, who were struggling up the craggy incline sixty yards behind him.

Wolf crawled toward the boulder, then heard something. He looked back at Chandler and Fulton and held up his hand, stopping them. He pressed a finger to his lips.

Wolf turned up the sound of the conch and stood bolt upright behind the boulder. He saw the three Deinos abandon the dead elk carcass. One took flight and the other two ran out of sight, their powerful legs churning them to safety.

As Wolf ran around the boulder into the clearing where the carcass lay, his backpack snagged on a sharp edge of the boulder, ripping the wires of the sound device from the battery pack.

Wolf seemed stunned by the silence. He looked over his shoulder, hands frantically reaching for the connecting wires. But he couldn't find them. He started to pull at the clips of his back pack to release it from his body so he could get at the conch shell.

He heard two snaps and pulled at the pack, but saw a flash of movement rush into the clearing with such speed and force that he knew he was in trouble before he could turn around.

Its jaws snapping at the air, the rogue alpha male stood before him. The talon on its left three-toed appendage was missing. Wolf knew it was the same creature that had confronted Chandler. Its massive wings fanned the ground, sending a damp spray of dust into a cloud of terror.

Fulton and Chandler, fifty yards away, only saw Wolf's back and stood in place waiting for his signal to join him.

A blood-curdling screech, and Chandler saw Wolf's body jerk from sight. Chandler unclipped his safety and charged the hilltop, Fulton following.

When Chandler reached the boulder, he saw the alpha male standing thirty yards in front of him on the other side of the crushed bones and torn flesh of what was left of the elk.

Wolf was still alive, his arms and legs flailing back and forth, trying desperately to free himself from the creature's jaws. Wolf screamed, but the Deino only tightened its sharp grip on his torso.

"Do something," shouted Fulton.

Chandler aimed the carbine at the alpha male's body, but it was facing him, backing up, keeping Wolf in front of him.

Chandler ran around the elk carcass toward Wolf. He stopped, stood rigid, carbine butt against his right shoulder, aiming at the Deino's head.

Again, it angled Wolf's body to get in the way, blocking a clean shot.

Chandler dashed to the right, but the Deino knew to keep facing him.

Wolf was saying something, but his voice was too weak for Chandler to make it out. It sounded like a chant.

Chandler moved closer, trying to get a shot.

253

The Deino's piercing yellow eyes stared at Chandler, tracking his every move.

Time was running out.

Wolf broke out of his garbled chant. "Shoot it," Wolf shouted in pain.

Chandler could not get a clear shot.

"Reconnect the wires on the sound device," Wolf managed to say.

Wolf's dying plea only aggravated the Deino. It violently shook Wolf's helpless body in defiance, sharp incisors cutting into flesh.

Blood sprayed the air.

Wolf gave a guttural shriek of pain.

"Shoot it, Scott. Shoot it now," Fulton cried. "Shoot its legs out."

Chandler charged the creature and it strutted backyard, never letting its eyes lose focus on him.

Chandler and Fulton didn't see the two Deinos that were in flight from behind them gliding on the mountain air current, talons extended, ready to strike.

Chandler sprayed the ground with a burst of automatic fire, trying to shoot out the creature's legs. But it was high kicking, leaping into the air and snarling. The sharp cracks of gunfire forced the two Deinos, thirty yards behind them, to veer off down mountain.

The closer Chandler got to the creature, the more it shook Wolf's body, like an angry pit bull whose jaws were clamped in a death grip on a human leg.

As Chandler took aim, the alpha male leapt into the air yet again, its wings flapping violently, and it shook Wolf's body in a gyrating vice grip.

Fulton heard a bone snap.

The air turned red with a shower of Wolf's blood.

Wolf's body hung limp from the Deino's jaws.

Chandler knew his friend was dead.

He aimed the carbine and pulled the trigger.

The alpha male exploded off the ground, wings flapping to gain lift. It was running sideways, trying to fly, but the burst from Chandler's weapon had torn into its wing, which hung from its side, touching the ground. Leaping like a gazelle in a zigzagging motion, it bounded out of the clearing into a distant clump of mountain bush.

Chandler tried to get another bead on it.

He emptied his chamber in a burst of eighteen bullets.

But the Deino vanished and his best friend was gone.

Chandler smacked a fresh clip into the gun and swung the barrel back and forth over the clearing.

Fulton looked up into the sky and saw nothing but distant cliffs above them and torrential rain sweeping over the mountains.

Chandler looked at her. The reality washed over his face, turning it into a mask of pain.

He felt Fulton's arms embrace him, felt the warmth of her body against him. They were alone.

Chandler fell to his knees in grief.

CHAPTER 44

THE STORM SWEPT OVER NOATAK NATIONAL PARK WITH INCREASED INTENSITY. Secretary Robinson paced, listening to the sound of rain beating the olive-drab tent.

Two hours before, in a conversation with President Barton, Robinson had convinced him they had to mobilize a Marine attack force and stand ready to invade Noatak's Fossil River.

"We have two teenagers lost in the Park, Mr. President. We think they may be near the oil field. We're trying everything possible, but we haven't found them yet. Secretary Conlon informs me the nation has only seventy-two hours before we suffer a massive nationwide blackout. If we can't find the kids in time, I want your permission to proceed with an invasion to sweep the Park clean from the predators so we can get at the oil."

"Proceed with the mission within twenty-four hours even if you can't find the teenagers," Barton said. "Our nation can't be without mobility fuel."

"Yes, sir. I'll make it happen, Mr. President."

Robinson placed an urgent call to Brigadier General Buzz Pine, requesting nine helicopter squadrons be mobilized to Noatak from Elmendorf Air Force Base and stand ready to airlift 848 Marines into the Fossil River area to do battle.

"They'll be in the air within the hour, sir," Pine said.

Robinson hung up the phone. "It's about fucking time," he said.

At 1500 hours, nine squadrons of Bell Viper helicopters lifted off the tarmac at Elmendorf Air Force Base, Alaska, swept to the west of Mt. McKinley at 20,320 feet, and headed northwest toward Noatak National Park. ETA: 1725 hours.

The orders from Lt. Colonel Skip Hargraves to Major Wong read: "Prepare battalion for heavy combat. Take out predator colony and secure area surrounding Fossil River to gain access to oil field. Await orders for invasion time." Lt. Colonel Skip Hargraves, U.S. Marine Corps.

The rain and wind were incessant. By the time Ken and Meghan reached the high cliffs above the Fossil River, every last drop of oil on their skin had washed off. They moved up mountain at a blistering pace, fearful that around the next boulder, tree, or outcrop the Deinos would be waiting. Nothing but the conch shell and the iPhone recording offered a modicum of safety. But how much longer did they have?

When they got up above the mountain incline, the sharp precipitous ledge they'd seen from below leveled off. The mouths of four caves yawned in the distance.

They walked to the one that had the largest entrance and stood under the eaves of the cavern. One thing was unmistakable: the strong scent of oil wafting out of the cave entrance. They knew they had to get to the source and rub oil back on their skin before it was too late. They hoped it would be inside the cave.

Ken turned on his iPod and saw the green energy bar showing one third battery power remaining. He turned it off and pulled out the large conch shell Wolf had given him.

"We've got to get to the oil, Meghan. As strong as the smell is, it's got to be somewhere inside the cave." Ken looked at his arms and held them outstretched.

She shook her head. "We're screwed if they're in there."

"I blow the conch shell the moment we go inside. You saw what happened when I played the recording back at the river. The sound of the conch scared them away. But I'm almost out of power on my phone."

"Jesus, Ken. I don't think we should go in there. There's no place to hide. What if they trap us? We're dead meat."

Looking back into the cave, Ken realized there was enough light to see the cave walls and shadows of bends within the cave tunnel. They stood still and watched the windswept rain wash over the mountainside.

"We camp out here until the storm passes," Ken said.

"Let's stay here, at the opening. Then we can escape if they see us," Meghan said.

"And be out in the open? No way. Without oil on our skin, they're going to smell us if they haven't already."

"So what do we do?" she asked.

"We go inside and find the oil and rub it back on our skin."

Meghan looked at Ken. "You go first," she said, grabbing his arm.

CHAPTER 45

Chandler tried to clear his head from the loss of Wolf, but it hung over him like a dark cloud.

His mind kept revisiting the past: memories of their times together managing Glacier National Park in Montana, then the transition to Noatak National Park, managing the wildlife, and the freedom they had together after hours enjoying a six-pack of Coors at the local bar, laughing about some of the crazy tourists who plied the Park in their RVs, bikes, and rafts, unable to get too far into the Park because of the sharp mountain range that encircled the Noatak River with foreboding steepness.

"I'm sorry," Fulton said, trying to comfort Chandler with his loss. "He was a beautiful man."

Chandler did not respond.

"We've got to find our son and Meghan."

Fulton's comment snapped him out of his mind-lock. He used his ICOM transceiver to report into Major Wong that a Deino had killed Brave Wolf. He didn't tell him it was the same alpha male rogue that had attacked his helicopter, or that he'd riddled the Deino with bullets and it was wounded, bleeding, and probably very pissed off.

Instead, he gave Wong his GPS coordinates and urged him to send in support troops to back them up as they ascended the mountain to the cliffs above.

"We know the kids passed through this site where we are now."

It took eight minutes to find Wolf's backpack. Fulton found it lying on the ground under a sharp edge on the left side of the large boulder Wolf had hid behind before he stood up and confronted the Deinos feasting on the elk carcass. Chandler held the backpack with his prosthetic hand and saw immediately what had happened. The red and black wires, positive and negative, had caught on the sharp edge of the boulder and ripped free from the battery pack running to the sound device. Chandler quickly reconnected the wires, turned on the recording device. The bellowing sound of the conch filled the air.

Chandler and Fulton stood in front of the boulder facing the remains of the elk carcass.

"Now we know what was killing our caribou and elk herd," Chandler said.

"They were defending their territory, Scott, and they've survived for over a hundred million years. Every living fossil has learned how to be at the top of the food chain. That's how they endure."

"Tough to appreciate."

Fulton reached out and touched his prosthetic arm, nodding in support. She hesitated. "You and I have a son, Scott. If he's still alive."

He looked into her eyes. "We'll find him."

He gathered up Wolf's backpack and Fulton helped him slide into it, the speakers hanging out of the flap covering the opening.

Rain and wind stung their faces as they trudged up mountain trying to find signs of where Ken and Meghan were headed. Without Wolf, they knew they would have trouble staying on track.

Ten minutes passed. No sign. Another ten minutes, no arrow. Then five more minutes and Fulton's voice broke the silence. "Over here," she said. "An arrow, Scott. I almost missed it."

"Thank God you didn't," he said.

Chandler walked over to her and looked down at the arrow. It was formed with rocks and branches from an elderberry bush, but there was no motor oil tipping the point. When he saw the point of the arrow he said, "We've got to hurry. We've only four hours of daylight before sundown."

A squadron of seven helicopters in tight formation passed over them. Chandler and Fulton looked up and waved.

Nobody saw them.

CHAPTER 46

KEN PRESSED THE CONCH SHELL TO HIS LIPS, POINTED IT TOWARD THE CAVE entrance, and blew into it as hard as he could.

They couldn't hear the commotion inside the cave, shadows darting in and out of the honeycomb maze of tunnels.

Meghan cupped her ears as the seashell made its haunting, deafening sound. She stared at him in wonder. "Where did you get that?"

"Brave Wolf gave me the shell and taught me how to use it."

Ken was staring into the cave. Meghan, focused on survival, was angry with herself for not controlling the fear she had felt in the dark rock crevasse.

"Stay close to me at all times," Ken said. "We hug the right wall of the cave. When I stop, you stop. When I move forward, you follow me."

She nodded. "I'm ready, Ken," and they entered the cave hugging the wall on the right. "If we see them in there, we drop to the cave floor," she said. It was the first time she affirmed their quest for survival, and Ken looked back at her acknowledging he had heard her.

The smell of oil intensified the moment they reached the first chamber, but there was another smell that was unsettling: decay. Straight ahead of them they saw something glistening. Ken inched his way forward, Meghan following in close step. There was enough light from the mouth of the cave to cast a dull glow inside the first small chamber and reveal something sparkling like diamonds on the walls.

"Phosphorous," she said.

They entered the next chamber, which lead into a massive cavern. Meghan stumbled and looked down.

It was a human skull.

She wanted to scream, but held herself in check. Ken looked over his shoulder.

"I'm okay," she said. "Keep moving."

"Follow me," he whispered. "Don't look down. Don't look back."

Meghan nodded.

On the wall behind her, Meghan could see blue and red stick figures, ancient cave paintings. She tapped Ken's shoulder. "Behind you."

Ken turned around and scanned the wall.

"Oh my God," he whispered. "Brave Wolf's legend's true."

Ken's mind was spinning. Meghan, for the first time, forgot about danger. She seemed transfixed by the story described on the wall. The stick figures were running from something. Ken pointed to a large conch shell etched in red dye that one of the stick figures was holding. He was blowing on it and there were beasts running away from the people—the winged beasts, etched in blue dye.

Ken turned back to Meghan. "These are the same as the figures on Brave Wolf's bowl."

When they turned around and looked across the cavern they saw pools of dark liquid bubbling to the surface.

"Oil," Meghan whispered. "The whole cave's filled with pools of oil."

Ken and Meghan moved deeper into the cavern, backs pressed against the damp wall. Then Ken froze in place. Something was there.

They heard a cracking noise. Ken could see across the cavern floor, beyond the pools of oil, an unnatural silhouette. Ken squinted. "Get down, slowly," he said.

"What is it?" Meghan whispered.

"A Deino."

"Where?"

"To the right of the big pool."

"What's it doing?"

"Sitting on a nest, I think."

"Oh my God. Does it see us?"

"I don't think so. There's another one to the left. Beyond the small pool on the right."

The phosphorous on the cave walls sparkled faintly, offering just enough light to create shadows and outlines. They heard another crack, closer to where they were standing. Meghan looked down. Eight feet from her position she saw a clutch of five large eggs, bigger than ostrich eggs. Bigger than any eggs she'd ever seen.

At that instant, a head broke through the eggshell. It let out a loud, cacophonous chirp that echoed through the cave. Ken saw the Deino to the right rise off its nest and take three steps toward them, still fifty yards away. It was snorting at the air, sensing something was amiss.

"Don't move."

"It sees us."

"I know."

"Ken…"

"Shhh." Ken clutched the large conch shell in his left hand. He thought about blowing it, but he was trembling so much he changed his mind.

When Ken had first sounded the conch into the cave entrance, it had caused a flurry of motion deep within the tunnels, but the hen Deinos continued to sit on their nests, protecting their eggs. His mind raced. Should he use the iPhone's recording instead? He knew the battery was low.

A loud crunching noise sounded off to the left, magnified in the large cavern. It was another Deino sitting on its nest, its massive teeth gnawing through a bone. When the Deino lifted its head to engulf more of whatever it was, Ken saw the faint outline of a leg and shredded pants, maybe a boot.

A military boot. A Marine boot. Ken felt a rush of bile fill up his throat and thought he would gag. He choked it off by clutching his hand to his throat.

"What is it?"

"Nothing. We've got to get to the oil," he whispered. "Follow me. Slow. Real slow."

"Yes," Meghan whispered. "Keep going."

Ken slid his foot to the right. He repeated the process until they reached a small bubbling pool of oil that was tucked up against the cave wall. They stood on a three-foot section of cave floor that spilled out from the wall to the edge of the pool of dark, thick fossil fuel.

As Ken bent down to poke his hand into the warm bubbling liquid, the Deino on the nest closest to them saw movement and sprang to its feet. Its head turned toward them and Ken heard it snort the air, searching for scent.

He pulled his iPhone from his pocket and flipped it on, the sound of a conch filling the cavern. There was a flash of movement in front of them and across the cavern on the other side. The Deinos deserted their nests and vanished deeper into the cave, some fleeing through the cave entrance. Then the iPhone's battery died—and the sound died with it.

A haunting silence spread through the cave. Everything was still, except the continuous methodical cracking of hatching eggs—and somewhere deeper within the cave, a raspy breathing, and the eerie sound like crickets.

There was a movement so quick that they saw only a faint blur. Meghan clutched Ken's arm.

"Cover your body with oil, Meghan. Now."

Meghan's hands thrust into the dark bubbling pond of fossil fuel, and she lathered her body with the thick liquid.

When Ken bent down to dip his hands into the dark pool, a shriek filled the cavern with such ferocity that Ken almost lost his balance. Meghan's outstretched hand pulled him back from the edge of the dark pool.

They were on their knees, desperately trying not to move. A Deino bounded into the cavern, jumping between pools, shrieking to announce its presence.

"Don't move," Meghan said.

"Don't worry," Ken said. "Its wing's broken."

"What's that in its jaws?" Meghan asked.

Ken leaned forward to get a better look, squinted hard, and winced. "A body."

"Jesus," Meghan said, her voice trembling.

"Shhh."

Meghan finished rubbing oil over her skin. As Ken leaned over to scoop up the oil and apply it to his skin, two Deinos appeared out of nowhere, one from the left, the other from the right, both on the other side of the pool flanking them. They were communicating to each other in a high-pitched chatter.

The Deino on the right made a different noise, a rattling in its throat, and three more Deinos ran over to the pool, two on the right, one on the left. Now there were five. Ken and Meghan's backs were to the cave wall. Three feet in front of them, on a thin ledge, was the oval pool of fossil fuel spreading out from the wall thirty yards across to the other side, the sound of black bubbling crude gurgling around them.

"They've got us trapped. It's over. Blow the conch," she said in one last hopeful plea.

Ken put the conch shell to his lips, sucked in a desperate breath of air and blew into the small hole of the shell. His lips were quivering and only a dull squeak poured out of the shell, agitating the Deinos. The large alpha male was across the cavern eating its kill, unmoved by the disturbance, its yellow eyes fixed on its prey.

The three Deinos on the left moved closer, jaws snapping at the air. The two on the right advanced. The conch shell had streaks of oil on it from Ken's hands and when he lifted it to his lips again, it slipped from his grip and fell on the cave floor.

"Give me the conch," Meghan demanded.

"You can't blow it," Ken said.

"Give me the conch."

CHAPTER 47

Cʜᴀɴᴅʟᴇʀ ᴀɴᴅ Fᴜʟᴛᴏɴ ʜᴀᴅ ꜰᴏᴜɴᴅ ᴀɴ ᴀʀʀᴏᴡ ᴀɴ ʜᴏᴜʀ ʙᴇꜰᴏʀᴇ, ɴᴇᴀʀ ᴛʜᴇ elk carcass. Since then, they'd crisscrossed back and forth, up and down, retracing their steps.

"Without Wolf, it's damn near impossible to know what to look for except the arrows. The storm's not making it any easier," Chandler said.

"They've got to be up there," Fulton pointed to the high ridge above.

"I hope you're right," Chandler said, climbing a sharp embankment, Fulton following.

The Deino on the left kicked its talons in the air, jaws snapping, snarling.

Reluctantly, Ken handed the conch to Meghan.

She pursed her lips and pressed the small aperture of the conch tightly to her lips.

Ken was already thinking about an escape. Their backs were to the wall and they were trapped. There was no way out, he concluded. But he refused to give up hope.

The sound was a raspy squeak, high in pitch, nothing resembling the conch. Ken watched her, his eyes wide in disbelief that she would even try to make a sound from the giant shell.

But the sound began to change. Meghan's eyes were wide. The high pitch began to change into a lower bellowing, coronet blast that filled the cave with euphony.

The expression on Ken's face washed into utter amazement as his girlfriend played the conch in a steady, eerie, almost musical pitch that ebbed and flowed as if she were the soloist in some kind of orchestral conch exhibition.

The Deinos vanished and Meghan pulled the conch away from her lips gasping for oxygen.

"Awesome, Meghan. How did you do that?"

"Four years of coronet lessons. Started in sixth grade."

"You never told me that."

"You never asked."

"Oh my God. That was incredible," Ken said. "You just saved our lives."

As Meghan raised the conch to her lips to make another blast, the shell slipped from her oily hands and rolled over twice, vanishing into the dark pool of bubbling oil.

"Oh my God," she said. "It's gone."

The first Deino to appear was a young male. It streaked toward them from the left, trumpeting a ghastly, high-pitched screech. Another appeared on the right. Maybe they were the same ones, Ken thought, but they were chattering a signal that ushered four more to join them from distant cave tunnels. They were surrounded yet again, only this time there seemed to be three more.

Ken had little time to think of options. There was only one left. His iPhone battery was dead. The conch shell lay on the bottom of a deep bubbling pool of oil, and their backs were up against a damp wall of the cavern.

He slowly turned his head toward Meghan.

"When I say 'drop,' fall toward me. We fall together. Same time. Bury your face on the ground away from the oil."

"What are we doing?"

"Just do as I say, Meghan. Do not look back at the pool. Understand? Just stay down with me."

Meghan nodded.

When the Deinos moved to within six yards on either side of Meghan and Ken, Ken fell to the left and Meghan fell with him.

The Deinos charged them, just as Ken's lit match hit the surface of the dark pool of oil.

With a loud concussion, a massive orange flame filled the cavern, and dark, billowing smoke gushed through the tunnel toward the cave entrance.

The heat was excruciating, but Ken and Meghan huddled tight against the cool wall, their bodies entwined, faces away from the fiery pond.

A terrible cry filled the air as two of the Deinos, disoriented, stumbled into the flaming pond. Clawing at the edges of the pool, they managed to pull themselves out and ran wildly, bodies aflame, screeching hideously. The first Deino zigzagged across the cavern, ran into a far wall, then stumbled into another small pool of oil and lit it on fire. Its head burst into flames. It bobbed up and down as it tried in vain to escape, then sank beneath the surface of the blazing pool.

The second Deino flapped its burning wings, trying to gain lift inside the massive cavern. It hovered off the cave floor for a moment, flew in a flaming circle, then crashed into a wall at the far end of the cavern. Its torso, tortured by the burning hot oil, it tried to stand, but kept falling over. The living torch burned for several minutes until its charred body fell over, useless talons rigidly pointing up to the cave ceiling. The creature gave one last thrashing jerk, let out a final cry, and went silent.

Chandler was the first to see the plume of smoke. "Up there. Jesus. They're up there. Come on. Let's go!" He broke into a run.

"What's happened?" she shouted.

"I don't know. Come on."

"I'm coming," Fulton said, her hands and mountain boots clawing at the lose shale, trying to gain traction.

"They're in one of the caves."

They ran toward the smoke and found the cave entrance. The heat escaping the tunnel was almost unbearable. Chandler pulled the sound device from his backpack and aimed it inside the cave. The bellow of the conch filled the cavern.

Chandler cupped his hands to his mouth and shouted, "Ken! Meghan!"

Inside the cave, Ken asked Meghan "Did you hear that?"

"No."

"Listen."

The faint cry of a human voice reached their ears. Ken sat up, pressing his back against the cave wall.

"Ken, Ken! Meghan!" Fulton was screaming.

Chandler pulled a bandana over his mouth. "Wait here."

"I'm going with you." Fulton pulled her shirt up to cover her mouth and nose.

"Hold my hand and stay close. Crouch down and try and stay below the smoke line." Chandler and Fulton ran into the first chamber, coughing, but able to breathe.

When they got to the second cavern, spilling out into a massive cave, Ken saw them and shouted, "Mom! Mom! Over here!"

Deino nests lay in every direction, surrounding each pool of bubbling oil. It was a maze Fulton and Chandler had trouble negotiating in an effort to reach the teenagers. Fulton scurried around the largest pool and ran toward her son, hopping over nests like she was in a hopscotch race. Chandler followed her, and finally they burst into a clearing, the four of them running toward each other. They embraced, standing between two dark pools of bubbling oil.

"Thank God you're alive," Fulton said.

"Follow me," Chandler said.

Fulton looked around the cave. Black smoke clung to the ceiling and flames licked the walls and floor of the cave as fire sought oxygen to stay aflame.

Chandler led Ken and Meghan toward the cavern exit. Fulton was snapping pictures as if her life depended on it: the nests, the eggs—some of them hatching. As baby Deinos ran toward a hidden chamber, she put her camera on automatic. Click, click, click, click.

Ken called back to her. "Look at the cave wall, mom. On your left. The paintings."

Fulton ran up to the wall and began to photograph the primitive images. Click, click, click.

They burst out into the clearing, gasping for air.

"How did you survive?" Fulton asked.

Meghan said, "It was your son, Mrs. Fulton. Without him, we wouldn't have made it." She threw her arms around Ken and hugged him.

"The Deinos are awesome, mom. We saw them hunt."

"And kill," Meghan added.

"Meghan plays the conch. You won't believe it. She's incredible."

"But I dropped the conch into the pool of oil."

"You were awesome."

"You're both amazing," said Chandler. "You two managed to survive by figuring it out. The Marines could have used you. Who would've ever figured that rubbing oil on your bodies could save your lives?"

Ken shrugged and a smile spread across his face. "Where's Brave Wolf?"

Chandler thought about not telling him, but changed his mind. "We lost him, Ken."

"Lost him?"

"The alpha male got him," Chandler said.

"No, no," Ken cried, tears streaming from his eyes. "Oh my God, no."

"So how are we going to get out of here alive?" Fulton finally asked.

"By helicopter," Chandler said. "Let's go."

CHAPTER 48

CHANDLER PULLED OUT HIS ICOM TRANSCEIVER AND PUSHED PTT. "SCOTT Chandler to base headquarters. You copy, Major Wong?"

"Roger that, Scott. Go ahead."

"We've found them," he said.

"Are they okay?"

"Roger that."

"Congratulations, Scott," Wong said, with a surge of relief.

Chandler heard the major shout out to his field sergeant. "They found the goddam kids. They're alive." Then, back over the radio: "What's your position?"

"Heading down to my chopper. Same coordinates I gave you before. We're now about a quarter mile below the cliffs on the west side of Mount St. Lincoln."

"Roger that. We'll send an escort to you. Be careful coming down."

"Thanks, major. Imperative Secretary Robinson stop second invasion. Tell him about the kids. We can get to the oil using sound devices. You copy?"

"Affirmative, Scott. Will do. Over and out."

"Over and out."

The trek down-mountain was faster, but Chandler knew they were being watched and tracked by the Deinos, keeping their distance only because of the sound device's constant eerie bellows.

When they got down into the tree line, Ken thought he caught a flash of movement off to his left; but it disappeared as quickly as he saw it.

Ken noticed it, too. "Just saw one over there. It's tracking us."

They heard helicopters in the distance and saw eight Bell Vipers round Mount St. Lincoln and hover over the billowing plume of black smoke belching from the cave above.

When they reached Chandler's Sikorsky, they lost sight of the other helicopters in the thick forest canopy, but could hear them circling somewhere overhead. As they broke into the clearing, a shroud of thick vog had settled in, and they could barely see the chopper's green fuselage. It was perched atop the flat cretaceous rock slab.

Chandler pulled himself inside to the pilot's seat. He unslung his backpack and turned off the sound device the moment he sat down. "We're safe now," he said.

He strapped himself in and snapped the buckles in place. Fulton did the same, Ken and Meghan slipping in behind them.

"I'm starving," Meghan said.

Ken pulled out a plastic zip lock bag and passed it over to her. "Take what you want," he said.

Ken and Meghan had run out of food during the late afternoon of their second day. Ken had sampled half of the slithery creature he had swatted off his leg in the rock crevasse. It was a red-backed salamander and it tasted good, he had told Meghan, who ate the other half without too much coaxing. They had collected other morsels on their trek through the mountain terrain.

Fulton looked over her shoulder and saw the plastic bag. "What's that?"

Ken passed it forward. "Have one, mom."

"You're kidding, right?"

"It's how we survived. We ran out of food two days ago. We had to eat something. They're not that bad," Ken said. "Especially when you're hungry. Just slip them into your mouth and don't think about the crunchy sound or the goo."

"Believe it or not, the white ones are good," Meghan chuckled. "They're not as crunchy as the others. Easier to chew."

"White ones?" Fulton turned to Chandler. "You see this?"

"What?"

"In the plastic bag." Fulton took the bag and held it up to Chandler. "It's what they ate over the last forty-eight hours. I can't believe it."

Chandler held the bag and studied the contents. "Good fare. You should see what we ate in Afghanistan after C-rations ran out. A lot worse. Whatever crawls over there stinks, but you can survive on it. Over here, some of them are actually sweet. Especially the white ones."

Ken took the bag back and held it open for Meghan. The moment she touched it, the grub coiled into a tight, dime-sized nugget. She extracted it from the bag and popped it into her mouth like a gumball.

"Yuk. Jesus," Fulton said. "How can you eat that?"

"That leaves three left: a newt, red backed salamander, and a couple of large black ants," said Ken. "Sure you don't want one, mom?"

Chandler looked at the bag and said, "Give me the orange one."

"Are you guys serious?" Fulton asked.

"Sure they are," Chandler said, swallowing the newt in one gulp.

Ken plucked another grub, this one dull amber in color, and tossed it into his mouth, bit down hard. He took three crunching chews and swallowed and it slipped down his gullet. He gave a loud belch and Meghan laughed.

Chandler saw movement. Fulton had yet to snap the safety harness around her, and was still looking down at the floor, trying to find her sunglasses. Chandler reached behind his seat where he put the sound device within easy reach. He felt a backpack instead, and his heart skipped a beat. "Where's the sound device," he shouted. "Give it to me."

"Where is it?" Fulton asked.

"Behind my seat," he said. "It's not there. Damn it. Hurry," he said, cursing himself for not keeping it up front in the cockpit. Unknowingly, Ken had casually draped his knapsack over the device, covering it up.

The Sikorsky rested on the ground, blades still.

When the alpha male impacted the Sikorsky it was clocking thirty-eight knots, hard enough to knock the flight plan book out of its holder and to send Fulton off her seat. The small glass window on the pilot's side blew out from the impact, and the dent in the hatch door almost touched Chandler's leg.

"Brace yourself," Chandler shouted. "Get the sound device, now," he screamed.

He reached for the starter key and gave it a quick turn. The powerful engine came to life, the blades taking a slow turn, then faster, faster until each blade became a gray blur of power. Now the second engine grumbled to life, a puff of exhaust filling the air providing full torque.

The alpha male ducked beneath the turning blades. Its three-toed feet locked onto the landing bars with an unrelenting grip as it had done in its first encounter with Chandler's chopper. The powerful forearms, jutting out of its winged shoulders, clutched the steel side grips made for hoisting passengers into the craft's cabin. What startled Chandler was the fact that the beast had learned quickly from their first battle.

Ken and Meghan held each other, eyes wide, hearts pounding. Ken looked at the Deino's eyes, studied its large-winged body.

"It's the same one that killed Brave Wolf," Chandler said. "It has a broken wing."

"I think it was the same one in the cave, too," Ken shuttered. "It had a body in its jaws."

Chandler thrust the stick forward and the Sikorsky strained to lift off the ground. The alpha male was banging its jaws and thick scaly head against the larger hatch window. A crack was forming. Chandler knew he had to get off the ground fast.

The chopper lifted five feet. Ten. Fifteen.

When the chopper reached thirty feet, the Deino thrust its head at the window in Chandler's door with such force that glass sprayed into the cabin flight deck.

A shard of glass sliced Fulton's left cheek, and blood spilled down her face. She wiped it off with the sleeve of her field jacket.

"Find the sound device," Chandler shouted again. "Turn it on, now."

Fulton lunged over the seat, desperately searching. "I can't find it, Scott," she screamed. "Where is it?"

"It was behind my seat."

Fulton saw Ken's backpack. "I don't see it."

"Keep looking. Ken, help her out."

Ken lurched out of his seat and dove toward the back, his hands rifling over supplies then he scrambled back over the rear seat and reached for his backpack. He yanked it off the floor. "I found it," he screamed.

Fulton reached back and pulled the device onto her lap. She punched the ON button and the wail of the conch filled the cabin, but it was too late.

In one powerful thrust, the Deino's head had already plunged through the glass. Chandler held up his prosthetic arm in defense. The Deino bit down hard and jerked at Chandler, but his seat belt held him in place. The Deino's eerie shriek of dread was so loud that Fulton flinched against the cabin door, and her left hand snapped the red positive wire from the brass connecter. The conch sound died instantly.

Chandler forced the chopper to its limit, increasing the thrust of power. He took the Sikorsky up to a hundred feet, then two hundred, trying desperately to shake the Deino's grip, then he sent the chopper into a free fall. The helicopter was yawing back and forth, up and down, sideways. He worked the craft toward the Fossil. The clearing over the river was his only chance to break the creature's death clamp.

Meghan and Ken were screaming. Fulton's eyes wide with terror. The alpha male shrieked and continued yanking on Chandler's arm like a rag doll.

Chandler saw the river and flew sideways toward it, trying to dislodge the beast from his craft by rolling it back and forth, circling up, then falling back down. The Deino had a firm grip, its powerful feet clutching the landing bars and its forearms locked onto the side bars for support. It was working Chandler's arm deeper into its jaws, twisting, turning, engorging.

Chandler brought the chopper within twenty feet of the Fossil when he made the only decision that made sense. He pushed the chopper up to one thousand feet above the churning river, then forced the craft into a sheer power dive.

As they plunged toward the Fossil, Fulton screamed. "God. What are you doing? We'll all die."

Ken and Meghan were clutching each other, Meghan screaming.

Chandler fumbled for something under his left arm. He found it and yanked it out of its sheath, then lunged back to the controls. The Deino increased its death grip on his arm with a guttural shriek that wrenched the cabin.

When the chopper was only twenty-five feet above the river, Chandler reversed torque. The craft jerked to a midair stop, tilting on the left side, drifting toward the opposite shore. The angle, Chandler knew, would be critical. At the same time, he thrust his right hand high above his head and rammed the ten-inch bayonet blade deep into the beast's yellow bulbous eye, twisting hard to the right. A painful, guttural screech filled the cabin with dread as eye fluid sprayed across Chandler's face. He shifted his body weight toward the beast, timing the move to take advantage of the sudden stop in the craft's fall. The wounded Deino fell into a cartwheel spin plunging into the Fossil.

The chopper's angle above the river was forty-five degrees.

The helicopter was in a death tilt and Chandler had to hold the arc to prevent it as well from crashing into the Fossil.

Everybody on board was screaming, holding onto anything that offered support. Kimberly clawed for purchase of a ceiling cross bar. She found it and clutched it for life.

The Sikorsky's engine whined to maintain torque as Chandler's right hand worked the collective trying desperately to find the right pitch. Then he pushed hard on the cyclic stick controlling forward movement, his hand moving frenetically in a calculated motion back and forth, back and forth.

The craft moved sideways at a forty-five degree angle and he could not pull out of the forced turn. He was living Newton's Third Law: an object in motion tends to stay in motion.

When the helicopter circled to the far bank then cut back again toward the opposite shore, Chandler saw something that defied description. Twenty feet into the Fossil River, the alpha male was standing, its broken wing dragging helplessly downstream in the current. It was waiting for Chandler to return, its head turned sideways to favor its good eye. The Sikorsky was set in motion no matter what Chandler tried to do. At a forty-five degree angle, the helicopter was heading directly into the Deino's path. With only one arm, Chandler could not work the collective and cyclic fast enough to break the craft from its trajectory. Each turn delivered higher altitude but not enough lift to avoid impact between beast and craft.

Chandler watched the beast leap from the water, jaws agape like a shark gone berserk, blood streaming from its left eye.

Only it was a fucking dinosaur in the middle of my Park, Chandler thought, and it killed my best friend.

He was on a mortal collision course with the Deino, and he could do nothing except hold on, grit his teeth, and hope for the best.

The best was bad, real bad.

They all watched helplessly as the Sikorsky flew directly at the Deino.

Fifty yards away, thirty yards, twenty, now fifteen.

"Hold on!" Chandler screamed above the engine roar. Ten yards out. "Hold on! Lean to the right!"

Only ten feet above the river, and the chopper was heading toward a death course impact without exit. When the chopper flew directly over the Deino, the creature's powerful legs unleashed like coiled springs, with enough power and lift to propel its entire body up out of the Fossil, dancing in the air atop the river as if it was walking on water. The alpha male made one last shrieking effort to grab hold of its prey.

When it made contact with the helicopter, the craft gave a shuttering vibration. But when Chandler looked down at the Fossil, the water was blood red.

Cut in half, the predator's body floated down the Fossil in two large pieces.

The windshield too was covered in blood, with barely enough visibility to see anything, except a piece of quivering muscle that Chandler guessed might be part of a once beating heart.

Fulton had her hands over her eyes.

Meghan had passed out from fear.

But Ken witnessed the entire event. Nervous, yes. Petrified, yes. Mind blown, absolutely. But his eyes never closed, never flinched. He took it all in with youthful wonder. It felt like a dream.

But it was real, thought Ken, and it happened today, happened this hour, this minute, this second—and he was alive to remember it all.

Chandler let the helicopter take its prescribed course, four more circles over the Fossil at a forty-five degree slant. On each completed turn, he pulled a little more firmly on the collective stick giving the craft more loft.

On the eighth turn, he was able to correct the flight pattern into a vertical lift, and they rose 1600 feet out of the dense fog into a brilliant sunset.

The storm that had swept the mountain range had blown itself out over the Alaska plateau of mountains toward the east.

Ken leaned forward and reached over the seat. He went to touch Chandler's left arm. The sleeve of his field jacket was in shreds. His heart thumped in his chest. Chandler had to be losing blood fast. But where was the blood?

"Your arm?" Ken shouted in distress.

"It was prosthetic. I lost it in the war."

"My God. I never noticed."

"It's hard to tell the difference, Ken. Military high tech."

All Ken could say was, "You rock."

"Thanks," Chandler said.

"Where did you pull the knife from?"

"A Marine's always ready for battle. When I got attacked, I strapped it on, just in case."

"Awesome."

Meghan's eyes opened. After a long moment of silence, as she regained her bearings, she said, "Nobody back east will ever believe me."

"Probably not," Ken said.

Chandler pushed the Sikorsky up toward Fossil River Falls and flew beneath the plunging falls, clearing his bubble glass as if in a car wash. When the chopper swept out of the falls around the volcano's north side, the windshield was sparkling clean.

"Wow. What a spectacular sunset," Fulton said.

In the distance, a wall of helicopters flew toward them. Off to the left a plume of black smoke touched a passing cloud left over from the storm.

Chandler's radio came alive.

"Here to escort you guys back to F&W headquarters."

"Affirmative. Thanks for the escort, captain," said Chandler.

CHAPTER 49

When Chandler set the Sikorsky down on the tarmac at Noatak Airport, a small crowd was encircling the landing area.

"Get ready," Chandler said. "The press is here." He pointed to a small black and white van opposite his craft. Large Red letters on the van read, "WNOT." It was Noatak's only television station, and two men were running toward Chandler's craft as the chopper blades feathered to a stop. One had a TV camera, the other a microphone.

"How could they know about this?" Fulton asked.

"Small town. How could they not get wind of it with military choppers flying all over Noatak?"

Chandler opened the hatch, took a deep breath of cool mountain air, and jumped to the ground. Fulton exited, the teenagers following.

When Ken stepped out of the helicopter, a man shoved a microphone into his face.

Sam Bassoul, Station Manager of WNOT, sat bent over, eyes riveted to the screen monitor back at Noatak's station, the sound of the station's generator humming beneath the building. He looked at his watch—six minutes to the six o'clock news.

Bassoul checked his monitor screen. The transmitter light was red, 5:57 p.m. He wondered how many of his viewing audience would have power to view his six o'clock news. Not many, he thought. His generators would keep the WNOT signal alive, but across America, Bassoul knew, based on rolling blackouts and dimmed lights, and Nielson's viewing research reports, maybe forty percent of the viewing audience might be lucky enough to have enough power to see a broadcast to its finish.

At 5:58 p.m. a commercial from ExxonMobil flashed on his monitor, talking about the huge investment the company was making in offshore drilling and renewable energy after Hurricane Juan.

At 5:59 p.m. General Motors advertised the Spark Five electric automobile, promising 120 miles of travel at sixty miles an hour.

At six o'clock p.m., Mark Palmer's voice broke the air.

"Good evening," the newsman said. "I'm Mark Palmer, and we're here live in Noatak National Park, Alaska with the Fish and Wildlife Agency Team of Park managers, a division of the Department of the Interior. We have a unique story tonight. Behind me you see a green Sikorsky F&W helicopter that, as I understand it, just survived a very dangerous situation deep inside the Park. We're told that it has something to do with why Noatak was closed to the public a week ago.

I have with me tonight Ken Fulton, his girlfriend Meghan Lastinger, the pilot Scott Chandler who's Noatak's Manager of Wildlife and Ecology, and Dr. Kimberly Fulton, the Curator of Paleontology at the Museum of Natural History in New York City. An interesting mix of people whom you'll hear more from on tonight's six o'clock news report."

The camera zoomed in on Ken Fulton and Mark Palmer held the WNOT microphone up to his mouth.

"Ken?"

"Yes sir."

"Tell us what you saw today inside the Park."

"Dinosaurs."

Palmer laughed. "Dinosaurs?" Palmer said in disbelief. "Seriously."

"Yes sir. Living dinosaurs. My mom calls them living fossils. They can fly."

Meghan stepped beside Ken. "It's true," she said. I saw them with my own eyes."

"How many were there?" Palmer asked in disbelief.

"A colony of them," Fulton interrupted sternly, and the camera zoomed in on her face.

"Could you explain this to our viewing audience, Dr. Fulton?" Palmer said.

"I'd be glad to, but we don't have the time. We've got many reports to fill out and if you'll excuse us..."

Mark Palmer stammered to keep her engaged, but Fulton held up the palm of her right hand and said, "Please. Maybe later."

"One last question," Palmer said.

"One," Fulton said, her voice laced with agitation.

"Do you have any pictures of what you saw?" Palmer pleaded.

Fulton took the camera from around her neck and brought up a picture of the alpha male Deino attacking the helicopter. "See if you can zoom in on this," she said.

Palmer took her camera and peered at the photo. Forgetting he was on the air, he said, "Good God, what the hell is it?"

Bassoul was almost drooling with excitement when his cameraman, Jerry Neumann, zoomed the WNOT camera onto the photo from Fulton's Canon. The live screen in front of him burst into a full color shot of something from a lost world. Bassoul, not known for profanity, said aloud, "Holy fuck. This is incredible." Even if the story's fake, Bassoul thought, he knew he had his viewers who might have the electric power to watch it, hooked from the teenager's first word.

Palmer poked the microphone back at Fulton's mouth. "So what is this...this thing in Noatak National Park, Dr. Fulton?"

"Only one question and I gave you the answer. We're done."

"Please," Palmer's voice pleaded. "What is it?"

"We're done," Fulton announced and she waved Chandler and the teenagers away from the camera.

Palmer's hand holding the microphone was visibly shaking. He was reporting live what was no doubt the biggest story of his life.

Palmer ran after them, pushing the microphone at Chandler's face. "Someone said something about finding oil in Noatak, Mr. Chandler. Is there any truth to that?"

"No comment," Chandler said.

"Meaning there is oil in Noatak?" Palmer persisted.

Chandler pushed the microphone away from him.

"How much oil was found in there?"

Chandler grabbed the microphone and threw it twenty yards.

Palmer ran to retrieve it, his cameraman Neumann following. He picked up the microphone, shrugged his shoulders, and turned toward the camera.

"We'll be hearing more about this story on our ten o'clock news. For now, I'm Mark Palmer for WNOT, live in Noatak National Park."

CHAPTER 50

WHEN MAJOR WONG CONVEYED THE NEWS TO CHANDLER AND FULTON THAT Secretary Robinson had called off the second invasion into the Fossil River, Chandler and Fulton hung up the phone with a celebratory shout. Chandler's Park was saved—and there was hope for the survival of Fulton's living fossil colony.

The raging oil fire that Ken Fulton had set to save his and Meghan's life was still belching smoke out of the cave entrance when a team of specialists, who had worked on Kuwait oil fires, arrived on the scene via a Boeing Chinook CH-D47. The massive helicopter was able to set down the rear of the craft on the edge of the cliff to unload heavy industrial equipment while keeping the front of the craft aloft above the valley below.

It took them only six-and-a-half hours to extinguish the three fires within the deep cavern, the sound of the conch recording keeping them safe.

When Ken lit the large pool afire, the Deinos had instinctively scurried through the flaming cave to move their eggs through a series of connecting chambers into a large cavernous hollow filled with old abandoned nests. The colony now had access to the outside through the fourth cavern entrance.

Chandler insisted he personally oversee the wildlife and environmental safety of his Park when oil technologists and supplies arrived at the fossil fuel field.

Thirty minutes before the first military chopper dropped its payload into the area, Chandler had flown his Sikorsky into the Fossil, arriving in the dark moments before first light, his sound device announcing his presence.

Fulton was back at Chandler's cabin with Meghan and Ken working on a plan for the future survival of the Deino colony.

First light came at 5:18 a.m., sunrise at 6:11 a.m. Alaskan Time. There was talk about bringing old Black Hawk and Apache helicopters out of retirement to help lift supplies and heavy equipment up into the Fossil River, but high command made the decision to engage 103 Bell Vipers that were already in Noatak National Park.

Now, supervised by Wong, they ferried their payload onto the Fossil River plateau: twenty-foot long oil pipes, three feet in diameter, and large industrial oil rigs, dropping their payload to the field engineers below.

Oil rig company employees from Schlumberger and Williams Company oversaw the assembly of oil rigs. Pumps, pipes, and large industrial connectors were put together in less than seventy-two hours and snaked over the Brooks range down-mountain onto the plains on the south side of Noatak River.

The bellowing sound of the conch from electronic sound emitters protected their flanks, powered by large generators that had been lifted into the area by Marine Bell Vipers.

Oil rig technicians, petrochemical and petroleum engineers, and geologists swarmed over the oilfield, blueprints in hand, reading charts and studying graphs that had been provided by the Department of Energy's research team, and the National Geospatial and Intelligence Agency.

By one p.m. of the fifth day after successfully laying pipes and pumps on the Fossil River plateau, the U.S. military, the world's largest consumer of fossil fuel at144 million barrels per year, had issued orders to all motor pools to mobilize its inventory of military oil tanker trucks to line up at the base of the southeastern sector of the Brooks range. A line of oil tankers stretched a mile long on a swath of newly created dirt road above the permafrost that had been hastily built to connect from point of delivery to the small town of Bettles. An extension of the

Alaskan Pipeline had just been completed from Pump Station Five at Gobblers Knob to Bettles. As planned, Pump Station Five along the Yukon River, was now ready to receive the high volume of fossil fuel being piped from Bettles, where it would fill up the main Alaskan Pipeline to full capacity and transport it south to the Port of Valdez. Then it would be picked up by oil tanker ships and taken south to twenty-six oil refineries in Houston, Texas.

Every major media network—TV, radio, and newspaper—was on the scene capturing the story.

The winter snowpack had melted and summer weather had arrived in the arctic. Forget-Me-Nots bloomed in glistening blue clusters across the landscape. The military caravan of large oil tankers moved in and out of the Brooks Range without incident, but environmentalists across the country were now awakened by the news, and a flood of emails began to rock the internet.

By three o'clock, the line of tanker trucks spanned five miles. As each military truck was filled to capacity, they headed in caravans, lights on, southeast to Bettles. The Department of Energy was working with contractors to complete the extended pipeline from Pump Station Five beyond Bettles so that it would connect with the Brooks Range pipeline coming out of the mountains from the Fossil River plateau. The DOE estimated that the extension would be completed within eighteen days when military oil tanker trucks would no longer be needed.

The pipeline extension was meticulously constructed, with Department of Interior's Zollar insuring that EPA's environmental code was contiguous with the Alaskan 800 mile pipeline.

By late afternoon of the twentieth day, lights across America burned steady again, and summer vacationers, filling their gas tanks to the brim, headed back to highways in record numbers. Commercial jets resumed full schedules, and Wall Street's Dow Jones Industrial Average, for the first time in recorded history jumped 1,011 points in one trading day, beating the October 13, 2008 point gain of 936 points.

President Barton saw his red phone flash crimson. He punched the speaker button.

Lucretia said, "I have Gao Ziying holding, Mr. President."

Barton flashed back to his last call with the arrogant President of China.

"Connect me," he said to his secretary.

"Yes sir."

"Mr. President. Gao Ziying," the interpreter said.

"Yes," President Ziying."

"Congratulations, Mr. President. I understand your country has discovered a large oil field." The interpreter's voice was crisp without emotion.

"Yes," Barton said guardedly.

"There is no end to our thirst for oil, Mr. President. Even with OPEC increasing our supply, we're in continued great need."

"I can appreciate that, Mr. Ziying. The United States was in that very position until our discovery," Barton said. "I'm sure you realize that your deal with OPEC caused us grave consequences."

There was a noticeable silence on the phone. "Yes, Mr. President. I do. But you do realize this is about our country's energy survival. It's business."

"Indeed it is, Mr. Ziying. Our survival as well," added the President.

"China would be very interested in buying oil from you, Mr. President."

"I am sure you would, Mr. Ziying."

"Then I can take that as affirmative we can do business?" the interpreter said.

Barton smiled into the phone, letting his silence penetrate Ziying's mind.

"Mr. President?" the interpreter said. "Mr. President?"

CHAPTER 51

IT WAS FULTON'S PLAN TO FLY BACK INTO THE FOSSIL RIVER TO MAKE SURE that the *Deinonychus* colony was safe and still thriving.

Chandler loaded the picnic lunch onto the Sikorsky. Fulton climbed into the front seat flight deck, and Ken and Meghan sat in the back. The damaged pilot window had been replaced, and the three dents in the chopper blades from contact with the alpha male Chandler had been hammered out with a large rubber mallet.

Chandler's new prosthetic arm in place, he turned on the ignition switch and worked the cyclic and collective with confidence. The craft lifted smoothly off the ground.

In the distance, Mount St. Lincoln glistened in the mid-morning sun, and the large volcanic mountain to the south of it belched plumes of smoke from its cone.

It promised to be another beautiful Alaskan day. Fulton and Chandler had vowed each other to return to savor the sheer beauty of Noatak Preserve.

When they landed, the thick fog had lifted and only a fine vog mist hovered over the plateau. Visibility was good enough for them to see the Fossil in the distance, hear the soft flow of the river against the pine-scented mountain breeze out of the west.

When Chandler opened the hatch, he heard the sound of the conch from the perimeter electronic sound emitters protecting the oil field a mile and a half away. He knew they'd be safe. He'd activated his own device just to make sure.

He could hear something else in the distance: the faint yet powerful thrust of oil pumps sucking fossil fuel out of the mountainside and pumping it down-mountain to awaiting military transports.

Fulton spread out a red and white checkered tablecloth on the slab of cretaceous rock and took an assortment of sandwiches, and snacks from the basket.

"Where are the salamanders, mom?" Ken teased.

Meghan said, "I hope you brought the slugs."

"Funny," said Fulton.

Chandler chuckled as he walked to the edge of the precipice and peered into the valley below. He heard a loud pop and almost stumbled from the precipice, arms wind-milling to regain his balance.

"Jesus," he said. "That was close."

He turned around and saw Fulton holding a bottle of Veuve Cliquot, pouring four plastic-fluted glasses to the brim.

"Nice touch," Chandler said. "Thanks." He took the glass from her. "Maybe we should give Ken and Meghan Poland Springs."

"Give us a break," Ken protested.

"Just kidding," Chandler said, chuckling.

Fulton handed a glass to Meghan and Ken. "Consider it a celebration. Under the circumstances, we'll overlook the age thing."

She held her glass up to a distant mountain. "To the *Deinonychus* colony," she said. "May they thrive forever."

Chandler thought of his best friend, the pain of his loss tugging on his heart and mind. He managed a "Hear, hear," but it was painful not having Brave Wolf with them.

They all raised their glasses and tapped them together.

They sat down on the picnic blanket and the sound of crickets filled the air. Chandler reached for his carbine. Ken laughed and said, "It's someone's cell phone. The iPhone has crickets as one of the ringtones."

Everybody looked at each other trying to find the source. Meghan slipped her hand deep into a jean pocket and extracted her iPhone.

She had it on speaker. A voice said, "Meghan?"

Fulton pressed her index finger to her lips. "Shhh," she whispered.

"Hi, mom," Meghan said.

"We're still in South Hampton. You okay?"

Meghan knew from the emails she had received from Julianna McGuire that her mother had called only once, midweek, to find out if her daughter was okay. Julianna had lied. "She's fine, Mrs. Lastinger. She's in the Park."

What Julianna didn't know was that her mom had tried calling Meghan every other day to check on her, but never got through. She had felt a modicum of comfort speaking with Julianna.

"Yes, mom. I'm fine," Meghan said.

"Dad and I'll be home on Sunday. Where are you now?"

Meghan's heart was beating in her chest. The expression on her face read guilty as charged.

"I'm in the Park, mom."

"That's lovely, darling. It must be beautiful in the Park. It's a gorgeous day in the Hamptons, too. Enjoy the day."

"Will do, mom. Thanks. I'll see you Sunday."

Meghan clicked off and everybody laughed. "I didn't lie," Meghan said. "I am in the Park."

Ken lifted his champagne glass. "I'd like to propose a toast to a dear friend who gave me great advice," he said. "If it wasn't for him we'd all be dead. To Brave Wolf, whose spirit will always live on."

Ken saw his dad's eyes well up in tears; his mom's, too.

"He's with us now. He'll always be with us."

Ken got up and walked to the edge of the precipice, scanning the distant horizon of mountain peaks and valleys. In the valley below he saw movement. It was a Deino foraging on a bend of the Fossil River.

"Mom, look!"

Fulton walked out to the edge of the cliff. "What a sight."

Three more Deinos came out to the river's edge. Two of them played harmlessly with each other, feigning attacks. The other one pulled a large Sockeye salmon out of the river.

"There are two babies behind them. Look, one's a male."

"They seem so peaceful," Meghan said.

"They are," Fulton said. "For now. Let's hope it lasts."

Chandler stood behind them taking pictures. "Turn around," he said. "Let me get your picture with the mountains in the background." They all turned around and Chandler clicked off three shots.

They came back to the picnic blanket and sat down, except Ken who walked to his satchel and pulled something out of it.

Ken returned to the edge of the rocky slab and stared out across the mountain range. The sun danced off the distant mountain peaks. He saw a lake out to the right. It sparkled cerulean blue in the Alaska sun. He didn't say a word. He raised the conch shell to his lips. It had belonged to Brave Wolf.

Ken blew into the massive sea shell and a billowing low sound echoed across the mountain range. He kept blowing, changing the pitch of the sound by thrusting his right hand into the chamber then slowly extracting it, back and forth. The haunting sound vibrated the champagne in Fulton's glass, sending a stream of bubbles to the surface. Meghan saw Chandler's conch sitting next to the cooler. She stood up and picked up the conch. "Mind if I borrow this?" she asked.

"You know how to use it?" he said with a questioning look.

She walked over to Ken and stood beside him as he continued to blow the conch. She inhaled deeply and blew into the massive shell.

The sound of both conches playing in harmony echoed across the mountain. Chandler looked at Fulton, a grin on his face. Fulton gave a thumbs-up.

Ken could no longer see the Deinos below him along the Fossil River. They had all vanished when they heard the sound.

Ken turned around and saw Chandler kiss his mom. Meghan saw it too.

Ken's face lit up with a smile. He felt a tingle of goose bumps skitter across his body and his eyes brimmed with tears.

It was a beautiful day in the Park.

THE END

Made in the USA
Monee, IL
13 January 2022

88894527R00173